TALES OF PANNITHOR

BROKEN ALLIANCE

Written by

Scott Washburn

Tales of Pannithor: Broken Alliance
Cover by Alan Lathwell
This edition published in 2022

Zmok Books is an imprint of

Winged Hussar Publishing, LLC
1525 Hulse Rd, Unit 1
Point Pleasant, NJ 08742

ISBN 978-1-950423-72-9 PB
ISBN 978-1-950423-87-3 EB
LCN 2021952953

Bibliographical References and Index
1. Fantasy. 2. Mantic Games. 3. Heroic

For more information
visit us at www.wingedhussarpublishing.com

Twitter: WingHusPubLLC
Facebook: Winged Hussar Publishing LLC

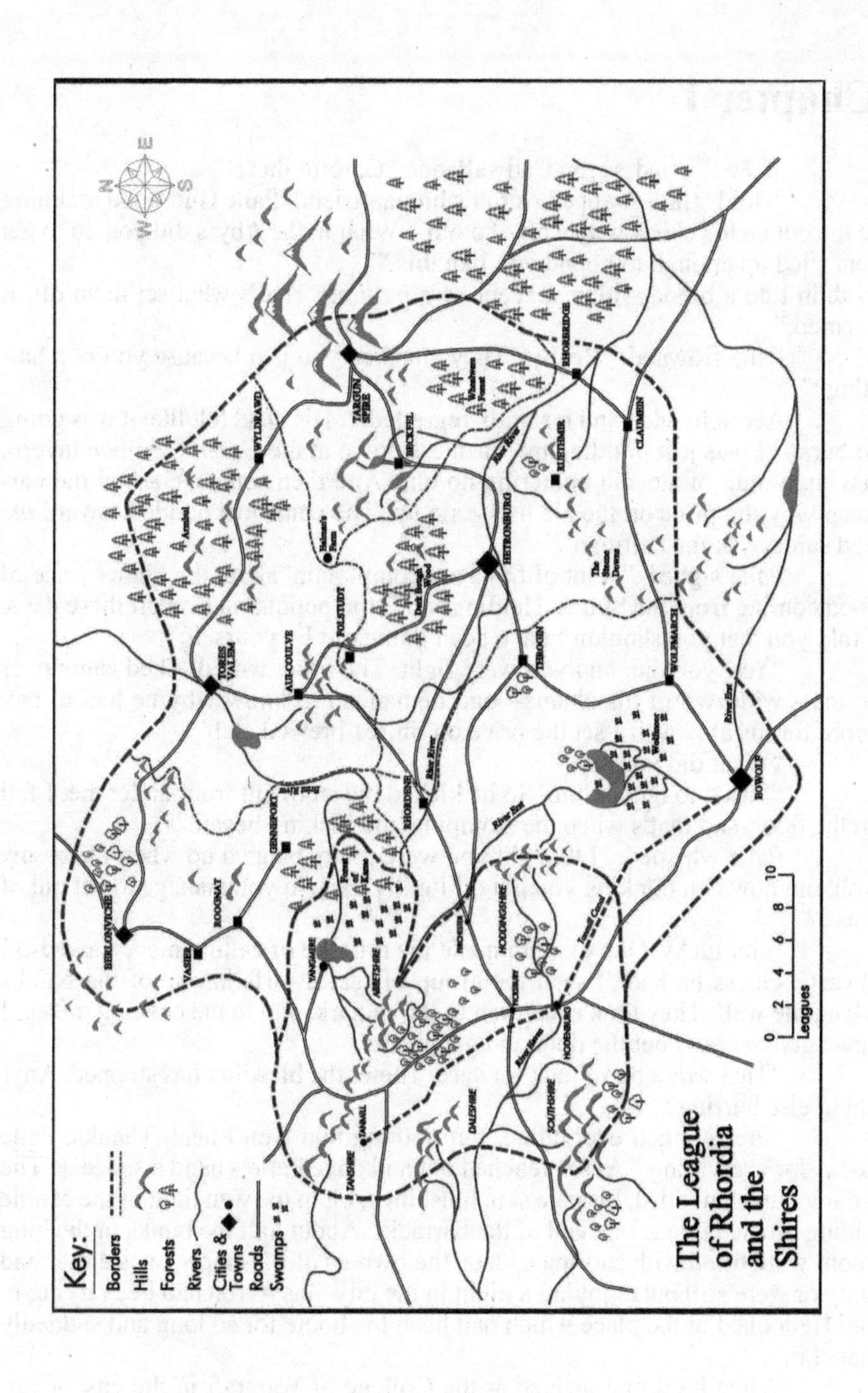
Key:
Borders
Hills
Forests
Rivers
Cities & Towns
Roads
Swamps
The League of Rhordia and the Shires
0 2 4 6 8 10
Leagues
N
E
S
W
BERLONVICHE
VASIER
ROOGNAT
GENNEPORT
TORES VALEM
AUI-COULVE
WYLDRAWD
Armbul
FOLSTUDT
TARGUN SPIRE
BECKFEL
YANGMERE
TANSHIRE
TANMILL
ABBETSHIRE
Forest of Karne
RHORDENE
Rhor River
DALESHIRE
HODDINGSHIRE
PICKSBURY
River Haven
SOUTHSHIRE
HODENBURG
Tunnell Canal
River Ent
HETRONBURG
THROGIN
RUETHMIR
The Steane Downs
RHORBRIDGE
CLAUMEIN
WOLFMARCH
Wolfmoor
BOWOLF

Chapter 1

"Ow!" cried Aeron Cadwallader. "Careful there!"

"Hold still!" snapped Aeron's human friend, Palle Gudmund, dabbing at the cut on his cheek with a bit of cloth. "What in the Abyss did you do to get 'em riled up enough to pound you like this?"

"I didn't do a bloody thing. Except be a *halfling*. That's what set them off, it seemed."

Palle frowned. "Really? They attacked you just because you're a halfling?"

Aeron nodded and instantly regretted it. His head felt like it was going to burst. "I was just minding my business down at the *Green Gryphon* tavern, having a mug of ale and bothering no one. And then someone asked the barkeep why the price on the ale had gone up. The churl just nodded toward *me* and said: 'Ask the halfman'."

Palle sighed. "A lot of folks are complainin' about the higher price of food coming from the Shires. Halflings ain't too popular in Eowolf these days. I told you that you shouldn't have been going out by yourself."

"Yes, you did, and you were right. The brute who'd asked came over to me - with two of his chums—and demanded to know why he had to pay more for his ale - as if I set the price on Shires-brewed ale!"

"What did you say?"

"I tried to ignore him. So he kicked the stool out from under me, I fell to the floor, and that's when the stomping and kicking began."

Palle whistled. "I thought you were pretty banged up when I first saw you, but now I'm thinking you got off lightly. How'd you manage to get out of there?"

"Got lucky. One of them made the mistake of calling me a 'sawed-off dwarf'. Guess he hadn't seen the group of real dwarfs in one of the booths along the wall. They took exception to the remark, and in the ensuing melee, I managed to crawl out the door and get away."

"That *was* a bit of luck for sure. There, the bleeding has stopped. Anything else hurting?"

"Pretty much everything, but nothing that won't heal. Thanks, Palle for… for everything." Aeron reached out and gave Palle's hand a squeeze. The young human nodded, his pale skin blushing a bit in the wan light of the candle sitting on the table at one end of the barracks. About half the bunks in the long room were filled with snoring cadets, the owners of the empty ones either had duty or were still out enjoying a night in the city—as Aeron had been trying to do. He looked at the place which had been his home for so long and suddenly hated it.

When he'd first arrived at the College of Warcraft in the city of Eowolf two and a half years earlier, he had been thrilled. For as long as he could remember he'd been fascinated with warfare and warriors. As a child, he'd dragged his mother and siblings out to watch the Shires musters, and the one time that a major force of the League of Rhordia had marched along the road that led by his farm he'd been so excited he'd nearly swooned.

This made him a bit... odd for one of the Shirefolk. His people were not nearly as peaceful and un-warlike as the other races believed, but most of his people thought of war as an unpleasant reality which needed to be dealt with—like fires or floods or hailstorms—and not something to exult over. Aeron exulted. When he was nine, he'd tried to join the Picksbury trained band—the local militia unit—even though he was much too young. The older members had laughed watching him try to hold on to a spear that was far too long and heavy for him. But they'd treated him kindly and put him to work fetching things and cleaning things and any other task that he was willing to do. As he got older, he was allowed to attend weapons training and eventually was like any other member of the band. Except the band only trained a handful of days a year. He'd started mumbling about trying to join one of the mercenary companies that the League employed.

His father, who was a well-off farmer/merchant, despairing of ever teaching him the trade - or any of the other trades common in the Shires - had eventually given in to the inevitable. He called in some favors the Shires' leaders owed him, and they twisted a few arms in the League Council; and to his amazement and delight, Aeron found himself traveling to Eowolf and the College of Warcraft. He wasn't the first of the Shirefolk to come there, but nearly all of the others had been artificers and engineers, there to study the arts of making war machines. Aeron knew a bit about machines, but his true interests lay with the art of war itself.

It had been intimidating and a bit frightening to come to this great human city and the nearly legendary College of Warcraft, but the headmaster, a white-haired human named Nedes, had taken him under his wing and made him feel welcome. And he *had* felt welcome... until recently.

"Come on," said Palle. "You can still get a few hours' sleep before roll-call."

The students, or cadets as they were called, were paired up in teams, and Aeron had been very fortunate to be paired with Palle Gudmund. He was the youngest son of a baron who lived in Duke Berlonviche's city-state off in the northern part of Rhordia. The human lad was quite short for his race and thus only a bit taller than Aeron, who was tall for a Shirefolk. They'd hit it off immediately and become fast friends. They helped each other and looked out for each other.

Aeron slipped off the too-large chair, groaning as a dozen throbbing aches blazed into sharper pains. Palle took his arm and half-carried him down to where their bunks waited invitingly. The human helped him into the lower bunk, said good night, and then hoisted himself into the upper one. Aeron lay back, resting his head on the pillow and pulled the blankets over himself.

He was exhausted, but sleep didn't come easily. While this was the first time he'd been seriously hurt, this wasn't the first incident of anti-Shirefolk feelings he'd encountered lately. When he'd first arrived at the College, he'd met some taunting, pranks, and nasty tricks from the older cadets, but he'd been expecting that. He was new, he was different, and he was smaller. It was normal. He'd put up with it, and with Palle's help, he'd made it through the first year. After that, he'd mostly been treated as one of the group.

But these new incidents were different. It wasn't just that he was a newcomer, it was because he was a *halfling*.

The League of Rhordia was a group of city-states almost smack in the middle of the Ardovikian Plain in the northwestern regions of Upper Mantica. The population of the League was overwhelmingly human, but they coexisted peacefully with families of Free Dwarfs who had found work in the cities, and even the occasional companies of mercenary ogres. The Halfling Shires had joined the League during a time of mutual crisis well over a century ago and had generally gotten along very well since then. But in the last few years, things had changed.

Even before he came to Eowolf, Aeron had heard grumblings around his village, in the taverns, or at the dinner table: the humans didn't really respect the People. They were just using them. They were cheating them of fair prices for the food the Shirefolk grew and humans needed so badly. They were taxing them too heavily. The troops the Shires sent to the League musters and to fight in the League's wars were just arrow fodder; sacrificed to save human lives. Aeron had heard it all but never gave it much credence. There were always grumblers, and grumblers had to grumble.

But now there were grumbles in Eowolf, too. He heard the talk in the taverns and at the market and around the mess tables at the College: the halflings were ungrateful, they were stingy and scheming. Everyone knew the halflings were getting more from the League than they were giving back in return. Why, the little moochers would never survive without the League's protection - although they had for centuries. At first Aeron had thought it was just talk, but now things were *happening*.

There were shouted insults and cat-calls in the streets, fellow cadets, even ones whom he thought were friends, were turning cold. The hateful term *halfmen* was being bandied about more and more openly. Acquaintances among the small Shirefolk community in Eowolf were talking of leaving, going home to the Shires. And then the incident tonight. Why was this going on? What was he going to do if it got worse? With those thoughts spinning in his head, Aeron finally drifted off to sleep.

Roll-call came much too soon.

Just as it had nine hundred-odd times before, Aeron's day began with Sergeant Osvald Rolf shouting at them to get up and get dressed while he flung open the shutters and banged on their bunks. Aeron tried to jump out of his bunk as usual and nearly fell flat on his face when his muscles proved so stiff from the previous night's ordeal that he could barely move. Moaning, he stood up, realized he had never undressed, and shuffled to stand at the end of the bunk. Palle thumped down from above, fastened his trousers, and said: "You all right?"

He nearly responded that he'd been worse, but he realized that probably wasn't true. "Ehhh," he moaned, then added: "How do I look?"

"Like you've been run over by a war horse. Bruises all over your face."

Rolf called them to attention and then strode down the aisle between the bunks, looking each of them over with an eye that missed nothing. As Aeron feared, when the sergeant came abreast of him, he stopped and looked closer. His huge, bushy eyebrows drew together in a frown. "What the demons happened to you?" he snapped.

"Got run over by a war horse last night, Sergeant," Aeron answered. He tried to say it quietly, but enough people heard that many eyes turned in his direction. *Great, everyone will want to know the story.*

"From the looks of you, it must have been a herd of them."

"Might have been, Sergeant, it was too dark to count."

The man's grizzled face smoothed out into an expression that might almost have been one of concern. "Do you need to see the chirurgeon, lad?"

"Don't think so, Sergeant. I'm a quick heal."

Rolf snorted and shook his head, but before he could ask any more embarrassing questions, his corporal, who held the roll book, said: "Looks like we have an empty bunk, Sergeant." Rolf's head snapped around and indeed, two bunks down a man was missing—Cadet Soren. Probably had too good of a time last night—unlike Aeron. The sergeant immediately forgot about him and stalked over to grill the man who was standing by the empty file about his missing bunkmate. Aeron sighed in relief. A short while later, Rolf determined that there weren't any more men missing and stood before them. "Breakfast at the first bell, weapons drill at the second. Dismissed."

The cadets relaxed and trooped down the aisle to the garderobe where they could wash and see to other necessities. Aeron winced, as did several of the people close by, when he stripped off his tunic and got the first look at the bruises that he was quite certain would be there. Black and purple blotches covered much of his torso.

"By the Children!" hissed Palle. "Maybe you *should* go to the chirurgeon, Aeron."

"Don't think anything's broken," he said, probing his ribs gently.

"But he might give you something for the pain."

"Having sampled Master Morten's potions before, frankly, I think I'd rather have the pain."

"Suit yourself."

After washing, Aeron went back to his bunk and unlocked the chest with his belongings and got out fresh clothes. He tossed the dirty ones into a basket which would be taken to the laundresses for cleaning. He was grateful about being in the Second Company now. Servants took care of routine chores. When he'd first arrived, he'd been in the Fourth Company with all the other newcomers and had to do all those chores himself. Now there were a dozen hirelings to keep the barracks clean and the hundred men in Second Company looking spruce.

A ray of sunshine stabbed through one of the windows and illuminated the opposite wall. A few moments later, a distant bell sounded and the cadets got up and moved toward the door that led to the stairs, automatically forming into ranks. In spite of his hurts, Aeron's stomach growled and he was eager for breakfast. The main building at the College of Warcraft was a huge structure, five stories tall with two long wings which met at right angles at a large central tower. The first floor had the refectory and other public spaces. The East Wing had the living quarters on the second through fifth floors. The North Wing had classrooms, laboratories, and the library. Humans seemed to love building this sort of thing. If you took a dozen of the largest structures in all the Shires, combined, they wouldn't be as big as this artificial stone mountain.

The head of the company reached the stairs but then had to pause as the First Company trooped past them down toward the refectory, four men abreast, marching in cadence. The First Company had seniority in all things. They would graduate this year and never missed a chance to remind everyone of it. *Next year that will be me,* thought Aeron, looking admiringly at the decorative silver braid on the seniors' tunics.

When it was their turn, Second Company went down the broad marble stairs, Now Third and Fourth Companies, on the lower floors, had to wait their turn. Aeron sometimes wondered why the prestigious First Company had to walk up four flights of stairs to get to their quarters. If he'd been in charge, he would have put them on the second floor and let the lower ranking classes do all that climbing. *I suppose they feel that being on top of everyone else is worth it.*

They reached the bottom of the stairs in the great entry hall and turned left into the refectory, ranks aligned perfectly. Their column of fours split into two columns of twos and then four columns of one as they took their places along either side of two long polished wood tables. First Company was already seated but sat motionless despite the large bowls of steaming food in front of them. Aeron found his spot and swallowed saliva at the sight of the oatmeal, bread, crocks of butter, eggs, sausages, and mugs of hot tea sitting before him.

But he and the others had to wait until all the cadets were seated and then wait some more as other people straggled into the room. These were the officers, the professors, the mages, and the students in specialist branches of the college. The College of Warcraft had four main sections. The most prestigious were the Military Magicians, or *Warmages* as they were commonly known. These were the rare individuals who could channel magic and were attuned to the sorts that had military applications. They were extremely valuable and were treated accordingly. No narrow bunks or harsh discipline for them! There were only a few dozen of them, and they had their own dining area on a raised platform aside from the rest.

Next in the pecking order were the Artificers. These were the folks who could make things. Not just ordinary things, but marvelous devices, often with magical qualities - war machines, mostly. They also worked with the dangerous *gunpowder,* which was becoming more and more common in the armies of civilized peoples. The only other Shirefolk at the College were among the Artificers, two students and one instructor. All Shirefolk - well, the males anyway - were innate tinkerers. They were always cobbling together strange machines to 'make their lives easier'. Most of their inventions were pretty mundane, but they had machines to plant, machines to weed, and machines to harvest. Thanks to these things, Shirefolk, despite their smaller size, could farm twice the land that a human could. But even among the Shirefolk, there were a rare few who took their tinkering to such limits that they were considered geniuses. Their creations were famous the world over, and the College of Warcraft was eager to have them.

Then there were the Engineers, they also built things, but mostly of a more ordinary type: bridges and siege works and fortifications. Lastly, there were the four companies of cadets. These were being trained as officers to command the armies of Rhordia - and with the addition of Aeron, the Shires.

Finally, everyone was there. The College Chaplain, a devotee of the Church of the Children, blessed the meal and everyone dug in. Despite the pains in his arms and shoulders, Aeron quickly leaned forward and filled his plate. While the discipline here was strict and the living conditions stark, they fed them well, for which Aeron was very grateful. Halflings might have been half the size of the humans, but they ate nearly as much. The bowls and platters were quickly emptied and refills called for.

As Aeron munched away, more of his fellow cadets got a good look at the bruises on his face and made comments.

"Aeron, did the husband come home early, or what?"

"Nah, he just was so drunk he fell all the way down the main staircase!"

"Hey, Cadwallader! Was that a male horse or a female horse that did that to you?"

"Dunno," he replied. "All I saw was a horse's ass." That got a laugh, but he couldn't join in. Aeron had to admit that the taunts and jokes were no worse than what would have been directed at any other cadet under similar circumstances. He'd joined in on a few occasions, himself. But somehow, this time every comment seemed to have an unspoken *halfling* attached. *You're being ridiculous. Stop it.*

Fortunately, at that moment, some of the stewards appeared carrying the second round of food, and one of them was the missing Cadet Soren. Kitchen duty was a common punishment for delinquent cadets, and it seemed that justice had caught up with Soren very quickly that morning. His classmates' jibes were instantly redirected to Soren, and Aeron was allowed to finish his breakfast in peace.

As things began to break up and the cadets headed back to their barracks to get ready for the day's activities, Aeron found himself walking up the steps next to Vadik Gulbrand, one of the pair of dwarfs in the company. "Vad," he said.

"Aeron," nodded Vadik, who then let out a loud belch. "Have a bit of trouble last night, did you?"

"You might say so." He hesitated and then went on in a low voice: "Have *you* had any trouble lately?"

"What do you mean?" replied the dwarf, a note of caution in his voice.

"I… I got beaten up last night just because I was a halfling. Has anyone given you any problem for being a dwarf?"

"Ha! I'd like to see 'em try!"

Aeron nodded. The dwarfs were shorter than men but broader and often stronger. They didn't take insults lightly - as he'd witnessed last night. Vad continued to stare at him as they continued up. "But I suppose I shouldn't laugh. Someone like you'd be a much easier target for cowards to pick on. And there have been some…"

"Some what?"

"Some incidents. Mostly with our women and children. Nothing serious, but still a bit… disturbing."

Aeron shook his head. "Why now? The Shires have been in the League for over a hundred years, and you dwarfs have been living here among the humans for a lot longer than that. Why's this trouble starting now?"

"Can't say," replied Vad, shaking his head in turn. "I've heard some say it's this 'humans first' poison coming from down south. That Lord Darvled character. But all I can tell you is to watch your back - and stay away from spots where you can get into trouble."

"Thanks, Vad, I'll try."

They reached the barracks and each went about getting ready for the day. First on the schedule, as usual, was weapons drill. Aeron took out his training gambeson, a close-fitting padded jacket meant to soften the blows that would inevitably land during training. He winced pulling it on over his bruises and then winced again as he thought about how those bruises were going to hurt when they got hit, despite the gambeson. Over that went a longer cloth tunic which was gray and emblazoned with the crest of the College and the sigil of the Second Company. Tall leather boots replaced his normal light shoes, and he tucked a leather helmet under his arm and waited for the call to fall in.

It wasn't long in coming, and soon the company was trooping back down the stairs, out through the main doors, and into the large practice yard. It was enclosed on two sides by the wings of the main building and by walls, stables, and workshops on the other two. The College wasn't meant to be a fortress, but it could become one if necessary. Out beyond the walls he could see the towers and spires of the city of Eowolf. In the distance, the palace of the Duke perched on the only bit of high ground around, the city being mostly flat.

The field was about a dozen hectares in size, divided into sections by carefully trimmed hedges. Each section was for training with certain types of weapons. But before they went to a specific section, Sergeant Rolf took them on a brisk trot around the perimeter of the fields, just to get them warmed up. Aeron and the rest of the company had gone through this hundreds of times, and it caused him no trouble, despite his aches and pains and the fact that he had to nearly run to match the trot of the long-legged humans. Then it was off to the hand weapon training section, where they were issued wooden weapons and told to pair off. Most of the humans favored wooden replicas of longswords, although a few liked the lighter rapiers. The dwarfs liked axes or large hammers. Aeron was obliged to use a short sword as the other weapons were much too long for him.

He would have preferred to spar against Palle, but Sergeant Rolf knew full well that buddies often didn't go all-out against each other, so he made sure they faced different opponents and rotated them frequently. Aeron's first match was against Cadet Casper Nimik, a tall young man from the north of the League. Casper had a ridiculous advantage in reach with his long arm and long sword, but Aeron was quicker and had learned to take advantage of that to get inside the guard of his opponent and score with his short sword. He still generally lost more often than he won. This time, slowed by his sore muscles, he lost all but two touches. Even so, Casper was gracious in victory and didn't crow over his small opponent.

Rolf rotated them around, and Aeron faced four other cadets before they were given a break. He lost to all of them but gave the last one a run until they were both sweating profusely. It was the tail-end of summer and still very warm. He and his last opponent, Vestor Kennet, sat down in the shade of one of the hedges to cool off. "Not bad, Aeron," said Vestor.

"Thanks. You were pretty good yourself."

"You're so fast; hitting you is like trying to swat a… uh, stab a fox."

Swat a bug? Aeron forced himself to accept the compliment for what it probably was and ignore the almost-insult. As he began to relax, he admitted that he really did enjoy this. Not just the swordplay, but the camaraderie. Sure there were nitwits among the cadets with the usual insults and bad jokes, but for the most part, they were good fellows. Fellows you could trust. For one of the first things Sergeant Rolf drilled into everyone was you looked out for your comrades, guarded their backs, and helped them when they needed it. Not because you liked them, but because they were your comrades. You did that - or you were no good.

Soon they were called back into ranks and started again, this time with an assortment of other mock weapons: axes, flails, and maces, just so everyone had at least some experience with weapons that were not their favorites. Again, Aeron had to use shorter, lighter versions of what the other cadets were using, but he still did all right. After another break, they went to another section and worked with spears and polearms. Aeron was quite good with spears. These were a traditional weapon of the Shirefolk; the perfect weapon to keep a wolf - or a goblin - at a distance while you dealt with them. Naturally, the humans were using longer spears than he had, but he still held his own.

Then just before the noon break, they worked with Aeron's favorite weapons: bows. Even more than spears, the bow was a favorite of the Shirefolk. While they couldn't match an elf with a bow, they could match - or better - just about anyone else. Aeron had to use a short bow instead of the longer bows of the humans, but within his range, say three hundred paces, he could put an arrow within a hands' breadth of where he wanted it, almost every time. Some of the others were also using crossbows, and the dwarfs were using the gunpowder weapons they had pioneered. After he had emptied his quiver, Aeron strode over to watch those dwarfs. Their muskets were scary things, giving off a flash and a bang and a cloud of acrid smoke. They didn't appear to be terribly accurate, but they could blow a hole the size of his fist through a target. The dwarf weapons were so large and packed such a load that the recoil would have knocked him, or even most humans, on their ass if they tried to use one. Humans did have such weapons though and used artillery. He knew that some of the tinkerers in the Shires had started experimenting with smaller gunpowder weapons, more suited to their size, but he'd never used one himself.

The noon bell rang out from the College tower signaling the midday meal. This featured bread, cheese, sliced ham and beef, and an assortment of vegetables, washed down with a not terribly good beer - definitely not Shires-brewed. Afterward, they went out beyond the College's walls to where most of the stables were located. The afternoon was spent with various riding exercises. The humans were on full-grown horses, while Aeron had a pony more suited to his size.

The dwarfs just looked on. They and their kin nearly all fought on foot. The rare few who did fight mounted did not use horses, but instead rode nasty creatures called *brocks*. They were like giant badgers with fangs and claws. They couldn't be mixed with horses, and the College had none in its stables. Aeron was comfortable on his pony but had no illusions that he could fight very well from atop it. Still, on a battlefield, the added height would improve his view of things and allow him to get from place to place quickly.

The humans rode around yelling and whooping and trying to hit targets with lance and sword. Aeron went through the motions, but even Sergeant Rolf, normally a bit of a perfectionist when it came to training, seemed to realize that Aeron was not suited for this sort of combat and didn't push things. The afternoon had turned quite hot, and by the time they were done, they and their mounts were dripping.

As the shadows lengthened, the cadets took their mounts back to the stables and spent nearly an hour tending to them. While most of the cadets would have servants or squires to handle this chore after they graduated, Rolf insisted they all know how to do it and inspected their work minutely.

The day was not quite over. The cadets marched back to their barracks, washed the day's sweat and dirt off themselves, and then dressed in their best clothing, including swords hung from their belts. Then it was back down the steps and out into the large courtyard just beyond the entrance doors. There, the four companies of cadets, along with a fair number of the artificers and engineers and even a few of the warmages, lined up for the evening parade. Aeron caught a glimpse of Dilwyn Brynmor, one of only three other Shirefolk at the college. Dilwyn wasn't exactly a friend—the artificers didn't mingle much with the others—but he talked with him from time to time.

Aeron wasn't quite sure why it was called a parade since they didn't go anywhere, they just stood there. As they lined up, Second Company was joined by its official commander, Sir Einar. The sergeants may have run the companies day to day and overseen their training, but the officers were the actual commanders. They were all knights, with a baron named Klemens commanding the entire group. They were all humans, too. About the only time the cadets saw them was at the evening parade or other ceremonial formations. Some of the officers would turn up on the training fields from time to time, but that was rare. The officers were all on horseback, except for Baron Klemens, who was riding an *aralez*, a rare beast which looked rather like a gigantic dog. They were difficult to train, but those that were became fiercely loyal. They were said to have magical qualities and a very few were even born with wings.

The few men to be bonded with an aralez were greatly admired and considered to be an elite. Horses didn't much like the aralez, so it was difficult to intersperse the two. In recent years, some of the herdsmen in the Shires had begun breeding a smaller version of the aralez which was much more easily trained. Many humans considered this to be almost a sacrilege.

The College of Warcraft had a small group of drummers, pipers, and hornsmen who were playing a martial air as everyone assembled. Finally, all was set and silence fell. After a short wait, Headmaster Nedes appeared. He walked slowly, leaning on a cane, to a spot opposite the center of the assembled people. The Chaplain accompanied him and once or twice it looked as though the man was actually supporting the elderly Nedes.

The Headmaster stood before them and nodded in their direction. This was a signal, and the cadets drew their swords and held them out, pointing toward Nedes. The musicians then gave a roll of the drums and then all the assembly roared out: *'Long Live Rhordia!'* three times at the top of their lungs.

And that was it. The ceremony was over and everyone sheathed their swords and filed back inside for dinner.

In spite of the seeming pointlessness of the parade, Aeron actually enjoyed it quite a lot. The music and the massed 'soldiers' sent a chill down his spine, and he shouted just as loudly as anyone. By the time his evening activities were finished, talking with Palle and some of the other cadets, writing a letter home, polishing his boots, and a few other things, he was feeling content. As he drifted off to sleep, the memory of the previous night's violence had nearly faded from his mind.

Chapter 2

The next day's activities were entirely different from those of the day before. Instead of physical training, the morning was filled with instruction. Instruction in *classrooms*. This was what made the Rhordian College of Warcraft so different from other training schools. The League of Rhordia was not particularly large, a mere fifty leagues east to west and north to south, compared to the two thousand five hundred leagues that the great northern continent of the world covered. Nor was it densely populated compared to the great cities of Basilea or Primovantor on the shores of the Infant Sea in the southeast, or the Successor Kingdoms far to the southwest beyond the Dragon Teeth Mountains. Rhordia's city-states were surrounded by many potential foes; the Young Kingdoms, a hodgepodge of greater and lesser realms pressed Rhordia's borders on all sides. Farther to the north were the rough tribes of the Mammoth Steppes, and the ever-present threat of raids by goblins or orcs from the mountains that ringed the Ardovikian Plain. The League couldn't hope to match its potential foes by sheer strength, so they had to do it by being *smarter*.

Many of the older civilizations had become hidebound, unimaginative, and stagnant in the aftermath of the God War which had torn apart much of the world in ages long past. They thought and acted the same way as their distant ancestors, and they fought their wars that way, too. Dogmatic religions stifled free thought, and innovation was discouraged or outright forbidden. The younger kingdoms were more dynamic but lacked the patience and discipline to conduct themselves in a rational or scientific manner.

Rhordia was different.

The League was not ruled by a king or emperor, but by a council of nobles from the five human city-states: Eowulf, Targun Spire, Hetronburg, Torffs Valem, and Berlonviche. Dukes, they called themselves, and while each ruled his own realm separately, in joint matters they all bowed to the majority wishes of the council. In addition to the five dukes, the head of the local Church of the Children had a seat on the council, and after the Halfling Shires joined the League, they, too had a representative there.

The League embraced science and encouraged innovation. Even the Church of the Children, the majority religion, was very open-minded and tolerant of other beliefs. This had led to a dynamic society with a strong economy and a military that was very powerful for its size. There were other schools in the world to train young nobles in warfare, but the emphasis was almost entirely on weapons skills and riding skills. The men were trained as warriors, not as soldiers. In most of those armies, tactics consisted of shouting: 'Follow me, boys! Charge!' Strategy was: 'Let's march out there and find someone to kill.' And logistics? Most had no clue what the word even meant.

In the College of Warcraft, they applied scientific methods to warfare. They studied past battles and campaigns, tried to determine why things had gone the way they did, who had made good decisions, who had made bad ones, and what lessons could be learned. Aeron found it all fascinating and enjoyed his time in the classroom; probably more than most of the other cadets.

On that day, they were in the History of Warfare class taught by Professor Egilhard. He was talking about the most famous battle ever fought by the League, the one which brought the League of Rhordia into existence: The Battle of Halman's Farm.

"You all know the basic facts about the battle," said the professor. "We raise our children telling them tales of it. The newly formed alliance, led by Alobart Rhor, met a vastly larger force of invading orcs and destroyed them utterly. How was he able to do that, gentlemen?"

Aeron looked around. All of his company was there in the third floor classroom; a large space with rows of hard wooden benches, a high ceiling with exposed wooden beams, and a row of narrow windows along one wall letting in the morning light. The other three walls were covered with maps and chalkboards filled with diagrams of troops formations. No one answered.

"Come, come, gentlemen!" snapped the professor. "You're not newcomers, surely you've learned something while you've been here!"

Finally, Vestor Kennet stood up. "Uh, he lured the orcs onto a trap, sir. Surrounded 'em and wiped 'em out."

"You make it all sound very easy, Mister Kennet," said Egilhard. "Do you think it was easy?"

"Uh, no, sir."

"So why was he able to do it? Anyone? How about you, Mister Yngve?" he asked, focusing on one unlucky cadet. Ketil Yngve squirmed in his seat, looking like he'd just woken up—and perhaps he had.

"Uhhh… orcs are idiots?" This got a few chuckles from the students, but Egilhard just snorted.

"They're not the only ones, Ketil," said someone loudly from the back of the room. This got a lot more laughs. The professor did not look amused.

"Anyone?" prompted the professor. His gaze moved across the class. Aeron looked around, but it didn't seem like anyone else was going to answer. He ran a finger nervously along a groove carved in the wooden bench; the initials of some bored cadet from long before. He didn't like to call attention to himself, but… he got to his feet.

"He knew his enemy, sir. He knew the orcs would be eager to attack and not stop to scout ahead. They would come straight on into the trap he'd set."

"Exactly!" cried Egilhard. "Alobart Rhor didn't just know his own army, he knew his enemy's. The orcs live for war and always favor the attack, even when outnumbered. Make no mistake, they can be cunning at times, shrewd even, but in most cases, their desire is always to close with the enemy as quickly as they can in a ferocious headlong charge.

"Knowing this, Rhor deployed his forces to take advantage of the orcs' aggressiveness. He sent out a screen of light cavalry to harass the orcs and draw them in. Then he formed his most steady infantry into a line in the center with orders to give ground in the face of the orc assault. Finally, he put all his heavy cavalry out of sight on each flank.

"His plan worked to perfection. The orcs charged after the light cavalry, and when they saw the line of infantry, kept right on going and smashed into them. The infantry slowly fell back, drawing the orcs in after them. But only in the center, the flanks remained anchored. Eventually nearly all the orcs were in a pocket, so tightly packed they could barely use their weapons. It was at this point—the Moment of Decision—that Rhor unleashed his cavalry. They swept around the ends of the infantry lines and hit the orcs from the rear, encircling them completely. The orcs were slaughtered almost to the last one of them. Sadly, Rhor, himself was mortally wounded, leading the cavalry charge. But his sacrifice led to the creation of the League." Egilhard paused and looked over the class. "So! What lessons can we learn from Rhor's actions at Halman's Farm, Mister Cadwallader?"

"Uh… don't just use your own strengths to your advantage, use your enemy's weaknesses against them?"

"Yes, well done, Cadet!"

"Thank you, sir," said Aeron, quickly sitting down and staring straight ahead. He could feel a hundred pairs of eyes on him.

"Professor?" Aeron looked up and was surprised to see Palle on his feet. His friend rarely said anything in class unless called upon.

"Yes, Cadet Gudmund?"

"How… how could Rhor be sure that the orcs would do as he expected? Suppose they did something else? What if this 'Moment of Decision' that you speak of never came?"

"Then we probably would not be having this conversation, and the League probably wouldn't exist. But no, I should not make light of this, for you do ask an excellent question. Alobart Rhor is widely considered to be a genius. Not just for his military skills, but for his diplomatic ones. Rhordia is very lucky to have had such a genius at such a critical time. But you can't always count on having a genius around when you need them, can you?"

"Uh, no, sir," said Palle.

"In fact, most of the time you are *not* going to have a genius handy. What do you do then?"

"I… I don't know, sir."

"You don't?" The professor looked out on the seated cadets. "I don't want to be insulting, but I haven't noticed any geniuses in this class—or in any of the others I've taught in recent years. A few have come close, but no. So lacking a genius, what are we to do in time of war?" Still no answer, and Egilhard did not look pleased. "Hmmph! Perhaps an easier question then: Why are you people here?"

This produced a lot of blank stares—and a long sigh from the professor.

"All right then, Mister Cadwallader, why are *you* here?"

"Me, sir?" said Aeron, taken by surprise.

"Yes, you, why are you here at the College of Warcraft?"

"To… to learn about warfare… to learn how to command soldiers in battle…"

"But you're not a genius like Alobart Rhor, so how can you hope to win?"

"I… uh," Aeron was becoming flustered, but he pressed on. "To… to take the things I learn here and… and do the best I can, sir."

Aeron expected Egilhard to ridicule his answer but was surprised when the professor leaned back with an expression of satisfaction.

"Take what you have learned and do the best you can? Yes, that's exactly it! That is what the College of Warcraft is all about, gentlemen! We study the past, learn from the successes, learn even more from the failures, try to understand why this was a victory while that was a defeat—and then apply those lessons in future wars. What we are doing here, gentlemen, is substituting collective experience and wisdom for individual genius."

A room full of blank stares met Egilhard's gaze.

"Well, I've given you enough to think about for one day, gentlemen. Class dismissed."

* * * * *

"Phew! Do you have any idea what old Egilhard was talkin' about?" asked Palle as they made their way down to the refectory for the midday meal.

"Maybe a little," said Aeron.

"Well then you're a better man… er… halfling… uh, cadet than I am."

"Aw, the old man is getting senile," said Ketil Yngve, looking back over his shoulder.

"I don't know, some of it did make sense…"

"Maybe to you! But then maybe you're a genius, Cadwallader, eh? Or maybe just *half* a genius!" Yngve laughed and moved on. Aeron frowned but said nothing.

After the meal, the company formed up, and Sergeant Rolf led them out through the College's main gates and into the city of Eowulf. They marched along one of the main thoroughfares toward the Duke's palace but turned off well before reaching it. Some of the people on the streets stopped to watch them, and a few even cheered, but most ignored them. This was a daily ritual and they had grown used to it.

Near the eastern gate there was a walled-off area with a number of long buildings which housed several regiments of League soldiers. The gates were standing open and the cadets marched in, Rolf exchanging greetings with the sentries standing there. Inside, there was a parade ground, and on the parade ground were groups of soldiers standing around. They were not in formation and were not carrying weapons or shields or wearing any armor. They watched curiously as the cadets marched up and were halted. "Oh, the Bloody Abyss! They're giving us raw recruits?" groaned someone further down the line from Aeron.

"Sure looks like it," said someone else.

"Silence!" snapped Sergeant Rolf. "For the past months, you've been practicing your command skills by drilling trained soldiers. Today we are going to see how well you can do with untrained men. Five of you will be assigned to each company, and at the end of the afternoon, we'll see how well you've done. All right, first five, that's your company over there. Second five..."

The cadet companies were organized with the tallest men at the right of the line and the shortest at the left. It looked prettier that way. This put Aeron and Palle and the two dwarfs at the very end on the left, so they were the last ones assigned. As things would have it, the company didn't have exactly one hundred men, so there were only four of them in the last group: himself, Palle, Vadik Gulbrand and his cousin, Hagen Felmann. They trotted over to where their assigned group of recruits was waiting.

There were only about fifty of them, so technically they were a sub-company, but they were all humans and they all looked very large in Aeron's eyes. He was more than a bit nervous. He'd done this scores of times before, but only with well-trained troops, used to discipline, used to following orders - even from young cadets. It was something he really enjoyed: closely spaced blocks of men all marching in unison to his word of command. It really made him feel like a soldier. But just at the moment, facing these men, who did not look the least bit impressed with the four youths standing in front of them, he didn't feel like a soldier at all. He looked vainly around for Sergeant Rolf. He could tell this gang who was in charge...

"You're senior, Aeron, I guess that puts you in command," said Vadik, grinning. "What are your orders... sir?"

Aeron grimaced. Yes, by the College's system of ranking, which was based on grades and demerits, Aeron had a higher score than the other three. He glanced to the waiting men and then back to the cadets, cleared his throat, and said. "Uh, right. And you are next in line, Vadik, so I'll make you my sergeant for today. Palle, you and Hagen are corporals so... get them formed up, eh?"

"Yes, sir," said Vadik, his grin growing larger. He turned to the men and shouted: "Attention! Get into ranks, you lunks! No, *four* ranks, dammit! Closer! So your elbows touch! Come on, move it!"

The men looked surprised, but none of them tried to argue as the two dwarfs started pushing them into formation. Palle tried to help, but in the end, it was the loud voices, confident manner, and impressive muscles of Vadik and Hagen that got the job done. Aeron held back and watched—as was proper for a company commander. Eventually, the men were lined up in a block four ranks deep and about twelve men wide. Vadik came up to Aeron, saluted and said: "Sir, the company is formed." He was still grinning, and Aeron wondered just how seriously he was taking all this.

Aeron put himself in front of the formation with his fists on his hips and tried to scowl like Sergeant Rolf would; he doubted he was succeeding. "Good afternoon, men," he said loudly.

No response.

Great.

Well, there was nothing for it but to push ahead. "Today we are going to learn the basics of the drill. The first thing is to learn how to march. Now, it's not as easy as you might think. Walking is not marching. People walk, soldiers march. Soldiers need to march. You men will probably end up being spearmen or pikemen, and to do that effectively, you need to be in a close, tight formation just like you are now. If you lose your formation, it will be harder to move and the enemy might be able to take advantage of any confusion in your formation. And in order to avoid losing your formation, you need to be able to march. You need to be able to have all fifty of you move like you were just one man." Aeron was dredging this all up from what his instructors told them in their first year at the college.

"The first thing is to keep your ranks. The way you do that is make sure your elbows are touching the man on either side of you. Don't let a space open up. Don't get too far ahead or fall behind. Keep those lines straight! The next thing is you need to march in step. Everyone steps out with their left foot first and then their right. Left, right, left right, all doing it together. Everyone understand? Let's try it and see. So with everyone moving their left foot first, company, forward… march!"

Naturally it was a disaster. Half the men started out on the wrong foot, and while trying to correct that, they forgot all about keeping their lines straight; and in a dozen heartbeats, the company was all in a jumble.

"No! No! Your *other* left! No! Blast it all… Company, halt!"

He and the others got them sorted out and back into formation and tried it again… with nearly the same result. They tried again… and again. By the time they took a break after an hour, they had made some progress. A little. Maybe…

"This is harder'n I thought it would be," said Palle as they sat together in the shade of one of the walls surrounding the parade ground. "D'you suppose they went and gave us the worst of the lot?" He gestured to where their men were resting a few yards away.

"I don't think so," replied Aeron. "I was watching some of the other companies. They don't seem to be doing any better than we are."

"So they're all a buncha idiots?"

Aeron snorted. "Come on, we didn't look much better the first time we were out on the field."

Palle chuckled. "No, I guess we didn't, at that. Well, break time's over. Let's see what we can make of 'em."

Aeron hauled himself to his feet and walked over to where Vadik and Hagen were sitting. Both the dwarfs were puffing away on their pipes. The dwarfs, all of them apparently, were avid smokers and always carried their pipes and tobacco pouches with them. Shirefolk enjoyed smoking, too, and the Shires were the chief source of tobacco in the League, but they weren't as obsessed with it as the dwarfs were. He stood before them and said: "Let's get back at it."

"Right." Vadik stood up, carefully knocked his pipe against his boot, and put it away. Then he began shouting for the company to fall in. There were a lot of groans and moans and grumbling but most of them got up, trying to remember their spot in the formation.

A few didn't get up.

The dwarfs and Palle were pushing the others into line and hadn't noticed the still-seated batch yet. Aeron walked up to them. "Break's over, men. Back in formation. We have work to do."

"Work?" snapped one of them. "Marchin' around like a pack of idiots, you mean! I joined up to fight, dammit! Marchin'?" He spat on the ground. "That's for marchin'!"

"You have to learn how to march before you can fight."

"I *know* how to fight. You know how to fight… little boy?"

"Get up," said Aeron as forcefully as he could. The man just grinned, revealing a mouthful of stained teeth and spat again.

"Make me."

A chill went through him. He'd never faced this sort of defiance before, and he had no idea how to deal with it. *You have all the authority of a real officer! Use it!*

Holding his voice as steady as he could he said: "Get up. Right now. Or, or you'll regret it."

The man's bushy eyebrows came together above glinting eyes and he smiled. "Oh, will I now?" He slowly got to his feet, towering over Aeron. "Will I now?" He stepped closer. His fists were as big as Aeron's head.

It took every bit of nerve to keep from stepping away. The man was unarmed, but he had no doubt that one blow from those fists would lay him out cold for a week - if he ever woke up at all. He had his cadet's dagger on his belt. A weapon almost long enough to be a short sword for him. But if he drew it, it would be an admission that he'd lost control of the situation. What should he do?

"What's the trouble here?!" snapped a voice, and he relaxed slightly. Vadik had come up beside him. Glancing back, he saw Hagen and Palle were there, too.

"None of your damn business - *dwarf*!"

"Your commanding officer has given you an order. Now get in formation."

"Or what?" said the man, not the least bit frightened. His companions, who had been watching with amusement, were now on their feet and coming up to support their friend. He grinned another nasty grin and pointed at Aeron. "An officer? Him? I wouldn't follow him to the outhouse! No way I'm following that piece of dung into battle! I'm damn tired of being ordered around by this… this *halfman*! You think you're so high and mighty, well we're not gonna take it anymore! Run on home, or you'll wish you had!"

"Get in line and shut your mouth," said Aeron, amazed that he could speak at all. "This is your last warning." He couldn't ever remember being so keyed up. Not even when he was getting the snot beaten out of him at the tavern. The man started to raise his fist…

Out of nowhere, a large shape came around his right side, and before he could move a muscle, Sergeant Rolf was there. His fist slammed into the man's jaw and sent him sprawling in the dirt. The other men drew back in shock. The man on the ground looked up, clearly dazed, tried to get to his feet, and fell back to the ground. He stared at Rolf in bewilderment.

Rolf loomed over his fallen victim. “Refusing to obey the order of an officer is a crime punishable by fifty lashes,” he said in an icy voice. He loomed a little more. “Threatening an officer with violence is a crime punishable by *death.*”

The man was nearly groveling now. Rolf loosened his sword in its scabbard and looked back at Aeron. “What do you think, sir? Should we make an example of this one?”

Aeron twitched. *He's asking me? Calling me sir and asking me? Is he serious?* It was true that he had been put in command of this company, which sort of made him an officer. But he couldn’t hand out death to this man just on his say so! This had to be some charade Rolf was playing.

So play along.

“He… he does have spirit, Sergeant. It would be a shame to waste that—providing he can learn discipline.”

Rolf slid the sword back with an audible click. “Seems this is your lucky day, you dog,” he said to the man. “Mister Cadwallader thinks you might be of some use to Rhordia. I have my doubts, and you may end up at the end of a noose yet. But for today, you still have your life—and you can thank the officer for that! Now back in formation! All of you!”

The men scrambled to obey. The ones who had already been in ranks had seen all of this, and when the sergeant walked by them, they snapped to attention. He went completely around the formation, scowling at every man, and then came back and saluted Aeron. “Everything’s in order now, sir.”

Aeron returned the salute. “Thank you, Sergeant.” And then in a whisper: “Thank you very much.”

Rolf nodded and replied just as quietly: “You’re doing fine, kid. Keep it up.”

They worked for the rest of the afternoon without any trouble from the men. Sergeant Rolf was never far off, although he spent most of his time helping the other cadets. Aeron’s company made progress, and even though they still looked pretty ragged, they could march around, change direction, and go for hundreds of paces without falling into confusion.

Despite the progress, Aeron wasn’t feeling terribly pleased and grew more and more silent on the march back to the College. Palle noticed and cornered him by their bunks after dinner. “What’s the matter?” he demanded.

“Oh, what happened today. What Sergeant Rolf did.”

“What do you mean? It was great the way he decked that guy!”

“But he shouldn’t have had to. I lost… I lost control. I shouldn’t have let that happen.”

“How were you… how were any of us goin’ to stop it? That brute was near as big as an ogre! Even Vadik and Hagen didn’t want to fight him!”

“An officer needs to command the respect of his troops…”

“Yeah, yeah, go right on an’ quote the regulations! But that guy hadn’t read the regulation. Probably never read anything at all. But you hadn’t known him for more than an hour and he hadn’t never seen you before today. You hadn’t had time to ‘command his respect’.”

"Maybe not," said Aeron with a sigh. "Still, once we graduate we won't have Sergeant Rolf to do our fighting for us."

"Well, you're still plannin' to head back to your home afterward, aren't you? Back to the Shires to help command their troops?"

"I guess…"

"What do you mean you guess? That's what you always said you were gonna do."

Aeron shrugged. "You know how unusual it was for me to come here. I'm not sure my own people will know what to do with me when I do get back. So who knows, maybe I'll end up with a mercenary company - full of tall humans. Or I could even make the Long Walk…"

"Long Walk? What's that?" asked Palle.

"Oh, that's what we call making the journey to visit our kin down in Ej."

"Your who? From where?" Palle looked totally puzzled.

"You don't know about them? It's not exactly a secret or anything."

"Maybe among halflings, but I've never heard of them."

"Well, our oldest tales say that the People used to be wanderers. Mostly herdsmen, although we might stay in one spot for a few seasons to plant crops and then move on again. I'm guessing it was to stay away from the worst troubles during the God War and later the War with Winter. There are still some of us who do that. But finally, two large groups decided to put down roots for good. One was here in Upper Mantica when Abbetshire was founded. And another one in Lower Mantica, away south of the Infant Sea. That's in the elf countries. Most of them settled around an elf city called Ej. They get along very well with the elves and have prospered.

"Anyway, there is some contact between them and us. It's over a thousand leagues from here to there in a straight line, and a lot father by the routes you'd have to walk. It can take as much as two years to make the journey, so not many do. The visitors are very welcome because they bring news and new ideas. A lot of our best tinkerers like to make the trip to see what our kin have come up with. So, if my military knowledge isn't wanted here in the north, maybe it would be in Ej."

"Well, I sure hope you don't do that. You'll probably find work with the Shires companies. And back there, you won't have to deal with brutes like that one you faced today. In fact, you're pretty big for a halfling, your recruits will all be scared of you!" Palle laughed and nudged him, and Aeron couldn't help but smile.

"I suppose you're right."

"Course I am. Now stop worrying and let's get some rest."

Chapter 3

The routine continued, and Palle's optimism seemed to be borne out. There were no further rebellions while drilling the recruits, and there were no other incidents either; although grumblings and rumors from the town did not subside. The Fall Equinox came and went and the weather turned cooler and the harvests began. The cadets broke out the cloaks and heavier clothing they hadn't used since early spring. As the days shortened, they did less work outside and more inside.

A course of lectures on Military Magic and Engines, which Aeron had been looking forward to ever since he heard about them, began that fall, and he found them fascinating. The lectures on magic were taught by actual warmages who demonstrated their powers when practical, or just described their effects if letting them loose within the college grounds was deemed too dangerous. Along with the demonstrations came advice on how to make the best use of them in battle, or what to do if you were on the receiving end of enemy spells.

Some spells, like fireballs and lightning bolts, while terrifying enough even when shot harmlessly straight upward from the roof of the college were, nonetheless, expected. All the tales spoke of such things and did not surprise the cadets. There were other spells, however, which did come as a surprise - at least to Aeron. There were spells which could produce a blast of wind strong enough to push men backward despite all their efforts to move forward. Another spell was similar, but the wind was so icy cold, that it could cause frostbite and slow a man's movement to a crawl.

One of the mages, a gray-haired and rather unkempt fellow named Hasbin, called Aeron forward to be the test subject for another spell. Being less than thrilled by the prospect, he tried to hold back. "Come, come, my lad!" said Hasbin. "It won't hurt. You'll probably even like it! There, now, don't be afraid. But we'll need someone else too… Let's see who would be… You there! The bearded chap in back!" Aeron looked and saw that the mage was pointing to the dwarf, Hagen Felmann.

Hagen came forward even more reluctantly than Aeron, but eventually the two of them were seated in chairs and facing each other across a table. "Now then," said Hasbin, "you two know how to arm wrestle, don't you? Good! Grasp your hands and get ready to give it all you've got when I say so."

Hagen looked sharply at the mage. "Sir, I've got twice the strength of Aeron! I don't want to hurt him!"

"Oh, you won't, you won't, don't worry. Now, I am going to count backward from five. When I get to one, I'll say *now* and you two go at it. Understand?"

They both nodded, but Hagen whispered: "Don't worry, I'll go easy."

Aeron smiled, but he wasn't sure that Hagen needed to go easy. Somehow there had to be magic involved here…

Hasbin started counting backward, but by the time he'd reached three Aeron felt something, something *strange*. A weird tingling energy seemed to be filling him. By one, he felt like he was going to burst.

"Now!" cried Hasbin.

Aeron threw Hagen across the room.

He was so startled he ended up throwing himself to the floor with the follow-through. He scrambled to his feet just as Hagen scrambled to his. Both the cadets—in fact all the cadets in the room—bore nearly identical expressions of astonishment.

"Are… are you all right, Hagen?" gasped Aeron.

"Arm's a little sore," said the dwarf, moving his shoulder around, "but all right otherwise. How… how'd you do that?"

All eyes turned to Hasbin, who was grinning from ear to ear. "It was a spell which can increase a person's strength. Or in a battle, a whole group of people's strength. You can imagine how useful that would be in combat. Sadly, the effects don't last long." Indeed, even as the instructor spoke, Aeron could feel the amazing sense of energy which had filled him seeping away.

"There is a similar spell which will weaken an enemy," added the mage.

"Sir," said Aeron. "Is there any way to protect yourself against this sort of magic? While it would be grand to have warmages helping us out, the idea of being burned to a crisp by a fireball; or left weak and helpless and not being able to do anything about it is rather… daunting."

Hasbin leaned back against the wall and seemed to be sucking on his teeth. "Well now, that's an interesting question. One mage, if he's good enough, and by that I mean powerful enough and quick enough, can use his own skills to counteract an opposing mage's spell - sometimes. But for a non-magic user? That's a different matter and a question that we mages have been puzzling over for centuries. Because it is true that a spell will affect different people differently. If I throw a fireball into a block of enemy pikemen, some of them are going to go down, killed or injured, while others, who are every bit as much inside the blast, will get away virtually unscathed. Why? No one really knows. Some theorize that it's a matter of will. That somehow a person can simply refuse to be affected by the magic and something inside him makes it happen. I'm not sure I really accept that theory, but I don't have a better one. But don't you young ones go out there taking crazy risks because you think you can just refuse to be hurt! That's a good way to get killed."

The other mages weren't quite as flamboyant as Hasbin, but their demonstrations were just as interesting - or alarming. Some of the effects of magical spells could be rather grisly. Master Mage Bhim one day took the class outside—despite the chilly weather - to where the college quartermaster kept some of the animals who were destined for the cooks' stewpots.

"Now I have already demonstrated the healing spells we can use to save the badly wounded from death and even put the more lightly wounded back into the fight," said Bhim. "But that sort of spell puts a considerable drain on a mage as he has to draw all of the power from himself. There is another way of doing it, which in a battle can be especially useful." At his direction, a large pig was dragged out of its pen and set before the assembled cadets. "Now, all of you gentlemen in the front rank. Please roll up the sleeves on your right arms." A murmur of surprise passed through the company, but they did as they were told. Aeron was at the left end of the front rank, and he rolled up his sleeve.

"Sergeant, if you would assist?" said Bhim to Sergeant Rolf.

The sergeant nodded and drew his dagger. He stepped up to the first man, grabbed him by the wrist, and drew a cut down the man's forearm. The cadet yelped a bit but did not pull away. Rolf moved to the next man. One by one he cut the cadets until his dagger was dripping red. As he got closer, Aeron could see that the cuts were not deep, just a shallow slice through the skin to draw blood. Vadik took his cut without even the tiniest flinch and seemed to be daring Rolf to cut to the bone.

Then it was Aeron's turn. Rolf's dagger probably wasn't as sharp as it had been when he started the exercise, but the cut was quick and sure, and he hardly felt it at first; but as the blood dripped down to his hand and then off his fingertips, it did begin to hurt. Not nearly as much as his beating in the tavern those months earlier, but it still hurt.

"All right," said Bhim. "My thanks to all of you for shedding your blood so readily for Rhordia. I shall make it up to you in just a moment." The man closed his eyes, spread his arms, and began a slow chant. Just like when Mage Hasbin had cast the strengthening spell on him, Aeron began to feel a strange tingling coursing through him. It concentrated in his injured arm, and as he watched, the wound closed up. He used his other hand to wipe away the blood and there wasn't even a mark left on him!

"Oh! Oh, look at that!" cried someone.

Aeron's head jerked up, and his eyes were drawn to where everyone else was looking - the pig.

The poor thing was squealing and thrashing about, tugging at the rope held by one of the quartermaster's men. As he watched, red lines appeared on the animal's pink flesh, and blood began seeping out of them. Line after line crisscrossed its hide and soon the beast was awash in blood. It squealed and grunted, and in a few more moments, it keeled over on its side. It gave a last shudder and was still. The man who had been holding it dropped the rope, backed off a half dozen paces, and made a holy sign to ward off evil. "Poor beastie," said Vadik.

"As most of you have probably guessed by now, I used my magic to transfer your wounds to the pig," said Bhim. "Not only does it take less of my strength, but in a battle, your wounds will become the enemy's."

The company that returned inside was very quiet. No one touched any of the pork served for dinner that night, even though there was no way to know if it came from the sacrificial pig.

The next day came a class Aeron had eagerly been waiting for: the one on war machines. It was taught by one of the legends of the College of Warcraft, one of the Shirefolk no less, named Paddy Bobart. In his youth he had been trained by dwarfs, and later, by the even more legendary Percival Arbuckle, who had died years ago. Bobart had taken his position at the college and was now quite elderly himself.

The first part of the lecture was on the theory and uses of war machines on the battlefield. While that was interesting enough, the really good part was when they got to go down to the armory and workshops of the artificers and actually see the things close up. Paddy Bobart was moving quite slowly, using a walking stick, but he was assisted by another Shirefolk, a fellow named Tomos Gerallt, whom Aeron saw only rarely. Following along was Dilwyn Brynmoor, who Aeron knew a little better.

Some of the workshops were in the main building, but those were for the smaller and safer items. The constructions which required furnaces and forges - which also contained powerful spells or gunpowder - were housed in a long building at the corner of the College grounds, fast up against the banks of the Wolfmoor River that flowed through Eowulf. It had three heavy stone walls and a fourth made of wood facing the stream. The theory was that if anything went seriously wrong, any explosions would blow out the wooden wall and spend their force over the river while the three stone walls protected the College. In Aeron's time there, nothing like that had happened, but he'd heard stories of when it had.

It was a chilly day with a biting wind, but inside the workshop it was uncomfortably warm. One of the furnaces was going at full blast, and as they watched, a stream of molten metal poured forth with a shower of gleaming sparks into a mold for a new cannon. Several finished cannon barrels were lined up, waiting for carriages to mount them on. There were elaborate decorations cast into the surface and mysterious runes carved in them.

"Nothing magical about cannons - usually," said Master Bobart. "Get a metal tube, put gunpowder in it, touch it off, and you've got a cannon. Most anyone can do it if they've got the tools. But here in our shop, we go the extra step." He ran a gnarled hand along the gleaming metal. "We put spells into them making the metal stronger so it won't burst like so many guns do after a while. This one, here, has another spell making the cannon balls fly straight and true. Cannon's not much good unless it can hit the target."

They moved out of the foundry into another part of the large building. This area had smaller forges for doing more detailed work with metal. A dozen or more people were working at anvils or grinding wheels or long tables stacked with tools; hammers banged incessantly. Off to one side was another table with people sitting at it.

"These are some of our novices," said Bobart pointing to some younger people seated along the work bench. "They're still learning the basics of manipulating matter." To Aeron's eyes, they appeared to be doing nothing except just be sitting there staring at chunks of metal. One of them, seemingly oblivious to the people watching, suddenly shook his head and slammed his hands down on the bench, making the bits in front of him jump; and then he cursed. Bobart moved up behind him and asked: "Trouble, Gallin?"

The man twitched in surprise and jerked around. "Oh! Master Paddy! I… I was just trying to join the pieces and they… they're fighting me."

"Heh, they'll do that sometimes. But maybe you're trying too hard. If you have the strength, you can make the rascals to do what you want with brute force, but sometimes it's easier just to coax them." He held out his hands and the pieces of metal on the table started to vibrate. They jiggled and bounced and slowly moved toward each other. They touched each other and for an instant glowed red; and when the glow faded, they were a smooth solid bar of iron. "See?"

"Y-yes, Master. I think..."

"Keep trying, you'll get the hang of it." He stretched out his hand again, and the bar shattered into pieces.

They moved along to get a closer look at the people who were working at the other tables.

"These people are working on weapons and armor which will hold enchantments when they are finished," said Dilwyn. "Swords and axes with uncanny sharpness, armor that can withstand blows that would pierce ordinary metal, arrows that almost never miss."

"Who gets this stuff?" asked one cadet. "Surely not the ordinary soldiers!"

Dilwyn shrugged. "Most of these things go to knights and other nobles who can afford to pay for them." His voice fell, and it was hard to hear him above the ringing hammers. "A lot of the College's funding comes from the sale of items like these."

They watched the people working, but after a while, Aeron came up to Dilwyn. "I heard that you have one of the big ... devices here. Are we going to be allowed to see it?"

Dilwyn smiled. "Last stop on the tour. I set it to warming up before the class started. It ought to be ready by now." He walked over and spoke to Bobart, and the old artificer nodded. They headed down to the end of the workshop and through a large set of double doors.

The room beyond wasn't large compared with the workshop, and that made the thing sitting in the middle of the floor seem all that much larger. It looked rather like a gigantic mastiff dog, or maybe a wild boar. Four thick legs, a round body with a high arched back, a head with eyes, a snout, and two long tusks, which reinforced the boar image.

But it had what looked like a pair of arms emerging from its shoulders and folded back along its sides...

...and what looked like a boiler and chimney on its back...

...and the whole thing was about twelve feet tall...

"An Iron Beast!" gasped Palle. The other cadets made exclamations in excitement and awe. The huge contraption was indeed mostly iron, but it had a lot of bronze and copper parts as well. A few of the outer panels had been removed, and Aeron could see that the innards were full of gears, pulleys, and other things he couldn't begin to identify. As he got closer, he could feel heat radiating off it. It creaked and groaned, and small puffs of steam spurted out of seams and joints. Moving around to the front, he could see that it was heavily armored, and the two metal arms carried a terrifying array of edged weapons. It was clearly a machine meant for war - or at least for killing.

Master Bobart strolled around the machine, looking at it closely and poking at something here, tugging at something there, until finally he seemed satisfied and had Dilwyn and Tomos replace the open panels. He then turned to face the cadets. "Well, what you see here is something I cobbled together over the last year or so. I call her Helga." This got a laugh, and the old halfling smiled. "She's all fired up and I can have her show off a little…"

"Excuse me sir," said Vadik Gulbrand. "You said 'fired up,' what does this machine burn? I can see some steam leaking out. Is there a fire heating a boiler?"

"There's *heat* producing the steam, but not exactly fire," replied Bobart. "What it is precisely is my secret, I'm afraid."

"So it's magic then?"

"You might say so. There's magic all through Helga. It makes her move, makes her do what I tell her. But enough talk! Let me show you what she can do." He walked over to stand in front of his creation which towered over him. He tapped a leg lightly with his walking stick. "Helga, time to wake up."

The machine moved. It seemed to straighten up, almost like a soldier snapping to attention. They heard scraping metal and clanking gears. An ominous red glow appeared in the thing's two eyes. "Ah, there you are," said Bobart, obviously pleased. "Helga, take two steps forward." The machine lurched and clanked two awkward steps forward. The cadets murmured appreciatively.

"Good, good. Now let's go outside. Helga, open the doors, please." Bobart pointed toward another set of double doors. The machine moved again, less awkwardly this time, and step by step approached the doors. Aeron expected the machine to push them open like a person would, but instead it suddenly lunged forward and the two tusks seemed to move outward from the head like thrusting spears, tearing both doors off their hinges! They tumbled to the ground with splinters flying everywhere. The machine stopped in the opening, apparently waiting for further orders from its creator.

Tomos Gerallt was standing close to Aeron, and he heard him mutter: "Why must he always show off like this? The carpenters get so angry fixing all the mess."

Bobart and Dilwyn herded the class around the behemoth and into an open courtyard behind the armory. A few dozen mannequins had been set up there: wooden posts with old coats of chainmail draped on them, shields hung from hooks, and rusty helmets set on top so they looked like soldiers. They were in two rows with a few dozen paces between the first row and the second.

"Gentlemen," said Bobart, "please stand to the sides, you don't want to get in front of her." The cadets quickly split into two groups, one on each side of the courtyard. Aeron and Palle moved over to the southern wall, with the machine to their right and the mannequins to their left.

When everyone was out of the way, Bobart stepped up to Helga, pointed at the first row of fake soldiers, and said: "Helga, destroy." Without hesitation, it moved forward, its arms unfolded from the sides, drawing back, ready to strike. It reached the row of mannequins, skewering two of them with its tusks, then the arms flashed into action, moving almost too fast to see. Helmets went flying, posts were snapped off, coats of mail were ripped to shreds, links spraying everywhere, and a loose shield went sailing over Aeron's head to bang off the wall behind him. Its head swung left and right, flinging the impaled mannequins off, and then it charged forward again along the line, trampling several more. Helga's clanking and squeaking rose to a roar, and clouds of steam almost engulfed it. In just a dozen heartbeats, the first row of targets were reduced to splinters. The machine swiveled back and forth looking for more targets. It seemed to spot the second line of mannequins and took several steps toward them before Bobart called out: "Helga, stop!" The machine instantly came to a halt.

"Wow!" gasped Palle. His reaction was echoed by almost everyone else there.

"Impressive, eh?" said Bobart, looking immensely pleased with himself.

Aeron was as impressed as anyone, but a question popped into his mind. "Uh, sir? Master Bobart?"

"Eh? What's that, young fellow?"

"Sir, In… in a real battle, things could get kind of… confused. How does… how does Helga tell friend from foe?"

Bobart blinked, and his bushy eyebrows drew together. He stared at Aeron as if seeing him for the first time. "And who might you be?"

"Uh, I'm Aeron Cadwallader, sir."

"Ah! Oh yes, knew your grandfather. What… what was your question, young man?"

"How does your machine tell friend from foe in a battle?"

"Oh yes. Good question, good question. And I'll answer it. Come over here." He beckoned toward his war machine.

"Over… over there, sir?"

"Yes, over there! Come, come, she won't hurt you."

Reluctantly, Aeron left the ranks of his fellow cadets and followed Bobart until they were standing right in front of the enormous thing. The red glow in the machine's eyes appeared to follow them. Bobart tapped the metal monstrosity with his walking stick and said: "Helga!" Again Bobart's creation seemed to come to attention. "Helga, this fellow here," he suddenly wacked Aeron with his walking stick, who yelped in surprise. "This fellow here is a friend. Helga! Friend! Understand?" The red glows seemed to focus directly on Aeron, who shrank back slightly. It made no other response that Aeron could detect, but Bobart said: "Good!" He turned back to Aeron. "All right, you go stand over there. Behind the row of dummies."

"Over there?"

"Yes, over there! You're not hard of hearing are you, Cadwallader?"

"Uh, no sir…"

"Then get a move on!" He pointed with his stick and seemed ready to whack him again. Aeron quickly walked where he was directed, passed through the line of mannequins, and stood about a dozen paces behind them—about as far as he could go due to the courtyard wall.

Bobart moved aside and then said: "Helga, destroy." And pointed toward the mannequins - and Aeron.

Once again the machine surged into motion. But this time, instead of watching from a - fairly - safe distance, Aeron was standing right in its path. The four huge metal legs were moving, the bladed arms were ready to strike, and it was coming directly toward him. Involuntarily, he stepped backward and bumped up against the stone wall; there could be no further retreat.

Helga reached the line of mannequins and, as before, cut them to shreds. Aeron was standing far too close for comfort, and he cringed down and shielded his head with his arms as bits of debris and wreckage spun away from the maelstrom and splattered the wall behind him.

As the noise died down, he dared look again, and there was Helga in the midst of her slain enemies. It turned from side to side - and then looked back directly at him.

It started moving again, right toward him. He could feel the tread of its mammoth feet as they struck the ground, coming closer and closer. He couldn't move, he just stared at its red eyes. Finally, it was just a few paces away, towering over him.

It stopped.

"F-friend, Helga?" he stuttered. "Helga? Friend?"

Helga leaned forward a bit, and he could feel the heat radiating off it. The red eyes were fixed on him.

"Friend?"

The machine suddenly straightened up, turned - the back legs nearly running over Aeron—and took three steps toward Bobart, then halted, motionless; except for a few wisps of steam drifting away.

Aeron wilted against the wall and let out a long, long sigh. Almost simultaneously, the cadets of Second Company began to cheer. They whooped and yelled and some tossed their caps into the air. At first, as he stumbled back toward his spot in the group, he thought they were cheering about the amazing demonstration of Helga's destructive power, but as he reached them, he was mobbed by his comrades and he realized that they were cheering for *him!*

"That was incredible!"

"Well done, Aeron!"

"I never would have done that!"

"Thought we was gonna have chopped halfling for dinner tonight!"

Hands slapped him on the back or ruffled his hair. Other hands demanded he shake them, and he could only mumble out incoherent replies.

Eventually order was restored and they marched back toward the main building. "Bravest thing I've ever seen, Aeron!" said Palle to him.

"Damn near wet myself," said Aeron. Palle laughed, but it was true. He was still shaking, and it wasn't because of the cold.

As the company was dismissed, Dilwyn Brynmor came up to him. "I haven't seen much of you lately, Aeron," he said.

Aeron shrugged. He'd never seen much of Dilwyn in all his time there. The artificers tended to keep to themselves. "Been busy," he said.

Dilwyn's voiced dropped to almost a whisper. "I heard about what happened to you last summer. In the tavern, I mean."

He shrugged again, not wanting to think about the ugly incident. "Over and done with."

"What did you do about it?" pressed Dilwyn.

"Stayed away from taverns."

Dilwyn snorted. "I imagine so! But say, Aeron, why don't you come down to the *Golden Ale* with me tonight? It's Shirefolk owned, y'know. We'd be welcome there, and we could have a talk."

About what? He wasn't sure what Dilwyn was up to, but suddenly he was very tempted. After the beating incident, he'd stayed in the College, even when he had time off from his duties. He was getting truly sick of the place and a chance to get away seemed like a grand idea. "All right. I don't have duty tonight."

"Good! I heard they've got a new supply of Shires-brewed coming in today. Be nice to have something better than the swill they serve in the refectory. I'll find you after dinner and we'll go."

* * * * *

After the meal was finished, Aeron put on his heavy cloak and met Dilwyn in the main entrance hall. They went out through the College gates, Aeron needing to show a pass, but Dilwyn's cloak had the red and gold braid of an artificer on it and the guard let him go through without a comment. It was almost fully dark, but the streets had lanterns hanging from poles and buildings at intervals, and they had no trouble finding their way. The streets weren't deserted, but the daytime crowds had mostly dispersed, and few people noticed the pair of small figures walking along the cobblestone streets.

The city's Shirefolk population was concentrated in an area on the northern edge, so it was a fair walk to get there. As they moved through the central parts, they had to pass human inns and taverns, and more people began to notice them. A few made rude remarks. "Are you armed?" asked Dilwyn.

"I've got my cadet dagger. You?"

"A knife. And I also have this." He tugged his cloak aside enough that Aeron could see something tucked into his belt. It took him a moment to realize that it was a gunpowder weapon, a *pistol*.

"You expecting serious trouble?"

"Not really, but I'm glad to not be walking alone. During the summer when it stays light so late I didn't mind, but now, in the dark…"

Despite their worries and precautions, no one bothered them, and they reached the Shirefolk enclave. This didn't look much different from the rest of Eowulf. After the Shires formally joined the League of Rhordia, a slow trickle of Shirefolk moved to the human cities. At first they were mostly just representatives of Shires businesses who were there to oversee the burgeoning trade. But with time, those representatives started bringing their families, and then more enterprising people arrived to do business directly with the humans or to provide services to the other resident Shirefolk. For the most part, these newcomers simply rented or bought the too-large human houses already there. Some, with the means, remodeled the structures, shrinking doors, lowering windows, or even adding additional floors. Most just left things as they were. A very few, somehow acquiring a vacant lot or some older structure that was on the verge of collapse, built Shires-style structures, but those were rare. The Shirefolk area could mostly be identified by the distinctive names on the storefronts or the brightly colored awnings on the windows.

The *Golden Ale* was one of those structures that was human-built but heavily modified for use by Shirefolk. The bright yellow front doors were large enough, and the main room had a ceiling tall enough, to accommodate humans if they chose to do business there; but most of the rest of the place had lower ceilings and smaller doors to suit Shirefolk. There was quite a crowd of their people there when they came inside. But instead of the expected sounds of merry-making, the place was filled with angry voices.

"Something has to be done!"

"This is an outrage!"

"We can't let the bloody humies get away with this!"

Aeron looked at Dilwyn in confusion. "What's happening?"

"I don't know. Let's find out."

They made their way through the crowd - the most Shirefolk Aeron had seen in one spot since he left home - and made it up to the bar. After several tries, Dilwyn managed to get the attention of the barkeep. "Oh, hi, Dilwyn," he said, "what can I get you?"

"Information, Dani! What in the Abyss has happened?"

"You mean you haven't heard?" exclaimed the fellow in surprise. "The wagon train! The one comin' from the Shires, it was attacked this morning! Not a dozen miles from the city walls!"

"Attacked by who?" demanded Aeron. The barkeep looked at him and scowled.

"This is my friend, Aeron Cadwallader," said Dilwyn. "Now who attacked the train, Dani? Bandits?"

"Pah!" spat the barkeep. "That's what these damn… *guardsmen* say! But they're lyin'! The survivors from the train say they didn't look like no bandits. Looked like trained soldiers."

"Survivors?" exclaimed Aeron. The word suggested that someone hadn't. "Anyone hurt?"

"Two of the teamsters were knocked around pretty good," said the barkeep, "but the wagonmaster tried to fight, and he was killed! Killed dead!"

"Missing Gods," hissed Aeron. "But a wagon train? Why weren't they using the canal?"

The barkeep shook his head. "It's the damn tolls the humans have levied. Damnation, *we* built the bloody canal! And the treaty we all signed when we joined the League says that Eowulf is responsible for the upkeep in their territory. They always levied a small toll to pay for it, but in the last year, they doubled it and then doubled it again. Still some traffic on it, but a lot of our folk are using wagons rather than pay."

"But it still could have been bandits, couldn't it?" said Dilwyn. "Some of those bands from down south are made up of discharged soldiers or deserters. They might look like soldiers."

"Maybe," said the barkeep, "but then explain how the stolen goods - and one of the wagons - were up for sale in the city market not four hours after they were stolen!"

"What?"

"It's true," said another fellow edging into the conversation. "I saw 'em myself. A Shires-built wagon, and the ale was still in their barrels with the Wictun brands burned into 'em! Saw other stuff that was sure from home, too. The folks doin' the sellin' didn't even try to deny it was stolen; they were braggin' about it! There were some of the city guards there, too, and they didn't do a thing!"

"Damn…" said Aeron, the word nearly falling out of his open mouth. There was no way the city guardsmen wouldn't have at least been suspicious of something like this. Why hadn't they done anything?

"So what is being done?" asked Dilwyn.

"Caradoc Lowri, our representative here, has lodged a complaint with the League Council," said the barkeep, shaking his head. "But all they told him was that they'd bring it up at the next session—which ain't for a month!" The fellow looked around at the other patrons. "Some folks are sayin' we need to provide our own armed escorts to wagon trains. Others—visitors from home who don't live here—are sayin' we ought to stop all trade with the humans until they put a stop to this sort of thievery. Can't say I'd be too happy with that, but something has to be done." He looked at Dilwyn. "So what can I get you?"

Dilwyn looked startled by the sudden change of subject. "Oh, uh, ale?"

"Got nothin' but local brewed. That all right?"

"Sure. Let us each have a mug." He slid a coin across the counter.

They took their drinks and found a table away from the crowd which was still very noisy. "So what do you think, Dilwyn?" asked Aeron.

"I knew there was trouble brewing, but I didn't think anything like this was going to happen. This is bad, Aeron. One of our people killed! Snubs and insults—and an occasional beating—are things that will be forgotten after a while. But not this."

"No."

"I don't know what's going to happen, but we haven't heard the last of it."

Aeron just nodded, unable to think of any reply. But Dilwyn was right: this was bad. And it was probably going to get worse. How much worse was anyone's guess.

Chapter 4

Thankfully, the initial furor died away, and the incident caused barely a ripple at the College, but things did not settle down. With the harvesting nearly completed, this was a time when there were usually fleets of barges, or long wagon trains from the Shires to the cities, bringing the surplus bounty of the Shirefolk's fields to become stores for the winter to tide the cities through to spring.

But the fleet and trains that arrived were much smaller than normal, and they were heavily guarded by grim-faced Shirefolk. The scarcity raised the prices, and the Shires slapped on a surcharge as well to pay for the guards. There was a great hue and cry among the citizens of Eowulf, and were it not for the guards, there might well have been riots. At first, the city guardsmen looked on as if they wanted to allow a fight, but eventually they stepped in to at least maintain the illusion that they were keeping order. Several tense weeks followed, but eventually the merchants and their guards departed, and a disgruntled calm took over.

Not much of this affected the College or its occupants. There was some grumbling about the 'haughty halflings,' but Aeron was still being toasted as the halfling who stared down an Iron Beast, and no one caused him any trouble. Still, he didn't venture out again and depended on Dilwyn for most of his news.

The news wasn't particularly encouraging, but Aeron's attention and that of all the other cadets were focused on the upcoming Great Muster. Halfway between the Fall Equinox and Winter Solstice was a gathering of the military forces of the League of Rhordia. The armies of each of the five duchies along with the forces of the Shires converged on one of the cities to be counted and inspected and paraded. It was as much a social occasion as a military one. There would be feasts and balls and festivals for one and all. It was seen as a unifying event that would go on for nearly a fortnight before everyone headed home in time to beat the first snows.

The muster was held in a different city each year on a rotating basis. This year was Eowulf's turn. It would be the first time Aeron got to see it. He was greatly looking forward to this, and he privately hoped that it would help calm all the recent troubles. The more practical aspects of the coming event were that the cadets were polishing their brass, blacking their boots, and making sure their tabards were clean and mended. But that wasn't the limit to their responsibilities. The cadets would be part of the muster, but they would also be used to make sure it ran smoothly. The cadets and the engineers would lay out the camps, locate the sanitary facilities, create supply dumps, and make sure everyone knew the schedule of activities. Their instructors said that it would be great experience for when they were on an actual campaign. Aeron realized that the instructors were probably correct - despite all the hard work.

Regular classes and instruction were suspended for the duration and for several weeks before, but the cadets were on duty from before dawn to well after sunset every day. Their duty assignments were rotated around so they would gain experience in all the different activities. Aeron most enjoyed his duty with the engineers laying out the camps. The engineers used sophisticated equipment to establish precisely straight lines that were an exact distance apart for the tents of the expected troops. Streets were established, areas were provided for the men to assemble, the cook tents, the sinks, everything was provided for. It was all laid out with wooden stakes, ropes with colored ribbons, and even chalk lines drawn on the ground. The size of the camps was enormous, and it was fortunate that the event took place after the harvest because a number of farmers' fields were now being requisitioned for the muster. Aeron looked forward to seeing so many troops all in one place.

The days he worked with the schedulers were not as interesting but also less strenuous. Messages came in from each contingent almost every day with departure dates, rates of march, the number of troops and animals coming, and their likely arrival dates. He had to organize the messages, report to his commander, and sometimes write out replies. He noted that there were no messages coming in from the Shires, but perhaps he'd been elsewhere when they came.

Working with the quartermasters was probably the most demanding - and the most awkward. The reduction in food shipments from the Shires was going to make feeding the arriving hosts more difficult. Some of the messages Aeron had sent out when working with the schedulers was to tell the expected contingents to carry more food with them than they normally would on such a march. But they couldn't carry enough for their whole stay, so parties of men were sent out into the city to find and inventory food stores.

He only accompanied two of these parties and he was rather appalled by the rough-and-ready nature of the operation. Men broke into private homes and businesses, gathered up food, and loaded it onto wagons, leaving behind only a paper receipt of dubious value.

They managed to collect enough food (he overheard an officer say that the problems were due to local hoarders rather an actual shortage) and a few days later, under sunny skies and a mild wind, the first of the troops began to arrive at the muster. These were the contingent from Torffs Valem, the second-most distant of the duchies, and most of the troops were mounted men. None of the duchies were bringing all their troops, of course, someone had to stay behind and guard things, and it made the most sense to leave the slower infantry.

Reports from the previous day had put the Valemers less than five leagues away at the town of Wolfmarch, and around noontime, lookouts in the towers along the north part of the city began to ring bells and blow horns and the word was passed that they were in sight. Aeron, along with most of his company, had been tasked with guiding these first arrivals to their camps and seeing that they had all they needed. He and his fellow cadets hurried to the North Gate and had to push their way to the front of the crowds which had gathered.

Standing on tiptoe, Aeron could see a cloud of dust on the Wolfmarch Road, and before long sunlight gleaming off lance tips. Moment by moment they drew nearer, and he could see more and more detail. The men from Torffs Valem generally used orange and black as their colors, and he could see that the leading company of knights had those colors on their shields, on their lance pennants, and on the caparisons of their horses. While not as showy as the colors of some of the other city-states, it gave a very warlike impression.

Aeron was still staring when Palle nudged him. "Come on," he said, "we've got a job to do."

"Oh, right, right."

They, and the rest of their detachment, moved out from the crowds to meet the approaching horsemen. Before them went one of the Duke of Eowulf's chief liegemen on horseback to welcome the arriving troops. This wasn't the formal welcome, which would come later, and was kept as brief as possible to allow the weary troops to get to their camps and rest.

Aeron couldn't hear what was said, but in short order the companies of Valemers were splitting off from the main column and being guided to their assigned section of the camps. Aeron and Palle had a company of mounted men-at-arms to conduct. They weren't knights and their equipment wasn't nearly as impressive, but they still looked like proud fighting men. Soon they had them where they belonged and informed the captain where he could pasture his horses and where to find all the things his men would need. Tents started going up in neat rows, and the soldiers were laughing and joking and appeared in good humor. A few looked in surprise at Aeron and one or two made unkind remarks, but he ignored them.

The next three days saw more and more troops arriving. The contingents from Targun Spire and Hetronburg marched in. Targun Spire's colors were dark blue and silver, and Hetronburg's were forest green and white. Hetronburg was the closest of the other duchies, and they had brought along a lot of their infantry: blocks of pikemen, companies of crossbowmen, and a mercenary unit of ogres. Targun Spire had a famed menagerie, and among the arriving contingent were two enormous mammoths, captured from the northern steppes and trained for war. The two beasts seemed impossibly large, but they were kept well under control. Horses, except for a few specially trained units from Targun Spire, were terrified of the mammoths, so cavalry had to be kept well away from them in camp and during the review itself. All the units were settled in without major problems. Aeron was very impressed by the efficiency of it all. The benefits of planning and organization, until now just something in his textbooks, was made very clear to him.

Berlonviche was the last of the human forces to arrive, and they took the road which led them through the middle of the Shires. Aeron half-expected the levies of his own people to follow along behind the Berlonvichers, but when the final companies of the yellow and sky blue-clad men marched in, the road was empty behind them. The Great Muster would officially commence in just one more day…

That night, right after dinner, Aeron found Dilwyn. "Where are the Shires levies?" he asked. "Have you heard anything?"

Dilwyn shook his head. “Master Bobart knows something, but he hasn’t said anything to me. He can be mighty tight-lipped when he wants to be.”

“It’s going to look really bad if no one shows up from the Shires.”

“I know. But there’s nothing you or I can do about it. Look, I have to go, I’ll see you tomorrow.”

Aeron didn’t sleep well that night, but the next day, a contingent of troops did arrive from the Shires. A very small one, just two hundred light cavalry on their ponies and a dozen supply wagons pulled by double teams. He wasn’t sure if this was meant to be a calculated insult or if it was to send some other message. But they were here and in time for the muster. He supposed that was the important thing. His duties kept him from going to see them that day, but he resolved to go talk with them when he had the chance.

The following day was the official beginning of the muster. Aeron and all the cadets, indeed every person in the College of Warcraft, donned their best: gray tabards embroidered with the proper colors for their branch and year, polished black boots and floppy black felt hats with a brass College badge and long colored feathers, again denoting branch and ranking. They marched out to the large field where everyone would assemble, the musicians in front, playing a rousing tune. The skies were clear, but a brisk wind blew down from the northwest, and Aeron pulled his cloak close around him.

The muster field was enormous. It was positioned between the city walls and the camps which had been set up for all the troops. There was a great crowd of people from the city and the surrounding countryside there to watch. Most just clumped together on the open sides of the field, but Eowulf’s nobility and wealthy preferred spots on the city walls which would give the best views and allow them to avoid rubbing elbows with the commoners. A large, elevated pavilion had been erected near the walls to hold the five dukes and their entourages. Large banners with the emblems of the duchies and the Shires flapped in the steady breeze. The Shires’ banner was an emerald green field with a golden plow in the center and flanked by shocks of wheat, tobacco leaves, barley spikelets, grape clusters, and hops flowers, all with a blazing sun overhead.

As the College’s contingent marched through the West Gate, Aeron could see the other troops massing on the edge of their camps. The College administrators along with the warmages, artificers, and most of the engineers marched over to a spot to the left of the pavilion, but the cadets had another duty. They were issued with small flags on poles and were to act as guides and markers for the various contingents to make sure they went the right way and ended up in the right spot.

The Great Muster would begin with the Grand Review. Each contingent would march past the pavilion to be reviewed by the dukes and other notables and then swing around the edge of the field, past the crowds, and then end up massed in a position facing the pavilion. The cadets in the Third Company were placed along the route the troops would march; the Fourth Company would be placed to mark the locations where each contingent would end up. First and Second Companies would be attached directly to the contingents themselves to make sure they went where they were supposed to. Aeron had pleaded to be assigned to the Shires contingent, and to his surprise, his request was approved. He picked up his green and gold flag and headed off toward the Shires camp. Palle and the dwarfs went with him. There had been about twenty other cadets assigned to the halflings, but when it was realized how few there were, they had been reassigned.

The cadets spread out as they trotted toward their contingents. The waiting troops were already in formation; serried ranks of infantry with glittering spear points, knights and cavalry on restive horses, stalwart ogres, bellowing mammoths, cocky archers, and flamboyant musicians. It was really rather magnificent. Aeron should have been thrilled, but he couldn't take his eyes off the tiny halfling contingent, standing quietly on the edge of a campground meant for twenty times as many troops.

He spotted the person who must have been the commander, sitting a somewhat larger pony than the others, out in front of the formation, accompanied by a banner-bearer. He was an elderly fellow, with gray hair, face creased with wrinkles. Dunstan Rootwell was his name. Aeron had heard of him but never met him before. He was a bit of legend in the Shires, and he'd fought in a good many battles over the years.

Aeron ran up to him. "Sir? Captain Rootwell? I'm the guide for your… your… force." He wasn't sure what to call it. Technically it was a company, he supposed, but that sounded much too… insignificant.

Rootwell, who had not been looking in Aeron's direction, twisted around on his mount and then looked down in surprise. "Who the blazes are you?" he demanded.

"Uh, Aeron Cadwallader, sir. From the College of Warcraft. I'm to be your guide."

Rootwell frowned. "Oh, right, Cadwallader. You still hanging around here are you?"

"Yes, sir. I have another year and a half at the College."

Rootwell cleared his throat and spat on the ground. "Let's get this over with."

Aeron wasn't sure if he was speaking to him, but he just nodded. "Yes, sir. They should fire the starting gun pretty soon, sir." Rootwell turned away and didn't say any more. He seemed angry. *But at whom?*

Aeron placed himself next to Rootwell. Palle and the dwarfs spaced themselves out along the column of cavalry. While they waited, Aeron looked them over and noted that while their weapons - spears and bows for the most part - were all in good order, the troopers were decked out for war, not a review. No colorful tabards covered their leather armor, no pennants decorated their spears, and those with shields had kept their canvas coverings on. Only the banner added any color to the formation.

They stood waiting for quite a while. From his position, he could only see people moving around by the pavilion, but not what was going on. Well, he supposed that there was bound to be delays for one reason or other. The review was supposed to start at the fifth bell, but it was long past that. Standing in place, he began to get chilled from the brisk wind.

Waiting, Aeron kept looking up at Captain Rootwell, trying to work up the courage to ask why the Shires had sent so few troops. But the older officer refused to meet his eye and the question died on his lips.

Finally, there was a blaring of trumpets from the direction of the pavilion, and a white puff of smoke erupted from one of the towers along the wall. A few heartbeats later, a loud *boom* rolled over them. Horns from the waiting troops answered back and the contingent from Torffs Valem began to move. The knights, all in orange and black, preceded by their general and banner-bearer, both mounted on magnificent aralez, and a mounted band of musicians, led the way. They turned to march toward the city walls and then swung left so they would pass directly in front of the pavilion. All the other musicians silenced themselves and let the Torffs Valems play alone. Company after company and regiment after regiment, they advanced. When the head of the column reached the pavilion, the musicians turned to the left and pivoted around so they faced the dukes. The general turned out to the right and positioned himself to the side of the pavilion to watch his command move by. Each unit saluted the dukes as it marched past.

Aeron was watching from quite some distance off, but it all looked splendid. When the tail end of the column left the camp, the next contingent in line, the ones from Hetronburg, started forward to follow. Their musicians were silent except for a lone drummer tapping out the cadence. When the last of the Toffs Valemers were past the pavilion, their musicians fell silent and wheeled into the rear of the column, joined by their general. Immediately, the musicians leading the Hetronburg troops began playing their own tune. By this time, the head of the first contingent was marching by the crowds of civilians, and their cheers threatened to drown out the music.

One by one, the contingents moved out and passed in review. Everyone seemed to hold their breaths as the two mammoths with the Targun Spire force lumbered by the pavilion. The beasts were notoriously edgy, and if one were to run rampant now, the entire leadership of the League might be wiped out. But their handlers had them under control and they moved on without incident. Next came the troops from Berlonvich in their yellow tunics with a blue trim that matched the chilly sky. It would be the Shires' turn next, and Captain Rootwell stirred and passed the word to get ready.

The tail end of the Berlonvichers left the camp, and Rootwell stood up in his stirrups, waved his arm, and shouted: "Troop! Forward at the walk!" and kicked his pony into motion. Aeron stepped out to remain abreast of him. After a dozen paces, they turned right onto the well-beaten path. Aeron reflected that by this time, his services as a guide were entirely irrelevant and a blind man could find the way just by the smell of all the horse-droppings. But he had his orders and he would carry them out.

They marched toward the city walls, and as the last of the Berlonvichers wheeled to the left, he could see the Eowulf troops massed inside the city beyond the open West Gates. As the host, they would be the last contingent to march. They would follow along after the Shires force.

The troopers wheeled left and approached the pavilion. The Berlonvich musicians fell silent, but the Shires troops had no music of their own.

In near silence, they rode past the pavilion. The Shires representative on the League Council, Caradoc Lowri, was there, too. He nodded toward Captain Rootwell, who touched his forehead in salute, but no honors of any sort were rendered to the dukes or the head of the Church of the Children. The humans looked back in growing anger. Aeron tried to not shrink under their gazes, but it wasn't easy.

The wave of discontent swept across the crowd, and by the time the Shires contingent reached the mob of spectators, the cheers had turned to boos. Before long, most of them were chanting *Halfmen! Halfmen! Halfmen!* A few started throwing things. The cavalry kept their eyes straight ahead and didn't react at all.

The ordeal ended when they reached their turning point and moved away from the crowd. By that time, the Eowulf troops were coming up behind them and cheers were resuming. Aeron guided them around to their spot. Like the camp, they only took up a fraction of the prepared space. Apparently some change had been made because the head of the Eowulf column squeezed in close beside the Shirefolk, shrinking the void down by half.

When all the troops were in place, swords were drawn and spears were angled toward the pavilion, and ten thousand voices roared out*: Long Live Rhordia!* Three times. The Shires cavalry made no move and spoke no word.

That ended the marching, but there were still speeches to be made and that dragged on for half the afternoon while Aeron slowly froze in the wind. After they had been standing there quite a while, Captain Rootwell suddenly spoke: "Cadwallader."

"Sir?" said Aeron, taken by surprise. "Yes, sir?"

"How long did you say you'd be staying on at the College?"

"I… uh, about another year and half. 'Til, 'til the spring after next, sir."

"And you're still planning to do that?"

"I, uh, well, yes, I…"

"Where do your loyalties lie, boy? The Shires or… Rhordia?"

The question took him totally by surprise, and his mind raced to find an answer. *Why can't I be loyal to both?*

But he'd hesitated too long. Rootwell scowled and then looked away.

*****

The long day of marching and ceremonies was followed by a long night of feasting and drinking. Huge fires were built in all the camps, and hundreds of cows, sheep, and pigs and thousands of chickens were sacrificed to the cooks. Mountains of bread and oceans of wine and ale were consumed. No one attending would have known there was a food shortage.

There was a great deal of coming and going between the camps; that was one of the purposes of the muster after all, to give everyone a chance to mingle and make friends. But hardly anyone visited the Shires camp, and none of the Shirefolk ventured away from their own fires.

Aeron, to his dismay, found he wasn't welcome anywhere. The Shires' insults to the League were a major topic of conversation in the camps, and the few places he tried to visit, he quickly left, lucky to escape unharmed. When he approached the camp of his own people, his College cloak and tabard won him cold stares and stony silences. He wasn't sure if his conversation with Rootwell had been passed along, but it probably wouldn't have mattered one way or the other. The night had barely begun before he gave up and made his way back to the barracks. None of the other cadets were there, and he lay in his bunk for a long time before sleep took him.

Where do your loyalties lie, boy?

* * * * *

In the morning, the Shirefolk were gone. He got the news at breakfast.

"Aeron," said Palle urgently, "have you heard…?"

"What?" He hadn't seen Palle since last night, and due to the celebration, breakfast was not done with the usual formations.

"The stinking little *halfmen* buggered off in the night!" said one cadet.

"Good riddance! After what they did - insulting the dukes and all - they got no business staying!"

"Well, look, there's one of them still here," said someone pointing to Aeron. Every face turned in his direction, and none of them seemed friendly.

"Hey, it's not his fault…" said Palle.

"Why didn't you leave with them?"

"Go on! Get out!" Someone threw something, a bit of food, and Aeron ducked.

"Oh, damn," hissed Palle. "Maybe we should get out of here."

"Yeah," said Aeron. "I'm not hungry anyway."

They retreated from the refectory with only a few spatters on their tunics. They went back up to the barracks and sat down by their bunks. "Sorry about that, Aeron," said Palle.

"Not your fault. And… and I can understand why people would be angry. It was… it was quite an insult. Wasn't expecting that." As he spoke, a great emptiness seemed to fill him. Rejected here, rejected by his own people. What could he do? Where could he go? The emptiness began to turn to panic.

"What are you going to do?"

"Don't know. Wait a minute…" A thought struck him, and he got up and headed for the door.

"Where are you going? asked Palle.

"Just want to check on something; be right back."

He left the barracks room, walked to the central stair, and then went down one flight and over into the other wing of the building. He went down a long hallway and came to a heavy door. He rapped on it and eventually it opened a crack. A human peered through, silhouetted by the light behind him. "What do *you* want?"

"Can I talk to Dilwyn?"

For a moment, he thought the man was going to close the door in his face. These were the Artificers' quarters after all, and mere cadets had no business here. And with what had happened, probably no halfling had business here either. But instead, he turned and shouted: "Hey, short stuff! Get over here, you got a visitor!" Aeron sighed in relief, he was afraid Dilwyn had gone, too. After a short delay the artificer came to the door and opened it wider.

"Aeron?" he said in surprise.

"Hi, Dilwyn. Can we talk?"

"Uh, sure. Come on, let's go outside." He came through the door and closed it behind him. The windowless corridor was dark except for a few wall sconces that didn't do much to lift the gloom. They walked back to the central tower and the grand staircase. With most people down in the refectory, it was quiet at this hour, the ticking of the great clock far overhead seemed unusually loud.

"I was afraid you'd left with the rest of our people," said Aeron.

Dilwyn looked around for any possible eavesdroppers before replying. "I nearly did. I was *supposed* to."

"What?"

Dilwyn's voice dropped to almost a whisper. "It was planned. The Shires cavalry wasn't here to attend the muster, that was just a diversion. They were here to get Caradoc Lowri, Paddy Bobart, and me, and Gerallt and take us home. Gerallt did go with them along with Lowri."

"Really?" said Aeron, shocked. "But why didn't you…?"

"Bobart wouldn't leave!" he replied in a hiss. "Damn old fool! He wouldn't leave without his precious Helga! He was determined to take it with him, but the College has it locked down tight, and there was no way we could get it out without everyone noticing. So Bobart is up in his study sulking."

"Why didn't you…?"

"Leave? I should have! But… but someone needs to look out for Paddy. He's brilliant at making things, but he doesn't seem to have a clue about the real world. If things come to a split, the League is not going to just let him walk away. He's too valuable."

"A split? You mean…?"

Dilwyn looked around again. "I've already said too much, but I guess you're into it as deep as anyone now. My cousin's on the Shires Assembly and he sent me a letter a few weeks ago, suggesting it might be time to come home. And then there was another message on the reverse side of the parchment using an invisible ink I developed…"

"Invisible ink?"

"For secret messages. No, don't ask me to explain why or how. Anyway, he told me that things are going to get a lot worse. The Assembly has decided to put a big tariff on any food sold to the League. They recalled Lowri. There's serious talk of pulling out of the League entirely. I've heard that the Shires contingents helping garrison the border posts in other parts of the League are being called home."

"Missing Gods," said Aeron. "That's going to be bad - especially about the food. The League depends on us for our surplus."

"Yes," said Dilwyn, "and not getting it is going to make a lot of these humans very mad. Even madder than they already are. So they wanted to get us out." When he saw Aeron's expression, he added: "I was planning to say something to you before we left, but things just got out of hand and I wasn't able to."

"So what are you going to do?"

Dilwyn shrugged. "Stick it out until someone can convince Paddy to leave without Helga. That might take a while. What are *you* going to do?"

Some of the panic he'd been feeling ebbed away. At least he wasn't totally alone. He had Palle and he had Dilwyn. And who knew? Maybe everyone on both sides of this mess would come to their senses and things could be smoothed over. But much of the panic remained. Bobart and even Dilwyn were valuable assets who the Shires wanted. Who was he? No one. The Shires didn't want him, and the Rhordians certainly didn't want him, either. If things fell apart completely, what could he do? Where could he go? Dilwyn was waiting for his answer so he said the only thing he could think of: "I guess I'll try to stick it out."

Chapter 5

He tried. It was hard; there was an almost unceasing barrage of insults and nasty remarks from most of the other cadets. Palle, and to his relief, Vadik and Hagen, never seemed to stray too far from him and that prevented any physical assaults, but they found other ways to torment him. His bunk was vandalized and his storage chest broken into. Even the laundresses seemed to be in on it, and he quickly learned he had better wash his own clothes if he ever wanted to see them again. Sergeant Rolf was as stern - and fair - as ever, and while on duty, Aeron had little to fear.

The Great Muster went on for its scheduled fortnight and then the contingents marched away, pursued by snow flurries. The College returned to its normal routines, although as the weather got colder, much of the physical training was held indoors or simply discontinued until spring. That meant more classroom instruction, which Aeron didn't mind a bit. Some of the instructors gave him a hard time, but for the most part, they pretended he didn't exist.

After the Winter Solstice, there was a month-long end-of-year break. The cadets from Eowulf went to their homes and any of the cadets from the other duchies could try to get home as well if they were willing to dare the weather. Many did, but a few stayed. The huge College of Warcraft building was nearly deserted. Palle decided to stay, and for some reason, the two dwarfs rotated who would visit their kin in the city and who would stay in the barracks. Were they doing that to make sure Aeron was protected? If so, he was very touched.

He considered going home. The border of the Shires were only a dozen leagues away and his home only ten more further along. There had been some snow, but the really bad weather was probably still a month off. He dearly wanted to get away, but he feared that if he left he might not be allowed to come back. Why? Why did he want to stay so badly? His dream had turned into a nightmare, and the only way out was to wake up. What possible difference would it make if he stayed and survived and somehow got his diploma? Who would that impress? Not the commanders of the human armies, and it was quite evident from Captain Rootwell's reaction it wasn't going to impress any of the Shirefolk either. Probably just the opposite. Why not just go and be done with it?

He thought and he dithered, but in the end, he did nothing.

For Yule, he let Dilwyn take him to the home of a friend he knew in town. It was nice to be out of the barracks and even nicer to be surrounded with people who didn't hate him. Good Shires cooking and even some precious Shires-brewed ale and a family with children scampering around and shouting was a very pleasant change.

Even better was getting a letter from his sister Mererid about a week after Yule. At least the postal service between the Shires and Eowulf seemed to still be working. Aeron, like most Shirefolk, came from a large family. He had three brothers and four sisters. He got along with most of them well enough, but Mererid was his favorite. They were the nearest in age and they had been very close growing up. She had been the one person in the family who didn't consider him crazy for wanting to pursue a military career.

His face lit up when Palle tossed the letter to him as he lay in his bunk. He immediately recognized the handwriting. He popped off the wax seal on the back, opened the envelope, and took out several sheets of vellum.

Dear Aeron,

I was so sad when you didn't come home, but I think maybe I understand why you didn't. Father and Mother were both expecting you and seemed surprised when you didn't appear. There has been talk around the town that all of our people living in the human lands would be coming home soon. I don't know if that is true, but if you do come home, rest assured that you will be very welcome.

The Yule celebration was very nice this year. Grandame Bloeuyn was here as well as Grandaunt Gwawr. Hefina came with the new baby—how cute! Cousins Nye, Rhordi, and....

Mererid went on to fill up a page and a half with the list of kin who were there and all the gifts that were exchanged and the meals eaten. Normally such goings on would have bored him, but he was so happy to have this one thin connection to home that he read every word and visualized every detail. When he neared the end, Mererid became more serious again.

I miss you very much, brother. We all do. Please come home if you can. You belong here with us.

All my love,

Mererid

He sighed and leaned back in his bunk. He missed her, too. Missed everyone. With all of his fears about being thrown out of the College and rejected by the Shires' military, had he forgotten that there was always one place where he could go and be welcome? *Home*. He suddenly found his eyes filling with tears. He sniffled and wiped them away. Pelle leaned down from his upper bunk. "Everything all right?"

"Yeah, yeah, it was from my sister, telling me about the holidays. Sounds like they had a jollier time than we did."

"Wouldn't be hard. This place is like a graveyard with so many people gone."

"I kind of like it this way, actually."

"Yes, I guess you would."

"What about you? Have you gotten any messages from home lately?"

Palle shook his head. "Nothing for a while. No one in my family is much for writing letters - not even me."

"My grandame always used to say: 'To get a letter, write a letter'." Aeron sighed. "I better answer this before I forget." He rolled out of the bunk and pulled out his chest. The vandals hadn't actually stolen anything, and they had not messed up his writing things too badly, either. He managed to write out a reply to Mererid that didn't sound angry or maudlin or said much about the current situation or his future plans. Which meant it didn't say much as all, actually. He re-read her letter and ended up mostly commenting on family matters she had brought up.

When he was packing things away again, he put her letter back in its envelope and was trying to decide where to put it where it would be safe from any future vandalism when he spotted the wax seal he had popped off. Wax was expensive and not to be wasted, so he would keep that and try to reuse it. As he picked it up, he noticed something and looked closer. One edge of the wax was curled up a little and discolored slightly. He frowned, took the envelope, and tried to fit the seal back where it had been. It looked as though…

Someone opened my letter!

They took a hot knife and pried up the seal. Maybe. He wasn't completely sure, but it seemed likely. *Why open my sister's letter? Do they think I'm a spy?*

Yeah, probably.

The more he thought about it, the more sense it made. Of course. He was a halfling in one of the League's most prestigious and important institutions. Of course he was a spy. In spite of his outrage, he had to grin at the thought of some League agent trying to puzzle out a secret message from all of Mererid's lists of relatives, meals, and gifts. His grin faded as he thought over the contents of his own return letter. Was there anything in it to arouse suspicions? Nothing he could see, but who knew what they - whoever *they* were - would think? Maybe he ought to ask Dilwyn about that disappearing ink!

Realizing that there was nothing whatsoever he could do about it if someone was reading his letters, Aeron eventually settled down and went back to reading a book on strategy he'd gotten from the library.

Eventually, the winter leave ended and the cadets started straggling back in. Instruction and classes resumed, and things returned to almost normal. The attitude of the other cadets toward Aeron was still nearly as cold as the barracks (it was impossible to adequately heat the enormous pile of stone), but the open verbal attacks mostly died away. The dirty tricks and vandalism did not resume; it was almost as if they didn't consider him worth the effort. After a few weeks, some of them actually started talking to him again, and once he even overheard someone recalling the time he'd faced down an Iron Beast. Maybe he could stick it out after all.

But then one evening, a month before the equinox, when he was talking with Palle and Vadik…

"Hey! Hey did you hear?" Casper Nimik appeared out of nowhere, shouting and startling everyone around.

"Hear what?" asked Palle.

"Nedes! Headmaster Nedes is gone!"

"Gone?" cried Aeron in surprise. "Gone where?"

"Retired! I have it straight from Sir Einar! The old man has had enough and is stepping down!"

"Wow," said Palle. "He's been here since forever. Who's replacin' him?"

"Don't know. I don't think Sir Einar even knew. Guess we'll find out."

"Well, that's a shame," said Aeron. "He was always very nice to me. I'm going to miss him."

* * * * *

It took Aeron a few weeks to realize just how much he was going to miss Headmaster Nedes.

Six days after the farewell ceremony for Nedes, the new headmaster arrived. A thin, black-haired, narrow-faced human named Jannik. No one Aeron knew seemed to have ever heard of him before, although rumor had it that Jannik had been a military advisor to the Duke of Hetronburg. He had no credentials as a military historian or theorist and no victories to his name as a soldier. The cadets whispered that he was just a political appointee, although why the College of Warcraft would become involved in politics no one could say.

For the first few days after Jannik's arrival there were no noticeable changes, although the new headmaster would show up without warning during their training sessions or in the classrooms. He would never say anything or interfere with the instructors. He would just watch for a while and then leave. But shortly afterward, things began to change…

"Corporal, where are the short swords?" asked Aeron. They were beginning another day of weapons exercises; the weather had turned milder and they dared venture outdoors again. His usual wooden practice sword wasn't in the rack where it belonged. None of the other short swords were, either.

"Orders, Cadet," replied the corporal in charge. "Headmaster Jannik, doesn't seem to like all the variety in the armory. Wants it standardized. Long swords for everyone now."

Aeron took out one of the wooden longswords and hefted it skeptically. It was at least a foot too long for him and considerably heavier than what he was used to. He could manage it with two hands well enough, but trying to wield it with one hand felt like he was trying to hold an oak tree. Glancing along the line of cadets, he could see that a few of the others, ones who favored rapiers or other weapons, weren't too pleased either. Vadik and Hagen, the two dwarfs, were snorting with disdain at the swords. They considered them puny compared with the battle axes they normally used.

"Ahh! How're we supposed to bash something with this twig?" demanded Vadik. "It'll snap off the first thing we hit!"

But their complaints fell on deaf ears. The corporal just shrugged and said everyone had to use a long sword. Aeron tried, but had a hard time of it and his opponents scored on him again and again, and he rarely managed to do anything in return. By the end of the session, his wrist felt like it was going to fall off. Later, when they practiced with spears, he was dismayed but not really surprised to find that his favored short spears were gone and he had to use a much longer spear meant for humans. Held in two hands like a pike he could manage it, but pikes were meant to be used by massed troops where you could present an impenetrable hedge of points to an enemy. In a one-on-one fight, you needed speed and maneuverability, and he had neither with this. His sparring partners had no problem getting past his guard and scoring.

"This isn't fair," said Palle during one of the breaks. "You do fine with a proper weapon. Why are they putting you at such a disadvantage?"

"I don't know," said Aeron, wiping sweat off his face with a handkerchief. "Maybe someone's thinking that in an emergency I might have to use a human-sized weapon and I should be trained for it."

Palle frowned over that for a moment and then shook his head. "But then shouldn't we all be trainin' like that? Force the humans to use halfling-sized weapons - or ogre-sized weapons for that matter! This doesn't make sense."

Aeron had no counterargument to that. No, it didn't make any sense. After the midday meal, they went back to work and he wasn't the least bit surprised when at the archery range his short bow was missing. The longer bows proved nearly impossible to use, and he ended up practicing with the lightest crossbow he could find—and even with that, he had to use one of the windlass contraptions to draw the string back to the loading position. It took so long to do, he only managed a dozen shots in an hour and his accuracy was poor - it was an entirely different sort of shooting from what he was used to. At one point, he spotted Headmaster Jannik watching him. He was too far away to be certain, but it looked as though he was smiling.

Naturally, his pony was missing, too, when they started the riding exercises. He'd never been on a full-sized horse, and even with the stirrups shortened as far as they would go, he could barely get his feet into them and he had to get a boost from Palle to even get aboard the enormous beast. Once mounted, he found that his spurs were useless, and he wasn't heavy enough to use his shifting weight to guide the animal. He was left with only the reins to control the horse and this wasn't nearly enough when he was supposed to be using a weapon at the same time. He managed to fall off only once, knocking the wind out of him, but he looked like a complete amateur.

The next day seemed almost normal with classroom instruction in the morning and drilling troops in the afternoon. The raw recruits at the city garrison were shaping up pretty well and he wasn't given any trouble, although Sergeant Rolf never strayed very far. But the following day at weapons training was like the one before and in some ways worse. He was paired up against the largest and strongest cadets, and it seemed like they were deliberately trying to batter him as much as they could. By noon, he had a mass of bruises that nearly matched what he'd had after the incident at the tavern. A couple of cadets he was friendly with tried to go easy on him, but for no reason he could see ended up on kitchen duty that night, and two days later, they were bashing just as hard as the others.

"Why is this happening?" demanded Palle one evening as he watched Aeron take off his shirt and examine the dark blotches on his torso.

"They're trying to drive us out, lad," said Vadik, coming over to sit next to them.

"What? Who?" demanded Palle.

"The new headmaster and his cronies," replied the dwarf. "It's all part of this 'humans first' crap that's spreading through the city."

"Has anyone been bothering you?" asked Aeron.

"Nothing like what they're doing to you, lad, but yes, there's been some incidents. Hagan had his chest broken into and some of his things ruined. Just like they did to you a while back. I think someone tried to get into mine, but I had a better lock."

"Well, it's not going to work, is it, Aeron?" said Palle angrily.

"Course not," he answered automatically. He wasn't sure he really meant it, though. He still had over a year to go before he graduated, and if this went on - or got worse - he wasn't sure he could stand it. He looked to Vadik. "What about you? Are you going to hang on?"

"For now. Don't like giving up. Not to the likes of these rats. Still, we came here to learn. If we can't learn, there's no point in staying, is there?" Vadik got up and went back to his own bunk.

"It's not right," said Palle. "I'm gonna write to my father. Maybe he can do something about this."

Aeron wasn't sure if Palle's father could do anything—or would want to even if he could. Or if Palle's letter would even get to him if what he suspected was true about the mail being opened. But what should he do? Try and stick it out? Like Vadik said, he was here to learn, but with each day becoming an ordeal just to survive, how much learning was he going to do? Still, it went against his grain to give up.

*****

Several relatively uneventful weeks passed, and Aeron began to think that perhaps he could weather this storm after all. The things being thrown at him were annoying, but not insufferable. He began to hope that if he simply refused to get angry or despondent, his tormentors - whoever they were exactly - would grow bored and give up on him.

But then Dilwyn's warning about the food tariff proved to be true and the news ran through the city like wildfire. The city had learned to cope with the reduced shipments, but this foreshadowed even worse events, and with the city's winter supplies running low, people began to panic. Aeron first heard about it at dinner one night when the usual ample servings were sharply curtailed. When cadets started complaining and asking why, some huge lout in First Company got up and pointed at Aeron.

"Because of them!" he shouted. "The little *halfmen* are trying to starve us!"

All eyes turned in his direction and angry mutterings quickly turned to angry shouts. Aeron kept his eyes fixed on his plate and did not react in any way. He just mechanically kept putting food in his mouth, chewing, and swallowing. He made no attempt to take seconds. Eventually the shouts died down, thwarted by his lack of response.

"Aeron, let's get out of here," said Palle. He didn't argue, and the two of them walked toward the refectory doors. This sparked a new round of shouts and catcalls, quite a number of which were directed at Palle rather than Aeron. 'Halfling lover!' 'Traitor!'

They made it outside and hastened up the stairs to their barracks, but it did not feel like any refuge. Tonight, all those bunks - well, nearly all of them - would be filled with hostile people. "I… I can't believe this is happening," gasped Palle.

"I can't believe it's happening so quickly," said Aeron.

"Yes! But what happened to all the talk about standing by your comrades?" said Palle angrily. "They drilled that into us from the first day we were here. Watch out for each other, help each other, guard your comrade's back! Damn hypocrites!"

Aeron looked around, but they seemed to be alone. "Palle… you might want to put some distance between us. You heard what some of them were saying just now. If they think you are going to side with me, they might start… hurting you, too."

Palle looked at him in astonishment. "Oh! So you want me to start being a hypocrite, too? I don't think so, Mister Cadwallader! You are my friend, and nothing is going to change that!"

Aeron smiled and shook his head. "Thanks, Palle."

They both slept lightly that night, but nothing happened. Several more days passed, and Aeron found that his sparring partners were growing downright vicious. At one point during a rest, he sat in the shade with a cloth held to his nose trying to staunch the bleeding. A nasty blow with a sword hilt had sent him sprawling. He hoped it wasn't broken.

"You got guts, kid, I'll give you that," said a voice. He looked up to see Sergeant Rolf standing over him. "Guts but no brains. You can't win this fight."

"So… so you expect me to run away?"

"Sometimes you have to run from a lost battle. Live to fight another day." Rolf turned and walked off. Aeron couldn't imagine Sergeant Rolf running from any fight, but if even he was suggesting retreat…

Aeron didn't think he could get much lower—but he was wrong. After dinner, he was in his bunk and jerked upright when he saw Palle being half-carried into the room by Vadik. "Palle! What happened?!" His friend was bruised and there was blood on his face. Vadik set him down on the edge of Aeron's bunk. "What happened?" he asked again.

"Oh, jus' got inna little discussion with a few of th' guys," mumbled Palle through swollen lips. Aeron looked inquiringly at Vadik.

"They beat him up for being friends with you, Aeron, I'm afraid."

"The bastards! Oh, I was afraid this would happen!"

"I'm alright," said Palle, waving a hand dismissively. "Had worsen' this a hunnert times…"

A fury was growing inside Aeron. How dare they! "Who was it? Who did this?"

Vadik shook his head. "Stop your thinking like that, lad. You can't take them all on. I'm thinking it's time for us to be going."

"Leave? You're going to leave? Give them what they want?"

"It sticks in me craw, for sure. But this is a fight we can't win, Aeron." He winced, that was just what Sergeant Rolf had said to him.

"If we stuck together…"

"Aye, we could last a while longer, that way, but how long? We can't be watching over our shoulders every hour day and night. We'd have to go to the crapper in teams! No, sooner or later they'd catch one of us alone, like they did poor Palle just now. Time to go while we still have our skins."

"Well… Well, there's nothing we can do tonight."

With Vadik's help, he bandaged Palle and put him into the lower bunk. He took the upper one and it took a long time to fall asleep. Give up? Run away? He didn't want to, but now that the humans were taking out their wrath on Palle, too... He hadn't counted on that. Did he have any right to put his friend at risk just to satisfy his stubbornness? Maybe he should go… Tomorrow, he would decide tomorrow…

* * * * *

But the next day, the decision was taken out of his hands.

Shortly after breakfast, he was summoned to the Headmaster's Office. He was escorted there by two of the College sentinels in full armor. Was he under arrest? He'd only been to this office a few times and never under circumstances like this. The office was paneled with old dark wood, skillfully carved with scenes of battle; brass hinges and hardware lent beautiful accents. The morning light streaming through stained glass windows gave a deceptively cheerful rainbow hue to the place. The Headmaster's secretary, also new, waved them through to the main office with barely a glance at Aeron.

Headmaster Jannik was seated behind an enormous desk that was cluttered with papers, which he was studying or writing upon. Aeron and his escort halted a few paces short of the desk and waited. Jannik ignored them for what seemed like a quarter-hour but which was probably less. Finally, he signed a paper, spread sand upon it to dry the ink, and then blew it off. Only then did he look up.

"Aeron Cadwallader."

"Sir?"

"I have just received news that the Halfling Shires have formally withdrawn from the League of Rhordia." Aeron sucked in his breath. "As you are now a foreigner, you have no place at the College of Warcraft. You will vacate the premises by noon today. Any clothing or equipment issued to you by the College must remain here. That's all." Jannik turned his attention back to the papers.

Aeron stood there quivering. He knew it was useless to point out that there were at least a dozen foreigners enrolled at the college; that would make no difference. Should he say something? After a dozen heartbeats, he could not come up with anything cutting enough, so he spun on his heel and left without a word.

The sentinels escorted him all the way back to the barracks and left him there. It was deserted; the rest of the company had already left for their morning instruction. A few moments later, the great clock sounded the third bell. Three hours. He had three hours to pack up and leave. Two and a half years of hard work and it all came down to three hours to gather his things and get out. He pulled out his chest, opened it, and then sat on his bunk staring for a long time.

The fancy dress tunic which he'd been so proud to receive, his work uniforms, the belt and dagger, his several hats, the boots, the books, the note paper, and a dozen other items would all have to be left behind. He had to dig down to near the bottom before he found the scant few items which actually belonged to him. A couple of shirts, a pair of trousers, three pairs of socks, shoes, a coat, a cloak, and a few dozen letters from Mererid and his parents. He pulled them out and slowly got out of his uniform and put on his own clothing. As he put on the coat, he noticed something in one of the pockets. He took it out and saw it was a piece of parchment: his official appointment to the College of Warcraft. He stared at it for a moment and then tore it up and flung the pieces on the floor. He wiped away a few angry tears, stuffed his remaining belongings in the same cloth sack he had brought them in, slung it over his shoulder, and stalked out.

In his state of frustration and anger, he nearly marched through the college gates without stopping, but then his feet faltered and he halted a few rods short of them and looked to the drill fields. Palle was over there, and there was no way he could leave without saying goodbye. But to go over there would mean every other cadet would see him leaving, see him running away. He could just imagine the sort of verbal abuse that would probably unleash. Maybe it would be easier just to leave. Maybe he could get a note sent to Palle…

No! He was going to say goodbye to his friend face to face, and not all the demons from the Abyss were going to stop him!

Turning, he headed for where Second Company ought to be. He had to pass by where Third Company was working, but most of them were so busy sparring, few of them even noticed the small figure walking by on the edge of the field. If any of them did, they were too afraid of their sergeant to break ranks and do anything. He found Second Company in the next field. He had no trouble spotting Palle as small as he was, and taking a deep breath, he walked straight over to him, which took him past a number of sparring pairs, most of whom stopped dead when they saw him. Palle had his back to him so he was able to get within a few paces before the sparring partner spotted him and stopped. Palle turned around and saw him, his mouth dropping open.

"Aeron! What… what's wrong? Why are you…? What's happening?!"

"I've been kicked out, Palle. I'm going home."

"Kicked out! Why? How could they?"

"You know why and you know how." His anger had been driving his feet and his mouth, but now it faltered. "This… this is goodbye, Palle."

His friend looked stricken, and the wooden sword fell from his grasp. Tears filled his eyes just as they were filling Aeron's. Without thinking, they moved into each other's arms and hugged hard. "It's not fair, it's not fair," whispered Palle.

"I know," Aeron whispered back, unmindful of the hoots and nasty remarks which started to erupt around them.

Almost as quickly as they started, the calls were cut off. The ensuing silence was broken by a single voice. "I believe I ordered you out of here, Mister Cadwallader." Aeron and Palle pulled apart and looked; there was Headmaster Jannik along with Sergeant Rolf. Aeron turned to face the headmaster.

"By noon," he said. "It's not noon yet."

"Don't you get impertinent with me, halfling!" snarled Jannik

"In case you've forgotten, I don't take orders from you anymore. You have no authority over me." Aeron felt like he was floating. Being impertinent to Jannik felt exhilarating.

Jannik's face turned red. "Perhaps not, but I am still in command within these grounds! Sergeant! Have this… creature escorted beyond our walls."

"Yes, sir," said Rolf. He took a step toward Aeron and then gestured at the gates.

Aeron deliberately turned his back on Jannik. "Goodbye, Palle, take care of yourself."

"G-goodbye, Aeron. Be careful going home. Write to me, will you?"

"Sure."

"Better send anything through my father," Palle added, his eyes darting to Jannik.

"Sergeant…" snapped the headmaster.

"Mister Cadwallader," said Rolf. Aeron nodded and turned toward the gates.

After they were out of earshot of Jannik, Aeron said: "You'll watch out for Palle, won't you? I hate to think of him getting into trouble because he was friends with me."

Rolf nodded. "I will, but this will pass. And with his father being a baron and all, I doubt anyone would risk doing anything too nasty to him."

"Thank you, Sergeant. And not just for this. You've been very fair with me over the years."

"You've been a good cadet. You deserved to be treated fair. Not like some of these nitwits." He paused and then said. "So what are you going to do now?"

"Go home, I guess. I've got nowhere else to go."

"Well, you be careful. There are a lot of angry people out there, and a lone halfling would be a damn tempting target. Have you got a weapon?"

"Just the little knife I brought with me. Good for potatoes, not much use in a fight."

"Hmmm, take this." Rolf handed over a dagger in a battered leather scabbard. "Might come in handy."

"Thank you, Sergeant," said Aeron sincerely. He didn't even feel tempted to refuse the gift. It was true, he might well need it. He tucked it in his belt, out of sight under his coat.

"Oh, and I heard tell that most of the halflings in the city are pulling out. There's a convoy of 'em assembling at the North Market Square. If I were you, I'd join up with them and leave when they do. Be a lot safer traveling in a group."

"Thank you again, Sergeant." They reached the gates. "Well, I don't suppose we'll meet again. Goodbye."

"You never know. Fare thee well, Mister Cadwallader." To his surprise, he stuck out his hand. Aeron took it and squeezed.

Rolf let go, turned around, and went back inside without a backward glance. Aeron watched for a few moments and then he, too, turned away and left the College of Warcraft behind.

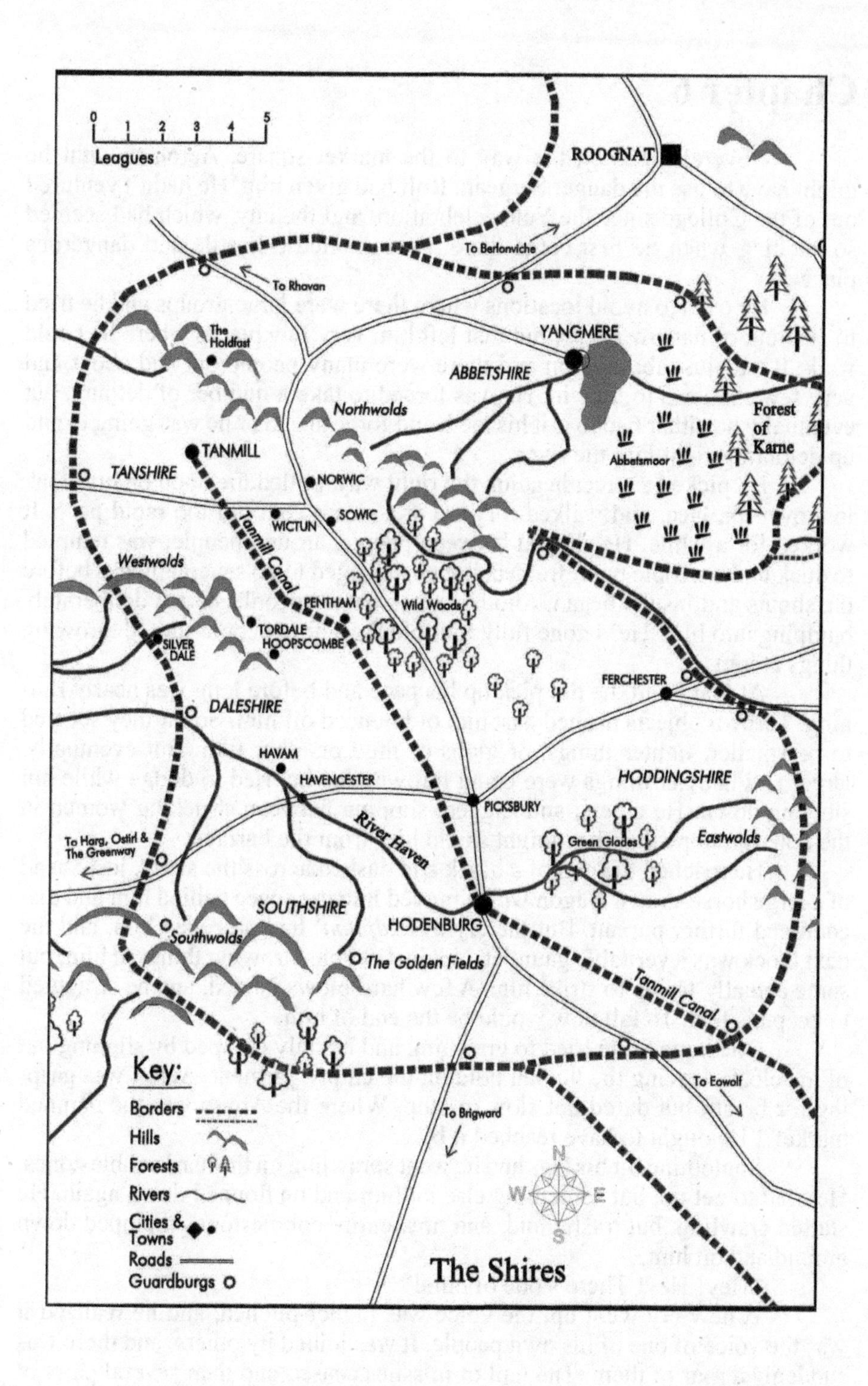
Leagues
0
1
2
3
4
5
ROOGNAT
To Berlonviche
To Rhavan
The Holdfast
YANGMERE
ABBETSHIRE
Northwolds
Forest of Karne
TANMILL
Abbetsmoor
TANSHIRE
NORWIC
Tanmill Canal
WICTUN
SOWIC
Westwolds
PENTHAM
Wild Woods
SILVER DALE
TORDALE
HOOPSCOMBE
FERCHESTER
DALESHIRE
HAVAM
HODDINGSHIRE
HAVENCESTER
PICKSBURY
River Haven
Green Glades
Eastwolds
To Harg, Ostirl & The Greenway
SOUTHSHIRE
HODENBURG
Southwolds
The Golden Fields
Tanmill Canal
Key:
Borders
Hills
Forests
Rivers
Cities & Towns
Roads
Guardburgs
To Eowolf
To Brigward
N
W
E
S
The Shires

Chapter 6

Several times on the way to the market square, Aeron thought he might have to use the dagger Sergeant Rolf had given him. He hadn't ventured out of the College since the Yule celebration, and the city, which had seemed so exciting when he first came there, now seemed a hostile and dangerous place.

He tried to avoid locations where there were large groups and he tried to stay out of narrow alleys, but that left him very few places where he could walk. It was just about noon and there were many people out and about and very few shadows to hide in. He was forced to take a number of detours, but eventually he either had to grit his teeth and forge ahead or he was going to end up detouring right into the river.

He picked a street heading the right way, pulled the hood on his cloak low over his face, and walked forward at a steady, but not too rapid pace. It worked for a while. He slipped between people, around people, was tempted to duck under people but refrained, but he managed to go several blocks before the shouts and insults began. Another block before people started deliberately bumping into him. He'd gone fully four blocks before people started throwing things at him.

At that point, he did pick up his pace and before long was nearly running. Thrown objects flashed past him or bounced off him. So far they seemed to be smaller, lighter things, or globs of mud or other filth. But eventually, larger and heavier things were being thrown, and he tried to dodge while not slowing down. He zigged and zagged, slipping between shrieking women in the not-vain hope that they might shield him from the barrage.

He reached the end of a block and dashed across the street, just ahead of a large horse-drawn wagon which moved into the space behind him and discouraged further pursuit. But the cry of *Halfman*! had preceded him, and the next block was a veritable gauntlet. Not just people throwing things at him, but some actually trying to strike him. A few hard blows landed, and he struggled to keep his feet. To fall now would be the end of him.

One huge brute tried to grab him, and he only escaped by slipping out of his cloak, leaving the human holding the empty garment. Aeron was gasping for breath but dared not slow or stop. Where the Abyss was the damned market?! He ought to have reached it by…

Something hit his legs and he went sprawling on the hard cobblestones. He tried to get up, but something else hit him and he flopped down again. He started crawling, but trash, mud, and now entire cobblestones thumped down around and on him.

"Hey! Hey! There's one of ours!"

A new cry went up, the voice was higher-pitched, and he realized it was the voice of one of his own people. It was joined by others, and there was suddenly a roar of them. The hail of missiles ceased and then several pairs of hands grabbed him and hauled him to his feet. He was surrounded by dozens of Shirefolk. Some held wooden clubs and others were throwing things back at the humans. He was half-carried into the North Market Square where a throng of halflings, a dozen or more large oxen-drawn wagons, and a few ponies were assembled. Looking back, he saw an angry mob of humans gathering on the edge of the square, exchanging missiles with equally angry Shirefolk. Now, finally, a squad of city guards came trotting up and got between the groups. They shouted for order and eventually got it. The human mob backed off and dispersed. The guardsmen had harsh words for Aeron's rescuers, seemingly blaming them for the incident, but they did nothing more than talk.

"Hey there, friend," said one of the ones helping Aeron, "are you all right?"

"A… a bit battered," he gasped. "But I'll live. Thanks to you folks. I thought I was done for."

"Well, you're among friends now, don't worry." Several of the people in the crowd patted him on the shoulder. One offered him a flask which he gratefully took a pull on. He was expecting water, but it was wine.

"Thanks… thank you."

"What in the world were you doin' out there anyways?" asked another.

"Just trying to get here. I only heard about the convoy a little while ago. Had to cross nearly the whole city."

The people around him grew quieter, and the one talking frowned. "From where?"

"Uh, the College of Warcraft. I am… I was a student there and…"

The people were all frowning now, and most of them turned away.

"It's that Cadwallader fellow," said one of them in a disgusted tone.

"Not worth the effort to save 'im," said another.

One of the older halflings didn't leave. He just scowled and then said: "No one here is happy to see you, boy. But we'll not turn you away, either. Come with us if you want. But once we reach the Shires, you're on your own." Now he did turn and walk off.

Great.

He stood there a while watching the others scurrying about loading things into the wagons. Some went off in groups down the streets leading to their enclave and returned bearing more items. Arguments broke out among family members about what could come and what had to be left behind. Many a child and more than a few adults were left in tears but looked all the more determined for them. Items which could not be taken were added to a growing pile. There was a lot of furniture in the pile, and the people made the effort to smash it up. At first he thought it was simply to deny it to the humans - although what use they could make of Shirefolk furniture he didn't know - but after a while he began to suspect it was actually to make *kindling*…

Eventually, he sat down in the shade of one of the wagons and examined his injuries - something he was becoming very good at. A few cuts on his head and hands, a new set of bruises all over, but withal, he had been lucky. Again.

As the day wore on, he got his breath back and made some attempts to help. At first he was rebuffed, but eventually he was able to lend a hand, heaving things up onto the wagons and tying things down. The wagons were all human-built and not in terribly good repair, clearly bought locally for the emergency (and probably at extortionist prices). To his eye, most of them seemed dangerously overloaded. There was one wagon that had a canvas top that was tied shut. He wasn't sure what that was carrying, but nothing more was being added to it. Another wagon was reserved for the elderly, very young children, and a few pregnant women. It looked like everyone else would be walking.

Finally, the wagons had as much as they could carry or as much as the oxen pulling them could handle. The fellow who seemed to be in charge - Aeron had no idea who he was, but people were constantly calling out questions to him, so he knew his first name was Trefor - mounted one of the ponies and began shouting for the people to get ready to move. Nearly all of them had enormous packs on their backs, even the younger children were carrying heavy loads.

The wagon drivers climbed aboard, others took the leads of the oxen, and most of the rest got themselves in order. A few went over to the pile of discarded belongings and looked to Trefor. He nodded at them.

They produced oil lanterns and splashed some of the oil on the pile. Flint and steel started a small blaze which quickly spread to the more flammable objects. The firestarters returned to the group, and at Trefor's word, everyone began to move. Aeron picked a spot in the line and walked along with the rest. He looked back at the fire from time to time. Some of the humans were clustering around it now, trying to drag out anything that might be valuable.

The train turned down the street to the North Gate and the blaze was lost to view, except for a growing column of black smoke rising above the rooftops. Crowds had gathered along their route, but they limited their abuse to the spoken word. There were close to four hundred Shirefolk in the convoy, and the numbers might have intimidated the humans enough to prevent anything else. Or perhaps they were distracted by the fire. Aeron noticed more and more of the humans starting off in that direction.

The North Gate wasn't far, and they all breathed a sigh of relief when they passed through and the gates slammed shut behind them. Aeron looked back and noticed that the cloud of smoke seemed to be getting bigger—and wider. "Is the fire spreading?" he said aloud. Other people looked back.

"We made sure it was well away from any buildings," said one halfling. "And there's almost no wind. If it's spreading it's because *they're* spreading it!"

"You mean our homes?" asked one woman. "But… but why? It's not like we'd ever go back. Why burn them?"

"Because they hate us," said another.

The column grew silent except for the clop-clop of the oxen's hooves on the hard packed road leading from Eowulf to the town of Hodenberg in the Shires. Hooves and the occasional sound of crying. Mostly from the children; they were too young to understand all this. But a few others, too. Aeron felt like crying himself.

But suddenly, a strong voice was raised in song. It was a song every one of the People knew, handed down for generations:

Many a place I've been, I've been,
And many a sight I've seen, I've seen!
But now I've turned my feet around—
I'm homeward bound! Homeward bound!

A dozen new voices joined in on the chorus:

Homeward bound! I'm homeward bound!

The world is large, and can be mean,
With pickings fat, or pickings lean!
But now I yearn for a welcome sound—
I'm homeward bound! Homeward bound!
Homeward bound! We're homeward bound!

There were more verses than anyone could count, and the song went on and on. Aeron listened for a while and then he, too, joined in on the chorus:

Homeward bound! I'm homeward bound!

* * * * *

The long train of wagons rolled, and the people walked and walked, but by the time evening was approaching, they could still see the taller buildings in Eowulf and faintly make out a dark smudge of smoke. They had come about three leagues, but on the flat plain, they could see a long way. A detachment of Rhordian cavalry, maybe twenty of them, had been following slowly behind, but when the halflings stopped to make camp, the cavalry wheeled about and galloped off, apparently to spend the night snug and warm inside the city.

Aeron and the others would be sleeping in the open, and it was still two weeks to the equinox. The weather had been a bit milder than normal and the snow was all gone except for in places the sun couldn't reach. But it was clear and it would get cold that night. The wagons were parked in a circle and fires built in the gaps between the wagons. There was a small woods a few hundred yards off the road, and it provided enough deadfall to fuel the blazes. It was going to be crowded in the space inside the circle, but that was probably for the better. Once the fires were going, meals were prepared, and Aeron realized that he hadn't brought any food at all. The cadets were forbidden to keep food in their barracks, and he hadn't dared to stop and buy any on his dangerous dash to get to the North Market Square. And somehow, he didn't think anyone was going to offer to feed him considering the way they'd acted toward him.

But someone did.

He huddled as close to one of the fires as he could without intruding on anyone's space and wished he hadn't lost his cloak. He looked longingly as the food was served out to the group by the fire, but after a moment he turned away, listening to his stomach growl.

"You must be hungry, aren't you?"

He turned around in surprise to find a Shires woman standing there with a wooden bowl. He didn't know what was in it, but at that point, he would have accepted stewed rat. "Uh, yes, yes I am, a bit. Haven't eaten since breakfast."

"Well, then here, Take this." She held out the bowl.

"Thank you! Thank you Missus...."

"Andras. Nesta Andras."

Aeron looked at the contents of the bowl. It was a steaming stew of some sort, the aroma made his mouth water. Definitely not rat. He started to bring the bowl to his lips when Missus Andras held out a spoon. "Careful, it's hot."

"Thank you, thank you again." He took the spoon, dipped it in the stew, and blew on it for a moment before putting it in his mouth. "It... it's good," he said, chewing and swallowing.

"Glad you like it." She handed him a piece of bread and he took that, thanking her again. "But there aren't going to be any seconds. We've got a lot of mouths to feed."

"I understand. And this mouth thanks you."

She sat down a few feet away and watched him eat. "You're that Cadwallader fellow, aren't you?"

"Yes."

"What the blazes were you doing at that War College thing? Were you one of those mechanic fellows?"

"The artificers? No, no, I don't have that sort of skill. I was training to be a military officer."

"Why?"

"To uh... learn how to fight better. Smarter."

"For the League?"

"Well, for all of us... the Shires and the League."

"The League hates us."

"I guess they do now. But until this morning, the Shires were part of the League. I thought.... I thought if I could help the Shires to fight better and smarter, it would help everyone." He ate some more stew. "This is really good."

"A lot of people are wondering why you were there at the League school. Living there, wearing their uniform..."

"All of *you* were living in Eowulf, too, weren't you?" he asked a bit too sharply. "What were *you* all doing there?"

The woman quirked an eyebrow. "Fair question, I guess. Me, I followed my husband here. He died last year of the ague, but instead of going home we stayed on, me and our two children, running his business myself."

"Why?"

She shrugged. "We were making money. Things weren't bad like now. Why not stay?"

"Well, we're all going home now, I guess," said Aeron, finishing the stew and handing the bowl and spoon back to her.

*****

It was a cold night, but they huddled together for warmth and kept the fires burning. They put the old and the little ones underneath the wagons and rigged blankets or canvas to create little enclosures which stayed a bit warmer. There were a score of spears and a dozen bows hidden in one of the wagons, and these were broken out and distributed, and a constant watch was set. No one could really say what they were watching *for*, but Aeron volunteered to stand a watch and they let him. He was really tempted to give some advice about how best to organize the defense, but he restrained himself, and that was probably a good thing. He walked around half the night to stay warm, but when his turn was up, he curled up on the ground as close to a fire as he could get and tried to sleep.

By morning there was a thick frost coating the ground, the wagons, and many of the blankets - and Aeron's clothing. He got up and couldn't stop his shivering, but it looked to be another clear day. The sun would be up soon to warm them. Meanwhile the fires were built up and breakfast was soon cooking. Trefor, the wagon master wandered about, urging people to hurry. "We've still got a long ways to go, and I don't want to spend one more hour in League territory than we have to."

Missus Andras fed him breakfast, which was a cornmeal mush, more bread, and unsweetened tea. When the march started, he found himself walking with her and her two children. In the daylight, he could see Missus Andras better; she was younger than he'd first supposed and quite a handsome woman. The girl-child, Elin, was five and looked at him curiously, but the boy, Gethin, seven, seemed as suspicious of Aeron as most of the adults. "The others say you are a traitor," he said to him.

"But we're traders, too!" protested Elin. "Is that bad?"

"Tray-tor, stupid, not tray-der!"

"What's a tray-tor?"

"Someone who, someone who… I'm not sure." The boy looked puzzled.

"Someone who betrays their own people," said Aeron succinctly.

"Like him," snarled a fellow walking a bit off to one side and indicating Aeron with a jerk of his head.

"You betrayed us?" asked Elin, her eyes wide.

"I don't think so. I was trying to learn things that I could use to help our people, and…" he fixed his eye on the one who'd spoken and raised his voice, "…the Rhordians threw me out the same as they threw all of *you* out. So it seems *they* don't think I'm a traitor to the Shires."

The fellow scowled more deeply than ever and snorted. But he made no reply and quickened his pace to move ahead in the line..

"Well, I don't think you are a tray-tor, Mister…"

"Call me Aeron. And thank you, Elin. Thank you very much."

Missus Andras had been observing this exchange silently, and when she met Aeron's eye, she nodded her head slightly.

Around mid-morning, their shadowing League cavalry caught up with them and lazed along a half-mile off to their east. Beyond them, sunlight glittered off the Tanmill canal and further away he could see a thick white mist hanging over the marshes of the Wolfmoor. The fields to either side of the road were still a sad-looking winter brown and dun color with no trace of the green that would burst forth in just a few more weeks. They passed farmsteads, whose owners came out to look at the strange caravan trundling by.

At noon, they stopped to rest and eat, Aeron guessed they had probably traveled about two leagues. Not a very good pace, but it was all that could be expected with the oxen and the old and the young. If they could do another three leagues before halting, that would put them perhaps four leagues short of the border and maybe they could get into friendly territory the following day.

By afternoon, they were all flagging; Aeron, with very little of his own to carry, took all of Elin's load and some of Gethin's as well. Their mother looked at him gratefully. As the day drew to a close, he saw the League cavalry head off toward a nearby human village. He thought that the convoy had probably done those three leagues he was hoping for. Everyone was tired, and they set up their camp as they had done the night before. Missus Andras had him sit with her family for supper.

"What will you do when you get back to the Shires?" he asked her. "Do you have somewhere to go?"

"We're originally from up near Ferchester in Hoddingshire," she replied. "My family still lives there. I'm sure they'll take us in, but as for what I'll do…" She trailed off and just stared at the fire.

"Were you able to salvage anything from your business?"

"Nothing but what we're carrying. Once they figured out what we were doing, the humans weren't willing to buy much of anything; I suppose they figured they'd get it for free when we left. So we've not much hard money at all."

"I'm sorry. I'm from near Picksbury. It's on your way, and you are welcome to stop and rest at my home if you want."

"Thank you for that. We'll have to see how things work out. What about you? What will you do?"

"I don't know," he said, shrugging. "My hope had always been that once I graduated I could come home and help the Shires Captains improve our troops. I doubt anyone is going to be interested in my help now."

"Just because you got your knowledge from Rhordia? Either your advice is good or it's not. What does it matter where it comes from?"

Aeron smiled. "I hope other people think that way, Missus Andras."

"Call me Nesta, will you?"

"All right…"

"And if no one will listen, then what will you do?"

Another shrug. "My father has a business and some land. I can always help him, or start a farm…"

"Neither of which appeals to you."

"No, that's why I went to the College in the first place."

"Well, I wish you luck, Aeron Cadwallader."

"And I you, Nesta Andras."

* * * * *

That night, after he stood his watch, Aeron headed for the spot where they had set up a trench to deal with necessities. After he had done his business, he was heading back and he met someone coming the other way. He seemed to be carrying a chamber pot. Well, maybe one of the older folks couldn't make it to the trench… The person clearly wasn't expecting to meet anyone and wasn't looking where he was going. They nearly ran into each other. "Oh! Pardon me," said Aeron.

"What? Oh! Sorry!" said the other person. The voice sounded familiar, and as he dodged aside, the hood of his cloak fell away and the firelight caught his face…

"Dilwyn! What are you doing here?"

"Quiet!" hissed the artificer. "Keep your voice down, Aeron!"

He looked quickly round but saw nothing but the watch fires with a few sentries silhouetted in front of them fifty paces away. "Why? Who are you afraid will hear us?"

Dilwyn shook his head and drew Aeron around the trench and further off into the dark. "Only Trefor and a few others know that we are here."

"We? You mean you and Paddy Bobart? You got him to leave?"

"Yes, he's in the covered wagon."

"Well, I know he didn't bring Helga with him, it's bigger than any of the wagons! How'd you get him to come?"

"Wasn't easy! And not just convincing him. I knew as soon as the word of the Shires leaving reached Duke Eowulf, he'd seize Paddy for himself. No way he'd let someone that talented just stroll off home."

"So you had to sneak him out of the College and join up with the wagon convoy? How did you do it? And once he was gone, this is the first place the duke would think to look. Why haven't they tried to stop us?"

"Ha! Tricked 'em! They don't even know he's gone yet—or so I hope."

"What? How'd you do that? Wouldn't they look to make sure he was still there, first thing?"

Even in the almost total darkness Aeron thought he could see the grin on Dilwyn's face. "Well, you know I'm Paddy's apprentice, don't you? I might not be up to building an Iron Beast yet, but I have learned a thing or two. I built a nice little simulacrum of Paddy and…"

"A what?" Aeron had never heard the term before.

"A duplicate; a double."

"Of a person? You can do that?"

"Oh, it could never pass a close inspection, but in dim light and from a distance, it will look like him. And I made it so it can move a bit and even talk a bit."

"But if someone gets close…"

"Yes, the game would be up in an instant. But I've left a friend there who will keep people at a distance for a while. He's telling everyone that Paddy is under the weather and needs rest. Paddy is notorious for refusing to let the healers near him, so my device is in his bed and our friend is handling the rest."

"Friend?" asked Aeron, confused. "But Gerallt's already gone. Who else there would help you?"

"A human. They're not all bad eggs, you know. One fellow, not going to tell you his name, safer that way, liked Paddy a lot and Paddy helped him out many a time. He's agreed to man the gates for us. Take in food, take out a chamber pot, let people get a glimpse of my gadget, and keep up the pretense as long as possible."

"A brave man."

"Yeah, I hope he doesn't get in too much trouble once it all comes to light. He helped us get out of the College building, too. The night before everything fell apart—we got an advanced warning about the Shires leaving before the official declaration arrived. By the time the word of it reached the Duke, we were safely tucked away in Trefor's basement."

"How'd you get Paddy to agree to go without Helga?"

"He's stubborn, but he's not stupid. He knew that once it all went in the fire, the Duke would try to grab him for himself. He didn't want that. And he didn't want Helga in the Duke's hands."

"But it is now, isn't it?"

"Maybe, but Paddy built it with a special spell to make it come to life. Without knowing what it is, it will take them a good long time to figure out how to make her run."

"Sounds like you've thought of everything. And by tomorrow, we'll be back inside the Shires."

"We're not there yet. So not a word to anyone, all right?"

"Surely you don't think any of our people would betray you to the League?"

"No, but why take chances? We'll stay closed up in our wagon, and you don't say anything."

"Of course."

"Good, now, I… uh… have to go."

"Oh! Right, sure. See you later." Aeron went back to the camp and tried to find a spot close to a fire.

* * * * *

The next day started like the previous one; breakfast, and a hasty departure. The wagon master, Trefor Trahern (he'd finally learned his last name), however, seemed edgier than previously. "Come on! Come on! Get a move on!" he shouted. "I want to be across the border before nightfall!"

Everyone was tired, but they moved as quickly as they could and were soon on the road. As the morning mists dispersed, Aeron could see some low hills off to the northeast, just gray streaks against the sky. They lay right on the border of the Eastwolds. They weren't headed that way, but somehow it felt good to actually see part of the Shires. Their road bent more to the northwest, but it couldn't have been more than four leagues to the border in that direction. Yes, surely they'd cross before nightfall.

The land had been sloping gradually upward as they marched along. Around noon, when they were thinking of stopping for a meal, they crested a miniscule rise and several people with sharp eyes pointed out something ahead. Squinting, Aeron thought he could see a dark shape rising a bit above the plain. *The watch tower of the guardburg on the road!*

The Shires maintained small fortified villages or sometimes just farmsteads at intervals along the borders. Depending on how large a threat the denizens of the lands beyond the border posed, the guardburg could be garrisoned by from a few dozen to a few hundred troops. In really dangerous areas, part of the garrisons would be made up of human troops from the League. Aeron wondered if all of those were being 'asked' to leave. Until recently, this area would have been considered a friendly border and the garrison here was probably a score or less—and all Shirefolk. With current events, there might be more now, but there was no way to tell from this distance.

As the people caught sight of it, there were a few cheers. A few even suggested that they skip the meal and push on, but they were quickly overruled. Everyone was hungry. The wagons halted, and Aeron looked around. Their escort of cavalry had returned, hanging back a half-mile or so. Would they follow them all the way to the border? But as he watched, he noticed a number of the humans standing up in their stirrups and few pointed back along the road to the south. Shading his eyes from the sun with his hand, he looked in that direction trying to see…

Cavalry!

A dark shadow was moving across the ground perhaps a league or a league and half behind them. Moving fast; they were raising a small dust cloud as they came. Right toward them. Light glinted off steel, banishing any doubts he might have had. He turned back to the folks around him, frantically trying to spot Trefor Trahern. There! He pushed past people and dashed over to him.

"Captain Trahern!" He'd never heard anyone call him that, but as he'd hoped the strange address immediately caught the halfling's attention. He twisted around and started at Aeron in puzzlement.

"What? Oh, you. What do you…?"

"Cavalry! Rhordian cavalry coming up on the road behind us! A couple of hundred at least, riding hard!"

"What? Are you sure?"

"Take a look!" Aeron grabbed him by the arm, pulled him a few paces until there was a clear view, and pointed. Trefor looked, frowned, leaned forward…

"Damn…" he hissed.

Others had seen them by now, too, and began crying in alarm.

"Get someone on a pony off to the guardburg," said Aeron. "Right now!"

"Right… right…" said Trefor. He looked around, spotted someone… "Hefin! Ride for the guardburg! Ride like there's a demon chasing you and bring back help!" The fellow nodded, waved, and a few moments later was galloping away. Aeron looked to the closer detachment of cavalry, half-expecting them to pursue, but they did not. Perhaps they hadn't seen the rider, or maybe they didn't know what was going on either.

"You'd better get the wagons in a circle," said Aeron.

"How do we know they mean us any harm?" asked someone.

"Maybe we should try to get to the guardburg," said someone else.

"We'd never get near it before they overtake us," said Trefor. "And the best way to make sure they don't mean us any harm is to be ready to fight. Yes, circle the wagons!" He began shouting orders, and teamsters and the ox-handlers began to turn their balky and cumbersome charges to form a circle. Fortunately, they'd already done this twice before, so they knew what to do.

"Get them as close together as you can!" cried Aeron. "Make the gaps between the wagons as small as possible!"

The grunting oxen and straining halflings shoved the wagons into something like a circle. It wasn't a very good circle, but it had an inside and an outside, and the gaps between the wagons weren't too big. Aeron looked apprehensively at the nearly thirty confused-looking oxen who had been unhitched and were now inside the circle. If it came to a fight, something would have to be done about them; if they panicked, they could cause untold damage to the people inside. They'd have to get them out somehow. But maybe it wouldn't come to a fight—and until it did, no one was going to listen to him.

While they had been creating the circle, the new group of cavalry met up with the small one which had been shadowing them. There was a brief discussion, and then several riders went off, one toward Eowulf and the other went off northeastward in the general direction of Hetronburg, although that was over twenty leagues away. Then the combined group, well over two hundred of them, came forward toward the wagons at a walk.

"Get the weapons out and distribute them," ordered Trefor, "But keep them out of sight."

While they awaited the arrival of the humans - to talk presumably, since they were coming so slowly - Aeron looked over the state of the defenses. They weren't good. They had an oval of wagons, about a hundred paces wide, with fourteen gaps between them. Twenty people with spears and a dozen with bows were not going to be able to stop a concerted charge, even by light cavalry as these were.

As he was inspecting, he came to the wagon with the canvas top. On impulse, he rapped on the side and said: "Dilwyn? You in there? I think you better come out and see this." After a moment, the canvas was pulled aside and his friend popped out. Aeron thought he caught a glimpse of Paddy Bobart in the gloomy interior.

"So they've come after us?" asked Dilwyn.

"Yes, over two hundred light cavalry. Looks like they want to parley, but I don't doubt what - or who they're here for."

"They must have caught on to my double of Paddy. Damn, if it had just fooled them for one more day - half a day!"

"Well, it fooled them for two days, you can be proud of that." Aeron looked off to the north. "We sent a rider for help. Maybe we should have sent you and Paddy."

Dilwyn shook his head. "Paddy's too old to ride. At least not at any sort of pace. The Rhordians would just swoop down and grab him like a hawk snatching a field mouse. Somehow we have to hold out until help gets here."

"Just as likely that any help to arrive will be more League forces." Aeron looked around at the women and children and sighed. "We could get a lot of our folks killed if we try to fight."

"We can't just hand him over to those bastards, Aeron!"

"I suppose not. Look, they're nearly here. Let's go and see what they have to say."

They walked over to the part of the circle nearest to the approaching horsemen and pushed their way through the crowd to get close to Trefor. The wagon master's eyebrows shot up when he saw Dilwyn, but then just nodded at him.

The cavalry halted about three hundred paces away - just beyond effective bowshot for the halfling's small bows. Then a half-dozen of the riders came forward. One was carrying a banner with the Duke of Eowulf's sigil on it and another was clearly the leader of the group. All the riders were wearing leather armor and helmets. They had curved swords at their sides and most carried spears and had bows and quivers of arrows hung from their saddles. The leader had a mail shirt and his weapons and gear glinted with polished brass, or maybe it was even gold. When the advancing party was thirty paces away, Trefor stepped forward and raised one hand. "All right, that's close enough," he said. "Who are you and what do you want?"

The leader halted his group and returned the gesture, raising his hand. "I'm Captain Lennart, one of the Duke's liegemen. Who do I have the *honor* of addressing?"

"I'm..." Trefor paused and glanced at Aeron and a smile tugged his lips upward. "I'm Captain Trahern. We are peaceful travelers returning to our homeland - which lies just yonder. We want no trouble. Depart, and we will be on our way."

"Nor do we wish for any trouble... captain. However, we need to search your wagons for any... contraband you might be carrying."

"Contraband! We've nothing here but our clothing and a few modest possessions. Nothing to concern you or your duke."

"No doubt you are right, but I must make the inspection nonetheless. Let me and my men carry that out and you may be on your way."

"You can't!" hissed Dilwyn. "Once they're inside the ring, there'll be no way to stop them from taking Pa... from taking anything they want!"

Trefor looked back at the crowd of his people - the people he was responsible for getting to safety. "Dilwyn," he whispered. "Look at them! I can't...!"

Aeron could see the anguish on his friend's face.

"But... but, we can't just turn him over!"

"Dilwyn, what can I do? You're asking too much."

Aeron looked at the cavalry, looked back at the halflings, and then looked at the circle of wagons. Suddenly he reached out and tugged Trefor's sleeve. "Keep talking. Stall for time. I've got an idea."

Chapter 7

Without waiting for a reply, Actca turned to the watching people. Some of them looked defiant, but most looked scared—especially Tessa. And, with Jim and Cedric, an icy feeling filled his stomach when he realized he might well get them—and everyone else killed. But a strange resolution filled him, [illegible] like when Mago Hakon had cast that strength spell on him.

"Friends!" he called as loudly as he could. "Friends! These men from Cowall are afraid that we have carried away some treasure from their city! They want to inspect all the things we are carrying. So let's let them have a look! Get everything out of the wagons," As he said the words, a look of skepticism swept over every face, and a wave of muttering arose. But he didn't falter. "Yes! Get everything out of the wagons and pile it up. Pile it up here and there, make a pile in front of each wagon so they can see it all!"

The muttering stopped, and some of the people realized what he was doing. "Come on!" he shouted. "Get the stuff out of the wagons!"

He saw that Cedric, at least, clearly caught on immediately. He ran to one of the wagons, opened up the rear gate, and started dragging things out. Within moments, nearly everyone else was doing the same.

Actca smiled in satisfaction and then turned back to see what Trefor was doing with Captain Demmon. "We can let you see all that we are carrying," Trefor was saying, "but we'll not let you inside the circle."

The Hammian's tone had turned colder. "That won't do, Hadling. We demand to search every wagon. There could be... secret compartments."

"Then once you look over our other goods, you can back off and send in a man or two to check. But we'll not let your whole mob inside the line."

Over three hundred piles of items were soon in the works and the wagons were emptying fast and the other, [illegible] they were rising higher and high-er, if they were [illegible] enough time.

Several people ran up to the two wagons Trefor, Tubby, and Aaron were standing between and started unloading. Actca waved them off. "Leave these two until last. And go get the oxen yoked up and pointed this way!" The people stared at him dumbfounded, but after a moment shrugged and did as he told them. Actca thought how if you looked like you knew what you were doing, other people would follow without question.

Looking to Trefor and Kanar, he saw that the talk wasn't going to go on much longer.

"Enough of this!" snarled Demmon. "You know perfectly well what we want! If you turn over the Artifact, Fanny Robert and all his possessions, you'll be allowed to go on unharmed. Refuse and [illegible], and I won't be responsible for the consequences!"

"And what would those consequences be, Captain?" shouted Tessa.

"Don't be a fool!" replied the Hammian. "[illegible] you think we're such a fool. Do you think there's [illegible] if you continue to take what we

Chapter 7

Without waiting for a reply, Aeron turned to the watching people. Some of them looked defiant, but most looked scared. He spotted Nesta Andras with Elin and Gethin; an icy feeling filled his stomach when he realized he might well get them - and everyone else killed. But a strange resolution filled him. It sort of felt like when Mage Hasbin had cast that strength spell on him.

"Friends!" he called as loudly as he could. "Friends! The men from Eowulf are afraid that we have carried away some treasures from their city! They want to inspect all the things we are carrying. So let's let them have a look! Get everything out of the wagons…" as he said the words, a look of skepticism swept over every face and a wave of muttering arose. But he didn't falter. "Yes! Get everything out of the wagons and pile it…. Pile it in between them! Yes, make a pile *in between* each wagon so they can see it all!"

The muttering stopped, and some of the people realized what he was asking them to do. "Come on!" he shouted. "Get that stuff out of the wagons!"

"He's right!" cried Nesta, clearly catching on immediately. She ran to one of the wagons, opened up the rear gate, and started dragging things out. Within moments, nearly everyone else was doing the same.

Aeron smiled in satisfaction and then turned back to see what Trefor was doing with Captain Lennart. "We can let you see all that we're carrying," Trefor was saying. "But we'll not let you inside the circle."

The Rhordian's tone had turned colder. "That won't do, halfling. We demand to search every wagon. There could be… secret compartments."

"Then once you look over our other goods, you can back off and send in a man or two to check. But we'll not let your whole mob inside the ring."

Over three hundred pairs of arms were hard at work and the wagons were emptying fast and the piles in between them were rising higher and higher. If they were just given enough time…

Several people ran up to the two wagons Trefor, Dilwyn, and Aeron were standing between to start unloading. Aeron waved them off. "Leave these two until last! And go get the oxen rounded up and pointed this way!" The people stared at him dumbfounded, but after a moment shrugged and did as he told them. Amazing how if you looked like you knew what you were doing, other people would follow without question.

Looking to Trefor and Lennart, he saw that the talk wasn't going to go on much longer.

"Enough of this!" snarled Lennart "You know perfectly well what we want! If you turn over the Artificer Paddy Bobart and all of his possessions, you'll be allowed to go on unharmed. Refuse and… and I won't be responsible for the consequences!"

"And what will those consequences be, Captain?" shouted Aeron.

"Don't be a fool!" replied the human. "And you truly are a fool if you think those pitiful barricades will stop us! If you compel us to take what we want by force of arms, there will be no mercy for any who get in our way. Now yield! I'll waste no more words on you!"

Trefor looked at Dilwyn and then at Aeron. "You really want to do this?" He looked around the ring. The barricades were going up fast. They might stop a horse, but would it be enough to discourage the humans entirely?

"We have to at least try, Trefor!" said Dilwyn.

Trefor looked at Aeron. "So, did you learn anything at that College of Warcraft, Mister Cadwallader?"

"I learned a few things, sir. Although they never taught us about a situation like this one!"

"Can we hold?"

Was Trefor really asking him his opinion?

"We can try. I can't promise any more than that."

"Halfman!" roared Lennart. "What's your answer, damn you?!"

Trefor turned to face the human, his face twisted in anger.

"You want him? Come and take him!"

The expression on the human's face was hard to read at this distance, but Aeron thought it was a mixture of frustration and satisfaction. He probably hadn't wanted a fight when he first got here, but after being given the run-around by Trefor, he was probably looking forward to it now. He jerked on his horse's reins, turned it around, and trotted back to where his men were waiting. He began shouting orders and the men started getting into a battle formation.

"So what now?" demanded Trefor, staring right at Aeron.

"We need more time to get the barricades formed. As soon as the humans start to advance, we need to stampede those oxen right into them." He pointed to where the animals were standing. The people he'd sent to get them ready had them pointed in nearly the right direction.

"Are you mad?!" cried Trefor.

Aeron didn't bother to answer. He spotted Nesta and called out to her: "Nesta! Have the older children grab every pot and pan they can find! We're gonna need some noise here in a few moments." She nodded and began gathering the youngsters. Then Aeron ran over to where the score of people with spears were standing. "We're going to stampede the oxen into the humans! You with the spears, form a cordon on either side of them to make sure they go right through that gap in the wagons. Understand?" The spearmen goggled at him and didn't move, so he grabbed one of them and pulled him where he wanted him. "Two lines! One here and one over there. When the oxen start moving, keep them heading in the right direction!" They finally got it and moved into position. "Like drilling those bloody recruits back in Eowulf," he muttered.

"Without the oxen, how are we going to move the wagons again?" asked Trefor.

"If we don't beat back the humans, are we really going to have to worry about that? And if we stop their first attack, they are going to start shooting arrows into here. Do you really want two score of wounded, terrified oxen running loose in the middle of us?"

Trefor was silent for a moment and then said: "Maybe you aren't mad after all."

"Don't judge too quickly. I might well be mad, you know," Aeron said.

"Aeron!" cried Dilwyn. "Here they come!"

"When I give the signal," he said to Trefor, "get the beasts moving. Have the children bang their pots together to scare them."

Without waiting for an answer, he dashed back to the gap between the wagons and looked. Yes, the Rhordian cavalry had formed up into a column, about a dozen wide by fifteen or twenty ranks deep. Not a usual formation for light cavalry at all, but apparently Captain Lennart was planning to burst right into the ring of wagons and overrun the defenders at a blow. It might well have worked, too. They were advancing at a trot, which ate up the distance rapidly. Aeron waved to Trefor and motioned him to get the oxen moving. A moment later, he heard a loud racket of metal on metal and dozens of voices shouting. The large, lumbering oxen started moving - right toward him.

The Rhordians were about a hundred yards away and quickening their pace to a canter. Most of them were still carrying their spears upright rather than in an attack position. Despite Lennart's harsh words, it seemed he didn't want a slaughter.

Aeron eyed the two oncoming masses of quadrupeds and hoped he'd gotten the timing right. Too soon, and the Rhordians would just avoid the oxen; too late, and they'd be penned up inside the ring before they could burst out. It was going to be close…

An instant before they were going to be trampled, Aeron grabbed Dilwyn and dragged him down under the rear of one of the wagons as the frightened, bellowing oxen thundered past. He rolled on his stomach and looked out from his refuge.

Perfect!

The oxen burst out of the ring of wagons while the Rhordians were still fifty yards away. The animals immediately started to spread out, and the startled cavalrymen, with their fellows coming up from behind, found themselves with nowhere to go. The front ranks tried to turn aside, but the following ranks, realizing what they were riding into also turned, bumping into them, and the forward part of the column disintegrated.

Then the oxen collided with them.

There were few actual collisions, although he did see some animals go down, but the cavalry was swept aside like leaves before a strong wind. There were shouts and screams and curses, and before long nearly all of them, oxen and Rhordians alike, were driven back down the gentle slope past the point where they had started from. He thought he could see Captain Lennart riding around frantically trying to get his men back in order. From behind him, he heard the people laughing and shouting and taunting the Rhordians.

No time for that!

He'd won them precious time, but they couldn't afford to waste it. He scrambled out from under the wagon and started shouting: "Get the barricades finished! They'll soon be back, and we have to be ready! Come on! Move!"

The people realized that he was right and went back to work with a will. Boxes and bags and pieces of furniture, barrels and crates and anything else sturdy and heavy were piled up in the gaps between the wagons. "As high as the sides of the wagons, at least seven feet high! Tall enough a horse can't jump over it! Make it as thick and sturdy as you can! Come on! We haven't much time!" He ran around from wagon to wagon, inspecting each barricade and making suggestions.

The defenses weren't nearly as strong as he would have liked, but maybe they would do. Some ingenious fellows were taking lengths of rope and running them back and forth between the wagons and interweaving them with the items in the barricades, binding them into a solid mass that couldn't easily be knocked over or pushed aside.

Others were working to create makeshift weapons. Knives were being tied to broomsticks to make spears, a meat cleaver strapped to a pole made a halberd. Boards were being pried off the inner sides of the wagons to make clubs. Other people were digging up rocks to throw.

The archers and those with real spears had gathered around Trefor, and Aeron went over to them. Trefor was saying: "They're getting ready to make another charge. You archers, start shooting as soon as they're in range. Those with spears…"

"Wait!" said Aeron, pushing into the crowd. "We can't fire on them!"

"What?" said Trefor, staring at him. "I've changed my mind again; you *are* mad!"

"No one's been killed, no one's even been hurt, except for a few bruises. But once we start shooting arrows. Once we start killing people, we've crossed a line we can't step back from. Do we really want to start a war?"

"Well, what do you want us to do? Just let them ride up and knock down our barricades and come right in? We're fresh out of oxen, in case you hadn't noticed!"

Aeron hesitated. He knew he was right about the larger consequences, but Trefor was also right about the immediate practical problem. "Uh… throw rocks! Throw mud! Use the blunt end of the spears; anything to drive them back. Keep the archers ready to fire, but make the humans fire the first shot!"

There was a great deal of grumbling and head-shaking, but Dilwyn suddenly spoke up: "I think he's right, Trefor. We're in League territory, and if we start killing League soldiers, it's going to send the whole thing up in flames. At least make them start the violence."

Trefor looked like he was going to explode. "This is crazy…"

"Well, you better decide right now," said Aeron, pointing, "here they come." The Rhordians had gotten themselves sorted out and into a new formation, only two ranks deep and as wide as their numbers allowed. A horn was blown and they started forward. "Looks like they're going to try all the gaps this time."

Trefor shook his head in exasperation but finally said: "All right! No shooting unless they do! Spearmen, use the butt ends of your spears. Everyone else! Throw rocks at their horses when they get close!"

"And cover all the gaps!" added Aeron. "They're gonna hit everywhere at once!"

The people surged out to each of the gaps, twenty or so to each one. Trefor sent a few of the spearmen to help but kept the rest and the archers in a clump close to him. Aeron looked around and realized that he had no clue what *he* ought to be doing. He pulled out the dagger Sergeant Rolf had given him and realized just how useless it would probably be in this sort of fight. No time to tie it to something and make a spear…

The Rhordians were *here*.

They rode up to the wagons and gathered at the gaps, their formation curling nearly all the way around the ring. They shouted and waved their swords and poked their spears over the barricades. The defenders shouted and poked the butt ends of spears back at them or clacked them against the spears of the cavalry, but thanks to the barricades they really couldn't get at each other.

But then, at the shouts of Captain Lennart, the horsemen began urging their horses right up against the barricades. Some of the stacks of boxes began to lean in alarmingly under the weight of all that horseflesh.

A number of the people with no weapons threw themselves against the inside of the barricades, trying to keep them from toppling. Others with the spears began to thrust and poke much more aggressively against the poor horses. And many more began to throw the rocks and mud they'd dug up. Bolder ones started hurling the copious droppings the oxen had left behind - and they weren't aiming at the horses.

As Aeron had hoped, the horses didn't like this treatment at all, and they began to rear and buck and back away from their tormentors. If these had been the warhorses of the heavy cavalry, they would have been trained to tolerate this sort of abuse, but the light cavalry mounts weren't meant for action like this. To add to the bedlam, Nesta had rallied her pot-bangers, and they were coming up now, clanging away like mad, and the horses started to panic.

Finally, one dung-spattered and angry trooper had enough. He stood up in his stirrups and hurled his spear over the barricade. It caught a mud-slinger in the shoulder, punched clear through, and knocked him over, pinning him to the ground.

A sort of gasp spread through everyone - human and Shirefolk alike. There was a held-breath moment of near-silence, and then the noise erupted twice as loud as before. Several more spears were tossed, but thankfully finding no victims this time, and then Trefor screamed at his archers to let loose. Only a half-dozen were still with him, the rest having been spread out around the ring, but they'd been ready and waiting, and they didn't waste a moment. A small shower of arrows lashed out. Some missed, others stuck in the men's armor, but one caught the rider who had thrown the first spear smack in the eye, and he reeled around and fell out of his saddle.

"Well, *that's* done it," said Dilwyn from next to Aeron.

And indeed it had. More arrows flashed out, and more spears came in. The halflings carrying spears flipped them around and were using the pointed ends now and connecting with them; sometimes against horses and sometimes against men. The thrown spears from the men, whether they struck flesh or the earth, were quickly picked up and used against their former owners. No more mud or dung was thrown, just rocks, and with the accuracy Shirefolk were famous for. But the humans were scoring, too.

Looking around the ring, Aeron could see that a dozen or more of his people were down, but the rest were fighting, and the human cavalry was in a position it simply wasn't meant for. Unable to use its speed or maneuverability, the men were easy targets, and one after another they fell. Until finally a horn was blown and they grudgingly retreated, pursued by rocks, arrows, and catcalls. A half-dozen lay dead; some of their wounded were able to ride away on their own and a few more were dragged aboard horses by comrades. Things slowly quieted down, except for the moans and cries of the wounded and the exclamation of those tending to them.

And the weeping of the kin of those who were dead.

There were only three of those; a light price for a fight like this, but there was no telling that to those who had lost someone. Aeron looked down in shock at a young lad who'd been hit right in the heart by a spear. His shirt was soaked in blood. He still clutched a rock in his hand. *If we'd just given up, he'd still be alive...*

"Have they given up?" asked Trefor, suddenly appearing next to him. "They haven't given up, have they?"

It was hard to think. He couldn't tear his eyes away from the dead youth. *He's about my age...*

"Cadwallader!" Trefor grabbed his arm and shook him. "They haven't given up! Look, they're rallying! What should we do now?"

"What? Oh." With a huge effort, he pulled his mind back where it belonged. He looked out from the barricade to where the humans were regrouping. They were three hundred paces away and it was hard to see exactly what they were doing, but he had a good idea... *Stringing their bows.*

"They won't charge again. Not until they've worn us down. They've got bows, and I expect they'll use them."

"So we should get people behind the barricades and the wagons...?"

"Yes, but..."

"But what?" demanded Trefor. The fellow was brave, Aeron could see, but he was far out of his depth here. *And you're not?*

"They'll hit us from all sides. Even if we're crouched here behind this wagon and safe from a shot coming from that way, an arrow coming from the other side of the ring can still hit us. We need to create some real cover."

"How?"

Thinking fast, he saw a possibility. "Take some of the stuff from the inside of the barricades. Shove it under the wagons, all the way to the side facing outward. Plug up the openings under the wagons. We can get the young and the old and the sick and wounded—anyone who can't fight—under there and they'll be relatively safe. The rest of us will just have to take our chances."

Trefor looked to Dilwyn, who nodded. "It's good plan. We should do it."

"All right," said the wagonmaster, who began giving order to have it done.

"I'm going to get Paddy out of his wagon and underneath it. He'll be safer there." He quickly moved away.

Aeron helped shove a few boxes under a wagon to create the little fortresses he'd envisioned. They actually looked like they'd be pretty effective. Arrows fired from a distance would go up and then arc downward at an angle that wouldn't allow them to find the space beneath the wagons as long as the outside face was filled up. There wasn't a lot of room, but maybe ten or twelve people could shelter there. With fourteen wagons, that was nearly half the total.

It wasn't until arrows started to rain down on them that he realized the Rhordians had returned. It was just a few at first, but then a steadier and steadier increase, like the approach of a heavy rainstorm. Soon the thunk and thud of arrows hitting wood and earth sounded like a hailstorm.

Two hundred horse archers with maybe forty arrows each comes to... eight thousand arrows? The circled wagons and the ground inside was going to look like a bloody pincushion.

It wasn't long before they suffered their first casualty, a fellow making an unwise dash from one bit of cover to another caught an arrow in his leg. He cried out and began crawling toward shelter. Another person ran to help him and was rewarded with an arrow in his arm. Both were dragged under an already crowded wagon and tended to. More cries soon followed from the opposite side of the ring.

The Shirefolk archers were firing back, but there were only a dozen of them and the enemy was now using the tactics they were trained for: ride in, fire a shot and then turn away, ride out of range and then do it again a few moments later. They were difficult targets for the defenders, although they did score a hit now and then. The area outside the wagon ring was a swirling mass of horsemen that despite its look of chaos was actually a well-drilled maneuver like some courtly dance.

Moment by moment, the defenders' casualties mounted. Some lightly wounded, quickly patched up, some more seriously hurt—and some dead. Aeron and Trefor moved from wagon to wagon, trying to encourage their people, but to what effect he didn't know. The defenders were frightened and angry, and a few were clearly demoralized. The enemy plan was working; by the time they ran low on arrows, the defense would be so battered and shaken, a charge would have little trouble breaking in this time. When he checked the sky, he was surprised at how far down the sun was. This had been going on for longer than he'd realized, several hours since they first sighted the enemy at least. But night wasn't going to come soon enough to help them.

He checked on Nesta and her two children; she had her youngsters crammed in under a wagon with a lot of other kids, but she was forced to stand more in the open. Several arrows were sticking in the ground dangerously close to her. She held an iron frying pan like a makeshift shield. He made a few idiotic remarks trying to encourage them, but there wasn't a thing he could do. Later, he found himself next to the wagon where Paddy Bobart had been hiding. The old man was there with Dilwyn, crouching under the wagon, looking a bit puzzled, but also angry. "How are you doing?" Aeron asked.

"All right so far. But this isn't looking good, is it?"

"Not really, no. If we don't get some help, we're in trouble."

"Any hope of that?"

"I don't know. The watchtower at that nearby guardburg has been sending up smoke for over an hour, so our rider got through. But how long it will take to assemble a relief force, I have no idea." He paused and nodded toward Paddy. "Is there anything he can do to help?"

Dilwyn shrugged. "We had to leave almost everything except his notes behind. He has some magic, but he's not really a mage and… and I think the whole situation has confused him. He's not a young man anymore, y'know."

"No, I'm not!" said Paddy suddenly. "But I'm not deaf, either! Nor helpless! Who are those rascals out there, anyway? And why are they shooting at us?"

"Paddy, I explained before: the Shires have left the League, and those are Rhordian soldiers. They want to take you prisoner and drag you back to…"

"Yes, yes, yes! I remember now. Take me back, eh? I'd like to see them try!" He came out from under the wagon and moved toward the barricade at the end of it.

"Paddy, you shouldn't…!" protested Dilwyn, taking hold of his arm.

"Leave go of me you whippersnapper! Cadwallader here—see, I can remember some things!—wanted to know if I can help. Well, I surely can!"

"You're not a warmage, Paddy!" said Dilwyn. "It's not like you can throw fireballs at them."

"Ha! Show offs! Don't need fireballs for something like this. I might not be able to toss lightning, but I can master matter! Just the thing!"

"What are you going to do?" asked Aeron, hope surging in him. "Break their bowstrings?"

"Pah!" spat Paddy. "They'll have spare bowstrings. Let's do something they'll find harder to repair." He leaned against the barricade with one hand, raised the other up, and pointed toward an approaching horse archer. The man drew back on his bow…

…and it snapped in two!

One end of it flashed back and hit the human right in the face, nearly knocking him out of the saddle. Paddy cackled with glee. "There! You see!"

"I did see," said Aeron. "That was wonderful! Can you do it again?"

"Can I? Just watch me!"

And he did it again. And again. One by one, he snapped the enemy's bows, rendering them useless. The riders stared at their ruined weapons in confusion and slowly drew away. When he had disarmed everyone near this particular part of the perimeter, Paddy toddled off to the next spot over. Dilwyn was nearly frantic, and Aeron was a bit worried himself, as arrows coming from the opposite side fell perilously close to the old man. They tore the tops off two barrels to create makeshift shields and moved along with Paddy, trying to guard his back.

When they reached the next barricade, Bobart peered through a gap in it and exclaimed: "Well! Look at that saucy fellow!"

Aeron looked and saw one of the Rhordian riders galloping at full-tilt up to only thirty paces away before loosing his arrow, turning his horse sharply, and galloping away again. It was some really impressive horsemanship, Aeron had to admit. Paddy stood there grinning and waited until the man came racing toward them again. Aeron expected Paddy to shatter the man's bow, but he had other plans. When the rider fired his shot and started to turn away, Paddy gestured, and the leather girth strap on the saddle parted. The horse went one direction and the rider and saddle went another; a moment later, the man was sprawled on the ground.

The Shirefolk nearby roared with laughter, but one of their archers wasn't laughing, and when the man tried to run, he put an arrow right into his buttocks, sending him sprawling again, shrieking in pain. The human was an easy target now, but no more arrows were fired at him. Crippled, he was no longer a threat and was allowed to limp away.

Meanwhile, Paddy was happily shattering more bows.

"Did you know he could do this?" asked Aeron.

"No," replied Dilwyn, "and I doubt the Duke of Eowulf knew either, or he would have sent along a warmage with his cavalry."

They continued to follow and guard Paddy as he went around the ring, disarming archer after archer. The amount of fire falling on the defenders grew less and less, although people were still being hit. Hope was starting to grow in Aeron, and also in the hearts of the other Shirefolk. Many who had been cowering in near-panic under the rain of arrows were now shouting and taunting the enemy.

"Maybe we can do this after all," said Dilwyn.

"Can he keep this up?" asked Aeron. "The mages at the College talked about the drain this sort of thing puts on them. How much strength does he have?"

"I don't know. He is looking tired. I'll try to make him stop and rest in a while."

But they were only a little more than halfway around the ring with Paddy when a horn began sounding from the enemy, and the riders quickly pulled back and formed up back near their original assembly point. "What now?" demanded Trefor. "They giving up?"

"I doubt it," said Aeron. "Their mission to get Paddy aside, they've taken losses and they're not going to let themselves be beaten by a bunch of 'halfmen'. They're angry, and that makes them more dangerous." He hurried over to the barricade closest to where the enemy was gathering. Trefor followed, but Dilwyn stayed with Paddy.

They had to push their way through a crowd of celebrating people, who clearly thought the enemy *had* given up, to get a clear view. Unfortunately, what he saw sent a chill down Aeron's spine. "They're dismounting."

"Why?' asked Trefor.

"They're going to attack on foot. The worst thing possible for us."

"But they're cavalry!"

"Doesn't mean they can't fight without their horses. They'd rather not do it this way, but they've got no choice, and I don't know how in the Abyss we're going to stop them this time."

"We've got the barricades… and every adult will be able to fight…"

"And every adult will be *forced* to fight! The barricades will give us a better chance, but this is going to be… horrible."

"So? You expect us to surrender now?" sneered Trefor.

"It's gone too far for that. They're mad as demons, and even if we did give up, the results would probably be worse than if we fought to the last."

"And how do you know that? You're just a kid."

"I read, I listen, and I learn. But enough of that. They're getting ready to attack. Get all the archers up here and everyone with a decent weapon on this side of the ring. At least on foot they can't suddenly sweep around and hit us from the other side."

The enemy's horn blew again, and the mass of newly-minted infantry came forward. They were tired and it was slightly uphill, so they didn't come at a run, it was barely a trot. A score or so remained mounted, including the banner-bearer, the hornist, and presumably Captain Lennart, and followed along behind the rest of the men. Some of the attackers had spears while others had slightly curved swords. They all looked ready to use them.

When they reached about a hundred and fifty paces, the halfling archers started firing. They were certainly tired, too, and many of them were forced to use scavenged, slightly overlarge, arrows that the humans had so kindly provided. Only about half of the humans were carrying shields, and the ones they had were fairly small and didn't provide much protection from arrows. Men started falling almost at once, but that did not seriously thin their line.

There are about a hundred and fifty of them, thought Aeron. *We've got almost twice that number who can fight. Can we stop them?* Twice that number? Really? Only if you counted everyone who wasn't too young, too old, or too hurt to wield a weapon. Only if you included youths and the women. And most of them only had the most makeshift weapons. *And they are so much bigger than we are.*

The humans weren't enormous, fortunately. Light cavalry usually had smaller riders, the big ones being reserved for the heavy cavalry or infantry. But even the smallest of the men coming against them was a full head higher than even the largest Shirefolk.

The defenders had tried to make up for that difference as much as possible. In the time they had to get ready, they'd rearranged some of the inner parts of the barricades and built steps to allow them to look over the top and strike at anyone trying to get across. The wagons were also filled with defenders, and the huge human-built wagons were almost like the walls of a stockade.

Nearly here. The humans were fifty paces away and quickening their step. A few of them still had bows and followed along, shooting at the defenders in the wagons. Thirty paces and they began to scream their battle cries and broke into a run.

Aeron was so mesmerized at watching the oncoming enemy he almost forgot to draw his weapon, Sergeant Rolf's dagger. The Rhordians reached the wagons and barricades and immediately started climbing over them. Shirefolk with spears rammed them into faces or bodies and tried to drive them back. The defenders in the wagons hurled rocks or any other large, heavy object they could get their hands on, smashing them down on the heads of the humans. A dozen or more were laid low in the first few moments.

But the Rhordians struck back with their own weapons, and their unarmored opponents began falling fast, too. Battle cries turned to cries of pain, and weapons dripped red. Still, the Shirelings fought on. Any time a real weapon fell—from the hands of an attacker or defender, it made no difference - it was picked up by someone without one and used against the enemy.

The Rhordians had focused their attack on just four wagons and the gaps between them, and their concentrated numbers began to tell. Men were getting up on the wagons or over the barricades, and in some spots they were tearing the barricades down from the outside. The first few men to get up or over were set upon by many times their numbers and usually cut down, but their sacrifice let more men follow, and the odds began to shift.

More people rushed to the danger points, but to Aeron's dismay, most of them were women and lads barely big enough to carry any sort of weapon. His breath caught in his throat when he saw Nesta Andras wielding her heavy iron fry pan among them. She lunged forward and smashed it down on the hand of a human trying to pull himself over the barricade. The man shrieked, snatched back his mangled hand, and disappeared behind the barrier.

Aeron rushed forward to help Nesta, just as another human vaulted over the barricade, knocking her to the ground. He was big and had the look of an experienced fighter, and he had a red tassel on his helmet. The man struck out all around him with a sword in one hand and a long knife in the other; several people tumbled away, clutching deep cuts. Nesta, struggling up, whacked the man in the leg with her fry pan. He cursed and brought up his sword to strike.

"Leave her alone!" shouted Aeron, charging forward. The man saw him coming and lashed out with his sword. Aeron ducked under it, inside his guard, and thrust with his dagger. The human knocked his blow aside with his knife hand, and then smashed the hilt of his sword into Aeron's face, knocking him back to his knees, stars dancing before his eyes. The man reared back, raising his sword for a blow Aeron had no hope of dodging.

But then the sword shattered into glittering fragments, and the man's stroke hit nothing - because all he was holding was the hilt of a sword.

Paddy!

It had to have been Bobart's doing, but there was no time to look to confirm that. The human was off-balance and right there, not two feet away. Aeron surged to his feet and thrust the dagger with both hands right into the human's throat. His enemy lurched backward, blood spewing from the wound as the blade was torn free, soaking the front of Aeron's shirt. The man's hands went to his throat, but he reeled backward, colliding with another man coming over the barricade, and went down. He wouldn't be getting up.

Aeron gasped for breath, trying to deal with the fact he'd just killed someone. But there was no time for that. More enemies were appearing. The barricade in front of him toppled over, and a dozen or more humans clambered over the remains. A score of Shirelings gathered to oppose them, but what hope did they have to stop them? A glance showed that the same thing was happening at the other points of attack. Dilwyn was half-carrying Paddy a dozen paces back, but the old halfling looked exhausted. Aeron pulled Nesta up to stand next to him. "You should stay back," he said.

"No," she replied, and didn't move.

The Rhordians didn't come charging at them in a mob. They were tired, too, and had lost a lot of their fellows. They got themselves organized and gripped their weapons, but they didn't immediately attack.

"Go on! Finish this, damn you!" roared a voice. Aeron looked and there was Captain Lennart on his horse with his bannerman, just the other side of the toppled barricade, gesturing with his sword. "They're done! Attack!" The humans seemed to draw themselves up and started forward…

A horn blew.

Then another and another.

Not the high-pitched, brassy tone of a human horn, but the throaty call of rams' horns. Shireling horns!

Lennart twisted to the right in his saddle and snarled: "What?"

Shouts and cries and the clash of battle came from the direction Lennart was looking. The men in front of Aeron all looked that way, too, and a few took steps backward. Then, through the gaps in the barricade, he saw a swarm of Shirefolk on ponies galloping into the flank and rear of the Rhordians! They were led by a fellow riding not a pony, but one of the miniature *aralez*—a massive dog-like creature nearly as large as a horse—that he'd heard about.

"A relief force!" he cried. "From the guardburg!"

The cries and shouts from outside the ring were immediately joined by more shouts from inside. The people around Aeron screamed in joy and started moving forward. The men in front of them began moving back.

"Stand! Stand and fight, you dogs!" roared Lennart, standing up in his stirrups. But as he did, he suddenly swayed to his left, and then he and his saddle slid off the horse and he fell.

Paddy again!

Aeron looked back and there was the old Artificer, grinning like a loon.

"Now!" shouted Aeron. "Charge!" He waved his bloody dagger and led the Shirefolk forward.

The Rhordians fled.

The humans had much longer legs and quickly out-distanced Aeron's pursuit. He and those with him were exhausted and decided to leave the chasing to their mounted kin. In fact, they stopped after only a score of paces when they found Captain Lennart trying to disentangle himself from his stirrups and saddle. He stopped struggling when he found himself ringed by armed and angry Shirelings.

The rest of his men were fleeing down the slope to where their comrades were holding all the horses. Unfortunately for them, when they saw the relieving cavalry, they mounted up and rode off, towing all the horses with them. The pursuers cut down a few of the fleeing men, and a dozen or so surrendered, but the rest, less than a hundred now, were allowed to keep running. Exhausted, and having cast off most of their weapons and gear to get away, they were no threat now.

Aeron looked around the chaos that remained and suddenly felt very light-headed. He began to sway, and only Nesta's strong hand on his arm kept him from toppling. "Are you all right?" she asked.

"Just tired."

"Tired and beaten to a pulp. Your face is a mess."

Oh, right, the sword hilt to his head. It was starting to hurt now. He touched it and flinched at the stringing pain. When he drew his hand away, there was blood on it. Nesta took his hand and drew him toward where her children were still huddled under a wagon. "I'll help you get that cleaned up and some bandages…"

But before they got halfway there, a half-dozen of their rescuers rode into the ring, the ponies stepping awkwardly over bags, boxes, and bodies. The commander in the lead wore a bright green scarf around his neck and an aura of authority. His aralez had blood on its muzzle, which it licked with a huge tongue.

"Get ready to move!" he shouted. "We can't stay here. There's more of those rascals on the way!"

Aeron spun around and stumbled back toward him. He saw Trefor Trahern trotting that way, too. The wagonmaster's left sleeve was torn away and the arm dripped blood. When they got close, Aeron shouted: "More? How many? How far?"

Almost at the same time, Trefor was shouting: "Move? Are you mad? We have wounded—and dead! The oxen are scattered! We can't move!"

The halfling on the aralez looked from one to the other, and then his gaze settled on Trahern. "Who are you?"

"I'm Cap… Trefor Trahern," he said, casting a glance at Aeron. "Master of this convoy. Who are you?"

"Conwy Macsen, commander of the guardburg up ahead. And I'm not asking you to move, I'm telling you that you *have* to move! My scouts report there's another batch of Rhordian cavalry coming on fast. At least five hundred of them, and they'll be here in two hours or less. Which means you and your people damn well better be inside the guardburg in less than three hours. Now move it if you want to stay alive!"

"But we've got a lot of wounded and old people and others who can't walk or ride! We've got to have at least a few of these wagons!"

"Can you round up some of the oxen, sir?" asked Aeron. "Most of them are just wandering around out there. If you could get a dozen or twenty, we could double or triple team three or four wagons."

Macsen looked and could see the injured being pulled out from under the wagons or helped where they fell. He shook his head and then cursed, but he shouted to one of his subordinates: "Lewys! Take your boys and round up as many of those oxen as you can catch and bring them here! Quick as you can!"

That man rode off with some of the others. Almost immediately, Dilwyn came up and grabbed hold of the leader's trouser leg. "Mister Macsen! I've got Master Artificer Paddy Bobart here! He can't be caught by the Rhordians - he's what they attacked us for in the first place! The Shires Assembly wants him safe. Can you get him out of here right now?"

Macsen seemed like he was about to explode. He looked around. "Anything else? You want these prisoners taken back with us, too? Maybe your grandmother's favorite rocking chair? There's no *time*, man! Missing Gods, we've got to get out of here!"

And they did.

It was a struggle and a mad scramble that nearly spilled over into panic, but they got moving in less than half an hour. Paddy and Dilwyn and a chest of his papers were strapped to ponies and sent off immediately with a small escort. They hitched up six oxen to each of four wagons and piled all the wounded, sick, and elderly into three of them. The fourth carried their dead - twenty-four of them. No one wanted to leave them to the questionable care of the Rhordians.

Naturally, there was no room for any baggage beyond what the walkers could carry and still move quickly. There was a great deal of cursing and wailing over that. Perhaps more than over all the dead, much to Aeron's disgust. Not that there wasn't a lot of wailing over the dead. And anger, too. When word got around that they were going to have to turn their prisoners loose, some were demanding they be executed on the spot. Aeron found himself an unexpected advocate for saving their lives.

"We won a battle," he said. "With any luck, that will be the end of it. But if you murder these men, you are going to have a real war on your hands! You really want that?"

There was much grumbling over it and a few nasty remarks about *Traitor Cadwallader*, but the prisoners were allowed to walk off after their fellows who had already fled. Captain Lennart stared at Aeron with a strange expression before turning to go.

At Macsen's frantic urging, they got moving. The oxen grunting and mooing, the wagons creaking and groaning, the wounded moaning in pain, and the rest cursing at what they had to leave behind. Maybe they'd be able to come back for it once the Rhordians gave up the chase, opined a hopeful few.

Aeron marched with Nesta and her children. Gethin was babbling excitedly about the battle he'd just witnessed, but Elin was strangely silent and gave him odd looks. Well, he probably looked pretty odd just at the moment; battered face and blood-covered clothes. He hadn't even had a chance to wash the Rhordian's blood off his hands…

They hadn't gone far before they could spot the new Rhordian cavalry off in the distance. Yes, definitely a lot more than the first group. They picked up their pace as much as they could, and the newcomers were lost to sight as the caravan descended from the tiny ridge they'd been on.

The sun slid down the sky and disappeared behind a bank of clouds building in the west. But all eyes kept looking back south, expecting the enemy to appear on the ridge at any moment. Aeron realized that even at a horse-ruining pace, it would be at least an hour before they could reach that point; but even so, he looked back as often as anyone else.

The guardburg drew closer and closer, and the abandoned wagons fell farther and farther behind. A few small bands of additional cavalry arrived from the direction of the guardburg. They went to confer with Conwy Macsen, and it was a mark of how tired Aeron was that he didn't even try to go and overhear whatever tactical information they brought. He was done, and just placing one foot in front of the other was the best he could manage.

Many others of the people were done, too. A few of the children were loaded onto the wagons, and some of the women ended up riding double with the cavalry. Nesta and her children stuck it out, and the four of them trudged along together. After a while, Aeron just stared at the ground a few feet ahead of him watching the withered grass and weeds glide past him.

"Hey! Hey!" came a sudden cry. "There they are!"

They all looked back, and there on the little ridge, now silhouetted against the sky in the sunset, was a swarm of black dots, barely to be seen. Aeron looked ahead, and to his surprise and relief, the guardburg was right there, less than a mile away.

"Keep moving!" shouted Macsen. "We're nearly there! You can make it!"

They couldn't pick up the pace, not after all they'd been through, but they kept moving and the guardburg got closer faster than their pursuers. All during the trek, Aeron had been worrying about just how much of a refuge the place would actually be. The last time he'd come through here, over two years earlier, it had only consisted of a stone tower, twenty feet square and thirty feet high. There had been a large stone inn with a stable and a few outbuildings which doubled as a resting place for the traffic that came through along the road and as a barracks for the small garrison. Not much protection against a real attack.

But there had been some changes made, probably in response to the recent troubles. Now, a stout wooden palisade, fifteen feet high and two hundred paces on each side, enclosed the tower and the inn. Several hundred Shires infantry armed with bows and spears manned the defenses, and more were milling around outside. Many came swarming out to assist the refugees, and the whole mob was brought inside while the Rhordian cavalry was still a league behind.

The wagons creaked to a halt and the walkers slumped to the ground where they halted. Friendly people milled around them with water and food and care. Aeron realized he hadn't eaten since breakfast and was suddenly ravenous. He wolfed down the bread and cheese and sausage he was offered. Nesta and her children had appetites to match his.

He hardly felt as though he could not move another inch, but when the Rhordians got closer and the defenders all came inside and closed the gates, somehow he managed to lever himself to his feet to find out what was going on.

Not much, as it turned out. The Rhordians stopped five hundred paces away and sent forward a small party. Just as Captain Lennart had done with the wagon convoy, they demanded that Paddy Bobart be turned over to them, and just as before, they were told to be off. But this time there was no fight. The cavalry obviously didn't like the looks of the stockade and were not equipped to attack it. They sullenly rode away and pitched a camp just across the border. Aeron went back to find Nesta.

It was nearly dark now, and bonfires were lit and torches set along the walls. Aeron peeled off his blood-stained shirt and dug another one out of his pack. He nearly tossed the old one away, but the blood was all dried, so he rolled it up and stuffed it in with his other clothes. Nesta found a bowl and heated some water, and they all washed their faces and hands. Aeron's face was very sore and swollen where he'd been struck.

The rescuing cavalry began loudly telling the tale of their glorious victory to the infantry which had stayed behind. Not to be outdone, the survivors of the wagon convoy told their tale, embellishing the truth a bit without shame. Before long, Conwy Macsen was being carried around on the shoulders of his cavalry, and Trefor Trahern was raised (and rather quickly lowered again) by the people of the convoy.

Nesta shook her head angrily. "Look at those fools. Trefor did a good job, to be sure, but we wouldn't have lasted a quarter hour if you hadn't been there to take charge!"

"It doesn't matter," said Aeron, barely able to keep his eyes open.

"It matters to me!"

"It's all right, Nesta. We're safe." He waved at the celebration. "It doesn't matter."

[illegible]

Chapter 8

But as it turned out, it did matter.

The next morning, they woke up feeling still tired and aching in every bone. One of the wounded had died during the night, and the sentries reported that there had been a large fire visible in the distance. Scouts came back shortly afterward saying that the Rhordians were all gone, and that they had burned the abandoned wagons and everything they had been carrying.

The jubilation of their escape was quickly replaced with anger over their losses of both people and property in the minds of the refugees. That inevitably led to a need for someone to blame. No one wanted to blame Trefor Trahern; he was well-known and popular. Dilwyn and Paddy weren't around to blame since they had been spirited away to Hodenburg before the rest of them even reached the guardburg.

That left Aeron.

Hadn't he been the one so eager to fight? Trefor had been trying to negotiate with the Rhordians, and it seems all they wanted was that Bobart fellow anyways. But Aeron was determined to fight. And now twenty-five of their friends and family were dead and a lot more hurt, and all their belongings burned up!

By mid-morning, no one would speak to him except Nesta and her children. And shortly after that, no one would speak to her or them, either. That was just the refugees, of course. The victorious cavalry, who had only lost a single person dead, didn't know Aeron from a hole in the ground, and he was just as happy to leave it that way.

The survivors spent the day resting, tending their wounded, burying their dead, and making plans to move on - without nearly all of their possessions. None of those activities sweetened their mood, and by that evening, Nesta said to Aeron: "I just had to break up a fight between Gethin and another boy. That's the third time today. Let's get out of here."

Aeron agreed, and so they were on the road to Hodenberg at the first glimmer of daylight the next morning. The capital was about six and a half leagues away by the road, and they weren't going to do it in one day. Fortunately, there were several inns along the way, and with luck, they could spend the night at one and reach Hodenberg by the next night. Aeron's father had sent him a generous allowance for living expenses at the College of Warcraft, and with his recreational activities severely restricted for quite some time, he had a fair amount of money with him. He could afford to get a room for himself, one for Nesta and her children, and food for them all.

When the sun rose, it revealed a pleasant countryside around them. It wasn't as flat as the stretch between Eowulf and the border, and the road gently rose and fell. The Tanmill Canal, which had usually been in view to their right, was now often concealed behind low hills, even though it was actually getting closer as both it and the road converged toward Hodenburg. Small farmsteads dotted the countryside, and they could see many people working in the fields, plowing and getting ready for the spring plantings. It was lush and fertile land called the Golden Fields for the way it looked when the huge wheat crops ripened. The open lands were dotted with windmills, mostly idle at this time of year; but when the harvests came in, their vanes would be spinning whenever there was wind to grind the grains into flour.

At first, they walked at as brisk a pace as the children could stand, but once the guardburg was out of sight, they slowed to an easier stride. Somehow, it felt like they were leaving at least a few of their troubles behind. The talk among the refugees was that they would probably not be leaving for several more days, and once parted from them, they could become a simple set of travelers on the road, anonymous and not the target of anyone's anger.

It occurred to Aeron that they could easily be mistaken for a family. Nesta was older than him, but not by all that much, he'd discovered. She was twenty-four and he was twenty. As they talked, he found himself liking her more and more.

"So, are you going to just push on after we reach Hodenburg?" Nesta asked. "It's only another three leagues or so to Picksbury, and your home, isn't it?"

"About that, although my home is a bit farther along," he replied. "But I think I may be staying on at Hodenburg for a few days at least. Maybe longer depending on what happens."

"What are you expecting to happen?"

"Well, I honestly don't know. I'm *hoping* that they will find some use for me there in the Shires military. If relations with the League get worse—and it's hard to see how they won't after what's just happened - then the Shires are going to need to strengthen their defenses. I… I think I can help with that."

"Because of what you learned at that college-place?"

"Yes. I hate to say it, but we halflings are really behind the times in military matters. I think I could teach them a lot… if I can get anyone to listen."

"Like what?"

"Oh, I don't want to bore you."

"I won't be bored," said Nesta. "And even if I am, I like listening to your voice."

Aeron blushed and smiled. "All right. Well, halfling armies for the most part fight in… well, the only thing I can call them is *mobs*. No, that's not really fair, they aren't mobs, but they aren't nearly as well organized or disciplined as typical Rhordian soldiers. We get groups of fighters together under a commander; usually with some sort of flag and maybe someone with a horn…"

"Wasn't that the same as the Rhordian cavalry?" asked Nesta.

"Well, yes, but you saw how the Rhordians could fight in different formations…"

"What's a for-mayshun?" asked Elin.

"Uh, it's the way the troops are arranged. Like when they first tried to attack us, they were in a formation called a column. Not that many men wide, but many ranks deep. Later, they formed a line that was very wide but only two men deep. And then, even later, they dismounted and fought on foot. To be able to fight in different fashions like that takes training. Most Shires troops can't really do anything like that. They just cluster around their leader and he says: 'Follow me!' and they run along behind him."

"But we won anyway, didn't we?" demanded Gethin. "All their fancy for-mayshuns didn't help them, did they?"

"Uh, well, we had a very good defensive position and…"

"I threw rocks at 'em!" said Gethin, making a throwing motion with his arm. "Hit one of 'em, too!"

"You did not!" said Elin.

"Did, too!"

"How could you have? You were under the wagon with me the whole time."

"Yeah, and you were crying the whole time!"

"Was not!"

"Children, hush!" said Nesta. "It's rude to interrupt Mister Cadwallader."

"It's all right, Nesta," said Aeron laughing. "I'm just glad both of you made it through all that without getting hurt." He paused, looking at Nesta, and then said: "All three of you."

Nesta blushed and looked away, and there was a short silence before Elin spoke up: "Mama, what's that coming?"

Aeron looked, and coming over a rise in front of them were several wagons with an escort of Shires cavalry. At first he thought that maybe it was a supply train for the troops at the guardburg, but after a moment, he changed his mind. Something didn't look quite right…

There was a small crowd of other Shirefolk, mostly children, following along on the sides of the road. They must have come from some of the surrounding farms. They were shouting and a few of them were throwing rocks at the wagons. *What in the world…?*

"They… they're humans!" said Gethin in surprise.

And so they were. A dozen or so humans of all ages and sexes were huddled in the wagons, trying to make themselves poor targets for the rocks. The escorts were making no effort to stop the rock throwers, and some even laughed at any throw that found a target. Aeron and Nesta and the children got off the road and let the wagons rumble by. The humans aboard the wagons looked scared and angry, and some of the children were crying. Gethin started to bend down to pick up a rock, but a sharp word from Nesta stopped him dead.

As the strange cavalcade moved off, Nesta asked: "Is that what we looked like when they drove us out of Eowulf?"

"Pretty much, I imagine," said Aeron quietly.

"I… I never thought about any humans living inside the Shires."

"There aren't many. Just a few looking after business interests in Hodenburg and few of the other larger towns, I believe."

"Tossed out, just like us."

"Why is this happening, Mama?" asked Elin.

"I don't know, child, I just don't know."

* * * * *

Aeron's plan to get two rooms at the inn that night ran afoul of a company of Shires infantry heading for the border. The leaders had taken every room but one tiny space up in the attic.

"There's room enough for you three," he said. "I can find someplace in the stables I guess…"

"Nonsense!" snorted Nesta. "The children and I will take the bed and we can get a truckle for you on the floor."

"I… uh… that wouldn't really be proper, would it?" he asked, his face turning red.

"We slept on the ground not five feet apart for three nights running, Mister Cadwallader."

"With four hundred other people all around us."

"Aeron, stop being silly. And in any case, I'll sleep much sounder knowing you're close by." There was no arguing with that, so after a filling but somewhat overpriced dinner, they went to the room and settled in. The place clearly hadn't been used for a while, and there was no way to heat it except for whatever warmth might seep in from the floor below. At least that meant it was free of any small vermin. The soldiers were quite raucous down in the tavern, but their noise was muffled sufficiently not to be a problem. The children fell asleep almost immediately after the long day on the road, but he and Nesta talked quietly for a bit after they'd blown out the candles and the room became almost totally dark.

"I'm not sure how long I'll be staying in Hodenburg," he said. "I can afford to put you up there for a few days if you'd like to rest and get yourself together before… you push on to your home."

"Aeron, I can't batten upon you anymore than I have. I'm not completely without resources. As for going home… I don't know."

"Know what?"

She sighed. "I never got along all that well with my husband's family. I think that was a big reason he decided to try his luck in Eowulf. I don't know how welcome I'd be with them."

"What about your own family?"

"I was the youngest child by quite a bit. My parents are both pretty elderly now. They'd take us in, but it would be a burden. I have several older brothers, married with children almost as old as I am. They would take us in, too, but it would be… awkward."

"Where else would you go?"

"Maybe I'll just stay in Hodenburg and try to find work. I have my letters and I can keep accounts - skills that ought to be valuable there."

"Yes, I would think so," he replied, thinking. "My father has a successful business. Maybe… maybe he could find a position for you."

"Oh, I couldn't ask you to do that!"

"Why not? You've helped me out, why can't I help you? And my father wouldn't mind, as long as you can do the work."

She didn't answer right away, and when she did, she said: "Tell me about your family, Aeron."

Not quite sure what to make of this change of subject, Aeron tried to comply. He rattled off a list of brothers, sisters, aunts, uncles, cousins, and various other relations, until he was yawning so badly he was afraid his face would split. Nesta sounded like she was half-asleep already, but she asked one last question: "Do you have a lady-friend back home?"

"Uh, no. No I don't."

He wasn't sure, but it sounded like her mumbled response was: "Good."

* * * * *

The next day, they made it to Hodenburg, the largest city in the Shires and also the capital. There were five Shires, the oldest being Abbetshire off to the north; Hoddingshire, of which Hodenburg was also the capital; Southshire to the west of Hodenburg; Daleshire to the northwest; and just north of that lay Tanshire. While at the College of Warcraft, Aeron had seen a document claiming that something like a hundred and sixty thousand halflings lived in all the Shires. That seemed an impossibly huge number to him, but perhaps it was true. The Shires didn't hold a lot of territory, but the villages and farms covered almost every bit of farmable land. Hodenburg was nearly as large as Eowulf, and thirty thousand people lived there.

As they topped a low ridge, the city came into view, and they all stopped to rest for a moment. As Aeron stared at the city, still nearly a league away, something seemed to click in his mind. "Huh… never noticed that before," he murmured.

"What?" asked Nesta.

"The way the city is laid out. Does it remind you of anything? Anything we've all seen recently?"

She stared and stared but finally shook her head. "No. What do *you* see?"

"The shape. What shape is the city? Can you tell me, Elin?" he looked to the child.

"It… it's kind of … round?"

"Yes, it's almost a circle. What other circular thing have we seen on this trip? Just a few days ago?"

"The wagons?" asked Gethin. "They were in a circle."

"Yes! Exactly."

The boy seemed pleased that he'd gotten the answer right, but then he shrugged. "So what?"

"Well, our oldest legends say that the halflings were nomads—they moved from place to place with their flocks and herds and didn't stay in one place for long. If they had wagons, or just tents, they might have arranged them in a circle for defense—just like we did. Once they decided to stay in one place, they might have kept the circle arrangement."

"So what?" asked the boy again.

"Maybe nothing," said Aeron, shrugging in turn. "Our cities don't have high walls protecting them the way human cities do. But see how Hodenburg is a series of circles one inside the other inside the other? I bet the first settlement here kept the old style layout, and as the city grew, they just added more circles, growing outward. You can see the main streets radiating outward from the center. If you blocked off those streets - like we did between the wagons - you'd have a pretty good defense, even without walls."

"You sure are smart, Aeron," said Elin.

"Yes, he is," said Nesta.

Aeron blushed and snorted. "Well, let's keep moving."

The city was further away than it looked, and it was mid-afternoon by the time they reached the outskirts. As they walked, Aeron continued to think about his earlier observation. Shires architecture was different from that of the humans. They were all into squares and rectangles, but Shires buildings tended to be more round, like their towns and cities. Not perfectly round, because timbers cut from trees tended to be straight and bending them into curves was a lot of work. But hexagons and octagons were very popular, and bigger structures could have even more sides. Structures with more than one story tended to have each upper floor smaller than the one below it, making the building resemble an egg or an apple that had been sliced in half. Out in the countryside, many houses had dirt thrown up on them with grass growing out of the dirt so that only the doors and windows were uncovered. Structures like that were called *cloctans* in the old tongue. Not many people built like that anymore; and in the towns, a good many square and rectangular buildings in the human style could be found. *But houses covered with grass wouldn't burn very well... build palisades between them and you'd have a pretty good defense...*

There was no gate to the city, but the main road from Eowulf had a small constable's station next to it on the outskirts, and a half-dozen sherrifs were lounging about watching the people coming and going. They didn't spare Aeron and Nesta and the children a second glance, and they walked right past.

"There's a really good inn that I know," he said. "My father would stay there when he came to the city on business, and he brought me along a few times. The *Blue Raven,* it's called. It's on the north side of the city, though, can you bear to walk a little farther?"

"I think so. But we don't want you to spend a lot of money..."

"Two rooms..."

"Ah."

"Feather beds..."

"Oh."

"A heated bath house..."

"Mmmm."

"A *laundry*."

"You have talked me into it. Lead on, Mister Cadwallader!"

He laughed and led the way through the streets. Streets so unlike those in Eowulf! Nothing but fellow Shirelings around them, not the slightest threat anywhere. For the first time in days, Aeron truly began to relax.

The *Blue Raven* was exactly where he remembered it, and it hadn't burned down or anything. A mention of his father's name got them the two rooms they wanted, and they spent the rest of the afternoon in the baths (one for each sex, although Gethin went with his mother). While they soaked their aches and pains away, their filthy clothes were washed. Aeron wondered what the laundress would think about the blood stains on his one shirt.

Their laundry wasn't quite dry when they were ready to leave the baths, so the inn lent them robes to wear back to their rooms. By dinner time, they had their clothes back and they went to the dining room to eat. They had a lovely meal, the best Aeron had had in ages. Soup, fresh-baked bread, fried potatoes, and roast beef, all washed down with some very good ale. Nesta and the children seemed to enjoy it every bit as much as he did. Between the bath, the large meal, and the days of marching - and fighting - he slept like the dead that night.

"So what is our - your plan?" asked Nesta the next morning at breakfast.

"Well, the first thing is I need to get a letter off to my father to let him know I'm all right and where I am. Would you like to send one, too, to your family?"

She shook her head. "Maybe later. After your letter, what then?"

"Well, then I need to arrange a meeting with the Shires Muster-Master."

"Who's that? I mean, I know what the Muster-Master is, but who is that?"

"Actually, I'm not sure. The position rotates around, with someone from each of the Shires taking the job for half a year. Not sure who has it now."

"I'd suggest you find out before you barge into his office," she said with a smile.

"Good idea," he replied, smiling in turn. "Although I doubt I'll be able to just walk in and see him in any case. I'll have to set up an appointment."

"Well, then, I'd also suggest you visit a tailor and get some new clothes. Even with the good washing they got, your attire is looking a bit ragged. You'll want to make a good impression."

Aeron looked down at himself and realized she was right. The cuffs on his jacket and trousers were fraying, and the knees and elbows worn thin. His boots had seen better days, too. "Yes, you're right. I'll find a tailor first thing after the letter. That will delay things at least a day, though."

"And that will allow your face to heal some more. You really do look a sight, y'know."

"Really?" his hand went to his face. It was still a bit tender; his tongue probed the chipped tooth he'd noticed. And it was true that people were staring at him… "All right, then I'll approach the Muster-Master tomorrow. What are you and the children going to do today?"

Nesta frowned and she looked worried. "I'm not sure. We really ought to push on toward… home."

"You ca… I mean, I wish you wouldn't. You can stay and rest up a bit until I find out if they'll accept my service. And I was serious about you taking a job with my father. I'll ask him about that in my letter, and I'd really like you to meet my mother and my sister, I think you'd get along really well and…" He was babbling and forced himself to stop. He looked anxiously at her.

A tiny smile appeared on her face. "How can I refuse such a generous offer? All right, we'll stay a few more days. But I'm paying for my own room and board."

He could see there was no point in arguing.

A little later, he headed out into the city after asking the innkeeper for the address of a reputable tailor. He found the place, *Ercwlff's Emporium*, without difficulty, and after a rather lengthy discussion with the proprietor about just what sort of clothing would be proper for an interview with an important official like the Muster-Master, got himself measured. Ercwlff promised his order would be done the following morning. A stop at a nearby cobbler found him a pair of low boots which fit him tolerably well and he bought them. Looking at the contents of his purse, Aeron realized that he only had enough left after this for at most a week more in Hodenburg. He'd either have to beg money from his father, find employment, or go home.

He went back to the *Blue Raven,* thinking to take Nesta and the children out to take a tour of Hodenburg. Unfortunately, they weren't there and a note she'd left told him that they had gone out with that very goal in mind. He hurried back outside in hopes of catching up with them, but despite walking swiftly up and down many a street, he could not find them. Disappointed, he decided to go to the very center of the city, where the great Assembly Hall sat, and just wander around there in hopes that she would find him.

The Assembly Hall was like an enormous *cloctan,* built in the ancient style with all curves instead of many straight sections. The lower floor was actually stone, but above that, huge curving wooden beams arched up to meet at the apex creating a beehive shape. The space in between the beams was wattle and daub, skillfully plastered and painted, with many small windows piercing it. There was an opening at the top from which a plume of smoke rose up, signally that the Assembly was in session. The Assembly did, sometimes, allow spectators. Aeron remembered his father taking him here when he was very young, and he was tempted to go inside and see if the visitor's gallery was open. But he didn't want to miss spotting Nesta, so he remained outside, slowly making his way around the circular park and window-shopping.

He wanted to find Dilwyn Brynmor, too. He'd heard nothing of his friend or Paddy Bobart, but he knew they'd been sent here immediately from the guardburg. Perhaps Paddy could help him in his quest to find employment with the Muster-Master.

The noon bell rang, and he was thinking about lunch when there was suddenly a commotion by the entrance to the Assembly Hall. People started gathering, and Aeron followed along. A fellow wearing a scarlet cloak and a tall hat with a feather had emerged and he was climbing a steep set of stairs to a raised platform. *A crier!* Aeron realized that some sort of official announcement was forthcoming. The crowd all fell silent and waited. The crier settled himself, took out a piece of paper, and cleared his throat.

"Harken people of Hodenburg! I bring tidings from our wise leaders!" The crier's voice was loud and carried clearly to the crowd. "In light of the ruthless and unprovoked attack upon a caravan of our folk, which left not less than five and twenty of them dead, the Shires Assembly declares that from this day hence, all trade, all commerce, and all dealings with the people of the League of Rhordia shall cease!"

A gasp passed over the crowd and then a small rumble as they took in the meaning of these words. All trade cut off? Who would they sell their surpluses to? Where would they get the metals they lacked? What about the silks and other luxury goods from distant lands? And how would the League react to having its food supply removed?

"Doubtless this will cause some hardships," continued the crier, "but our honor demands this. And our wise leaders have already taken actions to lessen the effects of these actions. Treaties are being brokered with some of the Young Kingdoms to our west! They will take our goods in trade for what we need. Have heart, good people! All shall be well!" The crier put away the paper, straightened his hat, and walked back down the stairs. As he did so, a number of boys ran off carrying sheaves of paper, apparently copies of the announcement to be posted throughout the city.

The crowd began talking noisily as it slowly dispersed. Aeron started to turn away when he felt a tug on his sleeve. It was Nesta with the children. "Did you hear that?" he asked her.

"Yes. What do you think?"

"I'm not sure. Trouble with the League for certain. I'm not sure how these treaties with the Young Kingdoms will fit into things."

"The crier didn't say which kingdoms, did he?"

"No. In fact if I heard correctly, there aren't *any* treaties yet, just negotiations. But if something could be worked out with a few of the stronger ones, it might be enough to give the League pause about openly attacking us."

"Most of those 'Young Kingdoms' aren't of much account, though, are they?"

"It's true that a lot of them just consist of a minor warlord calling himself a king with a few hundred men at arms to enforce his authority on the peasants - or plunder trade caravans or their neighbors. They're always fighting with each other and their 'kingdoms' come and go, split up, or get absorbed by their rivals. But there are some that are bigger, and some that are even respectable. Treaties with them would be worth something."

"But even with them as allies, it could still mean war with the League, couldn't it?"

"I hope not."

"I learned not to count on hope on the trip here from Eowulf," said Nesta, her face creased by a deep frown. "Tell me the truth, Aeron: this could mean war, couldn't it?"

He took a breath and nodded. "It could."

"Well then, you better convince the Muster-Master to take your help, ought'n you? Did you get those new clothes?"

"Yes, I can pick them up tomorrow morning," he smiled at the change of subject. Although it wasn't a complete change, he supposed. "Have you had any lunch?"

"No…"

"Well, let's get something then. Erin, Gethin, are you hungry?"

"Yes!" shouted the children in unison.

They found a tavern that was close-by rather than returning to the inn and had a pleasant meal. They could overhear a lot of the other patrons discussing the Assembly's latest actions. Most seemed in favor, but there were a few dissenting voices. Aeron and Nesta kept the discussion light for the children's sake and mostly talked about what they'd seen that morning. Elin had never been to Hodenburg, having been born in Eowulf. Gethin's only visit had been when he was not even two, so it was all new to him, as well.

After the meal, they walked about the city until the shadows began to lengthen when they returned to their inn for dinner. It had been a fine day, but in spite of the interesting sites and pleasant company, Aeron grew more and more nervous as he thought about what might come tomorrow. He lay awake in his bed for a long time before sleep finally took him.

*****

Following breakfast the next day, he went off to collect his new clothing and bring them back to the inn. With the advice of Tailor Ercwlff, he'd bought a pair of buff-colored wool trousers, a matching vest, and a dark green coat with brass buttons. A new white shirt went with them. He tried them on at the tailor's, of course, and a few final adjustments to the fit were made, but he took them off again, not wanting to risk getting them dirty on the walk back. He went to his room, put them on, and then rapped on Nesta's door to get her opinion.

"My! Look at you!" she exclaimed, smiling at him. She walked around him, tugging a bit here, brushing a bit there. "You look very fine, Aeron."

"Too fine, d'you think? I don't want to come off as some sort of fop."

"No, I don't think so. You look… respectable. And your face has healed just enough to not be repellant but still make you look like you've known battle."

Meaning it was *repellant before this?* He didn't like the sound of that. "Thank you."

"So, off with you! Go find the Muster-Master and let him know what you can do for him."

"Good luck!" cried little Elin. Gethin just stared at him.

Saying his goodbyes, Aeron left the inn and headed toward the center of the city. The Muster-Master kept a headquarters building on the circle near the Assembly Chambers. He had walked by there yesterday, but it had been closed up. He supposed the Master had been with the other Assembly members in their meeting. The building was of a more modern sort, eight-sided with the lower floor built of well-cut stone and the upper floor of wood.

Today, the door was open and he walked in - there were no guards. There was an entry hall which held a few paintings of legendary Muster-Masters and some tattered flags. A staircase straight ahead led upward, and there were several doors leading off to the right and left. He looked into one and it appeared to be a conference room with a larger table and several dozen chairs. The second door led to a small office with a desk, chair, and a person in the chair. The person was elderly, with shaggy gray hair. He was working with ink and quill on a stack of papers. He looked up at Aeron's entry and scowled.

"Who are you? What do you want?"

"Uh, I'm Aeron Cadwallader. I'd like to see the Muster-Master." He remembered belatedly that he still didn't know who, exactly, that was.

"You would, would you? On what business?"

"I would like to offer my services to him and the Shires."

"What *sort* of services?" The fellow was almost sneering now.

Aeron, determined not be browbeaten, drew himself up. "Who do I have the honor of addressing… sir?"

The fellow snorted. "I am Urien Yorath, secretary to the Muster-Master. And now I ask again: what sort of service?"

"Services as a military advisor, sir."

His eyebrows shot up. "Oh, really? Look young man, the Muster-Master is very busy, and he has no time for games or foolish requests from… from… whoever you are."

"Aeron Cadwallader, and I assure you, Mister Yorath, I am completely serious, and I believe thay my qualifications would be of great value to the Muster-Master."

"What qualifications?"

"I'll discuss that with the Muster-Master. When can I see him?"

Yorath snorted again, and his frown grew even darker, but he didn't shout at Aeron and tell him to get out as he expected. "He's not in the building just now. He'll be back later today. You are welcome to return later—for all the good it will do you."

"I'll wait."

"Suit yourself, but wait out in the other room, not here. I have work to do!"

"Certainly. Thank you for your help."

He left the office and found a hard wooden bench in the entry foyer. The chairs in the conference room looked more comfortable, but there was no good view of the entry from there, and he didn't want to risk missing the Muster-Master. And just who *was* that? It was ridiculous that he'd never heard anyone actually mention his name. He prowled around looking for something, a portrait, a scrap of paper, anything with his name, but found nothing. He could ask Yorath, of course, but that would make him look a fool - more a fool - in the secretary's eyes.

He sat or paced for an hour or so when Yorath emerged from his office and caught sight of him. He turned left and started down the hallway, but he stopped after a few feet and turned back. "The necessary is back here if you need it," he said, turned again, and continued on his way. *Well, that was kind of him.*

An instant later, as Yoruth disappeared, a thought struck him, and he sprang to his feet and moved to the office door as quickly and quietly as he could. Taking a deep breath, he slipped inside. He went to the desk and quickly looked over the stack of papers on it. There *had* to be something here with the Muster-Master's name on it! No… no… he dared to lift up a sheet and look at the one under it… *there!* "Missing Gods!" he hissed. *Dunstan Rootwell!*

He quickly retreated and got back to the bench and sat down before Yoruth came back. Just to confirm his discovery, he called out: "Where is Master Rootwell today?"

Yoruth didn't blink or hesitate and simply answered: "Meeting with the Assembly. Those things can last all day." And with that, he went back into his office. Aeron tensed, waiting for him to come back and angrily accuse him of burglary, but no such thing happened. Aeron slowly relaxed a bit, but only a bit.

Rootwell! Of all the luck. The same Dunstan Rootwell he'd met at the League Muster last fall in Eowulf. The one who seemed to hold him in such contempt. *'Where do your loyalties lie, Mister Cadwallader?'* Would he even give him the time of day now?

The day dragged on slowly. Aeron made use of the necessary several times and heard the hour bell ring outside again and again. He didn't dare leave for lunch, and his stomach was growling. Yoruth did go out at noon, presumably to eat, and locked his office behind him, but he didn't insist Aeron leave. Sitting there alone, he thought about how absurd it was that the headquarters of the Shires military had only one person working there aside from the commander himself. During one class at the College of Warcraft, they took a tour of Duke Eowulf's headquarters, and there had been dozens of people there, writing reports, sending and receiving messages, making plans, and doing all manner of things. Did Rootwell even know how many troops he had at his call - let alone where they might be or their state of readiness? If it came to a war, how could the Shires hope hold out with so little planning?

It was well into the afternoon, and Aeron was wondering if he was going to waste an entire day, before the front door opened and Master Rootwell stepped through, accompanied by another person. Aeron sprang to his feet and cleared his throat. Rootwell stopped in his tracks and demanded: "Who are you?"

"The young gentleman has been waiting since this morning to see you, sir," said Yoruth, who had emerged from his office silently. "He says he wants to offer you his services."

Rootwell ran a piercing eye over him, and Aeron nodded. "Indeed? Well, perhaps I can spare him a few moments when Captain Idwal and I are finished. Have him wait." With that, he and the other halfling went up the stairs and disappeared.

Yoruth nodded his head toward the bench, and Aeron sat down again.

The secretary went back to his room. *Well, at least he didn't send me packing right off. Maybe he didn't recognize me...*

Perhaps an hour went by before he heard noise from upstairs. The captain - who dressed no differently than anyone you'd see on the street - came down the stairs, poked his head into Yoruth's office, and then went out the door, only sparing Aeron a glance. After a few moments, the secretary came out and went up the stairs carrying a bundle of papers. Another half-hour passed before Yoruth returned. "The Muster-Master will grant you a quarter-hour." He turned and went back into his office.

Aeron was up, off the bench, and up the stairs at nearly a run. He slowed down at the top of the steps and saw a short hallway leading to an open door. Swallowing, he straightened his new clothes and marched forward and through the door.

Rootwell was seated at a large desk, covered with papers, and did not look up immediately. He was dressed in ordinary fashion like the captain, but he did wear a long red cloak secured by an ornate gold pin. Aeron halted two paces from the desk and came to attention. A dozen rapid heartbeats went by, and then Rootwell looked up at him and spoke:

~*'So, Master Cadwallader, have you decided where your loyalty lies?'*~

Aeron blinked and felt a moment of panic when Rootwell did not address him in the common tongue. What was…? *Ah!*

The Muster-Master was speaking in the People's ancestral language called *Tinker-tongue*. It was rarely used, except by the elderly in conversation anymore, and some of the younger folk had abandoned it entirely. But Aeron's grandfather had used it often, and Aeron, himself, having a knack for languages, had learned it at his grandda's knee. Still, he had to dig deeply into memory to craft his reply.

~*'There was never any doubt, Master. I am a child of the Shires, and my loyalty has always lain and always will lie here among its green hills and fair dales.'*~

He couldn't see any surprise on Rootwell's face at the reply, but his expression softened a tiny bit. "So, you haven't abandoned your heritage completely," he said in Common.

"No sir, I have not abandoned it at all."

"Some people suggest that you have."

"They are wrong. I went to Eowulf in hopes of learning things that will help our people. I had no way of knowing the League might end up our enemies."

"And now you come here offering to teach *me* what you have learned?"

"Knowledge is knowledge, no matter what its source. If we can improve ourselves by using Rhordian knowledge, we'd be fools to turn our backs on it. Sir."

"Book learning is not the same as real life, boy. How many battles have *you* fought?"

Aeron hesitated. He didn't want to seem like he was boasting, but now was not the time for false modesty, either. "One," he replied, and his eyes met Rootwell's. "And I won it, too."

"Really? All by yourself?"

"What commander ever wins a battle all by himself? But I was in command, and I did win."

Rootwell cocked his head. "I'm not a well-read man, so perhaps I missed that particular battle in the history books. What battle are you referring to?"

"The one just fought on the road to Eowulf. I took command of the refugee convoy and held off the enemy until relief arrived."

"Indeed? I have read several reports on that incident. Your name doesn't appear in any of them." His voice was filled with scorn.

"I'm not surprised. But just ask Paddy Bobart or Dilwyn Brynmor; they saw. They'll tell you."

Rootwell opened his mouth to reply but then shut it again, and his expression became thoughtful. "Bobart and Brynmor aren't in the city…"

"Where are they?" asked Aeron. He'd tried to find Dilwyn, but no one could tell him anything.

"Never you mind. But perhaps I will consult them. There were a few… oddities about the reports I did receive. Perhaps they can clear things up."

"Please, sir, I know I'm not a seasoned veteran like you. I've read about the fights you've been in against orcs and goblins, and I know you and Master Bobart defeated the Ratkin invasion of Berlonviche - Norwood, we call it - many years ago. But I'm no fool, and if it comes to war with the League, you are going to need my help! You know how we fight, and you know how the Rhordians fight. As allies, we made a good match: they provided the shock infantry and heavy cavalry while we provided the light infantry and most of the light cavalry. But if we fight them, do you think our skirmishers will be able break their blocks of pikemen, or our ponies stop a charge of armored knights? Our histories say that before we joined the League, we did have disciplined regiments of pike and units of armored heavy cavalry. But once allied with the Rhordians, we let those things lapse. We need to learn how to do them again. The times have changed, sir, and if we don't change with them, we are going to be swept away!" Aeron stopped for breath. He looked at Rootwell. Had he gone too far?

The Muster-Master was still frowning, but he was tapping his finger on the desk and glancing between the papers and Aeron. Finally he said: "Where's your home?"

"Uh, Picksbury, sir."

"Go home."

"Sir?" He could feel the blood draining from his face.

"Go home, boy. See your family. Get some rest. I don't think the situation is as dire as you make out, but I'll remember what you said."

Aeron couldn't make a sound.

"You've had your quarter-hour, now scat!" Rootwell waved his hand and went back to his papers.

Aeron stood there a while longer, and then turned and walked away.

Chapter 5

The carriage rumbled along the rough, rutted road, jostling its passengers. Aaron and Nosta endured it, but Tim and Elam thought it was a fine thing, and they laughed and [illegible] each time the vehicle lurched. The roads in the Shire were generally well maintained, at least between the major towns, but after the winter, they were definitely in need of work.

"I think I'd rather walk," muttered Aaron. "Or ride the canal."

"[illegible] that it was so kind of your father to arrange for the carriage. How could you complain?" asked Nosta. "And it's a lot faster. Walking or riding the canal would have taken a whole day, and it looks like it'll rain before nightfall. At this rate, we'll be at your home by noon."

"Yeah, great."

"Aren't you eager to see your family? It's been over two years, hasn't it?"

"Yeah, sure. It'll be nice to see them—well, most of them. But [illegible] how glad they'll be to see me."

"Now you are being silly, Aaron [illegible]," said Nosta. "You can't seriously tell me that they'll hold the fact that the Warden Master [illegible] against you."

"No, you're right, they'll welcome me [illegible] and take me in and all, it's just... well, when I set out for the [illegible] a lot of my family thought I was mad, and pretty much all of them expected me to come home in a few months a failure. I might have stuck it out longer than any of them expected, but I'm still coming back with my tail between my legs. I can't say I like it much."

Nosta didn't say anything and the coach fell silent except for the clop of the hooves of the six horses, [illegible] the creaks and groans of the carriage. [illegible] looked at the [illegible] and a dark bank of clouds was building there; Nosta was right about the rain.

The countryside looked entirely ordinary, peaceful, quiet. If any of the people he saw along the way realized how much of that could change if war came, none of them showed it. The only unusual thing along the road as the miles rolled past was a large group of soldiers headed the other way. And it was only [illegible] because it was a mixed group of Shirefolk and humans. About fifty humans on foot with a couple more on horses were being escorted by [illegible] number of Shirefolk, both infantry and cavalry. The humans must have come from one of the border posts where there was a [illegible]. They were clearly being taken to the [illegible]. The humans did not look particularly happy, but most of the Shirefolk seemed in good humor. The soldiers gave way before the carriage and flowed around it on both sides. Some of the mounted [illegible] and Elam laughed in delight. "They're so pretty!" she shouted. "Like great big puppies!"

Chapter 9

The carriage rumbled along the rough, rutted road, jostling its passengers. Aeron and Nesta endured it, but Elin and Gethin thought it was a fine thing, and they laughed and giggled each time the vehicle lurched. The roads in the Shires were generally well-maintained, at least between the major towns; but after the winter, they were definitely in need of work.

"I think I'd rather walk," muttered Aeron. "Or take the canal."

"But it was so kind of your father to arrange for the carriage. How could you refuse?" asked Nesta. "And it is a lot faster. Walking or taking the canal would have taken a whole day, and it looks like it will rain before nightfall. At this rate, we'll reach your home by noon."

"Yeah, great."

"Aren't you eager to see your family? It's been over two years, hasn't it?"

"Oh, sure. I'll be glad to see them - well, most of them. Not sure how glad they'll be to see me."

"Now you are being silly, Aeron Cadwallader," said Nesta. "You can't seriously tell me that they'll hold the fact that the Muster-Master didn't hire you against you."

"No, you're right, they'll welcome me - us - and take us in and all. It's just… well, when I set out on this whole… thing, a lot of my family thought I was mad, and pretty much all of them expected me to come home in a few months a failure. I might have stuck it out longer than any of them expected, but I'm still coming back with my tail between my legs. I can't say I like it much."

Nesta didn't say any more, and the coach fell silent except for the clop of the hoofs of the six ponies pulling it and the creaks and groans of the carriage. Aeron looked to the northwest, and a dark bank of clouds was building there; Nesta was right about the rain.

The countryside looked entirely ordinary; peaceful, quiet. If any of the people he saw along the way realized that all of that could change if war came, none of them showed it. The only unusual thing along the road as the miles sped past was a large group of soldiers headed the other way. And it was doubly unusual because it was a mixed group of Shirefolk and humans. About fifty humans on foot with a couple more on horses were being escorted by triple their number of Shirelings, both infantry and cavalry. The humans must have come from one of the border posts where there was a mixed garrison. They were clearly being shown the way home. The humans did not look particularly happy, but most of the Shirefolk seemed in good humor. The soldiers gave way before the carriage and flowed around it on both sides. Some of the mounted Shirelings were riding aralez, and Elin laughed in delight. "They're so pretty!" she squealed. "Like great big puppies!"

There was no doubt they were beautiful animals, and between their size - tall as a small horse and far bulkier - and their fearsome jaws, they were enough to give even human troops pause. Shirefolk had the same skill with animal husbandry that they did with crops, and in recent years, they'd been breeding these smaller aralez in considerable numbers. If ordinary cavalry were riding them now, those numbers must be growing a lot.

The soldiers were soon left behind, and a little later, they crested a rise, and Gethin cried out: "Look! A town! Is that it, Aeron?"

He peered ahead and nodded. "Yes, that's Picksbury."

"Are we going there?" asked Elin.

"We'll just pass through. My home is another few miles beyond."

The carriage started down the long slope leading into town, and Aeron studied the place with new eyes. It was laid out in the same circles-within-circles pattern as Hodenburg. Not nearly as large, of course, with only five or six thousand people, but the same layout. *If we blocked up the streets radiating out from the center, we could fortify the place pretty well. Not enough to stop an army with siege engines, but against raiders, it would probably do.*

He glanced at the passing farmsteads; most of them had some sort of walls enclosing a space connecting the house with the barn and some of the outlying buildings. A little work could turn them into miniature fortresses, too…

The rattle of hooves and wheels on cobblestone jarred him out of his musings. The central parts of the town had paved streets, and while the ride was smoother, it was also noisier. The coach pulled to a stop in front of a large inn that also doubled as the station for the coach line. The ponies would be changed here, and the passengers could get out and stretch their legs, eat, and attend to other necessities. His father had chartered this coach so there were no other passengers.

"You said something about your father owning a house here in the town," said Nesta.

"Yes, it's over that way a bit," he replied, pointing to the west. "It's not so much a house as a business office and warehouse with some living quarters. He'll stay there when he's here managing his business."

"And his business is trade and shipping?"

"Yes, that and farming. My grandda started it all really. He and his three brothers all owned farms north of Picksbury, and they had several years of very good harvests. This was just about the same time as the Shires joined the League and trade really started to increase. Grandda got tired of paying other people to ship his goods to Eowulf and the other League cities, and one of the brothers raised oxen, and a cousin was a wheelwright, so they started their own shipping company. Before long, they were shipping the harvests of other farmers, too. It just grew from there."

"Well, I'll be…!" said Nesta suddenly.

"What?"

"My… our business in Eowulf, we imported things from the Shires and resold them there. We had dozens - hundreds - of shipments over the years, and one of the chief shippers was Cadwallader & Sons! I never made the connection with you!"

"It's a pretty common name," said Aeron, actually quite pleased. "I'll bet that my father's records show a lot of things going to… what was your business called?"

"We just called it *Andras'*."

"Should be easy enough to find the records. You, uh… you didn't have any outstanding debts with Cadwalladers, did you?"

"No!" said Nesta, looking scandalized. "We pay our debts!"

"Good, good. I should have no trouble convincing da to give you a job."

"Aeron, I haven't decided whether I *want* a job with your father."

"Oh, of course. Sorry, I shouldn't make assumptions or put pressure on you. Come on, let's get something to eat while we're stopped." They went into the inn and got some food from the kitchen; just a light meal of ham, biscuits, and eggs, probably leftovers from breakfast. The children dug in enthusiastically, but Aeron ate slowly, casting glances at Nesta as he did so. He *had* been pressuring her to take a job with his father, hadn't he? He wanted to help her - she'd helped him after all - but it had to be her decision.

He really did like her. Quite a lot, actually. She was strong and tough and level-headed. And brave. He could still see her whacking at the Rhordians with a frying pan. Pretty, too. And he liked her kids. *So, what are your intentions here, Mister Cadwallader?* Good question, really good question…

Before he could supply an answer, the coachman stuck his head in the door and informed him that they were ready to move on. They finished eating, Nesta wrapped a few morsels for the children in a cloth, and they climbed back into the coach. "Only another half hour or so, sir," said the coachman.

"Hardly worth making the stop," said Aeron.

"Maybe not for you, sir, but I'm not done for the day. Need to get to Pentham by dark, and this was the last chance to change the ponies for five leagues."

"Ah, I understand."

The coach lurched into motion and smoothly rolled through Picksbury and out the north side. The cobblestones were left behind and rough road resumed. Now they were entering the countryside of his boyhood. Every farm, every copse of wood, every little stream was familiar and brought back memories. There was the Cadogan farm and there was Idwal's Pond where his da had taught him to fish and where he'd caught that bass near as big as he was.

And yet, as the furlongs sped by, he found himself getting tenser and tenser. He had no idea what would be waiting for him at home. He genuinely wanted to see his sister, Mererid, but he wasn't so sure about the rest of the family. He cringed at the thought of seeing his Cousin Madoc. The older boy had been a plague on him all through his teens.

Stop worrying. You've survived a battle, you can survive this.

All too soon, the coach reached the lane which led to the Cadwallader homestead and turned in. A row of elms lined the road, still bare of leaves from the winter, but covered with buds in promise of spring. Someone was out plowing a field off to the left, but he couldn't tell who it was.

They turned a bend and there in the distance was the house. It was very much built in the old style, but instead of a single *cloctan*, the place had sprouted several smaller ones over the years, budding off to the sides like a cluster of mushrooms. Grass covered most of the structure on the top, north, and west sides, but the south and east were uncovered, and many windows and several doors opened out on a green swath in front. A large barn and several smaller outbuildings formed a rough ring. They'd originally been connected by walls, but with all the expansion that had taken place, the walls had mostly been removed to make way for other things. Aeron frowned when he realized how vulnerable the place would be to attack.

But his frown became a smile when he saw the large crowd of people out in front, apparently waiting for his arrival. "My word!" he said.

"See?" said Nesta. "I knew they'd be happy you are home."

"Unless they are all here to tar and feather me."

Nesta chuckled and then punched him in the shoulder.

The coach swung around and halted right in front of the crowd. Aeron hopped out and just had time to help Nesta down before he was mobbed by his family. Mererid beat the others to him and wrapped her arms around him, but his mother was close behind, cheeks streaming with tears. Brother Owain along with sisters Tesni and Catrin, the three youngest, crowded close, while his father and older siblings along with two sisters-in-law, a brother-in-law, and a swarm of nieces and nephews and a cousin or two all hung back to await their turn.

"Aeron! Aeron!" cried both Mererid and his mother in unison. He hugged his sister and managed to reach out and pull his mother close to him, half-crushing his sister, who didn't seem to mind a bit. Eventually Mererid and his mother gave way to let the others come closer, and Aeron shook hands with his father and brothers Bronwen and Gwilym and exchanged hugs with sister Heulwen, and received back-pats from uncles, in-laws, and neighbors, and even some of the hired hands. The nieces and nephews, all quite young, tended to hang back from this near-stranger. To his relief, there was no sign of Cousin Madoc.

"Are you related to *all* of these people, Aeron?" said a voice. Looking back, he saw Gethin and Elin, still in the couch, staring wide-eyed at the throng.

"Nearly all!" he laughed. "But I guess some introductions are in order. Everyone! Let me introduce you to Missus Nesta Andras and her daughter Elin and son Gethin. We met on the way from Eowulf and, uh, had a few adventures together." He proceeded to point out and name everyone else, which took a while. They all offered welcome to Nesta and the children, although his mother and father eyed them a bit warily.

Eventually, the well-wishing winded down, "So, let's not all stand here waiting for the rain to soak us!" said Aeron's father. "Unless I'm mistaken, a fine meal is waiting for us inside!" A few drops of rain were, in fact, beginning to fall from the grey clouds moving in overhead, and he didn't need to repeat the invitation. Everyone began moving toward the door to the house, young Owain hauling their meager baggage for them. The coach turned around and headed back for the main road.

The inside of the house looked just as familiar as the outside. *I haven't been gone* that *long.* Everyone crowded into the large dining room that adjoined the kitchen. Aeron was seated at his father's right hand, but there was a bit of confusion about what to do with Nesta and her children, but Mererid took charge and, evicting several siblings, found places for them near her.

The food wasn't just a meal, it was a feast. Two different kinds of soup, good wheat bread with chewy crusts, duck, lamb, pork and beef, mashed potatoes, fried potatoes, sautéed mushrooms, it just went on and on. His mother must have close to emptied the winter stores to make all this. There was wine, three types of cheese, and ale, wonderful Shires-brewed ale. Aeron ate until he felt like he was going to burst.

Even though he was the guest of honor, there were oddly few questions about his time in Eowulf and the College of Warcraft or his journey home, and he was actually glad for that. He really didn't feel like talking about it just then. Any time anyone did ask a question, he was able to divert them simply by asking a question about what had been happening around here. And he usually got a very lengthy answer. Harvests and shipments, marriages, and grandchildren's first teeth were far more interesting to the family than distant events 'away-south'.

It was only after most of the eating was finished and someone lit some lamps because the drizzle had turned to a hard rain and it had grown quite dark in the house that his mother suddenly leaned forward and put her hand to his cheek and turned his head a bit. "What in the world happened there?" she asked staring at his face. "I thought it was just a bit of road dirt, but look at these bruises! Aeron, what have you been up to?"

Damn, the bruises from the fight. They hardly hurt at all anymore, and he'd nearly forgotten them. "I... uh... there was some trouble on the way home, Mama. I was with a wagon train of our folk coming home and..."

"You were in that?" asked Bronwen. "The train the humans attacked? They were talking about that at the tavern the other day. Sounded like quite an affair!"

"Yes!" Gwilym added. "Some folks got killed! Killed dead! And you were there?"

He nodded. "Yes. Me and Missus Andras and her children. We were all there," he said quietly.

"Didja kill any of those darn humans, Aeron?" said young Owain, waving a table-knife. The boy's mouth was spread in a wide grin. Clearly he thought he was making a joke.

Aeron started to shake his head, but then Gethin exclaimed: "He sure did! I saw him! One of the big ones knocked down my ma, Aeron came to help her and the human punched him in the face - that's where he got those bruises. But then Ma whacked the man in the knee with a frying pan and when he turned on her, Aeron stabbed him in the throat with his dagger and down he went!"

The expression on every face was suddenly wiped blank as if by a cleaning cloth, and dead silence filled the room. Aeron felt like every eye was on him, but somehow all he could see was the face of the Rhordian that he'd killed, the look of astonishment on the man's face, his gleaming green eyes, the hot blood spilling over his hands… For a moment, he thought he was going to lose his fine dinner, but he swallowed hard, looked down, and clutched the arms of his chair, and the fit passed.

When he looked up, his mother was staring at him, her hand covering her mouth. "Aeron," she gasped. "Aeron, it's not true is it?"

He couldn't quite meet her eyes, and he fixed his gaze on a small cameo on a chain she was wearing around her neck. He jerked his head a bit. "I'm afraid it is, Mama. It… it was an ugly thing, an ugly thing."

It took a while for any sort of conversation to start again, and the dinner wrapped up pretty quickly after that. The women-folk retreated to the kitchen while the males went to the parlor to smoke their pipes. Aeron could see that Nesta didn't know what to do. She kept looking toward the kitchen, but clearly didn't think she belonged there. Elin and Gethin huddled with her, eying the younger children who were playing tag through the house and making a lot of happy noise.

Mererid came to the rescue. She got Elin and Gethin into the other children's game and then took Nesta by the arm and escorted her into the kitchen. Aeron looked after her, smiling, and then reluctantly headed for the parlor. Things quieted down for a moment when he entered, but then his father offered him a pipe and tobacco, and he accepted it and the conversations resumed. Aeron had never been much of a smoker, but he found that the pipe gave his hands and mouth something to do and he managed to relax a bit.

He mingled as best he could, but the conversations were mostly about the condition of the fields, the likely weather, plantings, births among the animals, and all the myriad details of running a farm - things which interested him not at all. He tried to appear interested but made no attempt to tell them anything about his experiences at the College of Warcraft - or in the battle.

Eventually he sought out his father and the old man seemed as though he wanted to talk to him, too. "So, tell me about this lady you've brought home, Missus Andras," he said, before Aeron could say a thing. "Widow?"

"Yes, Da. Met her with the wagon train from Eowulf. I'd had to leave in such a hurry, I didn't even have a chance to pack any food. None of the other folk would give me the time of day, but she fed me and we became friends. She's a fine woman."

"And she really wacked that man with a frying pan?"

"Oh, yes! Distracted him at just the right moment. I'd likely be dead but for her." That wasn't exactly true, it had been Paddy Bobart shattering the Rhordian's sword that gave him his chance, but his da didn't need to know that.

His father chewed on his pipe stem, looking thoughtful. "Well then, the Cadwalladers owe her a debt of gratitude. What's her situation?"

"She and her husband owned an import and re-sale business in Eowulf. Oh, you probably have the name in your records, she says she did a lot of business with you over the years."

"Really? I'll have to check. Go on."

"Well, her husband died about a year ago, and she continued running the business. She has her letters and numbers. But when the Rhordians kicked us all out, she lost nearly everything."

"Couldn't she sell any of the business assets?"

"Apparently not. The humans, expecting to get it all in the end, wouldn't buy anything. It was the same story I heard from a lot of the people in the wagon train."

His father frowned. "The scoundrels! That's little better than thievery."

"They didn't get much in the end though," said Aeron with a grim smile. "The people burned everything they couldn't carry off. Except for any houses they owned - but from what we could tell, the humans took care of that and burned them themselves."

Da shook his head. "So she's destitute? What about her family?"

"She said she has a little hard money, but I don't know how much. Not a lot, I don't imagine. She said she could go to her people, they're up around Ferchester, I think. But she didn't seem too happy at the idea. Not sure why. I was thinking… I was thinking that perhaps you could give her a job."

"You were, eh? Well, I suppose something could found… no, I'm sure something could be found for her."

"I'd be grateful, Da, although I'm not sure she would accept. She seems awfully proud. To accept charity."

"Not charity. Payment for services rendered, boy. Your life is worth a job."

"Glad you think so."

His father snorted and reached out and ruffled his hair in a way he hadn't done in years. "So, we'll offer Missus Andras a job, and if she takes it is up to her. But what about you? If I offered you a job would you take it? Or do you still have other ideas?"

Aeron took a draw on the pipe and held the smoke in his mouth for a while before letting it stream out. "I don't know, Da. I'm not sure what I'm going to do now. I offered my service to the Muster-Master in Hodenburg on the way here, but he turned me down. So I guess I do need some way to earn my keep until…"

"Until what?"

"Da, I don't think the troubles with the League are over, I think they've barely begun. And it's going to be bad, and the Shires are going to need all the help they can get. Sooner or later, I'll be drawn into it. But in the meantime, I'll be willing to do anything you ask."

His father was silent for a while, looking first at him and then at where the rain was lashing one of the windows, and then back at him. Finally, he nodded. "We'll find you something, boy, don't worry about that."

* * * * *

Initially, what his father found for him was walking behind a team of oxen plowing fields.

Spring was upon them, and the plantings had to take place whether war was brewing on the borders or not. The Cadwallader clan held a lot of land, and even though it might have technically been owned by more than a dozen different branches of the family tree, the plots were all close together, and everyone from young to old pitched in to get the job done. Aeron had done enough of this before he went off to Eowulf, and he hadn't forgotten how.

Or how dull it was.

Still, dull was probably what he needed right now. Simple repetitive physical labor - *sort of like drilling soldiers, except the oxen are smarter* - was like a balm on his troubled mind. Working side by side with his family was a good thing, too. He was forced to admit he found that he actually liked some of his siblings more now than he had before he'd gone away. He was teamed with Owain; him driving the plow while Owain followed with the seed drill, a planting machine of halfling design which plunked down the seeds in a perfectly spaced pattern in the furrows Aeron cut. Owain had been an insufferable pest when Aeron was younger, but the boy had matured remarkably in the time since he'd last seen him. He even seemed to realize that he'd blundered with his unfeeling question at the welcome home dinner. Now, while he did ask some questions about Aeron's adventures, he didn't press when it was obvious Aeron didn't want to talk about it.

Day by day, the work got done. Aeron's father had hinted that he had a bookkeeping job in mind for Nesta, but for the moment, she was out there in the fields with everyone else. The kids were helping out with the same chores all the younger one worked on—milking cows and goats, tending the smaller animals, fetching things, carding the wool from the newly sheared sheep, and a dozen other tasks. She and her children were staying in a room in the big house, but he couldn't help but notice that her room was at the opposite end of the house from his, and his parents' rooms were in between. As far as he knew, she hadn't actually taken employment with his father—but she hadn't left yet, either.

The spring equinox came and went, and the trees began to show green at their tips. Cows and horses, sheep and pigs began having their babies. Still the work went on. Wheat and corn, potatoes and beets, tobacco and turnips, the crops went in. Aeron slept like a stone and woke up with muscles still aching.

One day during a rest, Mererid brought out a pitcher of apple cider to the menfolk. "Mama says we need to use this up before it goes bad," she said. Aeron sat down with his back against a rock wall a little apart from the others. When she was done giving out the cider, she sat down next to him. "I like Nesta," she said without preamble. "Are you sweet on her, Aeron?"

He nearly choked on his cider. "Uh, well," he said, coughing. "I'm quite fond of her."

"But are you *sweet* on her? Come on, big brother, don't try to fool me."

He smiled sheepishly at her and shrugged. "I guess I am."

"It would be grand if she became a part of the family. Elin and Gethin are sweet, too. So have you told her how you feel?"

"Not yet."

"What are you waiting for?

"Oh, for things to settle down, I guess."

"What things?"

He waved his hands at the fields and the plows and the standing oxen. "All the work here, for one. And I don't even know what I'll be doing once the crops are in. Da wants me part of his business, but I'm still not sure that's what I want."

"What else would you do?"

"If there is a war, I'd do what I was trained to do: be a soldier."

She looked upset. "Do you really think that's possible? War with the League? Do they really hate us that much?"

"I wouldn't have thought so until this all happened. Everything seemed normal, and then in only a few months, the hate was just bubbling up out of the ground, it seemed. A dwarf friend from the College said the poison was coming in from outside. Someone named Lord Darvled from down south is leading a 'humans only' campaign. But that's hundreds of leagues away. So I really don't know. War seems impossible, but the attack on the wagon train seemed impossible, too, but it happened. And if there is a war, it's my duty to help protect the Shires."

"If it comes to that, it's everyone's duty!" Mererid looked very determined, and Aeron had to remind himself that Shires women did sometimes join the militia companies - and not as cooks. *And if it comes to a war, we'll need every pair of hands which can hold a weapon.* The thought of his sister in battle sent a chill down his spine.

"Well, I'm sure Da and all the older and wiser heads are right and it won't come to that... Looks like the break is over. Got to get back to work." Mererid collected the mugs she'd used to serve the cider, and Aeron got the oxen hitched up again for more plowing.

* * * * *

Eventually the bulk of the tasks were done, and the Cadwalladers could start to relax—or at least begin to find different tasks. Aeron's father was already hard at work finding new customers for his wares outside the League. He seemed to think Aeron could help him.

"You spent two and a half years among the humans, son," he said one day in the office he maintained in one of the additions to the house. "You must have some grasp of how they think."

"Two and a half years among a bunch of cadets who were all thinking the same things: Drills and classes, how to keep the sergeants happy, blacking boots, shining brass, and when can I get a pass to visit the tavern and get some real ale? I didn't have a lot of contact with the sort of people you're interested in, Da."

"Still, with your classes on… what's it called? Strategy? You must have some knowledge of the Young Kingdoms. You studied maps and such, didn't you?"

"Yes…"

"Well then. What can you tell me?"

"All right. First, there are the Free Townships that abut the borders. They are human farms and hamlets that are more-or-less protectorates of the League. The League used them as buffers between us and the Young Kingdoms. I have no idea what their status will be now that we've left the League."

"They are pretty self-sufficient," said his father. "I doubt we'll be selling much to them."

"No, but if the League lays claim to them, we'll be completely surrounded. We won't be able to ship out anything without their leave."

"I hadn't thought about that. The Shires need to make sure that doesn't happen. I'm going to write to the Assembly and insist they do something."

"Good luck with that."

"I have some pull there. And since this will affect all of our exports, they'll listen. All right, what's beyond the townships? I know there are a half dozen or so Young Kingdoms around our western borders. I've made some inquiries with Brigward, Harg, Ostril, and Rhovain, but there must be more."

Aeron thought about it and wished he had some decent maps to consult, but the only one his da had was one that only showed the Shires and parts of the League. Of course, many of the Young Kingdoms came and went so quickly, it was hard to find any map that was up to date. He tried to remember what he's heard about the ones nearby. "Uh… I'd avoid Harg. From what I've heard, they are little better than bandits."

"So I assumed," said his father. "The response I got from them only talked about 'escort fees' and how dangerous the roads are. To me, it sounded like a threat to loot our shipments unless we paid them tribute."

"That's probably it, exactly."

"Unfortunately, they sit astride the quickest route to Ostril and the Greenway now that we can't go through Eowulf."

"The Greenway? You are thinking of going that far afield?" The Greenway was the great east-west road, a vestige of ancient times that ran all the way from Basilea in the east to the Straights of Von Terel in the west. It was said that it ran perfectly straight for leagues at a time with the surface made of precisely fitted stone blocks - at least the parts which hadn't been destroyed. It had once been lined with trees, hence the name, although most of the trees were gone now. At its nearest point, it lay fifty leagues to the south of the Shires.

His father shrugged. "It's a possibility. Could be a lot of new markets down that way."

"And a lot of trouble for unescorted wagons."

"True. But the thought struck me that if the potential profits were great enough, perhaps we could provide our own escort."

It took a moment for his father's words to sink in. When they did, his head jerked up and he found his father grinning at him. "Well, you did want to be a soldier," he said.

"You… you mean raise a mercenary company to escort our wagons?" The idea was… enticing. In his darker moments back at the College, when wondering what the future held for him, Aeron did idly think about joining a mercenary company—if any would have him. There were a lot of them wandering around the Young Kingdoms. Many of those kingdoms were so small they couldn't raise much of an army of their own, so many of them hired soldiers for defense or attack. Most weren't of much account and would have no need for a halfling swordsman with one fight to his credit, but a few of them had prospered and grown enough to almost be armies in their own right. Small ones, to be sure, but large enough to be known throughout the whole region. Organizations like Torvald Svendson's Legion or Markus Karsten's Free Company would be big enough to need quartermasters or even staff officers; jobs Aeron could do. But to raise his own company! To be in command… "That's quite a notion, Da."

"It's just an idea for now. But, as I said, it will depend on the potential profits. This is going to take a lot more investigation and thought. In the meantime, let's consider closer and safer markets."

So he worked with his father, collecting information, sending out letters, and making plans. Nesta did end up staying and formally took a job with his father - and continued to live in the house. They saw each other a lot, and Aeron's feelings for her grew, and he finally worked up the nerve to tell her how he felt. He was thrilled when she acknowledged that she had strong feeling for him, too. Neither of them knew quite what to do about it though. They'd only known each other for two months, and a betrothal seemed a bit premature. Still, her status as a widow gave her vastly more freedom to make her own choices than an unmarried maiden had.

"Let's just wait a bit and see how things go," said Nesta. He had to agree.

Later, he sounded out his mother on the idea of him marrying Nesta. "She's a lovely woman, Aeron," she said. "And her children are darlings. If she'd make you happy, I can't object. Your father, though…"

"What?"

"Well, I know he has other ideas about who you ought to be marrying."

"Oh, you mean the eldest daughter of a son-less landowner? So he can add another farm to his little empire?"

His mother frowned, but she didn't deny it. Eventually, she said: "I'll work on your father. Just be patient."

So he was. He continued to work with his father but grew increasingly frustrated by the lack of information about the geography beyond the Shires' borders. He finally convinced his father to let him go to Picksbury - and Hodenburg if necessary - to buy some better maps. The next morning he saddled up a pony and set out.

It was a fine day, and he let the beast have its head. He was in Picksbury before mid-morning, but as he'd feared, the only place he could find with maps was a tiny bookseller who only had two and neither was any better than the one he already had. So it was on to Hodenburg, which he reached slightly after noon. It took a bit of asking, but he finally found a much larger bookseller, and the man who owned it had an assortment of maps.

"Dear me, dear me, maps is it?" said the fellow, seeming flustered. "Not much demand for maps, you know. But let me see what I can find." He disappeared into a back room and was gone quite a while. Aeron occupied himself by looking at the books for sale on the shelves in the front part of the store. Not a single book on military topics could he find. But he did spy a thin volume which was a short history of the Shires. He decided to buy that for Nesta, who had developed a real interest in the topic. He also found an even thinner volume which was a primer for teaching children to read. It had some very nice hand-painted illustrations to attract a young eye. He took that too, for the children.

By then, the bookseller returned with an armful of papers and parchment, and even a few pyrographed deer hides. They spread them out on a table and they both looked them over for close to an hour. Aeron set aside any which didn't cover the areas he was interested in and then slowly examined them, weeding out ones which he could tell were inaccurate or long out of date. By the second bell after noon, he had a half dozen which he thought might be of use. Then it took nearly another hour to agree on a price for the maps and the two books. He paid more than he thought was fair, but the bookseller was adamant, and he finally had to give in. He counted out the coins, lightening his purse - filled with his father's money—a lot more than he'd hoped, but he had what he came for. At least the bookseller threw in a nice leather pouch to carry it all in and keep the papers dry and clean.

He stepped outside the shop, squinting against the sunlight. He had no hope of making it home until well after dark. He could probably make it to Picksbury, but he was of a mind to spend the night in Hodenburg at the *Blue Raven* and start fresh in the morning. That is, in fact, what he ultimately decided to do. He got a room, stabled his pony, took a bath, and had a fine meal. Afterward, he hung about the common room for a while, sipping ale and listening to the conversations going on around him. Most of the talk was about ordinary things, but a few folks were discussing the situation with the League and the likely effects it would have on business.

"So what are we going to do?" asked one.

"You worry too much," said another.

"But if we can't sell our goods to the League…!"

"Yes, we can't trade directly with the Rhordians," said the second one. "But there's nothing stopping us from selling it to someone else and if they turn around and sell it to the League, well, that's no nevermind of ours, is it?"

Aeron's ears perked up. Trading with the League via middlemen? Had his father thought of that? Was it even ethical, circumventing the decision of the Assembly like that? He tried to edge a little closer to the pair…

Before he could, however, the doors to the common room swung open and a fellow dashed in, breathless. "Say there, Tegid!" cried someone. "What's got you in such a hurry?"

The halfling tried to catch his breath as many of the people in the room crowded around him. Finally he gasped out: "The Assembly just announced that the Rhordians have attacked us!" The room turned to bedlam with a roar of voices. Aeron tried to push his way through the crowd, but could not get close. Finally things quieted down enough that he could catch some of what the fellow was saying.

"…somewhere up near Ferchester, I think."

Ferchester! That's where Nesta *is from!*

"…a bunch of human cavalry rode in between two of the guardburgs and raided some farms and a village or two. Stole every bit of food they could lay hands on and beat up any who tried to resist! Those that did resist had their farms burned, too!"

"Anyone killed?"

"Don't know. Maybe."

"What's being done?"

"Didn't stay to hear. But I bet they'll be calling for a muster."

"Damn well right! We'll give these humies a lesson they won't soon forget!"

The roar of voices was too much, and Aeron slowly backed off. He went outside to clear his head and breathed in the cool air. "Well, that's torn it," he said to the wind.

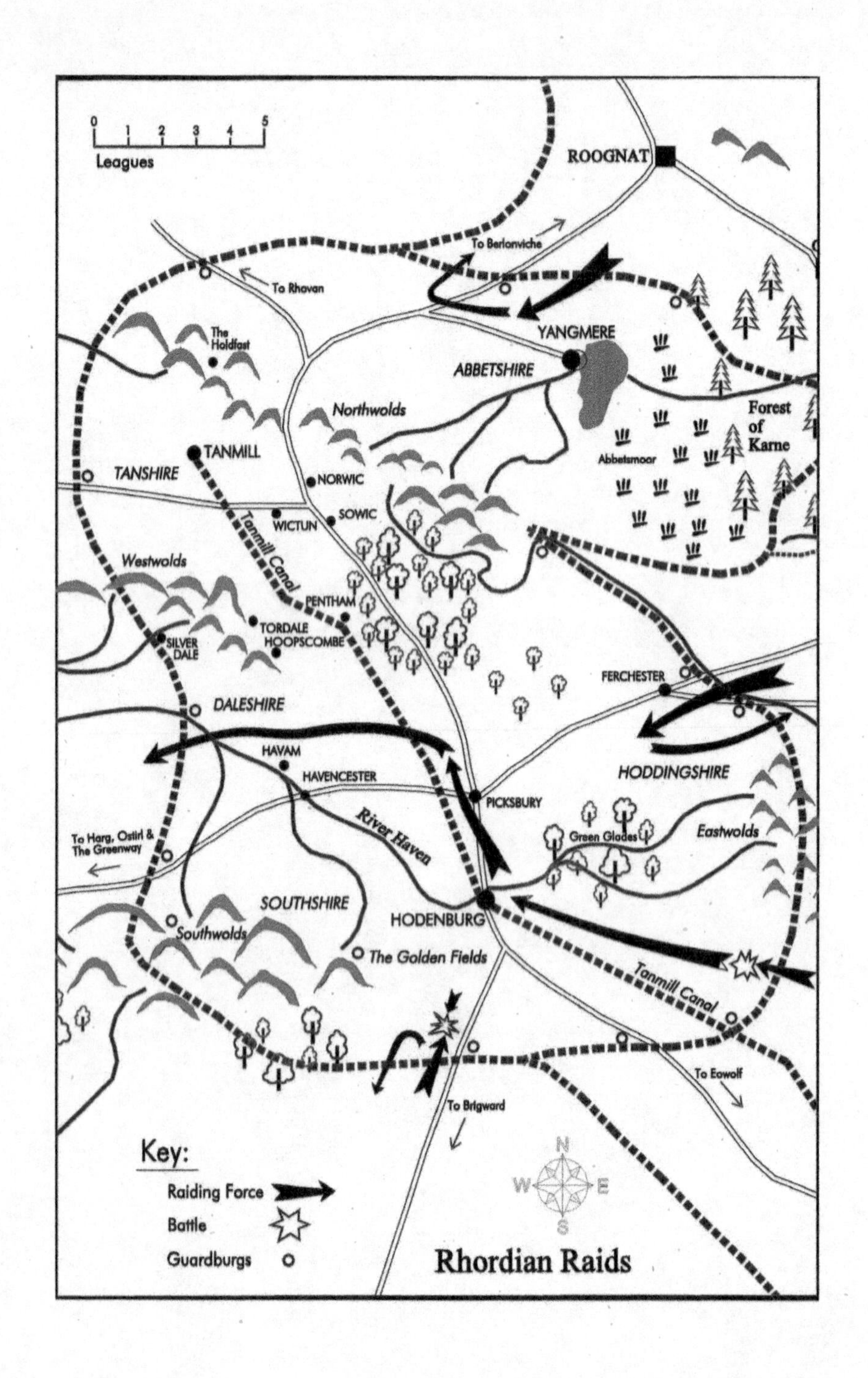
0 1 2 3 4 5
Leagues
ROOGNAT
To Berlonviche
To Rhovan
YANGMERE
ABBETSHIRE
The Holdfast
Northwolds
Forest of Karne
Abbetsmoor
TANMILL
TANSHIRE
NORWIC
SOWIC
WICTUN
Tanmill Canal
Westwolds
PENTHAM
TORDALE
HOOPSCOMBE
SILVER DALE
FERCHESTER
DALESHIRE
HAVAM
HAVENCESTER
HODDINGSHIRE
PICKSBURY
To Harg, Ostirl & The Greenway
River Haven
Green Glades
Eastwolds
SOUTHSHIRE
HODENBURG
Southwolds
The Golden Fields
Tanmill Canal
To Eowolf
To Brigward
Key:
Raiding Force
Battle
Guardburgs
N
W
E
S
Rhordian Raids

Chapter 10

He tried to see the Muster-Master again in the morning but wasn't surprised when he was turned away. Dozens of people were coming and going from his headquarters, but there were guards there now, and they wouldn't let him in. Rootwell must be up to his eyebrows in work.

Troops were assembling in the circle near the Assembly Hall, and he watched them for a bit. But there was no point in staying, so he got his pony and was quickly on his way. The news had gotten to Picksbury before him, and there was a large crowd gathered in the town circle. The local trained band was assembling, the same one he'd joined before he left for the College of Warcraft. He saw the band captain, Gwynfor Neirin, and tying up his pony, went over to him. "Ho, Gwynfor!" he shouted and managed to get his attention.

"What? Oh! Aeron! I didn't know you was back in town."

"What's going on? I heard about the attack up near Ferchester. Are they calling up the band?"

"Yes! Not just ours, either. All across the Shires, it seems."

"The word traveled fast."

"Yes, a fast rider came through from Hodenburg early this morning, changed ponies, and kept right on going. It'll be everywhere by nightfall." He looked him over. "You going to come join us again?"

"I just might. Need to get home to tell my folks, first, though. I was in Hodenburg, myself when this all happened. So, do you know if you'll be staying here or sent to the border?"

"No one's said anything yet, but I'm guessing the border." He shook his head. "Placin' a guard on the hen house after the fox has come and gone."

Aeron slapped his arm. "Maybe, but I have a feeling that more foxes are coming. You keep your eyes open, Gwynfor! Hate to see you get hurt."

"Thanks, Aeron, I will. And if you can come, we could use you."

Aeron smiled and took his leave. Gwynfor's words warmed him—someone not a family member who was actually glad to see him! He got his pony and rode the last two miles to home. Word had *not* reached there, and he had to explain it all to the family.

"Are they going to attack here?" asked his mother; she wasn't frantic, but clearly concerned.

"No of course not," said his father instantly. Aeron almost interrupted, but his father gave him a stern glance that silenced him. "That was way over on the other side of the Shires from here. They are calling up the Muster, and they'll protect us. No need for any of you to be worried. Now all of you get back to your chores. Off with you!"

Aeron did not go back to his chores and waited to get his father alone. "Da, I understand you didn't want to worry the others, but we might not be as safe here as you think."

His father opened his mouth with some quick reply but then stopped. He got out his pipe, filled, and lit it. "You think there could be a danger?"

"I do. Now it's possible that this raid was just some batch of hotheads acting without orders from the League. But if this is the start of some coordinated campaign, then nowhere is safe. A force of light cavalry could ride clear across the Shires in two days if they wanted. The guardburgs aren't near close enough together to actually seal the borders. A force starting from the border at dawn could be right here where we are standing before dinner time."

His father puffed on the pipe for a few moments. "So what do you think we should do?"

He gave a long sigh and then said: "Prepare."

"How?"

"Make the place defensible. Build a stockade wall that runs from the house to the barn, then to the hen house, the woodshed, and then back to the house." He swung his arm around pointing at each structure as he spoke.

"But… but… that's got to be twenty-five rods long!" sputtered his father.

"A bit over thirty, Da, I paced it off. But it needs to be large enough that we can bring in all the animals as well as the people. Don't want to leave them out for a raider to steal or slaughter. Or we could pick one of the other family farms to fortify. Uncle Hywel's place might actually be better. I'm not suggesting we fortify every one of the farms, we don't have the time, and if we are all spread out, we couldn't defend any of them even from a few score of raiders. But we need someplace safe for the family to take refuge. We'll need to get it done soon, too. And send out some of the younger lads on ponies as scouts every day to give us enough warning to get everyone to the refuge. With the whole family, we'd have forty or fifty capable of bearing arms. We might consider working with some of the other neighbors, too. Have them help with the work and then if there's trouble, they come and join us - more people to help defend. We need to get our bows in good repair and make some spears. A raiding party isn't going to want to fight a battle if it can avoid it. They see a heavily defended farm, they'll bypass it and hit some easier target."

His father just stared at him wide-eyed for a while, his pipe forgotten. "Well!" he said at last, clearing his throat. "Well! I guess you got something out of that College after all!"

"I guess I did, Da. But will you do it? I can't convince the rest of the family to go along by myself."

His father was silent for a while and relit his pipe. "It might be a lot of work for nothing, but if we don't do it, we could lose everything. All right, I know you just got back from a long ride, but get yourself a fresh pony and make the rounds of all the family holdings and tell them I want a meeting of all the elders tomor… no, let's make it tonight."

"Yes, sir!" said Aeron, delighted with the answer. He turned and headed for the stables. He was almost finished saddling the beast when Nesta found him.

"You're leaving again?"

"Just for a few hours. I'm rounding up the family heads for a meeting tonight. To, uh… make some plans."

"For defense, you mean? Things are a lot more serious than your da let on isn't it?"

He couldn't lie to her, so he nodded. "Probably, but we won't know for sure for a while." He hesitated. "Your… your own folks are up near Ferchester, but I'm sure they're okay. Only a few farms were raided so the chances of them being attacked is pretty small."

She nodded in return. "Yes, I'm sure you're right. From the tales we're hearing, the raid was south of Ferchster, and my folks are north of the town."

"If you want to go home, I understand. I can get Da to loan you a buggy and ponies if you want to go. I can probably get Owain to escort you." He'd prefer to go himself, but he had to stay here and oversee the events he'd just set in motion.

"No… no, we'll stay here. We've got a place and jobs to do, and if I were to suddenly show up there it would just … make a mess." She reached out and took his hand. "But shouldn't you get going? You're wasting daylight."

"You're right, I need to get going." She released his hand, he finished adjusting the pony's tack and he swung up into the saddle. "I'll be back soon."

* * * * *

The meeting ran far past dark, and everyone ended up staying the night. At first, it seemed to Aeron that the idea of preparing for a possible attack was going to be dismissed out of hand. But he and Da argued as forcefully as they could, and one by one, the other family heads of the Cadwalladers came over to their side. There were a few holdouts, but Aeron finally won them by pointing out that the first step was going to be collecting wood for the stockade, and the best source would be from a small pine grove that they had been talking about clearing for new cropland for years. It probably hadn't hurt that Mama had broken out some of the better wine and had been serving it freely as the night wore on. Finally, when all were in agreement, people settled onto sofas or just fell asleep in their chairs or slept in beds vacated by others. The candles and lamps were snuffed and quiet settled over the house.

In the morning, Mama and the girls produced a mighty breakfast, and afterward, the work began. The strong, brawny ones went off to the woods with the axes and saws and began picking out the trees they would need. They needed to be straight and not too thick. Aeron insisted that the palisade be at least ten feet tall, and that meant the logs needed to be thirteen or fourteen feet long so they could be sunk in the ground deeply enough to be solidly anchored. The younger boys and some of the girls handled the oxen which would drag the cut logs back to the house. It was agreed that it was the old family farm that would be fortified, even though Aeron thought several of the others would be a better choice. He knew when to keep his mouth shut.

Aeron himself made up more detailed plans of just how the fortifications would be laid out. He drew on the classes he'd taken in military engineering. By the end of the day, the first of the logs had arrived, and he had his plans pretty well finished. At dinner, he showed them to the others. "With the logs that have arrived and the ones you say can be delivered tomorrow," he said, "I think we can put a few people to work digging the trenches we'll need to anchor the butt ends. Then we'll need to sharpen the upper ends into a point."

"Why don't we just keep working on cutting trees for a few more days," said his father. "We've got a rhythm going, no need to break it."

"But..." Aeron started to object, but the look his father gave him put a stop to it.

After dinner, his father explained. "I don't think everyone is convinced of the need to fortify, Aeron. But they want to clear the woods, and what we cut can be used for firewood or lumber, so there's no waste. But once we start digging holes and planting the poles, the work is only for one thing."

"An important thing!"

"Yes, and I don't disagree, but as I understand your plan, the stockade won't do much good unless it's finished. Half-finished or three-quarters-finished isn't going to be any more use than not even started. So it takes the same amount of effort to cut all the trees now and place the logs later as it does to do some of each at the same time, correct?"

"Yes..."

"So let's do the cutting now. Maybe something will happen in the meantime that will change the situation."

Aeron didn't like it—he wanted to see some real progress—but he couldn't argue. So the next day, he helped cut down trees and trim off all the branches. The work got harder day by day because naturally they'd started with the easiest trees to get to and now had to go farther to find suitable ones. A few of the their neighbors came by to watch. Some of them made remarks that were very close to mockery. By the fifth day of this, a lot of his kin were grumbling.

On the sixth day, they stopped grumbling.

A messenger came from Picksbury with word of another attack. This time on the northern border near Yangmere. Details were sketchy, but it seemed clear that the first attack wasn't an isolated incident and that more could be expected. They went back to work with a will.

Two days later came news of another raid. This one was turned back by a force of Shires cavalry, but the very next day, they heard that a large force of Rhordians had routed a trained band very close to the guardburg where Aeron and Nesta and the survivors of the wagon train had found refuge and was pushing north toward Hodenburg.

The Cadwallader clan put every person it had to work on the palisade. Even a few of the neighbors who had been making fun pitched in in return for a place inside if it came to that. Unfortunately, despite all their working far into the night, by the next day the wall was far from finished and they were running short on logs.

That morning, a harried messenger came through pleading for every able-bodied halfling with a weapon to hasten to Picksbury to help in the defense there. Aeron was very tempted to go, but he could not bring himself to leave his family - and Nesta. So they kept working. He did organize some of the younger lads and lasses into scouts and watchers to give warning of anything approaching. Around midday, there was word that the invaders had bypassed Hodenburg and were heading for Picksbury.

The stockade was about two-thirds done, but they had used up all the logs, and it would take at least three more days to get all that was needed. "We'll have to do like we did with the wagon train," he said to Nesta, "form a barricade with everything we can find."

"I'll get the ladies organized," she replied without hesitation and immediately went on her way. Aeron rallied the men-folk and convinced them that tired as they were, they had to finish some sort of defense that very day. They grumbled, but they complied. Those from the surrounding farms hurried home, piled crates, boxes, furniture, and any family treasures into wagons and hauled them back. Aeron, his father, and brothers dragged anything large and solid out of the house and out of the barn, along with several wagons they owned, and began piling them in the hundred foot gap in the stockade.

By noon, there was something filling every foot, but only a few feet high in most places. They needed it at least six or seven feet to be of any real use. During the short noon break, his sister Tesni came galloping up on a pony shouting: "Da! Da! There's smoke, a lot of black smoke! It looks like it's the Islwyn place!"

Everyone sprang to their feet, yelling or asking questions all at once. Da shouted for silence and eventually got it. He questioned his daughter, and she made a fairly concise report of what she'd seen.

"D'you think we ought to go and try to help?" asked Uncle Hywel. Several voices spoke out in support of that. His father, uncertain, looked to Aeron.

Aeron swallowed and shook his head. "This raiding force must be cavalry. If they caught us out in the open - and they surely will if we go running off to help - they'll just ride us down. I like the Islwyns as much as anyone, but there's nothing we can do for them right now." There was some grumbling, but they could see the truth in what he said.

"All right then," said Da. "Aeron, you get a pony and ride back with Tesni and see what's happening. You know more what to look for than anyone. All the rest of us, get back to work on the barricade!"

"Da! Send out anyone you can spare to warn the other neighbors! Tell them to drop what their doing and come here as quick as they can!"

"Right, right. Now off with you!"

He was off in moments, riding beside his sister. He looked back and was glad to see everyone else frantically piling up stuff on the barricade.

"Do… do you think they'll come here, Aeron?" asked Tesni. She was clearly very worried.

"I doubt… I don't know. But this is probably another raiding force, looking for loot and not a fight. If we can get any sort of a defense arranged, they'll probably move on, looking for easier pickings."

"Oh, I hope so!" she said, and then she looked horrified. "But easier pickings will be our other neighbors, won't it?"

"Let's hope not. But come on, if we can spot the raiders, we might be able to tell which way they are going." They rode on, cutting across country, toward a low hill that was where Tesni first saw the smoke. Aeron could see it already, rising higher into the sky, but there was now a second dark smudge rising upward. "Uh oh, looks like something else is burning now, too."

They reached the top of the hill and came to a halt. Aeron shaded his eyes from the sun and looked out. Yes, there was one column of smoke off to the southwest that might well be the Islwyn place, although he couldn't actually see it because of a copse of trees. Due south, he could just make out Picksbury in the distance. There didn't seem to be any smoke coming from there. Apparently, it had put up a stout enough defense - or at the looks of one - that the attackers had bypassed it just as they had Hodenburg. The second smoke column was further to the west, and he couldn't tell what it was coming from.

"Do you see any of the raiders?" he asked Tesni. "You've got sharp eyes. Look for any sign of groups of men on horses."

"No, brother, I don't see any... *wait!* What's that there?" She pointed, and Aeron looked along her arm. At first he saw nothing, but after a moment, he saw a small group of people - Shirefolk - mostly on foot, but with what might be a couple of cows or ponies with them. They were a mile or so away, moving along the edge of a patch of woods.

"Looks like some of our folk escaping from troubles," said Aeron.

"They might be the Islwyns!" said Tesni. "They probably need help. Come on!"

He nearly stopped her. Their mission was to scout, to give warning to the family back at the house; but no, they had to go help their neighbors. He kicked his pony into motion and followed Tesni down the slope. They closed on the group quickly, and Aeron could see that it indeed looked like a family in trouble. Three adults towing another one on a pony. That one was slumped over like he was hurt. A half dozen children of all ages were clustered around, the largest one pulling a cow along on a rope. As they rode up, they could see that it was the Islwyn family, as they'd suspected. "Hallo, Mister Islwyn!" he cried. "It's me, Aeron Cadwallader! Looks like you need help."

Islwyn looked totally frazzled and blinked at Aeron for a moment before recognition bloomed on his face. "Oh, it's you, Aeron... hardly knew you. Yes, we could use some help. My boy, Meurig, here, they shot him! Those murdering scum shot my boy!" Aeron came up beside the lad on the pony, and indeed, there was the stump of an arrow protruding from his back, just below the right shoulder. "I snapped off the rest of it," explained Islwyn, "so we could move him, but I was afraid to pull it out."

"Yes, better leave that until we can get him to a chirurgeon." He looked the boy over. He was pale and obviously in a lot of pain, but he was still conscious. "But come on, you can come to our place, you should be safe there." He got them moving in the right direction.

"We'd hear the warning about the Rhordians, but we couldn't hardly believe they'd come all the way here," continued Islwyn. "But we didn't take chances, I had Meurig out on his pony to keep a lookout, just in case. About an hour before noon, he saw some riders and went to investigate - and they shot him! Can you believe it, they actually shot him?!"

"I can believe it," said Aeron. "What happened then?"

"Well, the boy galloped home and sounded the alarm. If they'd been willing to shoot him - an unarmed boy! - no telling what they'd do to the rest of us. So we grabbed what we could - not much - and set out to find someplace safe. I caught a glimpse of the monsters around our house, but I guess they didn't see us. And then... and then..." his voice trailed off in a choking sound.

"They burned our house!" wailed Missus Islwyn. "They burned our house!" She began to sob, and several of the smaller children did so as well. Aeron looked around nervously because of the noise she was making. He was just about to dismount and let Missus Islwyn and a child or two ride when Tesni hissed: "Aeron! I can see some Rhordians! They're coming this way!"

He twisted around in his saddle and looked where his sister was pointing. Sure enough, there was a group of horsemen, a score or so of them, about half a mile away. They weren't coming directly toward him, but they would pass close enough to spot them for sure. He made an instant decision.

"Tesni! Dismount! The rest of you stay as low and as still as you can. I'm going to draw them off. Wait until they've gone after me and then get back to our house!"

"But Aeron...!" objected Tesni, but he was already galloping away.

He picked a course that would cut across the front of the Rhordians, to attract their attention and hopefully distract them from Tesni and the others. The trick was then going to be to get away from them. His pony couldn't match the cavalry's horses for speed, although they had been on the move with this raid for two days and ought to be tired while his pony was almost fresh.

The first part of the plan worked without a hitch. He hadn't gone more than a furlong before the Rhordians caught sight of him. A half-dozen riders turned in his direction and increased their pace to a trot. He angled slightly to his right to keep the distance open and gave what he hoped they could see as a rude gesture.

They must have seen it—or at least assumed what it was - because a moment later, the whole bunch of them were coming toward him and increased their speed to a canter. The distance was narrowing rapidly, and he realized that he was going to have to get a lot closer to them than he wanted, because otherwise they would herd him right back toward where the others were hiding. He crouched down and kicked the pony and wished he had spurs.

Perhaps the mere fact that he *didn't* turn away took the Rhordians by surprise, because he managed to pass across the front of them at a distance of about a hundred yards. An arrow flashed by his head, but then he curved around a patch of large bushes and had cover for a few moments.

The enemy was in hot pursuit, but they were on his home ground now. He had grown up here, played with his friends and siblings here, and he knew every inch of it. Every stream and gully, every patch of woods, every wall, fence and hedgerow. So he led them on a merry chase, never giving them a straight run at him where their faster horses could have overrun him, or a clear shot for their arrows. Left, right, up, down, over fences, and under hanging boughs, he pulled them further and further from Tesni and the Islwyns.

But when another arrow came much too close, he realized he was pressing his luck. He needed to shake off his pursuers. Up ahead was a tall hedgerow enclosing part of the Yorath place. It curved away to his left, and if things hadn't changed, there was a narrow opening just around the bend…

He lashed his poor pony for one last burst of speed. He rounded the curve and… *there!* He reined in the beast savagely to stop right next to a narrow gap in the hedge. If you didn't know it was there, you'd never spot it—or at least he hoped so. He swung down out of the saddle and ruthlessly pulled his foam-flecked pony into the gap and through to the other side. A dozen heartbeats later, there was a thunder of hooves, and he saw between the branches the Rhordian horsemen pound by and onward. Aeron let out his breath.

He stayed there, letting his horse and himself catch their breaths for about a half hour, and then after scouting around on foot to make sure his pursuers had moved off, he led the pony back through the gap in the hedgerow and then mounted up and headed off toward home.

He rode slowly to spare the horse and also to allow him to keep a careful watch out. He saw nothing more of the raiders but winced when he saw another column of smoke rising up a mile or so to the west. *They couldn't catch me so they burned a farm instead…*

He chastised himself for thinking that way, but he couldn't help it. He quickened his pace, and he caught up with Tesni and the Islwyns just as home came into sight. Tesni was beside herself when she saw Aeron. "Oh! Missing Gods, Aeron! I was so worried! Are you all right?"

"Yes, yes, I'm fine. How's the wounded boy?"

"I'll make it," groaned Meurig Islwyn. "Just get me off this bloody horse."

"Almost there," said Aeron, and they were. The people at the barricade had spotted them and some came running out to help. They quickly got through the small gap they'd left in the defenses and then filled it in. Aeron was impressed by the work that had been done in the time since he'd left. The Islwyns were taken into the house and cared for. Aeron saw Nesta, and they gave each other a smile.

"So what do you think?" asked his father.

He looked over the barricade and nodded. "It ought to do. I saw some of the raiders, and it looks like they are splitting up into smaller groups to do as much looting and damage as they can. I think we should put our efforts into making more weapons now. Make as many spears as you can. Just sharpened sticks if we don't have enough knives to strap to poles. Make more than we need and maybe lean them up to stick over the palisade to make them think there are more of us."

"Good thinking." His father called everyone together and put them to work. They seemed more enthused by that task than by piling up boxes. By late afternoon, there was a spear for everyone and more. They had about a dozen hunting bows, too. Finally, they took a break. Aeron's mother and some of the other women and girls brought out food and apple juice and some beer. They kept a watch, of course, and about the time they were finishing up, his younger brother Owain gave a shout:

"Hey! Hey! I can see some of 'em! There they are! Comin' this way!"

Everyone leapt to their feet and hurried to the barricade, grabbing up their weapons as they ran. Aeron got there and looked out, and indeed, a group of cavalry was approaching. He sucked in his breath when he saw that there were at least forty of them, not the twenty he'd faced earlier. Still, there were at least sixty adult Shirelings to face them.

The humans rode up to about two hundred paces away and halted. They milled about for a while, talking and pointing, seemingly uncertain about what to do. Aeron and his kin and his neighbors watched in silence.

"So are you batch of chicken thieves going to just stand there?" shouted a loud voice. "Come on! We're not afraid of you!"

Aeron and everyone else turned, and to his amazement, it was Nesta who had shouted. She had a spear in her hands and she shook it in the air. Aeron smiled and then he too yelled and waved his weapon—the dagger Sergeant Rolf had given him. In a moment, everyone was shouting and brandishing their weapons. Some of the people with bows let arrows fly, although the range was really too long for them.

The horsemen drew back a bit, and for a moment, Aeron thought they might start firing back. He was about to shout for his people to find cover, but then the Rhordians turned their mounts and rode away. The last one paused for a moment and made a gesture that almost looked like a salute before he rode to catch up with his fellows.

As the enemy disappeared, the people cheered and shouted, and Aeron found that his arm was curled around Nesta's shoulder. Gethin was clinging to her skirts and Elin was clutching the leg of his trousers. "We did it! We did!" hooted Gethin.

"We sure did," said Aeron, ruffling the boy's hair.

The people eventually settled down and went to finish off their dinners, still talking excitedly. But this was soon cut off when the lookouts reported several new columns of smoke rising up. Members of the family and the neighbors who had taken shelter with them rushed to the barricades, and some of them began to weep or curse when they could tell it was their homes that were burning. "Looks like my place," said Uncle Hywel with a calm that amazed Aeron.

"We'll rebuild, Mac," said his father. "Don't you worry."

Thoroughly chastened, they set up a watch rotation for the night while the others tried to sleep. A few new fires could be seen in the dark, but they looked to be far away. When Aeron took his turn, he was pleased when Nesta came and stood with him. "I never… I never thought anything like this could happen," she said.

"Nor I. The last time the Shires were invaded by anything larger than some wandering goblins was long ago, before we joined the League. Everyone's forgotten what a real war can be like."

"But if they can do this again and again, how are people going to live?"

Aeron thought about it but didn't have a good answer. "We can fortify our houses. That will help, but it's not an answer. People can't spend all their time on guard; they have to work their fields and tend their animals. The only thing that can stop this is to build a real army that can be on guard and stop these raiders or hurt them badly enough if they do slip through that they'll stop doing it." He didn't mention what could happen if something more powerful than just raiding cavalry attacked the Shires.

"I'm frightened, Aeron. For my children. And for us."

Now he found both his arms wrapped around her. And hers around him. They held each other for a long time.

* * * * *

The next morning, they cautiously sent out some scout on ponies. Aeron went with them, and they found nothing but some smoldering buildings for several miles around. The enemy seemed to have moved on. About mid-morning, a large group of Shires cavalry, nearly three hundred of them, rode up and shouted a hello. The leader, someone Aeron didn't know, asked for information on the raiders. They told him all that they knew and asked for news in return. "They look to be running off to the west," said the leader. "We'll have them pushed beyond the border before sunset!" He looked over their defenses. "This is very impressive what you've done here. Good job."

"It was my boy's idea," said Da, pointing to Aeron. "The Rhordians took one look at it and rode off."

"I'm going to tell the Muster-Master about this. Well, we have to get going. Good luck." He ordered his troop into motion and they rode off.

They waited a bit and then sent off a rider to Picksbury to see if they could get a chirurgeon to come treat the Islwyn boy, but he returned to say that no one could come, as there was a flood of injured and wounded coming in from the surrounding farms and villages. Seeing that they had no option, they hitched up a cart and sent the lad and his father with a small escort to the town to get help for him. By nightfall, the escort returned to report that he was in good hands and was expected to recover. Missus Islwyn was very relieved but also very anxious to get back to see what remained of her home. There had been no more new smoke columns all day, and they promised they'd take her home in the morning.

At daybreak began the grim task of assessing the damage. Uncle Hywel's place wasn't as bad as they'd feared. The barn was just a pile of debris, but the main house was still standing. The raiders had looted the place and tried to set fire to it, but the fire had gone out and only done some minor damage. "We'll get this fixed up in no time," said Aeron's father. "Then we'll have a barn raising."

"That might have to wait," said Uncle Hywel. "There are other folks in worse need. Summer's coming, and the animals can do without the barn for a while."

Yes, there were definitely folks in worse need. The Islwyn place was almost completely destroyed, house, barn, and most of the outbuildings were burned to ashes. Missus Islwyn was stunned beyond tears, but her children made up for that and were in near-hysterics for hours. Most of the other Cadwallader properties hadn't been touched, but several other neighbors had some damage, although none as bad as the Islwyns.

They rallied around Missus Islwyn, promising all the help they could give. "You can stay with us during the rebuilding," said Da. "We'll have a solid place for you built before the first snows fly, rest assured." The woman was grateful but still in a daze. Aeron drew his father away.

"Da, the first thing we have to do is finish the stockade."

"But…"

"Da! The *first thing* we have to do is *finish* the stockade!" He stared at his father and did not look away.

The older halfling blinked first. "Aye, you're right. We would have been in a fix for sure if we hadn't had what we did when they came. All right. That's the first task before us. The rest will have to wait."

It only took a bit to convince the others of the need, but that afternoon, they were back to the pine wood, cutting down more trees. Some of the neighbors were proclaiming that they would do the same thing. Privately, Aeron thought that was a bad idea. They needed to concentrate their forces, not disperse them, but he said nothing aloud.

The following day, they were still cutting, but they had enough logs to continue work on the stockade. They were eager to replace the barricade, because some of the items being used oughtn't be left out in the rain.

While they worked, a pair of Shirelings on ponies and a few on aralez rode up, and Aeron saw that one of them was none other than the Muster-Master himself, Dustin Rootwell. They stopped beyond the remains of the barricade and shouted a hello. Aeron's father went out to meet them. Aeron deliberately held himself back.

"Well, Mister Cadwallader," said Rootwell. "I got a report about what you'd done here, and I have to say I'm very impressed. However did you get so much done so fast?"

"My boy here, insisted we do this as soon as the first raid happened. I'm sure glad I listened to him!"

"Indeed? And your boy is…?"

"Aeron, over there. He knows a lot about military matters. Went to that college in Eowulf." He paused and looked right at him. "Only a fool wouldn't listen to him."

Aeron winced, but Rootwell just chuckled. "Maybe so. Maybe so. But we are going to want to build other fortified homesteads like yours. Maybe one home in ten that all the surrounding families can retreat to if there's another attack like that last one. I'm going to send one of my clerks by to make a sketch and take notes on just how you built the defenses; what materials you used and how long it took. I hope you won't mind answering a few questions?"

"Not at all, we'll be happy to help."

Rootwell touched his hand to his forehead and then motioned his party to ride on. They watched them go for a while but then got back to work.

Chapter 11

Two days later, they had the stockade completed - just in time for Rootwell's clerk's arrival. Aeron took him on a tour and answered his questions. There were still things that Aeron wanted to add, like platforms so that they could shoot out over the walls as well as build a proper gate. Right now, they just had a wagon with boards covering one side that could be rolled out of the way and back again. There were other things too, like setting up watch posts on high spots all around the surrounding countryside with people always manning them and a signal system to spread a warning fast. He told all these suggestions to the clerk.

He also wanted to make more and better weapons; bows, arrows, shields, and some armor… But all that would have to wait for a while. The next thing on the minds of most people was to see about rebuilding the most critical of the destroyed structures. He could see there was no use in fighting against it.

Uncle Hywel's house was quickly cleaned up and some minor repairs made it livable again. A new fenced in area for animals took the place of the barn, which would have to wait. A new shed was built at the old farm inside the stockade for valuables and heirlooms from the other family farms. Until things settled down, there was no point in hauling them to the stockade every time there was an alarm. Aeron was pleased that no one was assuming there wouldn't be any more alarms.

The Islwyn place wasn't nearly so easy to fix. Almost everything would have to be rebuilt nearly from scratch. The house and barn had stone foundations which remained, along with a stone chimney for the house, but everything else was gone. The only bright spot was that most of their livestock had simply been run off rather than killed or stolen. Nearly all were eventually rounded up and returned.

Many willing hands turned out for a house raising - although not nearly as many as might have been expected for a normal disaster, the Islwnys were far from the only family in the area who needed help. Experience gained in cutting the trees for the stockade helped make quick work of assembling the needed lumber, but from there it became a lot more work. Some of the logs could be used as they were, but most had to be cut into limber, and that took a while. They were only two days into it when there was an alarm. A new raid had been spotted, but after a tense day, they learned that it was off to the east and had been turned away without doing much damage. They went back to work.

A week later, the frame of a house was in place and roofed over. It was an empty shell, but the Islwyn's moved in and their wounded son returned from Picksbury about the same time. The grateful family still had a lot of work to do to make it a home again, but at least it was something. A lot of people donated furniture and farming tools. It was a good start.

Several more raids occurred shortly after that, but again they were not close to Picksbury. Still, they were close enough that Aeron managed to convince the family to do the additional work on the stockade he wanted and then began working on improving their weapons stockpile.

"Never thought we'd own a bloody *arsenal*," said his father.

"Hopefully we'll never need them," said Aeron, "But better to have them and not need them than need them and not have them. When our wagon train got attacked, we didn't have weapons for more than a tenth of us, and a lot of folks probably died because of that."

"No arguing with that, son."

They set up a lathe to turn the shafts for spears and arrows. The children collected feathers to fletch the arrows. Spear points and arrowheads were a bit of a problem. The local blacksmiths were overwhelmed with orders from the Assembly, the Muster-Master, and the trained bands. Fortunately, they did have a small smithy right there on the farm with a bellows and an anvil. Aeron's brother, Bronwen, had a good hand for that sort of thing; and after a bit of practice, he started turning out serviceable points. They weren't pretty, but they would do.

Those with carpentry skills made wooden shields. Again, they weren't pretty (although some of the children tried their hand at painting warlike designs on them) but they would do the job. Armor was another matter. They didn't have the materials, skills, or the time for anything like chainmail, but after a few false starts, the women began turning out heavy leather jerkins that would be far better than nothing. Their attempts at leather helmets did not turn out so well, but again, they were better than nothing.

About the time they decided they had enough, the raids petered off and then stopped altogether. The optimists said that they'd bloodied the raiders enough to discourage them. Aeron wasn't nearly so hopeful. "They've just been probing for weaknesses," he said privately to Nesta. "They haven't committed more than a tenth of their force yet and none of their heavy units. If they are determined for war, it's barely begun."

"So what do we do?" She didn't sound scared, just determined.

He shrugged. "Keep preparing. I've heard that the Assembly is planning to build a whole series of fortified farmsteads like what we've done so everyone will have somewhere secure to flee to if there's a raid. They're also raising more trained bands."

"And you're going to join one?" Her question was direct and a bit of a surprise.

"How did you know? I haven't said anything to anyone."

"I'm starting you know you, Aeron Cadwallader," she said with a small smile. "You can't just stand by and leave things to others; you have to help. You've helped about all you can here, and with trade nearly at a standstill, I can't see you being much help to your father in that regard. So when do you leave?"

He looked away but took her hand and squeezed. "Picksbury is raising several new bands. One is going to be cavalry, but the recruits have to bring their own mount. I can do that - assuming Da will let me take one. If so, I plan to go into town the day after tomorrow."

He looked back at her, and now she turned away. "I… I'd go with you, except for the children," she said. "Sometimes they let women join, don't they?"

"Sometimes. But I probably won't be sent far away. We'll be used to guard the border and respond to raids. I'll probably be able to visit home quite a bit, and being mounted, I can get here quickly."

"But being cavalry, you'll be more likely to catch up to any raiders. So you're more likely to do some fighting."

"Probably, yes."

"Usually, I like the way you don't lie to keep me from worrying. Now, I'm not sure."

"I could lie if you want. But I won't be lying when I say I'll be just as worried about you as you are about me. It's not like staying home will make you safe." He squeezed her hand harder.

"Sometimes I lie awake at night," said Nesta, "thinking about how this awful mess brought us together. And now it will be taking us apart again." She shook her head.

"It won't take us far, and hopefully not for long."

"Hope. I don't put much trust in hope anymore." She moved closer. "I know you won't be leaving for a while yet, but kiss me goodbye now, Aeron. Right now."

Aeron held onto Nesta tightly, drawing her in, and doing as she asked.

*****

Two days later, he rode into Picksbury. He wasn't alone; to his horror, his cousin Madoc, Uncle Hywel's oldest boy, had decided that he wanted to join up, too. Madoc was just a few months older than Aeron and growing up had been a thorn in his side. Loud, boisterous, and a bit of a bully, Madoc was not the sort that Aeron would have chosen as his comrade-in-arms. In the time he'd been away in Eowulf, Madoc seemed to have matured a bit, and now he was merely annoying instead of unbearable. He seemed to think this was some grand adventure instead of the deadly serious thing Aeron knew it to be.

They did make an impressive pair, however. In addition to their ponies, they each had a spear, bow, shield, and armor - the best-looking the ladies had managed to make. Aeron also carried Sergeant Rolf's faithful dagger. Little Elin seemed particularly impressed with how he looked. People did make favorable comments when they passed.

"So where are we supposed to go?" asked Madoc.

"Let's find out." A few questions directed them to where the new mounted trained band was forming. It was on the outskirts of the town, in a large open field. He was heartened to see several hundred ponies and even a few aralez tied up there with many more people milling about. Clearly, some of the people were just spectators, but if there was one rider for every mount, it was going to be a respectable force. He had feared that they would arrive to find it was just a handful with no real use as a military unit.

He hailed a fellow who he assumed was one of the band by the short sword hanging on his belt and asked where they should go to sign up. He directed them to where a small pavilion had been erected. "Captain Einion is in there, he'll take care of you."

They tied up their ponies to one of the long wooden rails which were there for that very purpose and walked over to the pavilion. Two older people were seated at a table beneath it, and they appeared to be arguing with a young Shireling woman. She was dressed for riding and had several long knives stuck in her belt.

"Sorry, missy, but the rules is the rules, and we can't let you in," said one of the pair.

The woman had her hands on her hips and looked to be very angry. "What rules?" she snapped. "I saw at least two other girls out there with the troopers! They were armed and clearly part of your band!" She turned to the other fellow at the table. "Mister Einion, you're in command here, aren't you? What do you say?"

The other one, he must have been Captain Einion, looked more sheepish than annoyed. "Sorry, Gwenith, the rules say that no women can join unless they have a male relation in the band, too. Just wouldn't be proper otherwise. Your Da shouldn't have let you come all alone."

Madoc suddenly moved forward to get a good look at the girl's face. "Gwenith? Cousin Gwenith? Hey, it's me, Madoc Cadwallader! What are you doin' here?"

The girl spun around, face red with fury until she saw Madoc. Then her face lit up. "Madoc! It's you! Are you part of the band?"

"Just here to join up!" he said proudly, puffing out his chest.

"Perfect!" she cried. She seized Madoc by the arm and dragged him up to the table. "Mister Einion? This is my Cousin Madoc Cadwallader, he's my mother's sister's boy. He's joining up, and now I shall have a 'male relation' in the band! You have to let me in!" She glared at the other one.

That one rolled his eyes and looked to Einion. "Bevan…?"

Einion held up his hands. "Sign her up."

Gwenith squealed in glee and hugged Madoc, who smiled like a loon. Aeron stared at the girl. She had amber hair and lots of freckles and a snub nose. Not exactly beautiful, but cute. As he looked, he realized that he had seen her before, probably at some large family gathering, but she had been a lot younger then. He cleared his throat noisily and they both looked at him.

"Oh!" cried Madoc. "Uh, Gwen, this is my cousin, Aeron. Well, I guess he's your cousin, too, second cousins, right? Haven't you met? He's Uncle Howell's son."

"I think we did meet, years ago," said Aeron. "Probably don't remember me. And yes, we're second cousins."

She stared at him and then nodded. "Yes, I do remember. How grand! So I'll have *two* male relations in the band! You are joining, too, aren't you, Aeron?"

"Oh yes."

"All right then," she said turning back to the other man. "Please sign me up, Mister… Guto, wasn't it?"

The man frowned. "That's *Lieutenant* Guto to you… trooper. Make your mark here." He slid a ledger over to her along with a quill.

"I can write my name," she said, tilting her nose up. "And *Trooper Gwenith Parry*! That sounds so splendid!" She bent forward, took the quill, dipped it in the ink pot, and signed her name. She stood aside and Madoc signed next and then Aeron. He noted that there was nothing else on the ledger except names. He wasn't sure if they were signing a legally binding document or not.

Guto spun the book around, looked over the signatures, and nodded. "All right, that's done. I'm afraid there's no camp yet. The town fathers say they'll be deliverin' a bunch of canvas to make tents with later today. We're gonna set them all up in rows and make it all military-like. For now, just relax and don't wander off far. Oh, and they say they'll be sending forage for our animals, too."

"I, uh, I have some experience in laying out camps, sir," said Aeron.

"Do you? Oh, that's right, you're that fellow who went to the college in Eowulf, afore they tossed you out. Learned some things, did you?"

"A few."

"Indeed?" said Captain Einion. "Well, then you're just what I need. I'll make you the… the fellow in charge of tents and supplies and such."

"The quartermaster?"

"Yes, that's what it's called, isn't it? You'll be the quartermaster!"

"Yes, sir," sighed Aeron.

"And these two," said Einion, pointing at Madoc and Gwenith, "shall be your assistants."

"What?!" shouted Madoc.

* * * * *

And so Aeron became the quartermaster for the Picksburg Volunteer Light Horse. It wasn't the job he'd been hoping for, but he was certainly better qualified for it than anyone else. And it did give him a bit of authority - sort of.

In the Rhordian army, the position of quartermaster was considered one for a junior officer. In the Shires army, no one seemed to know what it was or how to treat the person filling it. Aeron decided to take advantage of that uncertainty by simply acting like an officer. If anyone questioned his authority, he said he was acting under the direction of Captain Einion and few people challenged him. The few times anyone did, Einion sided with Aeron, and that settled the matter.

On that first day, he sent Gwenith into town looking for wooden stakes and balls of string. She was very enthusiastic to be given the task. He sent Madoc looking for material to make tent poles and stakes. He wasn't nearly so enthusiastic. Gwenith was back around noon with the string and the stakes, and he and she spent the early afternoon laying out the camp. Some of the others watched and he even dragged a few of them in to help. With no direction to the contrary, he arbitrarily divided the band into two squadrons and each squadron into four troops and laid out the camp to fit that organization. Captain Einion came by to see how things were going, and Aeron explained what he and done. Einon just nodded and went on his way.

As the afternoon drew on, Madoc returned, followed by a wagon filled with poles and tent stakes, but there was no sign of the promised canvas. Dinner came and went - Aeron's next job was going to be organizing food supplies and cooking duties - but no canvas appeared.

Naturally, it rained that night. A hard, cold rain.

A few people huddled under the pavilion until it became apparent that it had been intended for festivals and wasn't really waterproof. Everyone soon retreated into the town to find shelter in taverns and inns. Aeron tried to stick it out to appear hardy and soldierlike, but soon realized that no one cared in the slightest, and followed the rest into town.

The next morning dawned chilly and foggy. It was only a month and a half after the Equinox, after all, but at least the rain had stopped. Captain Einion and Lieutenant Guto sent runners through the town to round up their scattered command and get them all back to camp for a morning inspection.

Still a bit soggy, the troopers finished their breakfasts and drifted back to the camp in dribs and drabs and spent the time seeing to their mounts. Aeron's pony gave him an accusing look, but it accepted a currying and an armload of hay. To his amazement and delight, Gwenith's mount was an aralez. He and Madoc crowded round to look at the beast.

"However did you get him?" asked Aeron.

"My father gave him to me, of course. And my father got him as a gift from a breeder he knows up in Abbetshire. Isn't he adorable?"

The beast was amazing, but not exactly adorable. It had about the same length and height as a pony, but its shoulders were nearly twice as broad and the head considerably larger. Its fur was mostly white but had a few patches of a light brown color. A huge pink tongue licked a giggling Gwenith, but Aeron's eyes were drawn to the large fangs the mouth held. They were easily as long as his hand. Madoc had spotted them, too.

"Wow, those could tear a person apart! What do you call him? Killer?"

"White Fang, maybe," suggested Aeron.

Gwenith looked scandalized. "Hmmph! The very idea! His name is Fluffy."

"*Fluffy*!" exclaimed Aeron and Madoc in unison.

"Why not? He *is* fluffy - when he's not dripping wet like now - poor boy." She started to comb out the matted fur.

Madoc shook his head, muttered something, and then went back to his own pony.

"He really is something," said Aeron. "How does his speed compare to a pony's?"

"Over short distances, he's as fast or faster," she said proudly, scratching him under his chin. "Over long distances, at a slow pace he can hold his own, too. It's at the middle speeds that he doesn't do well. A pony trotting or cantering will leave him behind pretty quickly. But we don't mind, do we,

Fluffy?" The beast gave a friendly growl and licked her face again. She produced some meat and a bone she'd gotten at breakfast, and Fluffy gulped down the meat and gnawed the bone enthusiastically.

A short while later, Einion called everyone to attention and had them line up in the open space in front of the bedraggled pavilion. Aeron looked closely at him and frowned. Einion had struck him the previous day as a good-natured sort, but he looked positively grim this morning. What had happened? A new raid? He stood out in front of them and began to speak:

"Comrades! You are all volunteers. Stout-hearted sons and daughters of our beloved Shires. You came here to help defend our land against the attacks of a ruthless enemy. An enemy who kills helpless farmers, burns their homes, slaughters their animals. If you had any doubts about fighting that enemy, put those doubts behind you!

"Yesterday, the Rhordians delivered a set of demands to the Shires Assembly. They say that if we yield to these demands, they will cease their attacks upon us. I've been given a copy of the demands to read to you." Lieutenant Guto handed a large sheet of parchment to Einion, who held it up in front to him. He looked at it for a moment and frowned.

"There's a lot of flowery words here that I won't bore you with, but the gist of it is this: the Rhordians demand a huge amount of our goods; wheat, barley, oats, corn, potatoes, turnips, cows, sheep, pigs, ale, tobacco, the list goes on and on. And not just a bit, huge amounts, some in the *thousands* of bushels. They want this delivered to them every year!" A growl arose in the ranks of the troopers as well as some angry shouts until Guto called for quiet.

"And that's not the end of it either," continued Einion. "They demand that we take down every one of the guardburgs on our borders with the League and raise no military force beyond what is needed to patrol our other borders with the rest of the world. We would also be banned from building any sort of war machines, or raising or keeping any aralez."

"What?!" squawked Gwenith from beside Aeron. More outraged cries came from the troopers, and this time, Einion and Guto let it go on for a while. Eventually it died down and their commander continued.

"The League has given us a fortnight to comply. The Shires Assembly has issued no formal reply as yet, but I have it on good authority that these demands will be rejected utterly..." Now a cheer erupted, a cheer that Aeron joined in. Einion waved for quiet and got it. "The Assembly is debating exactly what response they will give to the League, but I also have it on good authority that our reply will be written with steel and fire, not parchment and ink!"

The cheers rose up louder than before. Many had drawn weapons and were brandishing them. Aeron found that his blood was up like the others, but the rational part of his mind cringed at the thought of what was to come.

"We'll show those bloody-handed humies, won't we?" shouted Madoc.

"We sure will!" yelled Gwenith. "Try and take Fluffy away from me, will they?!"

When things settled down, Captain Einion had more to say. "Comrades, we have a big job ahead of us and not much time to get ready for it. I've been promised that the canvas for our tents *will* arrive today—in fact, I believe it's arriving right now." Everyone turned and saw that three large wagons were rumbling into the camp. "Our quartermaster, Aeron Cadwallader, has laid out our camp and now he will instruct you how to make your tents."

I will? Oh dear...

"I expect you to have our camp well-established by noontime. We will spend the afternoon getting ourselves organized and practice with our weapons and our mounts. All right, that's all. Let's get to it."

* * * * *

They didn't quite have it done by noon, but they were well along. Aeron stuck with the organization he'd set up yesterday: two squadrons with four troops per squadron. With the two hundred or so people in the band, that gave each troop around twenty-five, so he further divided each one into four 'comrades-in-battle' of six to eight. Each of these would have a tent, so that would be thirty-two of them, plus one each for Einion and Guto, two cook tents, one for each squadron, and finally one tent for the three women in the band.

The tents had to be simple things, and he used a design he'd seen in use by the troops at the Great Muster - although scaled down to suit Shirefolk. Each one was just a triangular shape about six feet high, eight feet wide, and ten feet long. There were flaps on each end to keep the wind and rain out. They could be made with a minimum amount of cutting and stitching.

He called for anyone in the band with experience in sewing and got a dozen or so and put them in charge of teams to do the critical work of cutting out the pieces and directing the stitching. He worked with them to make the first tent and then let them go ahead and make the rest. The other people he set to work cutting the poles and stakes from the wood Madoc had gathered. By the noon meal, they had about a half-dozen actually up, and Captain Einion was so pleased that he let the work go on after lunch; a few more hours saw them all done. The results were a bit sloppy and not all the tents were exactly the same size, but the camp as a whole looked very tidy and military. They even drew a small crowd of spectators.

Another hour was used up as the band sorted themselves out into their troops and comrades-in-battle groups. These were mostly decided upon by friendships and family connections. There were a lot of close relations in the band, as was very usual in Shires' trained bands. In the Rhordian forces, they just would have been assigned wherever the officers wanted them, but it couldn't be done that way here. Aeron and Madoc teamed up with four others who were from their neighborhood. Aeron didn't really know any of them closely, although he knew the family names and where they came from. Gwenith really wanted to stay close to Madoc and himself, but she couldn't stay in their tent—it wouldn't be *proper* - but Aeron had arranged so the females' tent was close to the commanders' tents, and he made sure he and Madoc had a tent near to there, so she was close-by.

Of course, at the moment there wasn't much *in* the tents. No cots or stools or tables, no real comforts of any kind. Just a few blankets thrown on the ground, marking the space of each person, with their small pile of personal belongings. This didn't seem to bother anyone at the moment, and some were talking about the items they could make or buy to make things 'more home-like'. Aeron didn't point out that if they got orders to move somewhere, any excess baggage they'd accumulated would have to be left behind.

By the time it was all done, there really wasn't much daylight left for any sort of practicing, so Captain Einion simply had everyone form up with all their gear on the 'street' in between the two squadron rows - which is exactly what it was intended for, a place to assemble - and looked everyone over. The variety of weaponry and equipment was far, far less uniform than their tents. Few of the recruits had as complete a set as Aeron and Madoc with their spears, bows, shields, and leather armor. Einion stopped and asked them about it, and Madoc proudly told him how all the Cadwalladers were equipped like that.

"Hmm, interesting," he said. "Maybe I should contact your folks about making more for us. The Assembly has promised weapons and gear for all the new trained bands, but the Missing Gods only know when we'll get it." Moving to stand in front of Aeron he said quietly: "Come to my tent and talk with me after dinner."

"Yes, sir."

Einion walked up and down the rows of troopers, looking each one over and talking to quite a few of them. By the time he was done, it was nearly dinner time, and he dismissed them to find their provender. As had happened the previous night, for many of them that meant going into Picksbury and eating at an inn or tavern. Aeron, Madoc, and Gwenith had all brough a fair supply of food with them, so they built a fire using the leftover scraps from the tent poles and stakes, and they cooked a fine little supper of their own.

"Only got enough for a few more days," said Madoc. "This army gon-na feed us or what?"

Aeron sighed. "As quartermaster, that's another one of my jobs. I need to set up a supply tent and get a commissary detail put together to handle the cooking and such. Speaking of which, I better go see the captain." He got up and headed for Einion's tent.

The captain and his lieutenant had managed to acquire a pair of stools and were sitting outside next to a fire. Aeron came up, decided he wouldn't salute, but came to attention and said: "Sir, you wanted to see me?"

"Ah, Cadwallader," said Einion. "Yes, we need to talk. Pull up a... well, pull up a log and sit down." There was a small pile of firewood, and he found one that set on end would make a reasonable seat. Einion handed him a jug which turned out to contain a rather potent cider. He took a swig and hand-ed it back. Einion took a swig and handed it to Guto. "Good job with the tents and organizing the camps and all," said Einion.

"Thank you, sir."

Einion snorted. "Can't get used to being called *sir.* You're about the only one who does it, though. I've been asking around after you, Cadwallader. I must say that I've gotten quite a variety of answers."

Aeron almost replied: *Sir?* but instead just looked attentive.

"There are some folks who think you're a spy from the League. Others that say you saved that wagon train and kept Paddy Bobart out of the hands of the damn Rhordians. There are a few who think you're a bloody-handed butcher who got a lot of innocent people killed by wanting to fight to save Bobart. Some others think you'll be worth your weight in gold if this mess comes to a real war."

Aeron sat up straighter. *Really? Who?* "I just want to serve the Shires as best I can, sir," he said aloud.

Einion nodded and then got out his pipe, filled it, and used a burning twig from the campfire to light it. He puffed for a few moments and then said: "I believe you. The stuff about you being a spy is sack of rubbish. I don't believe it for a moment. Missing Gods, what could you tell the Rhordians that they don't already know anyway? Not like we're good at keeping secrets around here. As for the rest, well, if you've got fighting spirit, that's what we need. And you've proved your worth here already. I'd be a fool not to make use of you."

"I'll be happy to do whatever you want, sir."

Einion nodded and blew a smoke ring from the pipe. "I was made commander of this trained band because my family is well-known and my uncle is on the Shire Assembly - not," he paused and looked straight at Aeron, "because of any military knowledge or experience I have." His gaze became piercing. "You, on the other hand, have both - and I need that knowledge and that experience."

"I'll help however I can," said Aeron.

"Good, good. So, if this was your trained band, Mister Cadwallader, what would you do to get it ready?"

Aeron signed in relief. He'd been trying to figure out a way to get Einion to listen to his advice, and here he up and asks for it! "Well, sir, the number one task in front of us is to turn this band into a *trained* band."

Guto snorted a mouthful of cider out through his nose and then went into a coughing fit. Einion looked on in amusement. "I think you've hit the hail on the head, Cadwallader. You all right, Folant?" Guto nodded and kept coughing. "So how do we go about training these folks? Most of them ride well enough - note that I said *most*. A few need more practice. Some can shoot bows, I don't know if any can shoot while riding. As for using weapons and shields, either on foot or mounted, your guess is as good as mine. So how do we start?"

Aeron marshaled his thoughts. *You wanted this and now you've got it!* "As you say, the first thing is to find out what our people can do. Since we're cavalry, riding should take priority. Tomorrow we can start out with riding drills, see who the best ones are, put them to work teaching the ones who need help. We can't ride all day without wearing out our mounts, so while they are resting, we can practice archery and weapons drill on foot. We'll need to set up archery butts and make some wooden weapons for drill. Later, we'll do the drills mounted. As we see who does best, we can appoint sergeants to command the troops, and corporals to lead the comrades-in-battle. Then…"

They talked for an hour or so, making plans, trading ideas, voicing their concerns. At least neither Einion nor Guto underestimated the amount of work that lay ahead. The one question none of them could answer was: how much time did they have?

Chapter 12

Training started early the next morning. Before going to sleep the previous night, he'd talked for a while with Madoc and Gwenith about what he wanted to do. The first thing he wanted was to sort out the best riders, but he wasn't sure how to do that. He didn't know more than a handful of the troopers by name, so how was he going to note who was who? It was Gwenith who solved his problem, and while the others were eating breakfast, they grabbed a couple of quick-eaters to help and set up their testing course on the adjacent field.

It was very simple, actually. They hammered a score of posts into the ground in a straight line with a dozen paces between them. The riders would take their mounts at a canter and zig-zag back and forth to the right of the first post, then the left of the second, back the right of the third and so on down the line. At the end, they would turn and gallop back the other way, jumping over fence rails set at varying heights held up by boxes and barrels. Aeron, Einion, and Guto would judge each rider as they went through the course. At the end, the best ones would go into one group, the worst would go into another, and the rest—probably the majority—would be sent back to camp. Names would be taken and the best would become riding instructors and the worst would get special training.

It was crude, but it worked. Testing two hundred riders took the entire morning, but everyone seemed to enjoy it. There was a great deal of whooping and hollering and laughing when riders fell off their mounts. Aeron looked on with great interest as Gwenith took Fluffy through the course. She did it very well, although he had to remind himself that it had been her idea. Had she done something like this before? The aralez wasn't quite as nimble as a pony, but it made it through the first part of the course only bumping a few of the posts. The loping stride of the beast wasn't as fast as a canter, but there was nothing for it. On the second part, he was amazed at how far Fluffy could leap, easily clearing the hurdles. It almost looked like he could have taken two at once if he wanted to.

The break for lunch reminded Aeron of another job he needed to get to work on. As usual, a lot of the troopers disappeared into the town to find food, and many of them were very late returning. He could see that Einion was as frustrated by that as he was, but at the moment, there was no way to enforce discipline. Everyone was a volunteer who had brought their own mount and their own equipment. The Assembly had not come up with any way to pay them yet, so anyone who got angry at the way things were done could simply up and leave, and there wasn't a thing to stop them.

The remedy for the extended meal breaks was to get a regular commissary for the band set up, so that meals could be served and consumed right in camp. The Picksbury town council had voted to supply rations to all the trained bands, but each band had to handle the details on their own. In this case, it meant that *Aeron* had to handle the details. After quickly eating his lunch, he spent the time going in search of future lunches for the band. A bit of asking led him to a harried scribe who worked for the council. He assured him that the bakeries in town were working day and night to produce bread for the troops, the dairy was turning out cheese, and the butchers were making sausage and curing meats. There was a warehouse where these things could be requisitioned, but each band would have to come and get what it needed. He'd need to get hold of some wagons and detail the people to help move the food and a place to store it in camp, and get some cooks to serve the meals, and... Aeron thanked him and hurried back to camp.

Once everyone was back, they got to work. The ones designated as trainers took charge of the ones most in need of training and spent the afternoon riding hither and yon and also going through the testing route again and again. After several hours of that, there were some marked improvements, although a few, in Aeron's opinion, were better suited to be infantry. The rest of the band, under command of Captain Einion, who was closely advised by Aeron, started learning some basic formations. Getting lined up, forming into a column of march, and then getting back into a battle line. It wasn't nearly as easy as it sounded, especially since the mounts were as untrained as their riders. Even Aeron was puzzled about what to do with the aralez. Being broader than a pony, they didn't really fit into the normal formations very well. Also, normal horses and ponies were quite skittish about the strange beasts. There were only four of them, so he couldn't put them all in their own separate comrades-in-battle group. Then he was struck with an inspiration. The Rhordian heavy cavalry had men called *guides* who carried small banners on their lances. One would be stationed on the ends of each battle line to help keep the alignment. Light cavalry didn't normally use them, but there was no reason why Aeron couldn't. So his four aralez riders became guides, one for each end of each squadron. Gwenith was delighted.

By the end of the day, everyone was tired, but most felt some satisfaction at the progress they were making. There was the usual mass exodus into town for dinner, and Aeron talked to Einion about getting the commissary set up. To his surprise, the captain said: "Lieutenant Guto will be taking over that duty, Aeron. I need you to stick with the training. When I was given this command, I was told that I could organize it any way I wanted to and appoint whatever subordinates I need, so I am making you my lieutenant in charge of training. You all right with that?"

"Yes, sir!" said Aeron, very surprised. "I'd be honored!"

Feeling very good about things, he went back to the fire where Madoc and Gwenith were cooking dinner and gave them the news. Gwenith clapped her hands and said: "That's wonderful! You deserve it!"

Madoc didn't seem nearly so enthused, but eventually nodded his head. "Well done, cousin. But don't you think I'm gonna start salutin' you and calling you sir!" Fortunately, he smiled afterward.

"Oh, I wouldn't expect that at all, cousin," said Aeron.

* * * * *

The days sped by. The mornings were spent on riding drill and the afternoons in weapons practice. After two days, the group of less-skilled riders had progressed enough that they didn't require separate training, they and their trainers were integrated into the whole band, and final adjustments were made defining each squadron, troop, and comrades-in-battle group. It would have worked very well, except for the fact that new recruits kept showing up. Nearly a dozen in the first week. Some were good riders and some weren't, and they had all missed the earlier training and had to catch up somehow. It was annoying, but there wasn't anything that could be done because Einion wasn't about to turn anyone away.

Sergeants were assigned to command the troops, but the corporals for each comrades-in-battle were selected by the people in them. Aeron foresaw trouble with that but also saw greater trouble if he tried to impose those leaders on them, so he let it go. By the end of the week, the band could form up, get into a march column, trot for a few miles, and deploy into a two-rank battle line faced in any direction with a minimum of confusion. It was good work. He was interested to see that the latecomers could catch on quickly by just telling them to stay next to a specific person and do whatever they did.

Weapons training in the afternoons was a bit more of a challenge. Almost no one had any experience with that sort of thing. A few score were decent archers, although fewer had done much shooting while mounted. Some had experience in using a spear from ponyback while hunting. Spearing a boar or a bear wasn't quite like fighting a human, but it was certainly better experience than none - which was what most of them had.

The archery butts served double purpose as targets for shooting on foot and while riding. For spear practice, they set up a number of targets on posts that the troopers could practice stabbing as they rode by at increasing speeds. Later, he intended them to practice on each other with blunt spears. But that would have to wait until they were better trained - and until they had some sort of armor and shields. Those items were not arriving quickly enough to satisfy anyone.

Then there was sword practice. Wooden swords did appear pretty quickly, being very simple to make, and Aeron, having far more experience than anyone due to his years at the College, became the swordsmanship instructor. He considered this vital training, not just to get their people used to using a sword, but to get them used to the very idea of fighting for their lives. Sergeant Rolf had described it as defeating the flinch reflex.

"This isn't a game," he told the trainees. "If you get into a fight, sword to sword or spear to spear with a man, to lose is to die. You can't hold anything back. That doesn't mean to charge in wildly with no plan, but it means when you strike, strike hard! When your opponent strikes at you, block it with all your speed and skill, and then hit back. Don't worry about bruises and scrapes. Yes, you'll get battered about and finish the day black and blue. But finishing the day *alive* is what matters!"

He then proceeded to whack the stuffings out of his trainees. At first, they were horribly inept, and he shuddered to think of taking them into real combat like this. They'd be slaughtered. Most of them picked themselves up, rubbed their bruises, and came at him again. A few whined that it wasn't fair for them to fight someone so much better than they were.

"So, when you find yourself up against a Rhordian, are you going to stop and ask him how good he is with a sword?" he sneered. "And if he is more experienced than you - and he almost certainly will be - are you going to ask him to let you go find someone more evenly matched? I rather think he'll just kill you and move on. Your only hope of staying alive is to get as good as you can as fast as you can. So take your lumps and get better!"

Most of them seemed to understand, but there were a few hardheads that he had little hope for. Others asked questions, and some of them were even good ones. "Aeron, I mean Lieutenant Cadwallader," asked one trooper named Nye Iolo, "You're pretty big, but you're nowhere as big as one o' those humies. How'n blazes are we supposed to fight someone twice as tall an' five times as strong?"

"Won't be easy," he replied, getting an exasperated look out of Iolo. A number of others gathered around, clearly wanting to hear a better answer. "There's no use in me telling you it will be easy. No doubt their size and strength gives the humans an advantage, but we have some advantages, too. Probably most important is that we're faster than they are. Their legs are twice as long, but they can't run twice as fast. And their reflexes are slower. Ever try to catch a cat that doesn't want to be caught? Or a fox, maybe?" He looked around, and a few of the watchers nodded. "Well it's like that for a human trying to catch one of us. I've fought many of them in practice fights like we are doing here, and I know what I'm talking about. Yes, they have a huge reach advantage, and if you try to fight them toe to toe, they'll hammer you into the ground; but if you can dodge their first blow and get in close, you can beat them."

"Is that how you killed that human in the fight at the wagon train?" asked someone.

"Something like that," he replied quietly. "Also, I had some help. That's the other advantage we have: being smaller, we can gang up on them. Right now, we are just working one on one to develop our basic skills. Later, we'll learn how to work in teams. If you can learn teamwork, then you can go after a human in pairs. One distracts them enough that the other can get in a killing blow."

It seemed like they were getting the idea, but it was hard to tell. He pushed them as hard as he could, but most of the time they were sparring with other trainees. He tried to spot the ones with a natural talent for it as future instructors to help him out.

By mid-week, Lieutenant Guto had managed to get the commissary going, and meals started being served in camp; the troopers were no longer allowed to go into town to eat. There were some complaints about that, but Aeron told them: "Sure, you could eat in town, but what happens when there's no town handy? We're cavalry, and that means we are going to get sent out to the border, maybe scout beyond the border. Out there, we're going to have to be self-sufficient; carry our own food, and be able to cook it under any circumstances." He pointed to the commissary tent and the food being prepared. "This is training, too! The same as riding and shooting and swordsmanship." Fortunately, several of the cooks were very good at turning the bland rations they were given into something worth eating.

After six days of hard work, Captain Einion held a review of the band and had many words of praise. As much as Aeron worried about what had not yet been accomplished, he felt the compliments were warranted. Einion gave them the following day off to rest, and that was warranted, too. Still, there was only one week left before the deadline the Rhordians had set for a reply to their demands. He had no doubt that the Assembly would reject them, but then how long until the Rhordians broke the self-imposed truce? How long before the Picksbury Volunteer Light Horse found itself in action?

They were halfway through the next week when he got his answer. They had just finished the day's training and were getting ready to eat when Captain Einion called Aeron and Lieutenant Guto and the troops' sergeants over to his tent. He was rubbing his eyes as though he had a headache. "Well, lads," he said when they were all there. "We have received our marching orders."

"Where to, Bevan?" asked a dozen voices, although Aeron said: *sir.*

"Up near Ferchester,"

"There have been a lot of raids up that way," said Aeron. "I guess we're going to be on guard against them?"

Einion shook his head slowly. "That would make sense, but I'm not so sure. I'm told that a lot more of our cavalry is being sent up that way. I think maybe something bigger is being planned. But in any case, we'll be moving out tomorrow. Tell your people, and have them be ready. I've managed to get us forty more ponies. We'll use them to replace any that might go lame, but they can also carry all our baggage and supplies. There'll be one assigned to each comrades-in-battle and the rest are for the officers and the commissary." He looked them over. "You have your orders. Let's get to it."

* * * * *

Dear Nesta,

I only have a short time to write this letter, as we will be leaving in less than an hour. Our orders to move came quite unexpectedly. I had hoped to get a chance to ride home and visit on our day off at the end of the week, but it is not to be. I am not sure where we are heading or what we will be doing when we get there, but I will try to get a letter to you when I have a chance. There probably is little point in you trying to write back, as I doubt there will be any delivery to us while we are in the field.

I'm guessing that our role will be defensive, helping turn back raids from the League. I don't want you to worry about me, just as I know you don't want me to worry about you. But I know we both will worry. I will take as much care as I can, and I expect you to do the same. Stay close to the house and don't let the children wander.

I will come see you as soon as I possibly can. Well, this has to go right now. Take care.

All my love,

Aeron

He hastily stuffed the letter in an envelope, sealed and addressed it, and hurried over to where a post service employee from Picksbury was waiting to take all the letters from the band. He had a bag which was full of letters from the others. He gave it to him, thanked him, and gave him a coin for his troubles. Sending letters was now free for volunteers, but he wanted him to have something anyway.

"Thanks to you," said the fellow. "And good luck dealing with those damn Rhordians!"

"Thanks to you, too, friend." He hurried back to where his tent used to be. The camp had come down immediately after an early breakfast. The tents folded, the poles bundled and tied to the backs of the spare ponies, along with any other loose gear the beasts could manage. With his promotion to lieutenant, he was now camping and riding with the officers. He looked over to where Madoc was finishing his packing. He couldn't spot Gwenith at the moment, but she was probably with the other two ladies.

A horn sounded and everyone rushed to finish up. The band now had three people who could blow a horn reasonably well, and Aeron had worked with them to come up with a few simple calls to give signals. One hornist would go with each squadron and one stay close to Einion. The call being played now was 'assembly'. Aeron went over to where his pony was tied. It was a gray-white gelding named Wyn. His sister, Mererid, had appointed herself the official namer of the animals at home. He hoped she wasn't too fond of this one, because the chief riding instructor at the College, a grizzled cavalry veteran, had told them that active service used up the mounts at a terrible pace.

He mounted and turned Wyn toward where the band was assembling. He spotted Gwenith on Fluffy with her guide flag posted on the left flank of the second squadron. The troopers were finding their spots with commendable swiftness, and the band was soon formed. Everyone seemed very eager and excited. Captain Einion rode up and nodded to him. "No time for any speeches," he said. "Let's get moving." He rose up in his stirrups and shouted: "Right by fours… Ho!"

Just as they'd practiced dozens of times, the band formed a column of march, four riders wide and about fifty long, with the baggage ponies following behind. It was smartly done. Einion spurred his pony and took his spot at the head of the column. Lieutenant Guto, who was commander of the second squadron as well as being the quartermaster, took his position about halfway down the column. Aeron had no specific spot, but on a march like this usually rode at the rear to prevent any straggling.

A sizeable crowd of people from the town had come out to watch them go and gave them a friendly cheer as they moved up onto the road to Ferchester. Einion ordered a trot and they picked up the pace, leaving Picksbury behind.

It was a fine day, and the road was dry. Ferchester was about seven leagues away, and they expected to reach there by the end of the day with no problem. Einion varied the pace and rested them for a while after every hour or so to spare the mounts. They took a break at midday and had their first meal 'in the field'.

By mid-afternoon, Ferchester came into sight with the Erst River, which marked the border, glittering in the sun just beyond. An excited murmur ran down the column. Aeron was at the rear talking with Gwenith, and they couldn't see the cause until they topped a rise and could see ahead. "Oh, look at all of them!" exclaimed Gwenith.

On the western outskirts of the town, the fields seemed to be filled with cavalry. He could see a half dozen camps already set up and several large groups were riding into empty fields, apparently to set up theirs. "Must be nearly every cavalry band in the Shires," said Aeron, impressed.

A courier was galloping up the road in their direction. He swung around to ride beside Einion, pointing a bit off to the right of the road. Einion nodded and the courier galloped back the way he came. After a bit, the captain shouted out: "Head of the column to the right... Ho!" The band left the road and cut across several fields - fields which looked to have been recently planted - to reach the meadow where they were to camp. They had to narrow down to single file to squeeze through several gates, but they finally got where they were going and now had the new experience of setting *up* their tents and camp in the field.

It took them quite a while; poles, stakes, and ropes which people were *certain* they had packed turned up missing or on a different pony. There weren't enough hammers to pound stakes, the field wasn't long enough to get nice straight rows. Can we graze the ponies here, or should we use that field over there? Where can we draw water? Where should we put the sinks? The results, while serviceable, didn't look nearly as good as their camp back in Picksbury. Dinner was quite late that night.

Well after dark, a messenger arrived summoning Captain Einion to the commander's tent, which was off closer to Fernchester. It seemed that the commander was the Muster-Master himself, Dunstan Rootwell. Aeron was tempted to tag along, but he was feeling unusually tired and decided to turn in early.

"So what do you think is happening?" asked Madoc as they sat around their fire.

"Maybe we'll find out when Captain Einion gets back," said Gwenith. "There sure are a lot of us here. What do you think, Aeron?"

He stared at the fire for a moment before answering. "Well, I can't believe that we're all here just to defend the border. With all of us here, who's guarding the other borders? So, I can see two possibilities. One is that somehow we *know* there is an attack coming here. Maybe our scouts spotted something, or we got word of it somehow."

"Spies, you think?" asked Madoc.

"Maybe. Or there might even be humans who sympathize with us who would send word. We do have some friends among the humans."

"You said two possibilities, what's the other one?" asked Gwenith.

He took a deep breath and let it out. "That we're here to launch a counter-raid. Into the League."

*****

"Comrades! People of the Shires! The League of Rhordia has violated our territory, burned our homes, and spilled our blood! Now they have demanded that we pay tribute to them and disband the means to defend ourselves! We shall not submit to this! Never!"

Muster-Master Dunstan Rootwell stood on a small platform in front of the massed cavalry which had assembled there. There were nearly two thousands of them, and they roared out a cheer at his words.

"The Rhordians have demanded an answer from us! Well, here is our answer!"

More cheers. All of the Picksbury Volunteer Light Horse was cheering around him, and although Aeron didn't actually say anything, he could feel his blood quickening in his veins. So he'd been right: a counterattack.

"The old saying is that what's good for the goose is good for the gander," continued Rootwell. "So it is your mission to pay them back for what they have done. Burn their farms, scatter their herds and flocks, make them suffer as they made us suffer!" There were more cheers, until Rootwell lifted his hands and got quiet.

"But we are not savages. We are not goblins or orcs… or humans. We want no senseless slaughter. If the Rhordians fight, then fight them. But if they are unarmed and don't resist, then leave them be. We will leave no dead children in our wake. I want this clearly understood."

A sober silence met these words and a few nodding heads. Some of the faces around Aeron were downright grim. Perhaps it was just sinking in that they might actually have to *kill* some people. There were other faces, however, that were still flushed with enthusiasm, and Aeron made a mental note of which ones. He was going to have to keep an eye on them once things got serious.

"Comrades! You have your orders. Carry them out!" Rootwell waved his arms, got one last cheer, and then he stepped down from the platform, got onto his pony, and gave a salute. Horns started blowing all through the host, and the bands started to move. They were leaving all their tents and baggage behind so they could move quickly. Each band brought a few ponies as remounts and to carry essential gear, but that was all.

Aeron urged his horse up next to Einion. The captain had only given the briefest summary of his meeting with Rootwell last night at breakfast that morning. "So what's the plan, sir?" he asked.

"It's all a bit fuzzy," said Einion. "We'll stay in a group until we're across the border. Scouts haven't found any significant Rhordian forces in the vicinity, but if we run into any, we'll send them packing. Once we're sure there isn't anything big waiting for us, we'll split up into smaller columns and do as much damage as we can. We're to meet up again near the town of Rhordenne tonight. In the morning, assuming we don't run into any big group of Rhordians, we'll do the same thing, split up and raise havoc, and then meet up back here tomorrow night."

"Simple enough," said Lieutenant Guto.

"Everything's simple until you meet the enemy," said Aeron.

"They teach you that at that College of Warcraft?"

"They did. But I've found it to be true from personal experience."

"If we stick together, obey orders, and do our job, it shouldn't be too bad," said Einion.

* * * * *

It *was* bad.

As Einion had said, the whole force stayed together until they had forded the Erst River and were well across the border. They didn't know what to expect, so they wanted their entire strength ready if they met serious opposition. But they saw nothing except a few small patrols of Rhordian cavalry who fled at the first sight of them. Aeron also noted that the guardburgs on the border were being strengthened and enlarged, and new ones were being built. By mid-morning, the commander of the force - it was that Conwy Macsen fellow who had relieved the wagon train, not Dustin Rootwell who had not come along - decided that they could safely split up and sent the individual bands on their way.

The Picksbury Light Horse veered a bit to their right until they were heading almost due east. The other bands spread out in a broad arc. Aeron noticed with approval that the long-established bands were more or less paired up with the newly raised ones, so there would be experienced troops close by to the new ones. On Aeron's advice, Captain Einion kept one squadron closely formed under his command while the other squadron split up into its four troops which spread out into a skirmish line a couple of miles wide. If they ran into any trouble, the formed reserve could move up to support them.

From that point on, it was smash and burn. When the scouts spotted a farm, they would swoop down on it, bunching together to give them a strong force. They would roust the owners out of their house and then set fire to everything that would burn. House, barn, sheds, smokehouse, chicken coop, everything. Others would drive off the cattle and sheep, taking any horses they could catch. They were too big to ride, but they could carry supplies and free up the ponies to be used as remounts. Pigs were generally killed, and the smaller ones slung on the horses for dinner.

At first there was no resistance; clearly the locals had not been expecting them. There was a good deal of weeping and wailing and cursing, but no resistance. By noon, that wasn't the case anymore. The alarm was spreading faster than they could move, and they found themselves being shot at from cover more and more often. At first the humans had the sense to only fire a shot or two from their bows and then flee. Knowing the ground, it was hard to catch them. But then they got bolder and kept shooting a bit too long, and some of them were ridden down before they could get away. Two were wounded and one killed that Aeron saw; speared right through the back as he ran. Their fire had wounded one of the ponies but done no other damage. They took the weapons of the wounded and just left them behind, they had no way to drag prisoners along with them. Maybe they'd get help from their neighbors after the band moved on, although Aeron doubted one of them would last long without quick help.

Sometime after noon, they came upon a small village of a dozen houses or so. Einion had two of the troops spread out around the place as lookouts, while the rest of the band formed up and charged right in. The humans had some warning, but not nearly enough to fortify the place. Some simply ran away, although the surrounding troops quickly caught them, more tried to hide themselves, but others tried to fight.

They didn't have a chance. Poorly armed, virtually unorganized, and outnumbered nearly ten to one they were swept away by the first assault. Aeron could admire their courage, but not their sense. Within moments, five of them were killed, another dozen wounded, and the rest were cowering on the ground surrounded by a hedge of spears. They did manage to wound several of their attackers and injure a pony so badly it had to be put down. Ironically, the most serious wound to the Shirelings was caused by a poorly-aimed arrow from one of the riders which hit a friend instead of a foe.

Aeron had struck no blow, but that was true of almost all the troopers - there just hadn't been enough enemies to go around. He, and a lot of the others, dismounted. He pushed up close to the prisoners to see if any of them knew anything about Rhordian troops in the area - and make sure they weren't injured any further. He picked one more less at random and went over to stand before him. "You there," he said. "Are you hurt?"

The man was on his knees, like all the others, but that put him at just below eye-level for Aeron. The human glared at him. "What's it to you?"

"If you're hurt, we can patch you up. We're not savages."

"No? Killing helpless people? Burning farms? That's not savage? We can see the smoke from here!" The man was getting angry. He started to rise up, but a trooper standing behind him rammed the butt end of his spear into the man's back and drove him back down again.

"Just giving back some of what you gave us, humie!" snapped another trooper. "Maybe we should drag you back to the Shires so you can *see* our burned homes! Burned by you Leaguies!"

The man glared at everyone around him but said no more. Aeron decided that this one wasn't likely to give him any information and moved on to a less defiant and more frightened one among the lightly wounded. "That doesn't look too bad," he said pointing to a bloody gash in the man's arm. "Once it's bound up, you'll be all right."

The man didn't respond but looked past him, and his face lit up. Turning, Aeron saw that the village's womenfolk were starting to emerge from hiding and many rushed over to see to their men. The ones who found their men dead began to weep, but the others started to tend to the wounded or cling to the unharmed prisoners. One woman came up to the man Aeron was talking to and began tearing strips off the hem of her skirt to bandage his arm.

"See?" said Aeron. "You'll be fine. We'll be leaving soon, and we won't hurt any more of you. But we do plan to stop here and eat our lunch. Be a shame if we were interrupted by Rhordian troops. If we have to fight a battle here, no telling who could get hurt." He nodded at the woman. "Think we'll be able to eat in peace?"

"I… I don't…" The man hesitated and seemed to realize what he was doing. His face scrunched up and he suddenly spat at Aeron. The gobbet fell short, but the trooper standing guard cursed and whacked him with his spear, and then suddenly things were moving much too quickly…

"Leave him alone!" shrieked a voice.

"Aeron! Look out!"

He spun around and a figure was rushing him, a knife flashing in his hand.

He barely had his dagger halfway out of his scabbard when a spear interposed itself, catching the attacker in the chest, and its own momentum pushed the point deep into the body. The figure stopped two paces away, the hand holding the knife slowly fell, the blade slipping loose. The figure toppled over sideways and crumpled to the ground, the spear still imbedded in the chest.

A boy. A human boy.

"Daichi!" Two voices screaming from behind him. Turning again, he saw the wounded man and the woman trying to come forward, shouting, crying, but the troopers converged and held them back.

Only then did he notice that the spear that had skewered the boy was held by Gwenith. She was the one who had shouted the warning, he dimly realized. She had a horrified look on her face and couldn't take her eyes off the boy.

"Lieutenant?" One of the troopers came up to him. "Sorry, I… I saw him coming, but I let him by because… because… well, he was just a kid, and I didn't see the knife and…" His voice trailed off and he turned away.

Aeron stepped between Gwenith and the boy, cutting off her view. "Gwenith? Gwenith? You did what you had to do. Thank you for saving my life. Gwenith?" He reached out and touched her shoulder. She jerked like she'd been struck and finally seemed to see him.

"Aeron? Oh… oh no… I didn't…. I didn't mean to…" Tears were filling her eyes. He gently pried her hands off the spear haft and turned her away from the dead boy and led her off. The parents were still screaming.

Madoc came rushing up. "What happened? Gwenith! Are you all right?" When she didn't answer right away, Madoc looked to Aeron. "Was she hurt?"

"She'll be all right."

"But what happened?"

He gently sat Gwenith down and then grabbed Madoc and pulled him away. "Just leave her be."

"But what happened?" he repeated.

"Ask one of the others, they'll tell you. But just leave her alone and don't ask her about it. Don't pester her; she'll tell you when she's ready - if she ever is."

There was no time for anything further because Captain Einion appeared and brusquely ordered everyone out of the village. "We'll eat our lunch in the field over there. No arguments! Get moving - *now!"*

There was some grumbling and then even more when he forced some of the ones who had been 'searching' the houses to drop bits of loot they'd picked up. Aeron had noted an alarming amount of thievery going on before houses were burned during the morning's ride, but he didn't feel he had the authority to stop it. Now he did.

The band got itself together and moved to the nearby field. "No time for cook fires," said Einion. Eat your rations cold. We need to get moving. And when we go, just burn the blacksmith shop and the mill. Leave the houses alone." As he stalked past Aeron, he heard him mumbling: "Too much… too much…"

Aeron sat with Madoc and Gwenith and forced her to eat something. She said she wasn't hungry and he believed her, but he still forced her to eat something. "If you're going to throw up, best to have something in there to throw."

She nibbled a piece of bread and a hunk of cheese. After a while she said: "I don't think I like this much. Not quite what I expected."

Aeron nodded. "War's only glamorous when you see it from a distance; in paintings or in books of tales. Up close, it's damned ugly."

"How… how did you feel when you killed that man during the fight at the wagon train?"

"Probably about the way you are feeling now - except it took longer. The difference was that the fight was still going on, and I didn't have time to stop and think until later. Then, yeah, I probably felt like you do."

"Not… not sure I want to do this anymore." Her eyes weren't focused on anything, just staring at the ground a few feet in front of her; the crust of bread forgotten in her hand.

"That's up to you. But remember: you only killed to keep me alive - for which I'm very grateful. You didn't kill because you wanted to, or out of hate, or because you enjoyed it. That's when things get truly ugly. Kill because you have to, but never because you want to. Hang to that, and you'll be all right."

"You're awfully wise for someone so young, Aeron," she said, finally looking at him.

"That's another thing about war: you grow up fast."

"That boy won't grow up."

"No. And that's yet another thing."

Horns started blowing and their lunch break was over. As they started to get up, Gwenith seized his hand and squeezed. "Thank you, Aeron." She got up and went over and climbed up on Fluffy. The aralez seemed to sense her distress and tried to twist his head around to lick her. She leaned forward and put out her hand to let him.

* * * * *

They left the village standing except for the two buildings Einion had ordered destroyed. They moved quickly for a while in a group but then spread out as they had done before, except this time the squadron which had been sent out as skirmishers was kept in reserve while the other one switched jobs with it. Since this was the squadron Gwenith was attached to, Aeron decided to tag along to keep an eye on her. She didn't speak much but seemed glad for the company.

More farms were raided, and even though no order had been given, Aeron noticed that often only the outbuildings were burned while the house was spared. Not every time, but frequently. It seemed as though the morning had sated a lot of the troopers.

The only thing out of the ordinary came about an hour after they left the village when a fast rider from the band to the right of them came hurrying up and asking for support from Einion's band. Rhordian cavalry had been sighted off to the south. The captain had the horns blow to gather everyone together, and then they followed the courier at a brisk canter until they found the commander of the other band. He shrugged sheepishly. "Sorry, one of our scouts got into a panic and reported a couple hundred of them when it was really only a dozen. Didn't want to take chances, so we called for you. We chased them off before you got here."

Einion assured him that it was no trouble and probably good practice. The Picksbury Light Horse went back to its own area and continued the sweep. By late afternoon, they were closing in on the rendezvous point near the town of Rhordenne. Nothing had been said in their orders about whether they were to assault the town or not, but when they arrived, they abandoned any such notion. The place was nearly the size of Picksbury with a stone castle, as the humans liked to construct, on some high ground. The town clustered around it, and even though it didn't have a defensive wall, the streets had been barricades and at least a few hundred armed men were defending them. To top it off, the castle and the bulk of the town was on the other side of the Rhor River. Aeron was very relieved that when Conwy Macsen arrived, he immediately saw that attacking the place would be far costlier than it could be worth. He ordered that any outlying farms or buildings be burned and the reassembled force should make camp about a mile to the west. With no tents or other baggage, this was a quick matter that just involved building some camp fires and finding a spot to throw down a blanket.

Fortunately, there was a chirurgeon with the main group, and they were able to get their wounded trooper treated, although he had to wait his turn as there had been other wounds and injuries suffered that day. One poor fellow had gotten a bit too enthusiastic about his arsonist activities and had badly burned both hands. Still, the total number was less than a dozen for the whole force, so the Shirelings were in a good mood that night, sharing tales of all they'd done to the 'damn humies'.

Aeron wanted to stay close to Gwenith but had to eat dinner with Einion and Guto to discuss the situation and the plans for the next day. They ate very well on various stolen - excuse me, *confiscated* - foodstuffs collected during the day, although the human ale always seemed very thin and watery. Afterward, they all sat on the ground, lit up their pipes, and puffed away in silence for a while.

"Does anyone else but me think this has been too damn easy?" said Guto after a while.

"The thought had occurred," said Einion. "Aeron, what do you think?"

Aeron puffed a few more times before answering. "It does seem strange we haven't run into more opposition. I mean, we know the Rhordians have most of their forces concentrated to the south, down by Eowulf, to watch the border near Hodenburg or up north by Torffs Valem to keep an eye on Yangmere, but I would have expected more in this area."

"Do you think they might be setting a trap?" asked Einion.

Aeron shrugged. "It's possible. Couriers could have reached the Eowulf forces by now, and if they moved tonight, they might be able to hit us in the morning if we're not careful."

"Or slip in between here and the border. Try to cut us off from home," said Guto.

"We'll have to keep a close watch tonight," said Einion.

But it seemed that they weren't the only ones who were getting nervous. Around midnight, messengers came from Conwy Macsen who told them to quietly wake their troops and get them ready to move out. They were told to keep their campfires burning. It took more than two hours to get everything ready in the dark, but by dawn, they were halfway back to the border. Scouts had been dispatched, but when they reported back, they said they'd seen nothing.

With no danger in sight, the bands spread out again and resumed their destruction. They also rounded up any cattle they could find and drove it ahead of them. By the time they reached the border around noon, they had several hundred of them.

There were hundreds of infantry waiting to welcome them back at the Erstford guardburg, and they reached their camp west of Ferchester well before dark. Everyone was in high spirits, and even Gwenith seemed to have shaken off her gloom. That night, Aeron shared a fire with Madoc and her.

"I still can't understand why there wasn't more opposition," said Aeron.

"Hey, don't look a gift aralez in the mouth, cousin," said Madoc. "If it was Rhordian stupidity or just plain good luck, I'll take either one."

"Can't argue with that. Except…"

"Except what?" asked Gwenith. "I can hear the wheels going around in your head. What are you thinking?"

"Well, stupidity or luck could certainly be possibilities, but there's one other possibility: they let us do it."

"What? Why would they let us burn a hundred of their farms if they could have stopped us?" asked Madoc.

"Maybe to get their people as riled up as we are."

"What do you mean?" asked Gwenith.

"So far, nearly all the killing and burning has been done by them. Not all the humans hate us, and with all the harm being done to us and the only harm being done back is higher prices on our goods and then the embargo, well, there could be sympathy building for is in the League. And maybe a lot of people who don't want a real war with the Shires. But now that we've done a lot of killing and burning ourselves..."

"That sympathy has probably vanished, and they now have an excuse for war," said Gwenith. "So you're saying they *did* set a trap for us, just not the kind we were worried about."

"I could be wrong, but if that was the trap they set, we walked right into it."

Chapter 13

Aeron had no way to know if his guess was right or wrong. After a day of rest, they returned to Picksbury to resume their training. They'd learned a lot of things during their first campaign, and they had to make sure those lessons stuck. More weapons training for sure, particularly shooting while mounted for their archers. The poor fellow who'd been hit by the mis-aimed arrow - and the even unluckier fellow who'd fired it - were made examples of the importance of accurate shooting.

Weapons drill took up about half of their days. The other half was spent on riding drills. Not just managing their mounts, they had progressed beyond that, but drills to practice using formations and quickly responding to horn signals from their commander. During their raid, small groups and individual troopers had gotten separated from the rest, and couriers had to be sent out to bring them back. There had also been problems with deploying the scouts and skirmishers or recalling them. It took too much time and was clumsily done. So they practiced, riding out from Picksbury and then deploying, recalling, changing directions, massing to the right or the left, all the things they needed to be able to do quickly and precisely in combat. A few more hornists were trained so that orders and signals could be quickly relayed from one part of the formation to another. By the end of a week, they were getting good at it.

More weapons and armor were arriving, too. Some of it came from the workshops in Picksbury, but a lot came from local farms, including from the Cadwallader farm. It was still a rather mismatched collection, and no one would ever mistake them for regulars by the looks of them, but they did look like soldiers now, not just a collection of eager bumpkins. Einion and Aeron were feeling pretty satisfied about it.

"Give us a few more weeks, and we'll be ready," said the captain.

Aeron didn't disagree, but he felt they needed far more real experience in the field. The deadline for the Assembly's response to the League had come and gone. He didn't know if any formal letter of rejection had been delivered, but surely the humans had already gotten the message. How would they responds? That was the question on everyone's lips.

At the end of the week, they finally got that whole day off they'd been hoping for, and Aeron rode home. He'd only been gone a bit more than two weeks, but it felt like months, and while he'd be happy to see his parents and siblings, his thoughts were mostly on Nesta. There had been a letter waiting for him when he got back to Picksbury, and he'd read it a dozen times in the following days, but he was terribly anxious to see her in person.

It wasn't all that far, and he didn't spare his pony. Wyn seemed nearly as eager as he was and was almost galloping by the time they turned into the familiar lane. His family knew he was coming, but they didn't know exactly when, so there was no big welcoming committee. His sister, Catrin, saw him first and ran screaming toward the house, announcing his arrival. By the time he brought Wyn to a halt, a crowd of people were swarming out of the house, out of the barn, and in from the fields.

The family gathered round, but they made a path for Nesta and her children, and they ran up and clutched him tight. All three of them. "Hey! Hey! I've only been gone a few weeks!" he laughed. "You're acting like you haven't seen me in years."

"It seems like years," said Nesta.

"We haven't *known* him for years, Mama," said Elin.

"But I want to," she whispered.

The presence of so many other people made any further conversation impractical, so Aeron looked around him and said: "It seems like you've been busy, too, while I was away. Look at this place. You could hold off an army now."

His father looked very pleased. "Yes, we managed to do all the things you were taking about. Platforms along the inside of the palisades to fight from, a ditch outside to make it harder for anyone to climb over, a proper gate, and we're turning out so many weapons we are giving the excess to neighbors and the people in Picksbury."

"Yes, my band has some of them. Well done, Da. Well done, all of you."

The welcome went on for a few more minutes, but then most of the well-wishers drifted off, back to their chores with promises to gather again for the noon meal. He and Nesta and the children strolled around the place with them pointing out all the changes to him. The amount of work done was really impressive, especially when he considered that all the normal work connected with running a farm still had to be done, too.

"Several of the other bigger farms in the area are being fortified, too," said Nesta. "If there is a raid, everyone will have a place to go."

"Good, that's good," said Aeron, remembering the destruction he and his troopers had inflicted on the humans. He had to admit that if their band had run into a place like this, they would have probably left it alone. But if they'd had a bigger force… he wasn't so sure.

Eventually, the children got bored and ran off and left Aeron and Nesta alone. "Missed you so much," he said to her.

"And I missed you," she replied. "I was so worried. Was… was it bad?"

"Bad enough. We didn't lose anyone, although a few were wounded, but… but we hurt a lot of people. Not soldiers, just people. Didn't like it much."

"I'm glad you didn't like it. Not sure I could love a person who did like that sort of thing." She pulled him closer and they kissed, not caring who might see them. When they stepped apart she said: "So what are we going to do?"

"Why don't we tell everyone when we meet for the noon meal?"

She smiled and nodded. "Good idea."

When all the local Cadwalladers, gathered in the big room of the house, had mostly finished eating, Aeron and Nesta got to their feet. "We'd like to announce something," he said. When he had everyone's attention he added: "I've asked Nesta to marry me."

"And I have accepted," said Nesta, face beaming.

Much applause followed with hugs, kisses on cheeks, and a great deal of hand-shaking and back-slapping. His mother came up to Aeron and hugged him tight and whispered in his ear: "Don't worry about your father, I've been working on him all the time you were away."

And indeed, when his father, who had held back from the other well-wishers, came forward, his face broke into a smile and he kissed Nesta and shook Aeron's hand. "All happiness to both of you," he said. "So when were you thinking to have the ceremony?"

Aeron looked at Nesta, but she seemed uncertain. "Not sure, Da. I'll be away a lot. I guess it would be better to wait until this is all over."

"That might be a while," said his father.

"Yes, it might. Well, I have to get back to the band first thing in the morning, so there's nothing we can do now. Why don't we see how things go and decide then?"

"Makes sense." His father paused and looked thoughtful. "But don't you worry while you're away. Even if…. If anything should happen… Bah, what I mean is, ceremony or no ceremony, Nesta and her children are part of the family now, and they'll be taken care of."

Nesta's eyes glistened with tears, and Aeron's throat was suddenly tight. "Thank you, sir. I truly appreciate that." Nesta gave the old man a hug which lasted quite a while.

Later, Elin and Gethin came up to them, Elin looking happy, but the boy had a wary expression on his face. "Does that mean you'll be my da now?"

"Well, your real da will always be your real da, gone though he is," said Aeron. "But I'm going to try to fill in for him best I can."

"And you'll make my mama happy?"

"I'll do my level best, Gethin, I promise."

The boy thought about that for a while and then nodded. "It's a deal."

Despite the betrothal, things still had to be kept 'proper,' so Aeron spent the night alone in his bed, alone in his bedroom. What would it be like to have someone share his bed; share his life? It was a tantalizing mystery that he looked forward to discovering the answer to.

He had to be back in camp in time for morning rollcall, so he was up before the dawn to have breakfast and say his goodbyes. "If nothing bad happens, I might be able to do this every week," he said as he climbed atop Wyn. "If I can't make it back, I'll write. You write back, too, all right?"

Nesta nodded but didn't seem to be able to say anything. She just squeezed his hand and nodded. And then he was off. The trip back to Picksbury went quickly, his thoughts somewhere else entirely.

Training resumed. There were a few grumblers, but everyone knew that it was only a matter of time before the Rhordians came again, and it might not be much time before they did. The Picksbury Light horse was shaping up nicely with everyone better equipped and better trained every day.

Aeron noticed that Gwenith seemed more focused and less light-hearted than before. She hadn't been much of an archer, but she now spent many hours at the butts, firing and retrieving hundreds of arrows. He gave her what help he could, using his favorite weapon. She often cut her dinner short to spend more time practicing until the light faded. Aeron suspected that she was thinking that it might be easier to kill someone from a distance than close up. Maybe she was right; Aeron didn't know. He wasn't going to say anything, and in any case, good archers were always needed.

A week passed with no attacks, but Rhordian cavalry patrols on their side of the border were dense and aggressive; scouting parties from the Shires had no luck penetrating them, and there were a few sharp skirmishes when they tried. "They must be planning something," said Einion. "Something they don't want us to see before they let it loose."

A few days later, Aeron got a real surprise. It was during the noon meal break from another day of training when one of the troopers came trotting up. "Lieutenant? Lieutenant? You've got a coupla dwarfs asking to see you? Should I let 'em in the camp?"

"Dwarfs?"

"Yeah, two big strong ones, beards an' all."

Intrigued, Aeron got up from the stool he'd been sitting on - their camp was much better outfitted with conveniences these days - and followed the fellow to the edge of camp where, indeed, two dwarf-like figures were waiting. "Who in the world…? *Vadik! Hagen!*" He could scarcely believe it, it was his two old comrades from the College of Warcraft! He ran forward and barely restrained himself from hugging them.

"Well, thank the gods, there you are, at last," said Vadik. "Thought we'd never track you down. But it's good to see you, Aeron." He stuck out his arm and they shook in dwarf fashion, grasping the forearm of the other. Aeron turned and did the same with Hagen.

"Nice to see you… *Lieutenant*," grinned Hagen. "Come up in the world a bit, have you?"

"A bit. But what are you doing here? Have you… have you left the College?"

"Yes, we stuck it out for a few months after you left, but it turned impossible," replied Vadik, all the cheer leaving his face. "The harassment and abuse just got worse and worse. Finally, Hagen had enough and pummeled one of the twits. He was given the choice of leaving or facing charges. I wasn't going to stay if he left, so we both did. Things were getting bad for our families in the town by then, so we all upped and pulled out."

"I'm sorry it came to that," said Aeron. "But are you families here with you? My home isn't far, I'd be honored to put you up there for a while."

Vadik shook his head. "No, we aren't staying. Our families are in a town off to the west, beyond the border. Harg, I think it's called. We couldn't come straight here because the League has your southern border sealed up tight and isn't letting anyone in or out. We snuck in from the west, although they have some patrols even out that way."

"If you aren't staying, why'd you come so far out of your way? I mean I'm pleased to see you and all, but you could have sent a message or something and saved yourself a good many steps. Where are you going, anyway?"

"Our plan is to head back east to our ancestral lands. Our grandsires left there to get away from all the fighting, but it seems like you can't run far enough to ever get away from hatred. But as for why we're here, it's to warn you."

"Warn me? About what?"

"The League is massing its forces around Eowulf. They're pullin' in almost everything they've got, it seems like. They're gonna hit you hard, lad, very hard."

Aeron nodded grimly. "That's what we were fearing. Any idea when?"

"Soon, I'd think. They're havin' trouble feeding the great host they've assembled. I'm sure they want to come up here and dine at your expense as soon as they can."

"Thank you both for coming here to tell me. I'll pass this along to our leaders right away."

"Least we could do for an old comrade," said Hagen.

Speaking of old comrades… Aeron asked a question near to his heart: "How… how was Palle doing before you left?"

Vadik shook his head. "He was right depressed for a while after they kicked you out. The others kept taunting him for a while until they switched all their attention to us. He seemed like he was pulling out of it about the time we left. He's damn angry at all that's been going on, but he's a lot tougher than he looks. He should be all right except…"

"Except what?"

"They were going to mobilize the 1st and 2nd Companies at the College and send them off with the army as junior officers. We could tell he was really disturbed at the thought of facing off against you on the field."

"Damn," muttered Aeron. It *was* a disturbing notion, the more so because he'd never even thought of the possibility. Very disturbing.

"There was one other thing, Aeron," said Hagen. "When we were leaving the College, that stinkin' Headmaster Jannik came to the gate to see us off—gloating he was. A couple of our kin were there to help carry our stuff. One of them, our Uncle Dagfin, has done a lot of traveling in his time. He's gone all over the place doing trading or crafting; one time he even took up with a band of mercenaries and…"

"Get to the point, Hagen," said Vadik.

"Oh, right. Well, one time, maybe ten years ago, he was down south on the other side of the Dragonteeth Mountains, he was in Valentica. There was some sort of to-do going on there, it was when that Lord Darvled succeeded his father when he died. Anyway, Lord Darvled was in a procession through the city with all his main vassals riding with him, and Uncle Dagfin swears that Headmaster Jannik was one of them!"

"Are you sure?" asked Aeron. "All these humans look alike, y'know." He tried to make it a joke, but Hagen said:

"He was sure. He has a real head for names and faces. He sees a person once, and he never forgets."

"Huh. I wonder how Jannik ended up in Eowulf?"

"They say he was an advisor to the Duke of Hetronburg for a few years before they gave him his new job," said Vadik. "With all that's happened, you have to wonder just what sort of advice he was giving him."

"Yeah…" Aeron tried to sort it all out in his head but couldn't seem to make any sense of it. But then he remembered his manners. "Have you eaten? You're not going to start back to Harg today are you?"

"No, what with dodging Rhordian patrols, it's a four day walk each way. So yes, we'd be happy to break bread with you and have a talk."

"Splendid! Come on, I'll introduce you to my captain."

But the following hours were anything but calm or relaxing. Once Captain Einion learned who Aeron's guests were and what they had to tell, he sent a fast courier off to Hodenburg, and by dinnertime, the Muster-Master himself had arrived to talk with them. They talked and ate and drank and smoked far into the evening while Rootwell drained every last detail of the Rhordian army out of them. It was grim listening.

"So ten or twelve thousands in all, you reckon?" asked Rootwell.

"I'd say so," replied Vadik. "But they say there's more coming from the other duchies. And that doesn't include the Eowulf city guards, although I doubt they'd be coming at you."

"Do you know who's in command? The five dukes have generally rotated who would command the field armies."

"We heard that it was the Duke of Hetronburg, but I can't swear to it," said Vadik.

"Siege engines?"

"Didn't see any out in the fields where they were camped, so I don't think the incoming contingents brought any. But there is the arsenal in the city and the College workshops. There could be a load of stuff there. We did hear a rumor that their mercenary company of ogres is *not* going along. Seems the Duke wants them there to keep order in the city."

"Warmages?"

Vadik shrugged. "No way to tell. They'd be staying at the College or be guests of the Duke. Won't know who's coming until the army moves out."

Rootwell looked grim. The Shires had very few who could wield magic of any sort and even fewer with the skills for battlefield magic. It would be a big disadvantage.

"And this Jannik, you're sure he was one of Darvled's men?"

"As sure as we can be. My uncle was sure. And that was ten years ago; no telling who he really works for now."

Rootwell shook his head. "I've met him a few times during meetings with the dukes over the years. Never said much. A damn cold fish, actually. Huh." He sucked on his pipe for a while and finally nodded. "I want to thank you two gentlemen for coming all this way to pass along the warning. I truly appreciate it." He turned to Einion. "Captain, I think our guests deserve a carriage and an escort to get them back where they want to be, don't you?"

"Indeed, yes, sir," said Einion. His eyes turned to Aeron. "You can arrange all that, can't you, Lieutenant? You'll command the escort."

"Yes, sir," said Aeron. "I'll make the arrangements at once, and we can be away before dawn."

"Thank you, sir," said Vadik. "We wish you all the luck there is in your coming trials."

And with that, the meeting ended. Rootwell hurried off, back to Hodenburg to make whatever preparations he could. Aeron found cots for the two dwarfs when they refused to be taken to an inn in Picksbury. Aeron scurried around to get the carriage arranged—the dwarfs not willing to ride a pony - and alerted one of the troops to be ready to move before dawn. He finally was able to get a few hours sleep for himself.

Dawn found them a league west of Picksbury, hurrying down the road to Havencester. It was ten leagues from Picksbury to the border, and with a change of ponies for the carriage at Havencester, they should reach the guardburg by late afternoon. They planned to stop and rest there until about midnight and then take to the road again hoping to get past any patrols in the dark.

"We could take you all the way to Harg, if you like," offered Aeron as he trotted alongside the carriage on Wyn.

"No, I'd rather you didn't," said Vadik. "No one's bothered us so far, but I'm not sure what would happen if people saw we were traveling with halfling soldiers. If word reached a Rhordian patrol, they might come scoop us up for questioning. Just take us as far as you can before dawn and we'll walk the rest of the way."

"All right. I don't like just dumping you out on the road, but you are probably right: secrecy is best."

They spent the rest of the ride talking about old times and recounting the good moments at the College, of which there were many. Jokes and pranks and some good fellowship. How had they lost all of that? It left Aeron feeling very sad over what might have been.

They reached the guardburg at the border, and Aeron talked to the commander about what had been going on in the area. He reported nothing but routine patrols by small groups of Rhordian cavalry. He let his troopers and the ponies rest, and after it got dark, he tried to get some sleep, but not quite trusting the commander to wake him at midnight he slept only fitfully.

When he was shaken awake, the moon was shining brightly overhead. It was just past the full and would lend enough light to travel quickly, but hopefully not enough to make them too noticeable from a distance.

They took to the road and moved along as fast as they could, eyes peeled for signs of enemy scouts or campfires. There were some farms on either side, and they aroused a few barking dogs, but nothing worse than that. "How much before dawn do you want to be let off?" Aeron asked the dwarfs.

"Coming the other way, there was a little pine woods near the road about five leagues from the border," replied Vadik. "We traveled mostly by night and we stayed there the day before we made our dash to reach the Shires. It ought to work just as well going the other way. Let us off there and we'll sleep through the day and then do a hard march the next night. That will put us far enough from the border that no one will take any interest in us."

They encountered no one on the road, and just as the moon was setting and the faintest streak of dawn could be seen in the east, they came upon the little wood, smelling faintly of pine in the dewy night. There was no time for a long goodbye, so Aeron embraced his friends and simply said *Thank you and good luck* to them both. They returned the farewell and quickly slipped off the road and disappeared among the trees. Something told Aeron that they would not meet again. He rubbed his eyes and swung aboard Wyn and said: "All right, let's get away from here before anyone spots us."

They made it back to the guardburg a bit after noon. They had seen a few people and what might have been a cavalry patrol off to the south, but they did not come near. Aeron let his people and their animals rest for the remainder of the day, and that night, and he slept like the dead. The next morning, they set a good pace that would not exhaust riders or their mounts and got back to their camp in Picksbury around dinner time.

As they got close, one of the lead riders shouted back to him: "Lieutenant? Somethin's goin' on!"

He spurred Wyn forward and saw what his trooper was talking about. There was a great deal of activity in their camp. Some of the tents had been taken down and looked like the people were packing up. He told the sergeant of the troops to take everyone to where they belonged and then he galloped straight to the headquarters area. He caught sight of Einion. "Captain!" he shouted. "What's happening?"

Einion looked up and saw him and an expression of relief passed over his face. "There you are, Aeron! I was afraid we'd have to go before you got back!"

"Go? Go where?" He reined in Wyn and hopped off. "What's happened?"

"A courier arrived this afternoon from Hodenburg. The League is attacking the guardburgs along the southern border in strength. They're holding out for now but desperately need help. The Muster-Master is ordering everyone south to Hodenburg for a counterattack. We'll be leaving before dawn."

"Missing Gods," hissed Aeron. "It's beginning."

"Aye, it certainly is."

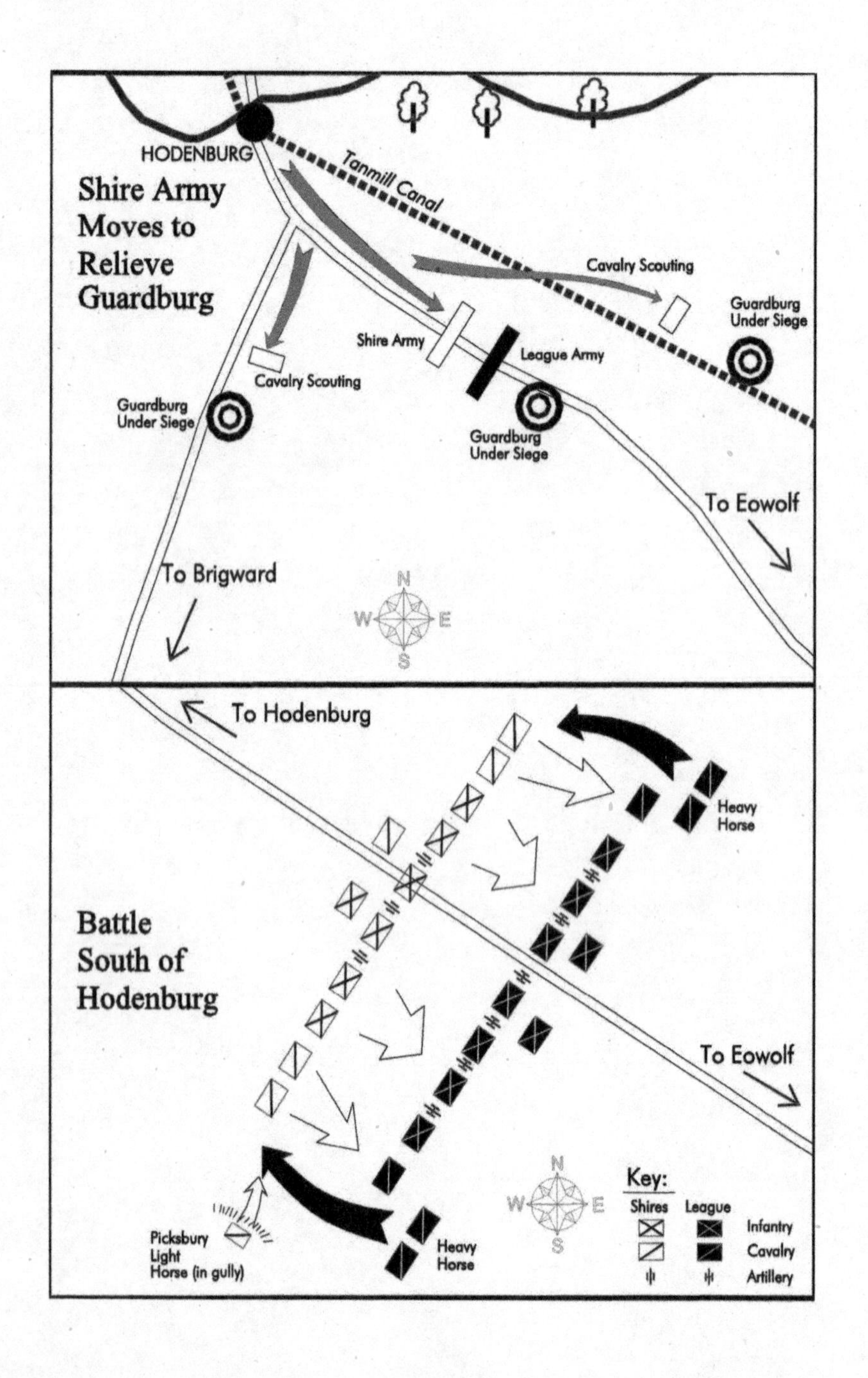
HODENBURG
Shire Army Moves to Relieve Guardburg
Tanmill Canal
Cavalry Scouting
Guardburg Under Siege
Shire Army
League Army
Cavalry Scouting
Guardburg Under Siege
Guardburg Under Siege
To Eowolf
To Brigward
N
W
E
S
To Hodenburg
Heavy Horse
Battle South of Hodenburg
To Eowolf
Key:
Shires
League
Infantry
Cavalry
Artillery
Picksbury Light Horse (in gully)
Heavy Horse

Chapter 14

The force that moved out from Picksbury looked pretty impressive as the sun rose to greet it. Close to two hundred and fifty in the Light Horse and nearly a thousand infantry, along with a modest baggage train. The infantry consisted of Picksbury's regular trained band, a new one which had been training just as the Light Horse had, and a third made of eager volunteers who had just shown up the previous day wanting to help out. How much use they would be with no training and only the sketchiest organization was debatable. Well, they could chop wood and draw water if nothing else. Word had it that several more bands would be coming from Havencester, Havam, and other regions to the north, but they weren't going to wait for them; they would have to catch up as best they could.

It was only three leagues from Picksbury to Hodenburg, so even allowing for Shirelings' marching paces, they expected to arrive that afternoon. The pace was a good one for infantry but quite slow for the cavalry. At Aeron's suggestion, Captain Einion used the time practicing deployments from march column into line and also sending out individual troops as scouts and flankers and then recalling them again using their horn calls. They were getting pretty good at it, and their activities drew the admiration of the foot-soldiers.

He kept his eye on Gwenith, but she seemed to be in good spirits; joking with Madoc and some of the others. Overall, morale was high and Aeron did nothing to dampen it, but privately, he was worried. If the entire force Vadik and Hagen had talked about was on the border, things could get very bad.

By noon, Hodenburg was in sight, only a few miles ahead. Aeron peered at it, shading his eyes with his hand. He had not seen the capital for over two months, and he was amazed at the changes. It seemed as though someone had read his mind when he had mused on the best way of fortifying the place. The outer ring of buildings now had stockades connecting them to form a solid wall enclosing the city. As he got closer, he could see that the outward facing walls of those buildings had been reinforced. Where roads entered the place, there were stout gatehouses. At intervals around the ring, wooden towers had been erected.

Outside the walls, a few of the buildings seemed to have been torn down to give clear lines of fire for the defenders. There were camps filled with tents outside as well, and the camps were filled with troops. Madoc whistled.

"What do you think, cousin? Five or six thousands?"

"Maybe. Hard to tell for sure."

"But a lot, right?"

"Oh yes, a lot." *But will it be enough?*

The head of their column was met by a rider who directed them to an area west of the town where they were to set up their camps. As they approached, they heard a faint rumble from off to the south. "Thunder?" said Madoc. "The skies are clear."

"We almost never get a thunderstorm at this time of year," added Gwenith.

"That's not thunder," said Aeron. "It's cannons."

"Missing Gods," said Madoc. "The guardburgs won't last long against that! If we're gonna help, we'll need to move right away."

"No they won't, and yes we will. You're learning, cousin."

But in spite of the ominous sounds, they didn't move right away. Dunstan Rootwell, the Muster-Master, was waiting for a few more trained bands to arrive, and then the army would march first thing the next morning. "It's six leagues to the guardburg on the Eowulf Road," said Aeron to Captain Einion. "The infantry can't do that in one day. The Rhordians will know we are coming and be ready."

"What else can we do, Aeron? The guardburgs were all reinforced, we can't leave those people to fend for themselves."

"No, I suppose not…"

"And you can bet they'll have us and the other cavalry out in front scouting for the army. You tell everyone to get as much rest as they can tonight - I expect we'll have a long day tomorrow."

* * * *

The next day brought one exasperating delay after another, and it was nearly noon before the Shires Army lurched into motion. It took more than an hour to get the whole column on the road, even though they were taking very little baggage. They had left their camps set up in the hopes that they'd be able to come back to them when the fighting was done. As near as Aeron could guess, there were four or five thousand infantry and close to three thousand cavalry. But except for one small band of armored cavalry which stayed with the main column, all the cavalry was light. The infantry likewise had very few units with any significant armor. Still, they had a lot of archers, which was a good thing. But there were only four light cannons being hauled by straining oxen, and as far as Aeron knew, no magic users. They could be certain that the enemy had far more artillery and at least some war mages, and they were surely going to do some serious damage when they got into action.

As Einion had said, the bulk of the light cavalry was spread out in a screen in front of the army to scout ahead and prevent any surprises. The Picksbury Light Horse was sent off to the right end of the screen, and when they reached the fork in the road that led off to Brigward, one of the Young Kingdoms to the southwest, they followed it toward the guardburg to see if anything was happening there. It was about four leagues off, and they picked up their pace, passing farms and windmills at a good clip. Some of those farms and windmills had been destroyed during the earlier raids, and the sights left everyone grim and angry. They reached the guardburg about mid-afternoon. All that time, there had been periodic rumbles from the direction of the other guardburg on the Eowulf Road, but nothing coming from ahead of them.

When they came into sight of the Brigward Road Guardburg, however, they saw that the Rhordians were already there. They halted about a mile away, on a slight rise, and took a long look. The guardburg, itself, appeared intact, but it was surrounded by human troops. Not a lot, maybe a thousand or so, mostly infantry, with maybe a hundred cavalry. They weren't attacking, they simply had the place invested.

When the Rhordians spotted the Light Horse, their cavalry came toward them, but then halted, apparently unwilling to attack the larger force of Shirelings. "So what do you think, Aeron?" asked Einion.

"Well, we're not going to relieve them by ourselves. But the Rhordians don't appear to be eager to attack the 'burg. Probably waiting for the big army to finish off the one on the Eowulf Road and then they'll come and take this one."

"But with only a hundred cavalry, these aren't any threat to our force," said Einion. "I'm going to leave one troop here to keep an eye on them with orders to send a messenger if anything happens. The rest of us should be getting back to report this to Rootwell."

"A good plan, sir," said Aeron. And it was; he was impressed.

The captain detached one troop with very precise instructions and then turned the rest of them around and headed eastward across the Golden Fields toward where the army ought to be stopping for the night.

It was starting to get dark by the time they arrived. The army had made camp maybe three miles from the guardburg, just out of sight of it behind a low ridge. They were directed to an open field, which looked to have been recently planted with rye. They pitched no tents and only made a few fires and had guards posted all around. Aeron turned his pony over to Madoc to rub down and then went with Einion to a commanders' meeting that had been called. He wasn't surprised that Einion didn't ask Folant Guto to come along; by this time, Aeron was second in command in everything but name.

A small pavilion had been set up as headquarters, but it couldn't hold all the band commanders and other officers who were clustered about, so Rootwell stood near a fire and everyone else arranged themselves in front of him. The first thing he did was to demand reports from his cavalry about what they'd seen. He had the most interest for the report of the cavalry scouting the Rhordian main army directly ahead.

"There certainly are a lot of them, Dunstan," said the fellow, obviously an old friend of Rootwell. "Six, maybe seven thousand infantry, only about a thousand light cavalry in a screen facing us. Looked like their heavy cavalry was off further to the south. Couldn't get a good count on them. Maybe a half dozen cannon mostly to the south of the 'burg. I know it takes a long time to load one of those things, but they didn't seem to be firing very fast. We were watching for over an hour, and I don't think they fired more than twice each."

"Any magic?" asked Rootwell.

"None that we could see. No fireballs or lightning or flashy stuff we couldn't miss. Anything more subtle… well, who knows?"

"But the 'burg is holding out?"

"Yes. We could see some places where the palisade had been damaged, and the new tower they'd build was all smashed up, but we could see our people still holding."

Rootwell then asked Einion for his report, and he accurately told of what they'd seen of the Brigward Road Guardburg. The commander of the cavalry scouting on the left end of the line then reported that the situation at the Tanmill Canal Guardburg was exactly the same: the place was surrounded but not under attack.

The Muster-Master was silent for a while but finally nodded. "We will attack in the morning." A sinking feeling grew in Aeron's stomach as they discussed the method by which they would attack. The plan that was developed was entirely conventional with the infantry massed in the center and the cavalry on both wings. It boiled down to going straight at the enemy and seeing what happened. How many battles had they studied at the College of Warcraft that were like that? Far too many. And in nearly every case, the army that was bigger or had better trained troops or better equipment prevailed. *The Rhordians have all of that.*

Speaking up at that moment was probably the hardest thing Aeron had ever done, but he simply could not remain silent with so much at stake. He waited until there was a tiny pause in the flow of words and then said: "Commander Rootwell, may I say something?"

"What? Oh, it's you, Cadwallader. You have something to add?"

"Uh, yes, sir. Sir, I think that to attack as we are proposing here will lead to defeat, if not an outright disaster." He swallowed and looked at all the eyes staring at him. *It's in the fire now...*

Rootwell did not answer immediately, but Captain Conwy Macsen did. The fellow who had led the cavalry force that came to the rescue of the wagon train had not changed much since the last time Aeron had seen him. "Oh you think so, do you, Cadwallader? Learned that at that damned college of yours, did you? Well, there's a lot more to fighting than a bunch of books! And here you are, a wet-behind-the-ears... *child!* Daring to question the judgment of a soldier who was winning battles before you were born!" There was a general growl of agreement from the others until Rootwell held up his hand.

"Easy, Conwy. Cadwallader might be young, but I've seen that he's no fool. Let him have his say." He nodded at Aeron to go ahead. He was sweating, despite the cool night, but he forged ahead.

"Thank you, sir. The plan that's been put forward wouldn't be a bad one against an enemy of equal strength, or if we could catch a stronger foe by surprise. But we know the Rhordians are stronger, and they know we are coming. In fact, I'm sure they were counting on us coming. With their cannons, they could have taken that guardburg two days ago if they'd wanted. The only reason it's still standing is because they want us to come to its relief. They want to fight us in the open field - make us *attack* in the open field - rather than have to attack us in our defenses at Hodenburg. They have set a trap, and we are walking right into it."

A number of the watching eyes got wider, reflecting the firelight, but others grew angrier more dismissive. "So you'd just abandon our kin in the guardburg and run back to Hodenburg like a pack of whipped dogs?" demanded one. Others made similar comments. A few of the comments got downright nasty, until Rootwell again gestured for silence.

"Interesting points, Cadwallader. But criticism is easy. What would you have us do instead?"

Yes, that was the truth of it: It was no good trying to dismiss one plan if you didn't have another to take its place. He'd been thinking about that all afternoon. A plan had started to materialize, but it wasn't complete in his head… until now.

"Well?" asked Macsen. "What grand design do *you* have to offer?"

Now or never. "We are doing exactly what they expect us to. They are ready and waiting. So instead we need to do something they *don't* expect."

"Like what?"

"The… the forces they have encircling the two other guardburgs, on the Brigward Road and the canal. They are probably there just to keep our garrisons from escaping until they can deal with them in strength. They don't expect a fight - so let's give them one. This night - right now - we send off all of our cavalry in two groups. Hit them just before dawn. Smash both of those forces and relieve the garrisons. The rest of the army falls back to Hodenburg and the cavalry rejoins them there. We whittle them down by a couple of thousands and then force them to come and attack us on ground of our own choosing."

"And abandon the garrison in the guardburg here?"

"They would have to surrender, yes, but we'd take twice as many humans prisoner, and we could make a trade to get them back. If we attack here and fail, we'll lose them all the same, with nothing to bargain with to get them back."

There was a long silence, and for a moment, Aeron had hope that they might actually listen to him, but then people started bringing up objections, and in moments, the tide had turned decidedly against him. A few, including Rootwell, were clearly thinking about what he had said, but in the end, the original plan was decided upon and the meeting broke up.

As they walked back to their camp, Einion said: "I think I agree with you, Aeron. Not so sure about your alternate attack plan, we'd only have about fifteen hundred cavalry against those forces around the guardburgs, but a direct attack like their planning seem like sticking your heads in the dragon's mouth. But what can we do?"

Aeron shrugged. "Follow our orders."

* * * * *

Aeron slept very little that night, and the wake-up call came well before dawn. He was tired but so keyed-up he didn't really notice it. He helped rouse the troops and get ready for a day that promised a desperate battle. Their position would again be on the right of the army.

In one concession to Aeron's warning about doing exactly what the enemy was expecting, the orders were to get formed up and start the advance while it was still dark, hoping perhaps, to catch the enemy at breakfast. But just as when the army marched from Hodenburg, there were the inevitable delays, and it was fully light by the time the army topped the ridge screening them from the enemy. The distance between the two forces also took longer to cover than they'd hoped, the deployed troops having to cross the fences and stone walls enclosing the fields of the farms that dotted the area. The enemy was ready and waiting by the time they closed to a half-mile.

The Rhordian Army was stretched out in a line that looked to be about three-quarters of a mile long. They stood between the Shires Army and the guardburg which was perhaps another mile to the rear. There appeared to be human troops still keeping the garrison contained. The center of the enemy army was composed of solid blocks of infantry with a few gaps between them in which cannons or catapults were placed. There was light cavalry on either flank, but not all that much; it seemed that was the one area where the Shire-folk had an advantage.

"Where are their heavy cavalry?" asked Aeron as he looked over the Rhordian positions.

Gwenth, who was riding Fluffy a short distance away, peered forward. "I can see a bunch of horses back behind their light cavalry, but there's no one riding them." Aeron looked closer and thought he could see the dark mass Gwenith was talking about. "Looks like they are dismounted and just holding their horses," she said. "Why would they do that?"

"To try to keep us from seeing them." He swiveled in his saddle to look to the northeast, toward the other flank of the enemy army. "I'll bet there's another batch of them over there."

"We can take that light cavalry in front of us," said Madoc, "but if there's a thousand heavy horse right behind them…"

As Aeron continued to look at the masses in front of him, a chill went down his spine and settled in his belly. *Missing Gods! It's the Battle of Hal-man's Farm all over again!* The classic battle that led to the formation of the League of Rhordia that they had studied at the College seemed to be laid out before him like a map in a textbook. A solid line of infantry in the center, wait-ing to draw in the enemy and then strong cavalry on either wing, ready at the right moment, to charge out and curve around the enemy flanks to encircle and destroy them. *And we're marching right into the trap!*

He jerked the reins of his pony and galloped over to where Captain Einion was riding. He quickly pointed out the situation and his fears for what was going to happen. Einion's face paled and then he said: "What can we do?"

"Get a messenger off to Rootwell to warn him. I don't know if he'll heed it or not, but we have to try. In the meantime, we need to take ourselves farther out to the right."

"Farther? But that will mean leaving a gap between us and the rest of the cavalry."

"I know, but then when the Rhordian heavy horse comes on, we'll be in a position to hit *them* in the flank. We won't be able to stop them, but if we can delay them long enough, the army might be able to escape."

"But we have our orders…"

"Orders that don't make sense anymore, sir. If I'm wrong, we still have enough light cavalry on this flank to handle the Rhordian lights. If I'm right and those heavies come on, it won't make any difference if we're here or not. Look sir, there's a gully over there on the right, a half mile away. We head over there, and they won't be able to see us, and maybe we can strike with surprise."

Einion looked very unhappy, but after a moment, he nodded his head and his expression became firm. "All right, I'll tell Guto what to say to Rootwell and send him off. You get the band heading toward that gully. I'll rejoin you shortly."

"Right away!"

Aeron found the nearest rider with a horn and had him blow the 'change direction to the right' horn call and blessed all the training they'd done because the band understood what it meant and did it. The band, which had been in a line facing the enemy, now wheeled into a column and picked up the pace to a canter and rapidly shifted to the right. Aeron thought he heard a cry from the next unit over demanding to know where they were going, but he ignored it.

They rode about a half-mile and then descended into the gully, and the opposing armies disappeared from view. He had no doubt that the Rhordians had seen them come over here, but he hoped none of them had worried about a few hundred light cavalry riding off, apparently out of the fight. He halted and dismounted and carefully crept up to the lip of the gully where he could see out. Captain Einion was riding up, and after leaving his horse in the gully, joined him. "Guto wasn't happy," he said.

"I expect not. D'you think he'll be able to get to Rootwell?"

"He'll try. So what's our plan?"

His reply was interrupted by a series of loud booms, one coming on the heels of the other. The Rhordian cannons had opened fire. Puffs of white smoke billowed up and hung in the still air. He thought that perhaps he could hear a few screams from the Shireling lines where the heavy iron balls had torn bloody gashes through the lines.

The Shires Army didn't falter, and the distance between the lines grew less and less. Aeron clenched his fists and muttered through gritted teeth: "Come on, Rootwell, don't be a fool! Don't give them what they want!"

He didn't.

Horns rang out and the army halted, still five hundred yards short of the enemy. Aeron let out his breath. Or at least a good chunk of the army halted. The spear-armed infantry halted and dressed their ranks, but the archers continued forward, not in neat formations, but in a swarm. They scampered forward at a run until they were just in range of the Rhordian lines and then let loose. Nearly half the Shirefolk had bows, and volley after volley, several thousand arrows in each, rained down on the enemy. The humans had archers, but not as many, and their targets were small and elusive. They had some troops with muskets, too, and these banged away, producing little puffs of smoke, but it was very long range for that sort of weapon. The light cavalry on the wings also rode up into range of their opposite numbers and began shooting but did not try to close.

For all the shooting going on, not many were falling on either side. The Rhordians had armor and large shields they could shelter behind, and the

Shirefolk were small, quick, and agile. Still, men and Shirelings - and horses and ponies - were going down. After a few minutes, the enemy cannons roared out again. Aeron thought he could see bits of...*something*...flying up from the freindly lines, but he didn't want to know what. After a while, the Shirelings' own small cannons managed to catch up, unlimber, and began to reply, flinging iron ball dangerously over the heads of their own archers to smash into the blocks of closely packed Rhordians.

This went on for quite a while, longer then Aeron would have expected, until the volume of fire began to diminish a bit; the shooters getting tired or running low on ammunition. "Why aren't they attacking?" asked Einion.

"They wanted to pull us all the way in, get our forces fully engaged, before they turned their heavies loose. But they are going to get tired of this pretty soon. Look, I think something's happening now." Mounted couriers were spreading out from a central point - probably wherever the commanders were - and heading off to pass on orders to the waiting units of the human army. Nothing happened immediately, but when a quarter-hour had passed, suddenly horns began blaring and flags were waved back and forth and things started to move.

The infantry blocks came forward, marching slowly but steadily to keep their formations aligned. Aeron could see some of the human gunners standing down; they wouldn't risk firing with their own troops in the way. On the flank closest to Aeron, the Rhordian light cavalry abandoned its long range archery duel and started forward at a brisk pace to engage the Shires cavalry facing them. And yes, the mass of horses Gwen had first spotted were indeed the missing heavy cavalry. The armored riders hoisted themselves onto their chargers and began their advance. He couldn't see what was happening on the opposite flank, but he was quite certain it was the same over there.

"Get ready!" he shouted back to the troopers in the gully. "Don't mount until I signal, but be ready to move!" The timing here was going to be every bit as vital as when he turned the oxen loose defending the wagon train. That seemed like a very long time ago now. Peering out from his spot, Aeron tried to take it all in, tried to spot that 'Critical Moment' his instructors had talked about.

As the Rhordian infantry advanced, the halfling archers fell back but continued to fire. More of the humans fell to this fire than before, because while moving, they couldn't keep their shields as carefully positioned to deflect arrows, but it did not stop their advance. The human light cavalry surged forward to engage their opposite numbers. Normally the Shires lights would have fallen back before them, but it seemed that they somehow understood what was happening and knew they had to hold. The fact that they outnumbered the humans by three to two probably helped them make that decision. They continued to fire their arrows until the enemy was just a furlong off, and then they launched their own counter-charge.

The two masses of cavalry smashed into each other, riders and mounts went down, and the formations dissolved into a swirling melee. The Rhordian heavy horse was coming now, sunlight reflecting off breastplates and helmets and lance tips. They weren't as colorful as they'd been at the Great Muster, where they and their mounts wore their fanciest livery, but they still looked imposing and deadly. Big men on big horses, heavily armed and armored, they could smash through any force of light cavalry foolish enough to meet them head on. But at the moment, the cavalry in front of them was a mixture of friend and foe. Not wanting to risk killing friends - and probably not wanting to spend their deadly momentum on some trivial target - the heavies swept wider to their left, probably thinking to swing completely around the fighting lights and then turn to smash in on the flank of the Shires infantry and crush them. But to do that, their own left flank would come within a few furlongs of the gully where the Picksbury Light Horse was waiting…

Perfect!

Or as perfect as this horrible situation could come. They just had to wait a little longer… "Aeron?" asked Einion. "Shouldn't we go now?"

"Almost… just let them get a little farther… so their flank is completely exposed… *Now!"*

He turned and screamed: "Mount up!" The troopers were ready and waiting, and they were up on their ponies and aralez in an instant. Aeron leapt onto Wyn's back, grabbed the reins, and took up his spear. A few more moments passed while they got their ranks straightened and then Aeron pointed at a hornist and he gave the signal to advance. Neither he nor anyone else seemed to question that Aeron was giving the orders now and not Einion.

The band surged up out of the gully and immediately started to canter. The left flank of the Rhordian heavy horse was ahead of them and a bit to their left. They would hit them not just on the flank, but in the rear as well. Aeron had the hornist sound the charge, and they broke into a gallop. "Ram it home! Give them everything you've got!" The troopers began to cheer.

Only now did the Rhordian heavy cavalry seem to notice them. Heads began to turn in their direction, and then their ordered ranks started to come apart as they tried to face this unexpected threat. But unlike an infantryman, a horse is a lot longer than it is wide, and in the knee-to-knee formation of heavy cavalry, it was simply impossible to turn a horse quickly. The Light Horse were on them before they could barely begin.

The distance closed with terrifying suddenness, and Aeron found himself heading right toward a human rider. The man wore a breastplate, but no backplate, and Aeron's spear punched right through the leather gambeson and into the man's lower back. The human screamed and reeled forward and slumped in his saddle; there was no room for him to fall. Wyn smashed into the rump of the man's charger and came to a sudden halt, nearly unseating Aeron.

All around him, similar scenes were unfolding as the Light Horse took full advantage of their position. Dozens of humans were killed or wounded in the first collision. The whole formation of heavy horse fell apart into a milling throng, all thoughts of advancing now gone as they tried to turn on the enemy savaging their rear.

Aeron wrenched his spear out of his first target and looked for another. There were plenty close by, but everything was in motion, and many of the Rhordians were succeeding in turning around. He thrust at one rider but had his blow deflected by a shield. A lance swung down at him like a club, and he blocked it with his own shield. Many of the Rhordians were realizing their long lances were useless in this sort of close-quarters melee and tossed them aside and drew swords or axes. The shorter Shireling spears were still useable and gave them a reach advantage, which they used to deadly effect. Aeron thrust again, and this time, his spear was batted aside by the man's sword. But an instant later, some friend's spear got through and struck the human right in the face, toppling him out of his saddle.

Off to his right, he saw Gwenith atop Fluffy and realized the aralez had one further advantage over a horse besides their teeth: they could *jump.* Gwenith was trading blows with a human when Fluffy suddenly sprang upward, propelled by his powerful hind legs, and knocked the human completely off his horse and landed right on top of him on the other side. And then he did it again to another one.

Shouts and screams, the neighing of horses, and the clash of metal all mingled into one horrendous sound. Any hope of passing orders or trying to control things was gone. It was just down to the skill and grit of the people involved. The Shirelings had grit, there was no doubt of that, but the enemy was getting over their surprise and bringing their superior training, equipment, numbers, and *size* to bear.

The Picksbury Light Horse were forced back, step by step. Not as quickly as they might have because, as Aeron could see through the jostling mass of horsemen, some of the other Shires light cavalry had disentangled itself from the Rhordian lights to actually join the fight against the heavy horse, forcing them to fight in two direction. But even with that help, the fight was quickly turning against them. Their weapons were nearly useless now against the armored fronts of the Rhordians, and their own leather armor and wooden shields could not take much punishment. Trooper after trooper fell and the line started to give way. The large warhorses of the Rhordians were another advantage they had. The beasts were trained to fight in a melee like this; kicking and biting. Wyn, jerked back as he took a nip.

A strange crackling sound rippled through the air, and it was followed by a loud boom of thunder. A moment later, a blazing ball of flame flashed out from the Rhordian lines and hit somewhere among the Shires army. Yes, this was the last straw, the Rhordian war mages were unleashing their powers. Things could not hold out much longer. The main battle line was breaking up, troops starting to flee to the rear. Was there any way he could pull his people out of here while there was anything left? He glanced around frantically, looking for inspiration.

Shifting his attention was a mistake. The Rhordian closest to him saw the opening and lashed out with his broadsword. The blade didn't actually hit him, but it hooked his shield and tore it away, snapping the leather straps, and very nearly dislocating his shoulder. The blade swept up for another blow, and he had no hope of dodging it.

A huge white and brown shape suddenly appeared from Aeron's right and there was Fluffy! Gwenith was on his back, screaming a battle cry. The beast slammed into the Rhordian and knocked him to the ground, landing on top of him…

…and also landing on the sword he was holding.

The aralez screamed a strange sound that cut through all the other noise. It didn't sound like a dog, more like a bear he'd once seen being speared after it had been caught killing livestock. Fluffy rolled away from the Rhordian who had been knocked senseless, and Gwenith tumbled to the ground. The sword was still stuck in the aralez's belly, its blood shockingly red against the white fur.

"Fluffy! No!" shrieked Gwenith. She lunged to her feet and then fell to her knees next to her beloved aralez. The fighting was still swirling all around them, but the Light Horse was soon going to be scattered. *I can't leave her here!*

He swung down out of his saddle but held on to the reins, dragging Wyn over next to the dying aralez. "Gwen! We have to go!" She didn't respond and just clutched Fluffy's fur and wept. He looked around frantically, his own people were falling back, and the Rhordians closing in. Where was Madoc in all this mess? He could get her to go…

He grabbed her arm and yanked her away from the aralez. "Gwen! You can't help him! We have to get out of here!" He literally threw the sobbing girl up on Wyn, despite the growing pain in his left arm. He was about to pull himself up after her when he saw a half-dozen Rhordians approaching from the sides. There was only a narrow gap through which they could escape, and Wyn would be too slow carrying both of them. He slapped Wyn hard on the rump and shouted: *"Go!"* The pony bolted off through the gap, leaving Aeron standing there alone.

He raised his hands as the Rhordians surrounded him.

Chapter 15

He half-expected to just be cut down right there, and a few of the humans looked ready to do so, but a sergeant rode up and ordered that he be taken to where the other prisoners were being gathered. One man dismounted and relieved him of his helmet and Sergeant Rolf's dagger, but didn't bother to strip off his leather jerkin. He bound his hands together in front of him with a piece of rope and then remounted and directed him toward the south. Only as they moved away from the scene of the fighting could he get a clear view off to the north. The Shires Army was gone.

He could see bodies, he could see the four abandoned cannons, and he could see some groups of prisoners, but the bulk of the army appeared to have fled beyond the ridge and was out of sight. Some of the Rhordian light cavalry was trotting up to the top of that ridge and disappearing down the other side, presumably in pursuit, but most of their army was halted and reorganizing. Close at hand, the enemy heavy horse was pulling itself back together. From all that he could see, it appeared that that his crazy plan had worked well enough to keep one jaw of the trap from closing on the army. Some, maybe most of them, had gotten away.

He looked at the closer bodies as he moved past them, recognizing a few of his troopers, but most were just lumps half-hidden in the grass. He hoped that Gwenith had gotten away. And Madoc. And Einion, and… Did the Picksbury Light Horse even exist anymore?

To his amazement, it was still well short of noon. The whole battle had lasted less than two hours. But with the small amount of sleep he'd gotten the last two days and then the morning's exertion, he was beginning to stumble as he walked. His shoulder was hurting more and more, too. His captor wasn't pleased with his slow pace and prodded him with a spear.

Eventually, they reached an area where all the other prisoners were being herded. There looked to be four or five hundred of them. The rider turned him over to the infantry guarding the captives and rode off. Aeron felt bad about losing Sergeant Rolf's dagger. He hoped its new owner took good care of it.

He didn't see any familiar faces among the other prisoners, but he didn't look at all that many. Fatigue and pain started to fill him, and he slumped to the ground and wished he had something to eat. His head was a whirling mass of thoughts and emotions. Fear at what might happen to him next, despair at the defeat of the army, sorrow over the probable destruction of the Picksbury Light Horse, some satisfaction that the sacrifice might have saved the rest of the army from annihilation, hope that his own sacrifice might have saved Gwenith from capture, worry about Nesta and the kids… It was hard to grab any one thought and hold it… he was so tired.

They sat there until around noon when there was some noise off to the south, and then the guards began yelling at them to get on their feet. Those that didn't move quickly enough got kicked or struck. Some of the prisoners were wounded and had to be helped along by their fellows. They headed along the road, and he saw that up ahead was the guardburg, and apparently it had surrendered. A long line of captives was emerging from the wreckage of the place and joining with the group that Aeron was part of.

They marched alongside the road rather than on it. The road was being used by the Rhordian army for its supply wagons. A long line of them were heading north. Aeron could only suppose that the Rhordians would move up and lay siege to Hodenburg. He doubted that it could hold out very long. After a while, the last of them were gone past and then came a convoy of wagons heading south, carrying the Rhordian wounded from the battle. There were actually quite a lot of them, both in the wagons and trudging alongside; men with bloody bandages, missing hands, and worse.

Some of the Shirefolk who were carrying or helping their own wounded called out, asking if they could be taken on the wagons. All they got for their efforts were kicks and harsh words. When a wounded Shireling a few files up from Aeron collapsed in the dirt, a Rhordian guard drove a spear through him before anyone could help poor fellow. Cries of outrage arose from the other prisoners, but most of them were bound like Aeron and could do nothing. By late afternoon, a dozen others had been similarly dealt with, and one fellow who tried to fight off the executioner got killed himself.

Aeron was as outraged as anyone, but he knew that this was the usual fate of prisoners who couldn't keep up, especially if the victors had their own wounded to care for. At least they hadn't been captured by goblins or orcs or ratkin who would often eat those they caught. But these Rhordians were clearly angry, and that could only mean that the Shirefolk, those despised *halfmen,* must have hurt them a lot worse in the battle than they had expected. The length of the wagon train of wounded proved that. A part of Aeron felt good about it, even though it probably meant his eventual fate might be a lot worse. What were they going to do with them? Slaves? Slavery wasn't common in the part of the world, but it wasn't unknown, either. Maybe they would just be used as bargaining chips to get the Shires to give in. Maybe he would see his home again - see Nesta again.

By dark, the entire group was nearing exhaustion, and even the guards were looking weary. They were now a couple of leagues south of the border. They were herded into a large field, and guards were posted all around them. The guards built fires and made meals, but the Shirelings had neither.

The guards also had wine.

Within a few hours, some of them were pretty drunk, and a few decided they were going to have fun with some of the prisoners. They hauled one poor wretch out of the crowd, cut his bonds and gave him a knife . They sent him up against some huge brute and told him that if he could beat him, he could go free. He had no chance, of course, and was soon bleeding on the ground. They didn't kill him, didn't even seriously wound him, but they kicked and beat him to an inch of his life and dragged him back to the other prisoners. Then they did it with someone else.

By the time that the third bloodied figure was tossed back with the prisoners, a strange, fey mood was gripping Aeron, a rage unlike anything he's ever felt before. He moved toward the edge of the group of prisoners facing where the unequal 'duels' were being held - while most of the others were trying to move away. When one human asked: "So, who's next? Any of you little scum want to give it a try?" he laughed and his comrades laughed with him. They were clearly surprised when Aeron shouted:

"I will! If any of you cowards have the guts to face me!"

There was a moment of stunned silence, then they laughed all the louder. "Oh, ho!" roared one of them, "You think you can match a whole soldier, halfman?"

"Shouldn't be hard. If you were *whole* soldiers, you'd be up front fighting and not back here beating up helpless prisoners."

Their laughter stopped and was replaced by cursing. He'd clearly struck a nerve. Several men came forward and roughly grabbed him and hustled him forward. His opponent was one of the bigger ones who had obviously been drinking, but sadly he was still steady enough on his feet. He was fingering his sword and grinning in a nasty fashion. Aeron knew he could probably give a better account of himself than the previous victims, but he knew he had little chance. And if somehow he did win, there was no chance at all that he'd be set free. Far more likely that they'd beat him to death for the affront. *So why are you doing this, you idiot? Don't you want to see Nesta again?*

One of the others was about to cut the ropes binding his hands, while another stood ready to give him his weapon, when suddenly a sharp voice from behind interrupted them: "I've seen enough of these damn ratlings! Insult us, will he? Soldier, I'm taking this one for myself, and I'm gonna teach him a lesson none of these vermin will forget!" A hand grabbed the back of his jerkin and another hand, holding a gleaming knife appeared a few inches from his face.

The soldiers seemed surprised, but they didn't say anything except, *yes, sir!* Aeron was jerked around and pushed away from the fire, away from the prisoners, and out into the dark field. He couldn't see who was behind him. An officer? What in the world had he gotten himself into now? Was this someone with a special grudge against Shirelings? Was he going to be taken somewhere and tortured? Or just have his throat cut and be dumped into a ditch? He tried to judge his chances to break loose. They were getting farther away from the other guards, so maybe…

They approached a small clump of trees. It had grown cloudy, and there was no light from the moon or stars. Maybe if he gave a sudden twist he could break the man's grasp and then run and lose him in the dark. He tensed…

"Aeron! Don't do anything! Just come with me!"

The voice sounded different than before. It was a voice he knew… they reached the trees, and he was spun around and he found himself facing…

"*Palle!*" He wanted to shout it out loud, but he had the sense to just make it a whisper.

In an instant, his old friend had his arms around him and was hugging him tight. Aeron's arms were still tied in front of him so he couldn't hug back, but he leaned into him and tried not to cry.

"Aeron! Aeron! Oh, thank the Children I found you!" Palle *was* crying, no doubt.

After a moment, he drew away and grabbed Aeron's arms. "Here, let me get you out of those ropes." The knife, which had seemed so menacing, now cut him loose.

"Palle! What are you doing?"

"Getting you out of here, what do you think?"

"But how did you find me? How did you know I was here?"

"I didn't know, how could I? But I was attached to this band of ruffians—I still wasn't too popular because of my friendship with you, so I didn't get assigned to an elite unit like the others. We just guarded the supply wagons and dug sinks and such. But when the prisoners started coming in, we got the job of guarding them, and I kept my eyes out for you—just in case. When I spotted you this afternoon, I almost fainted for joy. Couldn't do anything until now. But no more talk, you have to get away!"

Aeron wanted nothing more than to talk with his friend, but he realized he was right. If he was going to escape he had to do so right now. "But what about you? How will you explain…?"

"Explain what? I took an uppity halfling out to punish him and I came back alone. I'm an officer, Aeron, I don't have to explain anything to those men. But still, you're right, I need to make it convincing; need some blood on this knife." He started to roll up his sleeve.

"No! Cut me. Halfling blood looks like yours, but then you won't have to explain why you're bleeding."

"But…"

"No worse than when that mage, Bhim, had Sergeant Rolf cut us for his demonstration. No arguments, do it." He pulled back his own sleeve and exposed his arm. Palle snorted, but made a short shallow cut and then smeared the blood all over his knife blade and even made sure to get some on his hands.

When he was done, they stood looking at each other, just gray shapes in the dark. "Thank you, Palle. I'll never forget this."

"You'd do the same for me. I hope… I hope we can meet again in… in happier times."

"Yes, so do I. Take care of yourself, Palle. Oh, by the way, I'm engaged," It was a crazy thing to say, but it just popped out.

"Really? Congratulations! How did… no, if I start asking questions, we'll be here all night. You need to go. West would be best, I think. I heard that they are going to reduce the Tanmill Canal guardburg next while the main army continues on to Hodenburg, so you don't want to go east or north. Stay clear of the guardburg on the Brigward Road, we have that invested…"

"I know. I'll travel by night and slip through. Oh, one more thing! Is Headmaster Jannik still around?"

"What? Why do you care about…?"

"Just answer me! Is he?"

"Uh, he's here with the army, I think. Aide to one of the generals…"

“Well, Vadik told me - yes, I saw him recently - Vadik told me that he’s found out that Jannik is actually working for that Lord Darvled character from down south. Tell your father if you can. No time for more. Goodbye, Palle. ‘Til we meet again.”

“Fare thee well, Aeron - Oh! Wait!” He pulled a bag which hung over his shoulder on a strap and handed it to him. “Some food and water; I expect you’ll need it.”

“Thanks again, and I do. Uh, if there’s anything you can do for the other prisoners…”

“I’ll try,” said Palle. He reached out and squeezed his hand and then let go. Aeron turned and made his way through the small woods and then out the other side. He turned to what he hoped was northwest and set out at the best pace he could manage. The bag had some bread, a chunk of cheese, a few sausages, and a bottle of water. He ate and drank as he walked and thanked the Missing Gods for his friend.

* * * * *

As dawn approached, he was still well south of the border. He found a thick clump of bushes and crawled inside and slept. He woke a number of times when he heard strange sounds or moved his aching shoulder the wrong way, but nothing and no one came close. By mid-morning, it was raining steadily and the drips found him despite his cover. He ate a bit more around noon, but rationed what he had even though he wanted to eat it all. He peeped out from his hiding place and saw no one. He was tempted to try to move on, but even though he doubted that anyone was looking for him specifically, the Rhordians were sure to have scouts out all through the area. He forced himself to wait until dark.

His shoulder was hurting worse than ever, and he fashioned a sling to keep it from moving while he walked. As he emerged from his hiding place, he saw that the skies had cleared and there were stars he could steer by. He wasn’t sure how far west he’d come from the Eowulf Road, but he hoped it was far enough to avoid any patrols along it. He chose a course just a bit west of north and set out.

There were a few rumbles and flickers of light off to the east, probably artillery smashing the Tanmill Canal guardburg to splinters. There was nothing from the direction of Hodenburg, though. He wasn’t sure if that was a good sign or not. Surely whatever was left of the Shires army had made it back there by now. It seemed likely the Rhordians would put the place under siege as soon as they could.

The strain of the last few days had taken a greater toll on him than he’d realized, and he wasn’t able to move nearly as quickly as he wanted. He stopped about midnight for a rest and some food. He suddenly woke three hours later and could only make a few more miles before he had to find a hiding place for the day.

It took him a total of four nights to get to Hodenburg, and the last two were without food and nearly without water. He passed a number of farms and mills - some intact, others destroyed - but didn't dare to stop and beg for food. He had not seen a soul except for Rhordian patrols, so he had no idea if the farms were deserted, but he knew that they'd make ideal places for enemy outposts or just places for tired soldiers to sleep for the night. No, it was far too dangerous. He'd just have to tighten his belt.

At the start of the fourth night, he angled more to the east to head almost due north and directly for Hodenburg. It was probably hopeless to try and get into the city, but he wanted a look at the situation. If he later found friendly forces further north, he wanted to have something useful to tell them.

Therefore, he was surprised when he topped a ridge and found a huge expanse of tents and campfires spread out due east of him. For a moment, he thought he'd made better time than he'd thought and already reached Hodenburg and its besiegers, but then he spotted another group of lights miles off to the north and realized that was Hodenburg. The Rhordian army had stopped short of it. Why?

He puzzled over it for a moment but then realized he was in a dangerous location. The ridge he was on was a natural place to put a few picket posts. He turned west and moved away as quietly as he could until the enemy camp was out of view. He went west for another mile before turning north again. As he walked, he did indeed spot some campfires further along the ridge he'd just left. He'd been lucky.

He pushed on, refusing to take any breaks. He had nothing to eat anyway. A few hours after midnight, the glimpses he caught of the Rhordian camp was well to the south of him. Hodenburg wasn't that far ahead now. Maybe he could make it before…

"Halt! Don't you move or I'll spit you!"

Aeron froze in place, but instantly realized his challenger was a Shireling. "It's all right!" he called. "I'm one of you, I was captured during the battle and escaped!"

A person appeared and then two more. One had a small, hooded lantern which he, no, make that she, flipped open briefly to look at his face and then shut again. "Who are you?" the first one asked.

"Aeron Cadwallader. Lieutenant Cadwallader of the Picksbury Light Horse. I need to get to Hodenberg and back to my band."

"Good luck with that! The whole army went running back there, and it's a demon's own mess there right now."

"It's not as bad as all that," countered the woman. "They're getting things sorted out." She turned back to Aeron. "You hurt? Hungry?"

"Yes, and yes. Shoulder's banged up, and I haven't had any food for two days."

"Well then, Lieutenant, we better get you back to the city. The healers can look at your shoulder. Food we can give you right now. Come on."

One of them escorted him back to where the pickets had made a little camp without a fire. He got Aeron some food - just some dried meat and bread - and some water, which he ate and drank while they headed toward the distant city. "How'd you get captured?" asked the fellow, whose name was Yale.

"Someone in my band got dismounted. I gave her my pony. Sure hope she got away."

"She? Yeah, you did the right thing, there. Don't think these damn humans would stop at nothin'! So how'd you get away?"

"The guards were drinking and not paying as close a watch as you were. Managed to slip off in the dark. There were so many other prisoners, I guess they didn't notice." He decided there was nothing to be gained by mentioning Palle, so he didn't. "I was expecting the Rhordians to have Hodenberg surrounded by now."

"Yeah, so were we. No one seems to know why they stopped."

"I didn't see much after I got caught. How many of the army got back here?"

"Don't really know. I was with a band of spearmen near the left. A whole passel of Rhordians on horseback plowed into the fellows to our left and then we was all runnin'. Didn't have time to count, but I think a good lot of us made it out. All gatherin' back in town, now. They sent us out t'keep an eye on things."

"Lucky I ran into you."

"Yup. Even luckier that Arwel—he's one of our usual group—wasn't here tonight. He carries a bow and tends to shoot at anything that moves. Be a damn shame for you to get shot by friends just as you made it to safety!" The fellow laughed like it was a huge joke.

"Yeah, it would have been."

They reached a larger camp where the picket posts were commanded from, and his escort turned Aeron over to his boss. He seemed suitably impressed when Aeron said he knew the Muster-Master and needed to see him right away. The pony they used for running messages was put at his disposal and he rode double with the beast's owner into Hodenburg.

He hadn't actually intended to go see Dunstan Rootwell, he'd just said it to get the ride, but as they jogged into town, he realized that he really did want to see him. Rootwell could tell him what was going on, where was the remains of the Picksbury Light Horse, if Einion survived, if Gwen was okay… lots of things. But it was far past midnight and he really didn't have the energy. So he had the rider leave him at where the city's healers had set up a hospital, and after thanking him, tried to find someone to look at his arm. But there was an incredibly fine-looking cot sitting there empty, and before he knew it, he was on it and fast asleep.

* * * * *

It was nearly noon before he woke up, and if it weren't for certain bodily necessities, he might have slept until nightfall. After seeing to things, he managed to find a healer who could look at his shoulder. While few Shirelings could wield powerful magics, there were some who could wield the more modest sorts used in healing. By this time, five days after the battle, there was not such a frantic demand on them, and Aeron was able to find one with the strength to use on him. It only took a moment, but the results were amazing.

The pain was nearly gone, and he could use his left arm easily.

He also managed to get some food and was generally feeling much better. He started thinking about searching out Rootwell but then stopped and looked at himself. He was a mess; filthy, stinking, bloodstained. He had left nearly all his baggage back in the camp the Light Horse had made up outside of town. They had left it set up when they moved out, thinking they would be returning to it after the battle. Was it still there? Would any of the band be there? One way to find out.

He trudged outside of the city, discovering that he wasn't quite as well as he'd first thought, and wobbled his way toward the field where the camp should be. There were dozens of other camps that had also been left behind, but most seemed to be in the process of being dismantled. He spotted where his had been and breathed a sigh of relief when he saw that some of it was still up and there were people there taking the remains down. When he got closer, he realized that he recognized some of them. The Picksbury Light horse still lived!

He moved faster and soon reached it and was nearly mobbed when the people there recognized him. "It's Cadwallader! Look! Captain Einion! It's Lieutenant Cadwallader!" It was a happy reunion and he thrilled when Gwenith rushed up to embrace him.

"Aeron! Aeron! Oh, Missing Gods, I'm so glad to see you!"

"And I you! I didn't know if you'd gotten away or not."

"Just barely - thanks to you. I almost tried to come back for you, but Wyn was smarter than I was and wouldn't let me. I'd never have made it out except for you after… after…" Her smile faded and her voice faltered.

"So sorry about Fluffy." He looked around at the crowd. "Madoc?"

Gwenith shook her head. "No one knows. He hasn't made it back, but no one saw him fall. Maybe captured…"

"I was captured - for a while - but I didn't see him, or anyone else from the band with the other prisoners. But there were a lot and I could have missed them."

"Well, Gwen told me how you came to be captured, Lieutenant," said Captain Einion pushing his way through the crowd. "Good work that. But how did you escape and return to us?" Einion was sporting a bandage on his head.

Aeron told the tale in as few words as possible, again leaving out Palle's role, and then said. "But I really want to see Rootwell and… discuss some things. I thought I'd come back here first and see if I could get a wash and a change of clothes before I did."

"Oh, so if you didn't look like something the cat dragged in, you wouldn't have even bothered to come here and let us know you were alive, Mister Cadwallader?" said Gwen in mock outrage. "How dare you?" They all laughed, but soon he had all he needed and was on his way back into the city, Einion coming with him.

"I didn't see Guto with the crowd," Aeron said. "Did he make it?"

Einion shook his head. "No."

"How… how many did? Make it back, I mean."

"We had about a hundred and fifty in the camp this morning. About a dozen are still in the hospital in town. We... we actually had a few more than that when we got back here. Some... some just couldn't take it."

Meaning they'd deserted. Well, that was understandable, even if it was regrettable. But only a handful lost that way. It could be far worse. "Maybe they'll come back when they've had a chance to get their wits back. The battle must have been a shock to a lot of them."

"It was surely a shock to me," said Einion. "Aeron?"

"Yes?"

"Thanks."

"For what?"

"For taking command when you did. I never would have thought of the things you did. If we hadn't gone off and then hit the Rhordian knights from behind, it would have been a complete disaster. Rootwell had a commanders' meeting when we got back, and I made sure he knew what you did. He... he said it was a shame you'd been lost."

"Well, I hope he's glad to see me come back."

He meant it as a joke, but Einion grabbed his arm and said: "He damn well better! If he has any more doubts about you, I'll straighten him out right quick!"

They reached one of the new gates that had been built. Aeron noted that there were swarms of people working to dig a ditch in front of the palisades and the buildings that made up the outer defenses. He was pleased to see that they weren't just scattering the dirt they dug, they were laboriously hauling it inside the walls - or over the top of them using buckets and ropes - and packing it behind the palisades to reinforce them. Some of the dirt was even being taken inside the houses to fill up the lower floors. With that, maybe they could stand up to artillery and magic for a while longer.

"Looks like we're getting ready to make a real fight of it for Hodenburg," he said.

"Yes. You can see we're taking down the camps and are going to bring all the troops inside."

"Odd the Rhordians haven't invested the place yet."

"Yes, but don't look a gift aralez in the mouth. Every hour they give us is a blessing. Reinforcements from all over the Shires are coming in every day."

"Are they? Well, that's good... I guess."

They reached Rootwell's headquarters, and as expected, the place was a beehive of activity. Einion sent a message that they wanted to see the Muster-Master and they had to wait less than a half-hour to get in to see him. They found him in the same office Aeron had met him in when he was coming back from Eowulf. It seemed like a long time ago. But looking at Rootwell, it might have been years. The fellow looked aged. Hair much grayer, with strands of white, than he remembered him having—even from the commander's meeting before the battle, just a week ago. He looked up from his desk as they came in.

"So, your lost lamb has returned, eh, Bevan? No worse for wear?"

"The better for the wear, I'm thinking. If you'd just *listen* to him, I imagine you'd think so too, Dunstan."

Rootwell held up his hand. "You don't need to rub it in. I've had a dozen different people rubbing it in since the battle." He looked Aeron in the eye and said: "Cadwallader, you were right and I was wrong. Satisfied?"

Aeron rocked back, totally surprised. "I… I… it's all water under the bridge, sir. We need to worry about what we do now rather than what we did then."

"Hmmph!" snorted Rootwell. "You're more generous than most of the people I've been dealing with lately. Smarter, too. But we need to talk. Bevan? Would you excuse us?"

Einion nodded and took his leave. Rootwell was silent for a moment and then said: "Let's take a walk." He got up and led him not to the main stairway down, but through a back door, past a tiny garderobe, and then through a door which opened on a circular staircase which took them down and out a back door into a narrow alley. "My private escape route," he explained. "To avoid unwelcome visitors. Perhaps we can avoid interruptions this way."

They went out through the alley and into a main street. The place was bustling with soldiers, workers, and scared-looking civilians. None of they paid any attention to the person who was responsible for their defense. Aeron noted that Rootwell wasn't wearing the fancy red cloak he usually did. They walked in silence for a while before Rootwell spoke: "I had just received a message from one of the light cavalry commanders on the right flank, complaining that the Picksbury Light Horse had run off and left his flank open when the Rhordians launched their heavies at us. I was looking right at the batch on our right when your Light Horse hit them in the rear. I remember thinking: *well that was lucky.* It wasn't until I talked with Einion afterward that I learned it hadn't been luck at all. That was quite a job you did."

"One of my troopers noticed all the empty horses behind their light cavalry, and I had a hunch what it was. We sent off a messenger to you, to try and warn you, and then I… we took the only course we could think of."

"You keep saying *we*, but Einion's an honest man. He tells me it was all *you.*"

Aeron shrugged. "My view was a tad limited once we charged. How did you fare with the other attack from the left? You obviously managed to get the bulk of the army out. How'd you stop the other heavy horse?"

"Didn't exactly stop them, but I sent the Shires Knights against them. Slowed 'em down enough to allow us to pull back. Almost none of them came back, though."

Aeron nodded. The Shires Knights were the army's only true heavy cavalry. They weren't knights in the same meaning as the League and most human kingdoms. They were large people on actual horses, all armed and armored like human knights, but that's where the similarities ended. They held no title of nobility or anything like that. They were mostly used for ceremonial activities, but they surely earned their title in this battle.

"I thought… I thought that maybe with what they - and you - did that maybe we could hold, but then the magic started hitting us and it all came apart. Can't blame the troops, they could see we were in a vise, and with fireballs and lightning bolts hitting them, they just broke. Anybody would have." He shook his head and mumbled something Aeron couldn't catch. "Then we ran faster than they followed - what was left of the light cavalry did a good job guarding our rear - and we got back here in a lot less time than it took us to march out there."

They reached the city's new defensive walls and Rootwell went up a ladder into one of the towers which had been built and Aeron followed. There was a good view from up there. The defenses did look pretty strong. Not as strong as stone walls would have been, but still not bad. A solid line of stockade walls connecting the fortified buildings. Ditches in front of most of the sections. A dozen platforms for the cannons that had been too heavy to drag along with the army, and towers at intervals along the perimeter. In the surrounding fields, the tents from the camps were nearly all down now, and lines of troops, horses, and wagons were bringing them and all the other gear into the city. Aeron could see other convoys bringing in what appeared to be food from the surrounding countryside.

"How many troops do you have left, sir? The Picksbury Light Horse lost about two-fifths of what we had to start."

"Hard to get exact numbers, but it looks like we got about six thousands back from the wreck. But we have more than that now."

"Oh?"

"I think with the loss of the battle, people are really starting to take this seriously."

"They weren't before?"

"Oh, those who got hit by the earlier raids knew, but that wasn't really all that many of our people. Now the rest realize this is for real. The people here in Hodenburg are all rallying to the defense. We've gotten almost three thousand new volunteers to fight, and we're getting them outfitted. A lot of the rest are helping with constructing the defenses. And the word is spreading all through the Shires. We've had five hundred troops march in from the north, and messengers tell us there are another three or four thousands on the way."

"Trained troops, or just volunteers?"

"Mostly trained."

"They must be stripping the defenses from everywhere else, aren't they?"

"Not everywhere, but yes, a lot. They know that if Hodenberg falls, the Rhordians can go anywhere they want and take every village and town one by one. We must stop them here! And when all those troops get here, we'll be able to."

Aeron looked out at the distant hill, the one that separated them from the enemy army. "And the Rhordians are just letting you do it…" he whispered.

"What's that?" demanded Rootwell. He tilted his head toward Aeron who had noticed that the Muster-Master was a bit deaf.

"The Rhordians must know that if you are able to get all those reinforcements, it will extremely costly to take the city. And yet there they sit, two leagues away, letting our people just march in. I'm sure they know it's happening: they have their own scouts out, but they are making no effort to stop you. Why? They could have surrounded the city the day after the battle. Dug trenches and erected stockades so that no one could get in or out. And yet they didn't. Why not?"

"Maybe they needed to reorganize. Maybe we hurt them that badly."

"Did we? You saw it better than me. Did we really hurt them that badly?"

Rootwell's face had gotten quite red, and it looked like he was about to make some sharp reply when he stopped, took a deep breath, and slowly let it out. "No," he said. "No, we didn't."

"So they are letting you do this."

"And why do you think that is, Mister Cadwallader? Einion wants me to listen to you. So, I'm listening. Why do you think the enemy is letting us reinforce Hodenburg?"

Aeron was suddenly sweating. *You wanted this, you wanted to be an advisor to the Muster-Master. Time to give him some good advice!* But did he have any? Why *were* the Rhordians doing this? If they were letting all these reinforcements reach Hodenburg it must be because…

"Well?"

"If… if they are letting you do this, it's because they want all our troops here."

"Why? Do they think they can lure us out into another battle in the open field so they can finish us completely? Do they expect me to make the same mistake twice?"

"No, I doubt that…"

"Then why?"

The pieces all clicked into place. "Because if our troops are all here, it means they aren't anywhere else."

"What do you mean?"

"Once they think they have the bulk of our forces inside Hodenburg, they'll move in and lock the place up tighter than a drum. Like I said, trenches and stockades and every other sort of field fortification they can construct to seal us in—us and all of our trained troops."

"What does that gain them? They still can't take the place and we'll have enough food stored here to last for six months."

"Their gain, sir, is that once they have established their siege lines, they can keep what's here penned up with just a fraction of their forces. The rest will be free to go wherever they want. And with all of our other strongholds stripped of the troops they've sent here, there will be nothing left to stop them. They can subjugate all the Shires and leave us here to starve at their leisure!"

Rootwell's eyes had gotten very large. He looked at Aeron, looked around the city, and then looked out in the direction of the enemy. "And I used to be a rat-catcher," he whispered.

"Sir?"

"Oh, years ago, when I was as young as you, my job was being a rat-catcher. Never any lack of rats in towns and cities. I got to be pretty good at it. The experience even served me well after I became one of the Shires captains. But I had forgotten all those lessons, and now I'm the rat in the trap!"

"The trap hasn't closed yet, sir," said Aeron.

"No, you're right, it hasn't. So what do we do to get out of it? And don't tell me to evacuate the city, we simply *cannot* abandon the capital without a fight!"

"No, we can't do that, it would shatter the morale of everyone. We have to make a fight of it. But tell, me what's the minimum number you would need to adequately man all the walls and towers and to crew the cannons and to have at least a small reserve to replace losses or reinforce danger areas?"

Rootwell stood there for a while, thinking. He got out his pipe, filled it, and lit it, using a little flint and steel contraption which was a Shires-made invention. He puffed on it a few times and then said: "Four thousand of the trained troops, plus all the new volunteers, so seven thousand altogether."

Aeron gave a silent sigh of relief. That had been about his estimate, too, and he'd feared Rootwell would insist on a lot more. "All right. Then we need to get everyone else—plus as many of the young, the old, the sick and wounded, and any other useless mouths we can manage to move. We make Hodenburg the bait to trap the Rhordians instead of vice-versa."

"But will they bite? As soon as they see what we are doing, they'll close in on the city right away and go after any convoys we send out."

"Then we don't let them see. We keep the reinforcements coming in during the day, and every night, we send troops and people right back out again. We put all of our cavalry to work to drive back their scouts so they don't get wind of it. Get everyone back to Picksbury and then any not needed to defend there, send further north or east."

"The Shires Assembly is going to have a fit when they hear what we want to do," said Rootwell.

"Can you convince them?"

"You mean can *we* convince them. You're in this now, lad - up to your neck!"

Chapter 16

Rootwell was right: the Assembly did have a fit.

He demanded and got an emergency session - not that they had any other kind these days - and told them what he planned to do. Told them, not asked for permission. They objected, of course, but Rootwell was relentless, and he called on Aeron frequently to back him up. As the argument went on, Aeron's own conception of the plan continued to evolve.

"It's not just that we need to garrison our other strongholds," he said at one point, "we need a *mobile* army in the field, too. As long as we have a force that can move and strike where we want, the Rhordians can't put every one of our cities under siege. Our army could fall upon each besieging force in turn and crush it. If they get careless, we could even come back here to Hodenburg, and combined with the garrison we leave here, smash them. As long as we are not all penned up under siege, we can make the Shires a trap for the Rhordians."

A number of the members of the Assembly could not seem to grasp any concept other than building walls and hiding behind them. But Rootwell continued to hammer at them, and one by one, brought them around to their side. He never got it unanimous, but he got enough.

It was late afternoon before they emerged from the Assembly chamber, but there was no rest for them. The plan had to be put into motion immediately, that very night. "So who do we send? Some of the cavalry to escort whatever civilians we can round up?" asked Rootwell.

"Eventually all the cavalry should go, except for a few dozen left here to run messages and such, but they ought to be the last to go. We'll need them as scouts and picket screens until the last. Let's send about five hundred infantry."

As it turned out, the infantry was the easy part. Trying to get a few thousand civilians to up and move on such short notice proved almost impossible, and so for that first night, the infantry was escorting nothing but wounded carried in wagons and such camp followers who didn't actually live in Hodenburg. But they made it out, unmolested and hopefully unobserved.

The next night went much more smoothly, and two thousand civilians made it out escorted by another five hundred infantry. The reinforcements continued to come in, and they made sure the Rhordians saw them come, but each evening the cavalry sortied from the city and drove back any enemy scouts that might spot the secret exodus.

This went on for another four nights, but then the incoming reinforcements petered out and the scouts reported that it looked like the Rhordian army was preparing to move. Aeron and Rootwell conferred as soon as they heard that news.

"So far we've been lucky," said Rootwell. "But let's not push it. We send out everything else that's leaving tonight."

"Agreed," said Aeron. "All the cavalry, and everyone who can walk or that we have wagons for on the road. Anyone who can't walk or fit in the wagons can go in the barges."

"And you, too, Aeron."

He'd been half-expecting this, but it still surprised him. "But not you?"

"Someone has to command the bait, and that will be me. I have another job for you."

"Sir?"

"I convinced the Assembly members to leave. We can't have the leadership of the Shires bottled up here. So they will be going, and I want you to command the escort that will be guarding them."

"Sir, any competent cavalry commander could do that."

"I know, I know, but there will be new orders given you when you get to Picksbury." He reached out and put his hand on Aeron's shoulder. "Son, I need someone I can trust, someone who understands what needs to be done out there. You are that someone."

Genuinely moved, Aeron nodded and said: "I'll do my best, sir."

So, in addition to getting that night's sortie prepared, Aeron had to get his own affairs in order to leave. Fortunately, that didn't involve much. All the items he'd acquired to make camp life more comfortable: cot, stool, table, lantern, and a dozen other items would have to be left behind along with the tents. There would be no room for any of that. All the Picksbury Light Horse's baggage ponies would be carrying people that night. Aeron just bundled up his spare clothing and a few personal items into a roll that he'd tie on the back of his pony - his new pony. Gwenith had become so attached to Wyn, he gave him to her and found another. The girl was still mourning the loss of Fluffy, but she was made of stern stuff - sterner now.

"So where are we headed?" she asked when they saw each other.

"For tonight, just Picksbury. After that, I'm not sure."

"You're not? Then who is? All the rumors say that you're practically running things now and will be once Rootwell is left behind."

Aeron snorted, annoyed that everyone seemed to know that Rootwell was staying, even though it was supposed to be a secret, and even more annoyed that rumors that he was in command were floating around. "Well, there's this little thing called the Shires Assembly? Y'know, our elected leaders? They might want a say in things."

Now she snorted. "That pack of fools helped get us into this mess. No one has much confidence in them anymore. Not anyone in the army, anyway. But now that the word's gotten around about what you really did in the battle - and before the battle - they have confidence in you, Aeron."

Now he really was shocked. "You're joking."

"No I'm not. Just look around, Aeron, you can see it if you just look."

Flustered, he took his leave to see about the final arrangement. The hours before dark were very tense. If the Rhordians moved faster than expected and advanced on the city that day, it could wreck all their plans, and they might have to fight their way out. But the sun sank lower and lower, and the enemy did not appear except for their scouts on the distant ridge.

Shortly after sunset, hearty meals were served to those who were leaving. They would need the energy for the dash they would make that night. Aeron ate with Rootwell and discussed the final details of the evacuation. Finally, he got up the nerve to ask: "Sir, when we get to Picksbury, who is going to be in command of the army? You'll still be here, and you'll soon be under siege. You can't command under those conditions, so who will? Who do I report to?"

Rootwell frowned, emptied his mug of ale, and then got out his pipe, as he often did when marshaling his thoughts. "If it was up to me, it would be you, Aeron. You're the most qualified officer we've got. But it's not up to me. The Assembly has the final say, and while they admit that you know what you're doing, they think you're too young and too… impetuous for so important a command."

Aeron nodded, both disappointed and relieved. "I understand. Then who?"

"They've decided to put Conwy Macsen in command. Now don't frown! I know the two of you don't get along so well, but I've had a talk with him and made him realize that he really needs to listen to you. I think he will. But that will come later. Once you reach Picksbury, I have another job for you."

"You mentioned something about that earlier. What job?"

Rootwell pulled out a sealed envelope and handed it to him. "Your orders are in here. Don't open it until you reach Picksbury. And then follow your orders."

"Yes sir." He took the envelope and tucked it inside his coat. They both got to their feet, and Rootwell stuck out his hand. Aeron took it and they squeezed. "Good luck to you, sir."

"And to you, Aeron. I'd ask the gods to look out for you except…"

"Except they're missing," finished Aeron. It was almost a traditional farewell. They both smiled. "We'll try to keep you informed about what's going on out there, either by swimmer along the canal or by pigeon. Of course it will only be generalities in case the messages go astray. Unless I ever meet up with Dilwyn Brynmoor again and he can spare us some of his magical ink."

"Who knows? Maybe you will. Goodbye, Aeron."

He left and made his way out to the central circle where the expedition was assembling. There was a thousand cavalry and over two thousand more people on foot. Over a hundred barges, loaded with the old and young who couldn't keep up to the pace they'd have to set, were in the canal, ready to move, each with double teams to pull them. An even greater crowd of the people of Hodenburg who would be remaining had gathered to see them off. A great many tearful farewells were taking place all around.

Over a thousand more cavalry were either already outside or lined up by the south gates. Their job was to make a strong demonstration against the Rhordian sentries and give them something else to worry about than the folks heading north. It was the dark of the moon and all the riders, walkers, and bargemen had been forbidden any sort of light that might give them away. There were plenty of lights burning in the city, but beyond the walls, it was very dark.

The Assembly members were all mounted, of course, them and their families if they had any in Hodenburg. Aeron had decided that the Picksbury Light Horse would be their escort, and he made his way to where they were assembled. He found Macsen there, talking with some of the Assembly. He greeted Aeron cordially enough and then added: "I trust you won't allow them to get lost along the way, eh, Cadwallader?"

"No, sir, we'll deliver them safe and sound." Macsen touched his hat to the Assembly and moved off.

"So when do we get going?" asked one of the Assembly members. Aeron still couldn't match names with faces for all of them, despite the time he spent before them with Rootwell.

"When the Lieutenant Muster-Master says so, sir," he said, gesturing after Macsen. "The diversionary force won't be sent out for a while yet, so I imagine we'll be waiting another hour or so." The fellow sniffed and looked peeved. Aeron didn't stay around for any more comments or complaints and nudged his pony over to where Captain Einion was waiting. "Evening, sir," he said to him.

"Stop that, Aeron," said Einion. "I ought to be calling you sir!"

"Why? The only rank I hold that anyone's ever told me about is lieutenant in the Light Horse."

"Pah! You've been practically running things for a week."

"You sound like Gwenith! Don't let Macsen hear you talking like that."

"I don't care if he hears or not. He's a good fellow, but everyone here knows who ought to be in command."

"Well, this isn't the time to be talking about it. We've got a job to do. Look, they're sending out the cavalry to hit the Rhordian pickets. We'll be moving soon."

A wave of motion was sweeping through the masses of people. Some of the cavalry began moving southward and disappeared from the circle fairly quickly. The rest were heading north and did not move nearly so fast. In fact, several hours went by before the Light Horse and the Assembly members made it through the gate. They were some of the last ones out at the Assembly's insistence. They didn't want to be accused of being the first to flee. But once outside, all being mounted, they moved off the road and picked up their pace, passing most of the column by.

It was a long column, stretching for a mile or more. It was mostly adults, nearly all the smaller children having been sent out previously. Only a few wagons were present, as they, too had gone with the earlier convoys. All of the people carried large bundles on their backs, and the scene reminded Aeron of the flight from Eowulf. A few fools were carrying impossibly large loads, including pieces of furniture. Aeron was sure they would be left by the roadside before long. It was too dark to see the people's faces clearly, and he was just as glad for that. There wouldn't be any happy faces among them, he was sure.

Only a handful of infantry were coming along, a group in front and another behind, but strong forces of cavalry were on either side, and when the troopers who had been sent off to harass the Rhordians to the south rejoined them it would be a powerful force indeed.

After riding a while, there were some low shouts, and they looked back. Beyond Hodenburg, there was a reddish glow in the sky. "Looks like our cavalry did more than just show themselves and run," said Aeron to Gwenith, who was riding close by.

"Set fire to their camps, do you think?"

"Maybe. Sure hope they don't get in over their heads, we can't afford to lose them."

"Just so they hurt the bastards!" said Gwenith fiercely. She clearly wasn't over losing Fluffy. And maybe Cousin Madoc, too.

It was only three leagues to Picksbury, so they ought to be there well before dawn, but that wasn't the end of the journey for most of the refugees. It was too close to Hodenburg for comfort and it was possible the Rhordians might try to put both cities under siege; they didn't want all those civilians trapped there. Most of the troops would stay, to keep a close watch on Hodenburg, but the plan was to send as many civilians as possible further north into Daleshire.

They kept up a good pace, and as Aeron expected, a lot of excess baggage got dumped. By midnight, a few of the walkers were having trouble keeping up and ended up riding double with some of the cavalry. About that same time, challenges started being shouted by the riders guarding the flanks and rear, but it was the troopers who had been sent to harry the invaders catching up with the column. *They* were in very good spirits and were boasting about how they had routed the Rhordian pickets and penetrated right into their camps and set fire to some tents and wagons. That cheered everyone, even Aeron, but he couldn't help wondering if the Rhordians had really been surprised or if this was another trap. It seemed like they had been ahead of them every step of the way so far. Was an ambush waiting for them up ahead?

But no ambush appeared, and several hours before dawn, they saw the lights of Picksbury not so far ahead. A cavalry patrol from the town challenged them and then led the way. As the first streaks of dawn appeared in the east, the head of the column plodded through the newly built South Gate. Citizens of the town were there with food and drink for everyone. Some of the tension flowed out of Aeron; they had made it.

"So now what?" asked Gwenith. "Do we stay here or go somewhere else?"

"I suppose that will be up to Macsen," he answered. But then he remembered the envelope Rootwell had given him. Drawing aside, he pulled it out of his coat and opened it. By the light of a lantern hanging on a pole he read it through and then frowned. It simply said that the Assembly members were going on to Tanmill, about fifteen leagues further north, and he and whatever force he wanted to take along should escort them. It ended by saying that upon reaching Tanmill, he would be given new orders.

He went over to where the Assembly was eating his breakfast and sought out the head member, Heilyn Culhwch. "Sir? Muster-Master Rootwell gave me orders to escort you and the others to Tanmill. I, uh… I assume you were aware of this?"

Culhwch nodded. "Yes, we knew, but we didn't want to spread the news around until we were away from Hodenburg. I guess we'll leave tomorrow morning. Give everyone a chance to rest up."

"Very well, sir. I'll have us all ready to go at dawn."

So more travel. He found Einion and gave him the news. "Are you and the Light Horse willing to keep going? I know everyone was hoping to spend some time at home. I was hoping for some, too."

Einion didn't look too pleased, but he nodded. "They all realize this isn't some sewing circle where we can come and go as we please. We're part of the army and we'll follow orders. I'll let everyone know."

"Thank you, sir. But give them all the day off. Let them see their folks and relax a bit. Just make sure they're back here ready to go at dawn tomorrow."

"Certainly. But you get yourself home, too, Aeron. You've earned it as much as they have."

He realized that he desperately wanted to get home. So he found Macsen and told him what he was going to be doing.

"Hmm," he said. "Well, I'll be sorry to lose you, Cadwallader. You and those cavalry, but orders are orders. Any idea when you'll be back?"

"The orders didn't say. I suppose if the Assembly doesn't have any more need for us once we're there, we'll come back."

"All right, but keep me informed, eh?"

"Yes, sir." Aeron took his leave and then rode out the north gate for home.

It was a happy homecoming, and he held Nesta closely to him for a long time. But not as long as he would have liked. Her children and his siblings and parents and some nieces and nephews soon swarmed around demanding an account of the big battle. From what he could make out from his babbling relatives, they knew that there had been a fight and it hadn't gone very well for the Shires, but beyond that, they had nothing but rumors.

Aeron tried to reassure them without actually lying, but it was hard. And then his father asked what had happened to Wyn, and he couldn't explain that without telling them about Gwen and Fluffy, and that led to the charge of the Picksbury Light horse, which led to *why* the charge had happened, which led to the Rhordian trap, and with one thing leading to another, they got pretty much the whole unabridged tale out of him in half an hour - except for his encounter with Palle, he left that out again. They were simultaneously elated that he'd made it through alive - and a hero - and appalled at the Shireling losses and the dangerous situation now facing the Shires. And then there was Madoc.

"No word of him at all?" demanded his mother. "Oh no, oh no!"

"I'll have to tell Hywel. He's not going to take it well," said his Da.

"He might have been captured," said Aeron. "A lot of our people were. So don't give up hope yet."

"You said that you were captured but got away, Aeron," said Mererid. "Maybe he did, too."

"Then why hasn't he made it home yet?" demanded Mama. He tried to be as encouraging as he could, but everyone realized it didn't look good. After a while, his father left to go talk to Uncle Hywel, and Mama and some of the girls went to prepare a midday meal that would have been a homecoming celebration except for the news about Madoc. Things were further dampened when he told them he would be leaving before dawn in the morning.

"You can't stay?" asked Nesta. "And you won't even be in Picksbury? Where are you going and how long will you be gone?"

"I'll be heading up to near Tanmill. I don't know how long I'll be there. I'm sorry, Nesta."

"I hate all of this. This war!"

"Yes, but if this hadn't happened, we never would have met. Remember that."

"I guess that's true, isn't it? But enough of my moping, we have a day together, let's not waste it."

So, they spent the day strolling together, interrupted only by the noon meal and periodic demands from Elin and Gethin for attention. It was a lovely day with a pleasant breeze and puffy white clouds floating across the sky. The fields were full of newly sprouted crops or grazing animals. Except for the sight of the fortifications around the house and stacks of weapons, it was almost possible to pretend there was no war. Almost.

His father had not returned for the noon meal but was back for supper. He looked very subdued after his talk with Uncle Hywel. There was little of the usual good humor around the table. The war was hitting closer to home now. Even the fright of the earlier raid didn't quite compare to this. Madoc? Dead? It didn't seem possible to most of them.

Aeron had hoped to spend the evening with Nesta doing more strolling - or something - but with a full meal in him, he suddenly couldn't keep his eyes open, and he reminded himself that he had not fully recovered from his ordeal after the battle or the frantic preparations for the evacuation. And he had to be up well before dawn the next day. Nesta seemed to realize this and despite a few feeble protests on his part, he was tucked into bed before it was even fully dark. He was asleep in moments and slept like a log until he was shaken awake three hours before dawn.

He dressed, ate quickly, kissed Nesta and his mother goodbye, and was out the gate in less than an hour. He reached Picksbury before any blush of dawn tinted the east. He found where the Light Horse and the Assembly members were gathering, where, to his annoyance, he learned that a dozen members of the Horse had not returned. Whether just extending their time at home a bit or gone for good, no one could say. With only a little over two hundred people and mounts to deal with, there were only a few delays, and they were on the road, heading north just as the sun appeared on the horizon.

It looked like it would be a good day for travel. The plan was to take the main road to Sowic today. If they pushed, they could probably get all the way to Tanmill, but with the Assembly members' families with them, they were going to take it fairly easy. It would only be a short jaunt on to Tanmill the next day and then…

"Aeron! Hey, Aeron!"

The sudden shout jerked him out of his musings and he looked around. A group of people were standing where a lane intersected the main road. With a shock, he realized it was the lane leading to his home which he had come down just a few hours earlier on the way to Picksbury, and the people were his family! They had come to see him off; he felt warm all over.

But they looked strange, and he saw that all the adults were wearing the leather armor and carrying the spears and shields that the household had been manufacturing. Nesta, too. And some of the younger ones had bows. "Don't you worry about us, Aeron!" cried his mother. "We'll handle things until you get back!"

The members of the Light Horse were all smiling or laughing at the display, and many were looking at Aeron to see his reaction. He forced himself to laugh, but the sight of his mother and Mererid and Nesta armed for battle sent a chill through him. Could it really come to this? Every single person drawn into the fighting?

He couldn't stop, and it was probably just as well. He waved and smiled and twisted in his saddle to keep looking at them as the riders moved past them along the road. Finally they disappeared around a bend, and Aeron let out a long sigh. Many of his comrades and even a few Assembly members joked with him for a while but eventually let it drop.

As they rode on, most of the missing members of the Light Horse caught up with them and apologized for their tardiness. Einion growled at them a bit for form's sake, but that was all. The leagues fell away behind them, and they entered a forest called the Wildwood. It wasn't really all that wild these days, although there were still many a scary story from long ago told about it. The wood ran almost five leagues north to south, and the road passed through it for much of that distance.

"My brother tried to scare me with stories about trolls and ogres hiding in the woods when I was little," said Gwenith. "It looks pretty tame here close to the road, but I hear there are a few spots deeper inside where it's very wild."

"There *are* trolls in the marshes east of Yangmere," said Aeron. "But from what I hear, they aren't all that fearsome. Some of the folks in Abbetshire actually trade things with them."

"Have you ever seen one?"

"No, never been up that way. In fact, when we get to Sowic, that will be as far north as I've ever been."

"Me, too. Actually, the raid we made into the League was the farthest east I've ever been. Sure seein' a lot with this here war."

It was late afternoon by the time they emerged from the Wildwood, and they were glad. It had been getting very dark under the trees, and they saw that there were clouds gathering in the west bringing an early dusk. Sowic was only a mile ahead, and they got there around dinner time.

Rooms in several inns had been reserved for the Assembly members and their families, but the Light Horse would have to camp out, and because of a shortage of baggage ponies, they had not been able to bring their tents. The town was already housing nearly a thousand people who had been evacuated from Hodenburg, so there were no other lodging available. They found a spot in a nearby orchard and made camp there. Still feeling very tired, Aeron rolled himself in a blanket and was soon asleep.

He was awakened sometime in the night by water dripping in his face. The clouds they had seen at sundown had arrived and brought rain. He got up and sat down again near one of the fires and dozed fitfully until dawn. The troops ate breakfast and broke camp wet, tired, and grumpy. They met up with the Assembly members who all looked dry, rested—and grumpy. Aeron had to remind himself that they were going into exile, while like as not, he and the others would be heading back to Picksbury.

It was still another five leagues to Tanmill. They headed out the north road, and after a mile or so, turned west on the Rhovan Road. They passed the town of Wictun, and a few miles further on, came to the Tanmill Canal which, following the easiest route for water, had swung farther west after passing Picksbury. They turned north along the tow path and reached Tanmill shortly after noon.

Tanmill was a good-sized town, probably larger than Picksbury. Just beyond it were the Northwolds, not exactly mountains, but the tallest hills in the Shires. They were riddled with mines and provided most of the home-produced metals. Tanmill, itself, was home to many smelters and foundries, and dozens of tall chimneys rose skyward, spewing black smoke. The town had a gray, grimy look to it.

They rode into the town circle, and there was a small party there to welcome the Assembly members. Aeron doubted there was anyone to there to welcome him or the Light Horse. No matter, his job was done. He wearily dismounted and began tending to his horse.

"Well! It's about time you got here!"

The voice came from close behind him and he spun about. A familiar face was grinning at him.

"Dilwyn!"

[illegible] families, but the Light Horse would have to camp out, because of a shortage of lodgings. [illegible] they had [illegible] their [illegible]. The town was already [illegible] people who had been evacuated from Hattiesburg, [illegible] available. They found a spot [illegible] and [illegible] still feeling very tired, Aaron curled himself in a blanket and was soon asleep.

He was awakened sometime in the night by [illegible] on his face. [illegible] He got up and [illegible] the fire and [illegible]. The [illegible] and [illegible] Aaron had [illegible] himself that they [illegible] while [illegible] and the others would be [illegible] back [illegible].

It was still [illegible] to Tarnhill. They [illegible] the road, and after a [illegible] west on the [illegible] road. They passed the town of [illegible] and a few [illegible] to the Tarnhill [illegible], including the [illegible], for [illegible] passing Pickbury, they turned north along the [illegible] Tarnhill [illegible] after noon.

Tarnhill was a [illegible] larger than Pickbury [illegible]. Beyond it were the [illegible], not exactly mountains, but the tallest hills in the [illegible]. They were [illegible] with [illegible] and [illegible] most of the [illegible] metals. [illegible] was home to many [illegible] and dozens of [illegible]. The town [illegible].

They rode into the town [illegible] and there was a small party there to welcome the Assembly members. Aaron [illegible] there was [illegible] for [illegible] Light Horse. [illegible] had begun [illegible].

"Well, it's about time you got here."

The voice came from close behind him and he spun about. A [illegible] face was grinning at him.

[illegible]

Chapter 17

Aeron stood staring for a dozen heartbeats and then gasped: "So this is where you've been hiding! You and Bobart disappeared right after we got to the guardberg, and I wasn't able to get any word at all about where you'd gone to! But Tanmill? What are you doing here? Is Bobart here, too?"

Dilwyn Brynmor, the Shireling artificer he'd known from the College of Warcraft, stood there with his fists on his hips and laughed. "Well met, Aeron! You always had a head full of questions. Yes, I'm here with Paddy. Well, not here, but up in those hills there." He pointed up into the Northwold. I'd like you to take a little trip with me and all will be explained."

"I need to get my people settled in first and…"

"Bring them along."

"What? Look, Dilwyn, I was told I'd be receiving new orders when I got here."

"And I'm giving them to you."

"You?"

"Well, I'm passing them along. Paddy asked Rootwell to have you sent here. Rootwell arranged it with the Assembly, and well, here you are."

"And no one thought to inform me?"

"Couldn't. This is secret, Aeron, I mean really secret. No, come on, get your cavalry together and we'll go."

Mystified, but intrigued, Aeron went to Einion and told him they still had a bit farther to go. Neither he nor the rest of the Light Horse were happy, but they did as they were told. A half hour later, they were on a road that led up into the hills north of Tanmill.

At first, the road seemed to be one that served the mines, and they met several wagons carrying ore coming down. But after an hour, they took another road that split off from the main one and they saw no more mine traffic. The hills were covered with tall pine trees, and the road wound back and forth through them, higher and higher.

"Where in the world are you taking us, Dilwyn?" asked Aeron in growing impatience.

"We're almost there," replied Dilwyn. "In fact, we *are* there. Look." He pointed ahead.

The road leveled and then started down. The trees opened out and ahead of them, Aeron saw a wide valley surrounded by hills. The valley floor was a mile or more across and was filled with a few buildings, a lot of tents, and a lot of…

"Soldiers!" exclaimed Aeron. "Who… who are they?"

"The Shires' secret reserve," said Dilwyn, grinning an infuriating grin.

Totally gobsmacked, Aeron just gawked. There were enough tents for a couple thousand troops, maybe more. He could see companies drilling in the open areas, and to his amazement, a company on a firing range practicing with muskets!

"But… but how?"

"It was all Paddy's idea. He created this place almost twenty years ago. He calls it the *Holdfast*. His idea was that it would be the Shires' equivalent of the League's College of Warcraft. Even that long ago, he was worried that someday there might be a split."

"Twenty years! How did he keep it secret for so long?"

"Well, for the first nineteen years, there wasn't much here except the main house—you can't see that from here, but once we get closer, you will. Paddy tried to get the Assembly to fund and expand the place, but they didn't see the need and wouldn't go along. Paddy used his own money—he had quite a bit from all his inventions—and got the place started, but it pretty much languished for a long time. All the locals knew about the house, but there were only a handful of Paddy's helpers here at any given time, so they ignored it.

"But about a year ago, when relations with the League started to sour, he managed to get the Assembly to agree to really invest in the place. Now the Holdfast has workshops and laboratories and a lot of talented people. We get the metals we need from the Tanmill foundries, and we've been recruiting volunteers to train in using the things we make. It's quite a thing."

"Sure is," said Aeron. As they rode down the path into the valley, a smaller side-valley came into view, and on a promontory overlooking it, there was a large house with many windows and a stone tower rearing up behind it and attached to the tower was… was…

"What in the Abyss is *that?"* exclaimed Aeron. His cry was echoed by nearly everyone else in the column as they caught sight of it. Attached to the tower near the top there was a long shape. The lower part of it looked like a ship of some sort, made of wood. Above it was a cluster of round, golden objects that looked like a bunch of enormous grapes. But the whole thing appeared to be just floating in the air! *Floating!* It was attached to the tower by some tethers, but there was nothing supporting it at all.

Dilwyn was grinning again. "My words exactly when I first saw it."

"But what *is it?"*

The people from Ej call it an *airship,* and I suppose that's a good name for it. It is like a ship and it sails the air instead of the water."

"People from Ej? Our kin from down south? They're here?"

"Some of them. You know that we've kept contact with them for generations, but only through the long and dangerous routes over lands and seas. This thing - it's called the *Windwalker* - arrived a few months ago. It's something new the Ej dreamed up, and it can make the journey in less than three months."

"That's… that's incredible. And they're here to help us?"

"Well, that's not exactly why they came - they had no idea what was happening here when they left - but they are certainly willing to help us now. With this and a lot of other new ideas. Wait until you see them!"

Aeron's mind was racing. "This would be an amazing help just for reconnaissance alone! We could track the movements of the enemy armies. How high can it fly? Above shot or spell? How fast can it go? How many people can it carry? Can it…?"

Dilwyn laughed. "Easy, Aeron, easy! You'll get all the answers you want, but first let's get your people settled and then you and I can go talk to Paddy."

"I can see why you went to such lengths to keep this secret. If the League found out, they probably would have struck sooner and marched straight here rather than bothering about Hodenburg."

"Yes, that was our biggest worry - especially after we snuck Paddy away. I'm sure there are some in the League that suspect we've been up to something like this. That's why we didn't send any help down to you before the recent battle. What little we had ready wouldn't have tipped the balance, but they might have tipped off the Rhordians to what we're up to."

They reached the valley floor, and suddenly Gwenith exclaimed: "Oh look! Look! Aren't they adorable?"

Aeron wrenched his eyes away from the airship and looked for what had caught Gwenith's attention. He didn't have to look far. In a fenced-in enclosure was a cluster… herd… *pack!* …of aralez. Adults and younger ones and puppies. Lots of them. He had to admit that the puppies were about the cutest things he'd ever seen - even though these 'puppies' were the size of adult sheep.

Gwenith kept staring, and Aeron saw a tear trickle down her cheek. "What's the matter with her?" asked Dilwyn.

"She had an aralez of her own, but it was killed in the battle. It hit her really hard. I don't suppose you have any to spare?"

"Well, maybe," said Dilwyn, looking at Gwenith. "Who is she? Is she part of your unit? She's really cute, isn't she?"

"She's my cousin. Second cousin, actually. Her name is Gwenith, and if you want to win her favor, getting her another aralez would be about the best way you could go about it."

"Really? Well, we were thinking about outfitting an entire unit with them. Maybe it could be yours. I'll talk to Paddy about it."

He wasn't sure if he was joking or not, but no more was said on that subject. They reached an empty piece of land, and Dilwyn told them they could set up their camp there. "I'll see about getting you some tents, forage, and rations." He waited while things got organized and then tugged on Aeron's sleeve. "Come on, your people can handle this. I want to get you up to see Paddy before he takes his nap."

Aeron didn't need to be asked twice. He was very eager to see Bobart again and maybe - finally - get some answers about why he was here and what was going on. He told Einion where he was going and then followed Dilwyn.

Their path took them through the heart of the Holdfast. Workshops, storage sheds, furnaces, and forges all were beehives of activity with people running hither and yon, carrying things or running errands. There were barracks for the workers and kitchens to feed them. "I'll give you a proper tour of the place tomorrow. We work in shifts, all day and all night," explained Dilwyn.

There were rows of cannons parked outside. Some were of the conventional sort, but others had multiple barrels. "Volley guns, we call them," said Dilwyn when Aeron asked about them. "Smaller shot, but they can send out a hail of them. Not so good at knocking down walls, but they'll sure knock down infantry or cavalry." He pointed out another odd one with just two barrels. "That was an experiment that didn't work. The idea was to have two cannon balls connected with a stout chain. Fire off both barrels aimed a bit apart, and the balls and chain would slice through a whole formation of troops like a scythe through wheat."

"Why doesn't it work?"

Dilwyn shook his head. "Can't get both barrels to fire at exactly the same time. They share a common touchhole, but there is still something wrong with the timing. Either the chain breaks or the balls and the chain go flying off in some totally crazy direction. More dangerous to our side than the enemy. No time to fiddle with it now, though, we have other things to do."

"We sure could have used some of this during the battle," said Aeron, shaking his head.

"I know, and we all felt really bad not being able to help. But most of this stuff has only been finished in the last couple of fortnights. We don't have trained crews for most of them, and damn, we don't even have the horse teams and limbers to haul them yet. Yes, we could have sent off eight or ten of them, but we've seen reports of the battle. Do you really think a handful of cannons would have changed the outcome?"

Aeron though about it and had to realize that Dilwyn was right. "No, they just would have ended up captured by the Rhordians."

"Exactly. We need to save these until we can use them in force and at some decisive moment."

They walked on, past all the activity, and then started up a winding road that led to the big house on the hillside. As he got closer, Aeron realized it really was an immense structure, probably one of the biggest in all the Shires. It was built along the old traditional lines of the *cloctan,* with round walls tapering as they went up. But this place was partially built into the hillside so the walls didn't go completely around—or at least the outsides of them didn't, perhaps inside they were round and delved back into the hillside. But there was layer after layer going upward and smaller *cloctans* budding off on either side, attached to the main structure but also a part of the hill. The uppermost layers curved in on themselves to form the roofs. It looked rather like a strange clump of mushrooms. Scores of windows pierced the walls at many different spots. And there were a few doors opening out at the upper levels to small balconies carved out of the hill. At the rear was a tall stone tower reaching skyward, and tethered to the tower was the incredible airship.

"None of that is new," said Aeron pointing to the building. "Paddy must have had big plans for this place."

"Yes, like I said, he wanted it to be our counterpart to the College of Warcraft. He calls it *Golwg Bell* in the Old Tongue. He dreamed of having dozens of mages and artificers and engineers all working and studying here. And not strictly Shirefolk, either, it would have been a center of learning for the whole region. From what I understand, there has usually been someone here over the years, even if just as a caretaker. But since the troubles began, Paddy sent out the word to recruit anyone and everyone in the Shires who might be able to help out. It went slowly at first, but in the last few months, it's become a flood and things have really started moving."

"How long have you known about this?"

"About two years. One winter, I escorted Paddy home for a visit, and he took me here. It was all covered with snow - beautiful here in the winter - with just a couple of people taking care of the place. That's when he told me about all his plans - and his disappointment. Didn't think all that much of it at the time, but now all of his plans and dreams are starting to bear fruit."

"So why am I here? I mean it has been fine seeing you again, but I'm not a mage or an artificer or an engineer."

"Wait until you talk to Paddy."

So he held his tongue and tried not to trip over his feet as he stared at the airship. "What holds it up?"

"All of those golden globes, there."

"What's in them?"

"Nothing."

"You mean it's a secret and you can't talk about it?"

"No, I mean there is literally nothing inside the globes, a pure vacuum."

"And that's capable of lifting up a big thing like that?"

"Sure. Things float in water because they weigh less than the volume of water they displace. It works the same way for air. The trick is that to keep the air from crushing a sphere with a vacuum inside, the sphere, if it was made of metal, it would have to be so thick and heavy that it wouldn't float. The spheres up there do have some metal in them - gold actually - but it's incredibly thin, and what is really keeping the sphere from being crushed is a magic spell. Understand?"

"No. But it obviously works, so that's good enough I guess. And as long as... *Missing Gods! What's that?!"*

A dark shape had launched itself from the side of the airship. For an instant, Aeron thought it was some person trying to kill themselves, but then two enormous wings unfolded from its back and it looked like a huge bird of some sort. It didn't fall, it soared; turning and banking exactly like a bird. And then its wings began to flap and it gained height for a bit, and then the wings folded back and it went into a dive and swooped down toward them. He could see it clearly now, and it was a Shireling with mechanical wings strapped to it! The thing came out of its dive and flashed past them, not a rod overhead. "Hey Dilwyn! Watch this!" cried the flier as it went past. The contraption, moving at what seemed an incredible speed, zoomed upward, higher and higher, until it was going almost straight up and had slowed nearly to a stop; then it tilted over on its back and went downward again, gaining speed and flying off to the south.

"Show off," muttered Dilwyn. "That was Hazad B'deen, one of the people from Ej, they brought us a bunch of interesting gadgets - like those wings."

"How many do you have? How far can they fly?" Aeron's amazement just kept growing.

"Not enough and not too far. They've got a little magical steam generator to power them—sort of like how Helga worked—but they don't last long, maybe a half hour or so. Not much use for scouting, but we're working on some small bombs they could drop. Ought to come as a big surprise to the Rhordians."

"They're certainly a surprise to me!"

They reached the doors to the big house and went in. There were no guards. The entry hall was all done in fine woodwork, intricately carved, stained, and polished. Several portraits hung on the walls, but Aeron didn't recognize the subjects. Doors led to two large rooms on either side and two corridors ran off toward the rear. A grand staircase, right in front of them, led upward. Dilwyn started upward and Aeron followed. "It's quite a climb to Paddy's study," he said.

"How does Paddy manage it?

"Oh, he's not so frail as he tries to make people think, but there is a winch and pully system built into the back of the place for him when he needs it."

They went up the stairs to the second floor. The stair got narrower but continued on up as did they. Aeron noticed that the fine woodwork and portraits did not extend above the first floor. Higher up, the walls were simple whitewashed plaster, and the door frames and hand rails were painted wood. Some of the plaster was cracked. The construction of the building seemed to match the history of Paddy's dream: a grand beginning and then… nothing. But now a rebirth, it seemed.

There were a number of wall sconces to give light, most of them appeared to be magical, emitting light with no flame. Several cleverly positioned windows also let in light to the stairwell. At each landing, corridors led off to Aeron knew not what.

Finally, they reached the top floor of the main building, but they weren't done yet. A corridor led back to where the walls became stone, and Aeron realized this must be the tower he'd seen. A much smaller, circular stair led upward, and by the time they reached the top, he was puffing. They paused for a moment to catch their breaths, and then Dilwyn rapped on a heavy wood door.

"Come in! Come in!" came a muffled voice that Aeron recognized as belonging to Paddy Bobart. Dilwyn pushed the door open and they went in. Paddy was seated at a desk piled with papers and small devices of unknown function. This room had the same sort of finishes and decorations as the entry hall and would have been quite elegant except for the piles of… junk that cluttered almost every horizontal surface. Paddy caught sight of them, and his face brightened. "Ah! There you are at last. Sit down! Sit down!" He gestured to several chairs in front of his desk.

Dilwyn ruthlessly evicted a large orange tabby cat from one of the chairs while Aeron had to move a very odd-looking potted plant from another.

They sat down facing the ancient artificer. "So, Cadwallader, what do you think?"

"Of this place? It's amazing, sir. But how soon can we get some of your devices out in the field to help the army? As I'm sure you realize, we are in a desperate situation."

Paddy looked to Dilwyn and grinned, his old, wrinkled face wrinkling even more. "See? What did I tell you? Came right to the point, didn't he?"

"No surprise to me, sir," replied Dilwyn.

"No, I suppose not, you've spent some time with him, haven't you? But in answer to your question, young sir, it will all depend on how quickly we can turn all of the equipment and inventions you've seen into an effective fighting force. I love my gadgets, but even I know that such things aren't any better than the people who will be operating them. So I'll turn your question around and ask you: How soon can you hammer all this into an effective field force?"

"Me?!" said Aeron in shock.

"Yes, you. Why in blazes do you think I asked Dunstan Rootwell to send you here?"

Aeron tried to catch his breath, but his throat felt like it was cutting off the air. Him? *He* was supposed to take these wonders and turn them into an army? Or part of an army? "I… I…" he gobbled.

"Well?" said Bobart.

"Paddy, you're hitting him with an awful lot all at once. Give him a chance to digest this," said Dilwyn.

"Maybe. But he said himself that the situation is desperate."

"What…? What do I have to work with?" asked Aeron, trying to pull his thoughts together. "I need to know numbers. Equipment, people… And what sort of authority do I have?"

"Dilwyn can supply you with the numbers," said Paddy. "As for your authority…" He looked around his desk and then started rummaging among the papers. "Where is that blasted thing?" Dilwyn watched him for a few moments and then leaned forward and pointed. Paddy frowned at him but snatched up the paper and looked at it. "Yes, this is it. This is a letter from Rootwell, giving you complete authority to assemble and organize and command whatever force we can create here and then lead it to a rendezvous with the forces commanded by Conwy Macsen, at which point the combined force will be jointly commanded by the two of you."

"Jointly?" said Aeron in amazement. He almost reached out to grab the paper, but restrained himself. "Will Macsen agree to that?"

"Why would he have anything to say about it?" asked Dilwyn.

"He… uh, he doesn't much like me."

"Do you think he'd disobey a direct order from the Muster-Master?" asked Bobart.

"No, probably not…"

"Well then don't worry about it! You've got a lot more things to worry about right now—and I suggest you get to it, Mister Cadwallader."

Dilwyn got up and motioned Aeron to do the same. The cat immediately repossessed the chair. "Come on, I have an office set up for you. All the figures are there, and you can have a look at them before dinner."

They went back out into the hallway, and Dilwyn led him down several flights, back into the main part of the building, and then along a short corridor and through a door into a spacious, but very plain office with several desks and tables, a number of chairs, and a large set of doors with glass windows leading out to a balcony, which overlooked the valley.

"Over here, I've complied lists of what we have right now and what we think we'll complete in the next couple of months," said Dilwyn. "And over there are lists of the people we've got working with us and how many more we can expect to arrive."

Feeling overwhelmed, Aeron sat down and started going through the documents. Dilwyn helped explain it all, but much of it didn't make sense on the first go through. "Now I know what Rootwell meant," he mumbled.

"What? What did he say?"

"He told me I was in it up to my neck!"

* * * * *

After several hours, he felt like he was getting a grasp of what was going on and even starting to get some ideas about how to organize and employ this unexpected boon. As the afternoon turned toward evening, Dilwyn said: "Let's take a break. I'll show you your room and you can get cleaned up for dinner. There are some people you need to meet."

Aeron's room was right across the hall from his office. He was still trying to grasp the idea that he had a room and an office. He was simultaneously unsurprised and appalled that his belongings were somehow already in his room. The room itself was cozy, with a bed, table, chest of drawers, and a small window (which didn't show much except the hill rising behind the building). "I feel like some stray sheep the dogs are chasing back to the flock. You seem to have everything planned out for me, Dilwyn."

The young artificer laughed. "I think Paddy started making plans for you the day you stared down Helga back at the college."

"Poor Helga. Has Paddy built a replacement for her?"

"He's started working on one. I'll show it to you tomorrow. But here, why don't you wash up and get changed? There's a little garderobe just through that door. I'll meet you down on the main floor in a half hour?"

"All right, thanks." Dilwyn departed.

Aeron stretched out on the bed and tried to let his wits catch up with all that had happened. It was hard; things were moving so fast. In spite of his excitement it had been a long couple of days and he was exhausted. He nearly fell asleep right there but roused himself, washed and changed clothes, and made his way down stairs to meet Dilwyn. He had intended to ask Dilwyn to send a messenger to Captain Einion to let him know what was going on, but there was Einion himself in the entrance hall, along with quite a group of other people.

Everyone turned as he came down the stairs, and he felt very self-conscious. But then he took a closer look at some of the others and his attention was immediately focused on them. They were of the People, but unlike any he'd ever seen before. Their skin was much darker, with a reddish glow to it, sort of like a strong tea color. Their hair was also dark, ranging from dark brown to a shiny black. *People from Ej!*

Dilwyn came over and took him by the arm. "Here are some of the people I wanted you to meet." He drew him over to the crowd. He did know a few of them, Paddy; Einion; there was Tomos Gerallt, the other artificer from the College of Warcraft; and also Heilyn Culhwch, head of the Shires Assembly - he must have come from Tanmill later in the day - but the rest were strangers.

Dilwyn took him right up to one of the Ej people and said: "Anas, this is Aeron Cadwallader, the one I was telling you about. Aeron, this is Anas Macadrian, the head of the Ej delegation." The fellow was of middle years, shorter and stouter than Aeron, but he had chubby cheeks and a wide smile. Aeron extended his hand, and Anas grabbed his arm near the elbow and shook, dwarf-fashion.

"A pleasure! A great pleasure to meet you, Ser Aeron!" he exclaimed. There was an odd accent to his Common, but Aeron could understand him easily enough.

"And you, sir," said Aeron. "An honor to meet distant kin from so far away."

"The honor is all ours. Here, let me introduce you to my colleagues. This is Lachen Panchali, Golsing Sagira, Chafik Gaetan, and Wiam Cadalaria." The names came so fast Aeron knew he'd never remember which one went with which person, except for the last which belonged to a woman, the only one in the group from Ej.

Dilwyn then pointed out and named a dozen other people, all apparently from the workshops and laboratories of Paddy's Holdfast. He had no hope of remembering any of the names, but he supposed he'd be working with some of these people and would learn them later.

Bobart then announced that they should seat themselves for dinner and led the way into a spacious dining room off the entrance hall. A long polished table could accommodate enough chairs to seat everyone. Dozens of glowing crystals - obviously magical - hanging from above or mounted on brass rods like candlesticks on the table provided a strong clear light. Bobart took the seat at the head of the table, naturally enough, with Anas Macadrian on his right and Heilyn Culhwch on his left. Aeron was placed on Anas's right with the Ej woman, Wiam, to his own right. Directly across from him was another of the Ej people, Golsing... Golsing something or other...

"Honored guests," said Paddy loudly, getting everyone's attention. "Welcome to the Holdfast. We have gathered here in a time of crisis. In a time when all our people are threatened. Some of you come from nearby, while others of you come from an almost unimaginable distance. Here, working here together, we shall meet every challenge and overcome the threat. But enough talk! Dinner awaits!"

The diners all applauded, and then people appeared bearing plates and bowls and platters of food, pitchers of ale and bottles of wine. What followed was a feast such as Aeron had rarely enjoyed. The food was truly excellent. Soup, salad, fish, meat, potatoes, vegetables and a golden bread which tasted better than any he had ever had. When the dinner had first started, he wondered if he could manage to stay awake, but instead of the food making him sleepy, he found that he was fully alert and filled with energy. He had no trouble following and even participating the swirl of conversations going on around the table.

Much of the talk was about things happening at the Holdfast; topics involving engineering and magic that he could scarcely understand. Even more involved the current war, and he was able to provide some first-hand accounts of the disastrous battle and the defenses being built at Hodenburg.

But he also managed to strike up a conversation with Wiam about her journey here from Ej. "Dilwyn said that your voyage in the airship only took about three months. Is that correct?"

"It took a bit more than three months," she said. "The *Windwalker* can go from ten to twenty leagues a day, depending on the wind. It's a thousand leagues from Ej to here in a straight line, but we were obliged to take a more roundabout route. We didn't want to stray too far from land in case we ran into trouble - the airship is brand new and often requires a good bit of tinkering to keep it working. We did have to land several times to make repairs or take on fresh water, but we found deserted islands or inaccessible mountaintops. Several times we encountered bad storms that forced us to land - we can't fight a really strong wind. Once we were north of the Infant Sea, well, we didn't want to let everyone know we existed, so we tried to stay over sparsely inhabited lands as much as possible. People did see us, of course, but hopefully just small groups who no one else will believe."

"Why the secrecy? You didn't know about the war yet."

Wiam shrugged. "Anas insisted on it. He says humans are greedy, and if they knew we had such a thing, they'd try to take it away from us. I wasn't sure I believed him, but once we got here and found out about what was going on, I can see he was right."

"Well, I'm surely glad you are here. Dilwyn tried to explain to me how the golden balls made it float, but what makes it go where you want and not just drift on the wind?"

Anas, overhearing, turned and said: "Tomorrow we shall take you aboard and show you, Ser Aeron. If you like, of course."

"I would like that very much, and thank you."

"Excellent! I look forward to hearing what the Shires' master strategist has to say about our device and how it can help in this war."

"Master strategist?"

"That is what you are, isn't it? That is certainly what I have been led to believe by Master Bobart and Master Dilwyn."

Aeron took a large gulp of his wine. "I think… I think they may have been exaggerating a bit. I have learned some things and sometimes I have ideas which I think are good. But master strategist? That does me far more honor than I deserve!"

"Your modesty speaks well of you. A doer rather than a boaster. But you are the one who will decide how the things being made here will be employed in the coming battles, is that not so?"

"That is the plan, Anas," said Bobart, joining in. "But don't put so much pressure on the lad. He's just started his task and will take a while to feel his way into it, eh?"

"Ah, I see," said Anas. "A thousand pardons if I have overstepped myself." He made an odd little gesture, touching his chest over his heart, then his forehead, and then spreading his fingers toward Aeron.

"Uh, no apology needed, sir," said Aeron, trying to take everything in.

There was a stir at the far end of the room as several people wheeled in a cart on which an enormous pudding sat. They were followed by a stout Shireling woman with gray hair and a flour-covered apron protecting her dress. She was smiling broadly.

"Ah there you are, Beata!" cried Paddy. "You should have been here enjoying your art with us instead of creating more!"

"None of that from you, Paddy!" she replied, laughing. "If it is my art, as you say, then I'll be the one to judge when it's finished."

Paddy laughed in turn and then got up from his seat. "Friends! Not all of you have met the creator of our fine feast. Allow me to introduce Beata Glyndwr, or 'Momma Beata,' as she likes to be called. She is not only a cook beyond compare, but a practitioner of what I call *Gastromancy*, food mixed with magic. We savored one of her special creations tonight, and I imagine you felt some of its effects. I certainly did! I feel like I could go all night."

Aeron realized the feeling of energy he had experienced earlier must be the magical food! He had heard of magic potions and the like, but never magic food. The pudding was served, and he looked at the portion on the plate in front of him. It smelled delicious, and he quickly found that it tasted as good as it smelled. A warmth in his belly made him wonder if there was spirits in it, even though he had not tasted anything like that. The warmth seemed to spread all through him, and all his cares and worries seemed to melt away. There was war and battle ahead, but somehow he knew they would be victorious. The people around him here were friends and allies he could count on. Working together, they could not fail! He looked around at the people at the table and smiled.

Paddy was smiling back at him.

The pudding!

He suddenly knew that this strange euphoria must have been cause by the pudding. The knowledge did not change the feeling, but at least he understood it. "An… an army eating food like this would have a real advantage, wouldn't it?" he asked to the room in general. "Strength and endurance, good morale… what other effects can be had?"

"We're still experimenting," said Paddy. "But you don't miss much, do you, Cadwallader?" He turned to the rest of the diners. "Friends, I can tell you are all sharing the good feelings, but as Mister Cadwallader has discerned, they were caused - at least in part - by the marvelous pudding provided by

Mama Beata. Her special foods cannot only aid a person's physical well-being, but their spiritual as well. The bread you ate earlier increased your strength and stamina, the pudding here will lift your spirits. We plan to produce enough of these—and others—for the army. With all of the other wonders we are tinkering together here, we can expect to go on to victory!"

Whether it was Paddy's words or the pudding, everyone cheered, and soon they were on their feet giving toasts to the Shires and to the Ej and to each other. Aeron had far more wine than he should have, and even Mama Beata's bread couldn't counteract it entirely. The dinner dishes were swept away and replaced with a selection of cheeses, the pipes came out, and the room was soon filled with more pleasant aromas. The people mingled and talked as the moon rose high in the sky.

After a while, Dilwyn took Aeron aside and herded him across the hall to what was a meeting room. Paddy and Anas and Heilyn Culhwch were already there. Dilwyn shut the door after them. Paddy was sitting on a well-upholstered chair, and all of the good humor he had displayed that evening was missing.

"Well!" he said, huffing out his breath. "Three messages have arrived, one almost on top of the other. The first, from Dunstan Rootwell, was expected: the Rhordians have surrounded Hodenburg and are constructing siegeworks. The second is from Conwy Macsen saying that the enemy is pushing out a screening force toward Picksbury but have not attacked yet. He is watching them carefully."

"And the third?" asked Culhwch.

"The third," said Paddy with a long sigh, "was forwarded to us by Macsen. It is a list of demands sent to us by the League; it arrived in his camp only an hour after he sent his first message. On the face of it, it is outrageous. They demand that we completely disband our military and submit to occupation of all our cities and major towns by the forces of the League."

"What?!" cried nearly everyone at once. "That's impossible! We'll never submit!"

Paddy made a motion to quiet down, and they did. "The interesting thing about the demand is that they give us a *month* to reply. Note that they are *not* proposing any sort of truce in the meantime. I'm not entirely sure what that all means - or what is going to happen when the month is up." He paused and looked from face to face.

"What it does mean is that we have got an enormous amount to do and no more than a month to do it."

Chapter 18

The next morning, Aeron was given a whirlwind tour of the Holdfast. They started out with a short flight on the *Windwalker*. "Best to do it early when the winds are lighter," said Dilwyn. "It can handle a moderate wind, but coming back here to hook on to the tower is difficult and easier to do if it's calm."

Anas and the Ej crew were already aboard and waiting. Actually, getting on the airship was the scariest part. A narrow wood and rope walkway had been strung between the ship and the tower, and they had to walk across one at a time while it jiggled and swayed beneath them. Once aboard, the walkway was reeled in, the other ropes holding the ship in place were cast off, and the *Windwalker* drifted away on the gentle breeze.

Anas spoke a command, and several of the crew ran to the metal rods that rose up from dozens of locations and connected to the golden balls above them. They did something - Aeron could not tell what - and the ship began to rise rapidly, the tower of the *Golwg Bell* seeming to fall away below them.

"What makes it go up and down?" asked Aeron to Anas. "Dilwyn tried to explain to me about your golden balls filled with nothing, but I'm afraid I didn't really understand it all."

"Well, I don't really understand *how* the lift spheres - that's what they are called - are made. Our master artificers back in Ej created them, but their art is far beyond me. They work by displacing the air, and the more air they displace for their weight, the more lift they have. By manipulating the spell that creates the sphere, we can make it expand or contract. Bigger and we go up, smaller and we come down. Simple, see?"

"I think. But what about moving forward? How does that work?"

"That is really quite a lot simpler. Come over here." He motioned Aeron toward the side of the ship. The only thing like a ship Aeron had ever been on before was one of the barges on the Tanmill canal, but he had seen drawings of seagoing vessels. The main hull of *Windwalker* was shaped very much like one of those: long and narrow, pointed at the front and blunt at the back. Gingerly looking over the side - they were really quite high now - he saw that there were a series of panels attached to the hull. On Anas's command, there was a clank and a squeal of machinery, and the panels all swung out on hinges until they were sticking straight out from the hull. Then they all quickly swept back against the hull again. The motion repeated again and again, like the oars on a galley. As he looked closer, he saw that there were flaps on each of the panels which opened as they moved forward and snapped shut when they went back, catching the air.

"Sort of like the fins on a fish," he said.

"Yes, exactly," said Anas. "Here, come below and you can see how it works." He led him to a small stairway going down into the hull to another deck. It was dim down there, although there were some small windows letting in light and a few of the glowing crystals like he'd seen in Paddy's house. As his eyes adjusted, he could see a bewildering array of shafts, rods, and pulleys lining the inside of the hull. They were moving rhythmically, and he had to assume they were what were making the panels on the outside move. "Sorry about the noise. Our engineers are trying to do something about that, but no luck so far." Anas had to speak loudly to be heard. "A magically heated boiler provides the power."

"Like on Paddy's Iron Beast?"

"Very similar, yes. Come, let's go back up."

Up and away from most of the noise, there was a noticeable breeze now created by the airship's motion. The valley was now far below, and Aeron could see over the hills to Tanmill and beyond. The Wildwood was a dark patch in the distance. He peered off to the south, hoping to see Picksbury, but the far horizon was just a haze. *Windwalker* was circling, which prompted Aeron to ask how it was steered.

"We can move the panels on each side at a different rate," explained Anas, "just like an oared water vessel. Make the right side ones go faster and we will turn to the left."

"This is truly amazing, sir," said Aeron, "and as much as I'd love to fly around with you all day, I really need to get back to work."

"Yes," said Dilwyn, who had been silent the whole time. "We all do."

Docking the airship was a lot trickier than launching it had been, and it took quite a while to get it lined up properly, toss ropes to some waiting people on the tower, and then haul it in and tie it up and get the walkway rigged. Dilwyn was getting impatient and grumpily suggested that they just land on the ground, but Anas only laughed and insisted that this was good practice for his crew. Finally, they were off the ship and back into the tower.

"I want to show you our other operations in more detail this morning," Dilwyn said to Aeron as they went down the stairs. A pair of ponies were waiting for them outside the front doors, and they mounted up and rode off.

One by one, they inspected the workshops. All of them were producing weapons and armor and other items. Most of the things had something special or magical about them. "We have workshops in Tanmill producing non-magical weapons, too, of course," said Dilwyn. "Obviously it would be wonderful for all our troops to have the special gear, but that's simply impossible. It takes too long to make and requires materials that are in short supply. But we hope to be able to equip some of our troops with what we make here. I talked to Paddy and Culhwch about giving your Picksbury Light Horse the aralez. We had been thinking of spreading them around so that commanders would have them and a few for each cavalry unit. Do you think concentrating them all in one group is a good idea?"

"I saw how effective the ones we had in the Light Horse were during the battle," replied Aeron. "I really wished we had more. Spreading them around would help out each unit that had them a bit, but not a lot. But if we had a whole unit of them, with the riders properly armed and armored, we'd have something that could take on the Rhordian heavy horse head on and win. So yes, I think it's a good idea."

"All right, I'll see what I can do. And if it makes that Gwenith happy, who knows?" He smiled at Aeron.

They continued the tour. One shop they came to had several magic-wielding artificers working on things that did not appear to be weapons. They were strangely shaped metal objects on poles. "What are these?"

"Ah," said Dilwyn, "these are new. As you know, we are seriously short on warmages. We have a very few who can cast battle magic and a few more who can block spells cast by enemy mages, but in a major battle, we'd be badly outmatched. These are meant to balance things out."

"How?"

"These objects are being imbued with powerful counter-magic. If they work properly, they should cancel out any spell aimed in their general vicinity. We are planning to use them like battle standards and issue them to as many units as we can."

"That would be excellent," said Aeron. "In the battle south of Hodenburg, the Rhordian magic turned our retreat into a rout. If we had something like this… well, we still would have lost, but not as badly. And in the next fight, they might help us win."

They kept moving, and Dilwyn took him to another building that had a locked door. He produced a key and let him inside. "You were asking if Paddy was making another Iron Beast. He is, but the work is going slowly. I doubt he'll have it ready in time. Take a look."

Aeron walked in to a poorly lit building that had cluttered workbenches along the walls, chains on pullies hanging down from the roof beams, and a huge shape standing in the middle. It looked a bit like Helga, but it was clearly unfinished. Side and top panels were off, and the innards had a lot of empty spaces where he assumed machinery would go. "It looks like a different design than Helga," said Aeron.

"Here is what it's supposed to look like when it's finished." Dilwyn picked up a sheet of parchment from a bench and handed it to him.

He looked it over. "This looks like drawings I've seen in books, not so much like Helga."

"Yes, this is a very conventional design. Four legs, the head with long tusks, and a command cabin on top with room for a small cannon and a few other weapons."

"Helga didn't have a command cabin and didn't have any weapons except the tusks and the two arms with all the blades and such. Why the difference?"

Dilwyn looked uneasy and glanced around even though no one else was there. "I wondered that myself for a long time. Then one night, just before we fled Eowulf, Paddy had a little too much to drink and I found out the truth."

"Truth? What truth? You make it sound like some dire secret."

"Well, it is, really." His voice fell to a whisper. "Helga was no ordinary Iron Beast. Paddy was… Paddy was dabbling in necromancy."

"Necromancy!" exclaimed Aeron.

"Shhh! Don't ever mention this to anyone! I probably shouldn't have even told you."

"Well you did, and now you're going to have to explain it all. Come on, Dilwyn, give!"

Dilwyn sighed and shook his head, but Aeron thought he looked like someone who desperately wanted to get something off his chest. Finally, he spoke: "Paddy was trying to build an improved Iron Beast. That's the way he is: always trying to do things better than before. One of the weaknesses of the traditional Iron Beasts, like the ones the dwarfs make, is that they need a crew to drive them. In the control cabin, there are valves and levers to make it move and fight. If the crew gets killed, the beast is helpless. Paddy was looking for some way to make an Iron Beast that could control itself. Something you could just turn loose against an enemy army and let it raise havoc. So he dispensed with the control cabin and the cannon and added the mechanical arms."

"That *would* be something devastating," said Aeron, imagining such a thing rampaging through throngs of packed troops. "But what's necromancy have to do with it?" He knew very little about that dark and usually forbidden art that somehow raised and controlled dead creatures.

"He couldn't make it work! He tried all sorts of things to allow his beast to do what he wanted, and while he managed a few tricks with clockwork mechanisms and such, nothing really did the job. This is where it gets strange. Paddy had a little dog, just a mongrel he found somewhere, but he was very fond of it. Its name was Helga."

"Helga! The same as the Iron Beast?" A sudden horror filled Aeron. "You mean he… he…?"

"He didn't kill the dog if that's what you were thinking. He'd never do that. But Helga was dying of old age, and apparently Paddy had some knowledge of necromancy—don't ask me how—and somehow he managed to capture the poor critter's soul and lock it into the Iron Beast."

"Missing Gods…"

"This was all before I arrived at the College, mind you. From what some of the others there told me, Helga acted *very* strangely for a long while, and Paddy had to disconnect a lot of it to keep it from hurting anyone. Eventually, he got it under control. Or mostly so."

"Is… Is he going to try again with this one? But no, you said it was going to have a normal control set run by people."

"He was thinking about it, but I told him there was no way I'd help with such an abomination, and he gave up on the idea. He really does miss his Helga, though."

I wonder if Helga still misses him?

They went back outside and Dilwyn locked the building up again. Now they rode toward the camps and training areas where the troops were working. "I read your reports on the numbers of soldiers you have, but it didn't really mention where they were coming from," said Aeron. "Where are you getting all these troops?"

"Well, a lot are locals who have volunteered, we've pulled out almost all of the troops from the guardburgs on the western and northern borders, and others are coming from Abbetshire. We've stripped the garrison of Yangmere to the bone."

"Is that wise?" asked Aeron. Yangmere was the second largest city in the Shires. "What if an attack comes down from the north? The League has a lot of forces around Hodenburg, but they still have troops they haven't committed yet."

"It's a risk," agreed Dilwyn, "but it is seeming like Duke Berlonviche's heart really isn't in this war. He was always the one on the best terms with us of all the dukes. He's made no move against us during all this and has sent very few troops to join the forces coming against us from Eowulf."

"Could be a ruse to make you weaken your defenses facing him."

"Could be, but we are going to have to take some chances if we are going to make this work. But then you are in command here, *Lord Cadwallader*, do you want me to tell those troops to go on home?"

"Call me that again, and I'll hit you, Dilwyn. But no, don't send them back. If we can't beat the army around Hodenburg, it doesn't really matter what happens at Yangmere."

They spent the rest of the morning looking over the troops drilling and practicing with their weapons. Spearman and archers, musketeers and the cannoneers with their guns. They were enthusiastic, but except for a few of the trained bands from Yangmere, looked awfully inexperienced. He went over to where the Picksbury Light Horse was camped and gave them the news about the aralez. Gwenith was thrilled. Most of the rest were receptive to the idea, although a fair number were unhappy about giving up their horses.

"We'll get you matched up with your new mounts as soon as we can, so you can start drilling with them, Captain," said Aeron. "But in the meantime, I want to borrow your best sergeants and corporals to help with training these other troops. They really need some help."

"Uh, but they're all infantry, Aeron. Not sure what our people can teach them."

"They've seen the other infantry drill. They know the basic moves. And they can teach them discipline and let them know how important that is in a fight. It will be better than nothing. I'm going to set up a school to train officers and sergeants, but this will do until I can get that going. All right?"

"Yes, sir."

They went back to the *Golwg Bell* for lunch. Afterward, they met with Paddy, Anas, Golsing Sagira, Heilyn Culhwch, and Mama Beata for a strategy meeting. To Aeron's delight, there was a large map spread out on the table and a batch of colored blocks to show where troops were located. They used this sort of thing all the time in the College of Warcraft, but this was the first time he'd seen this in the Shires. "I assume I have you to thank for this, Dilwyn?" he asked.

"I thought it might come in useful."

"It surely will!" He peered at the map and nodded. "This is the most detailed map of the Shires I've ever seen. It looks new, too. Where did you find it?"

"I put some of our apprentices to work making it soon after we arrived. They collected every map they could find and then did some actual survey work and then put all the information together to create this. I've got them making smaller copies right now to use in the field."

Aeron's opinion of Dilwyn's abilities, never low to begin with, ticked up another notch. It was becoming clear that he wasn't just Paddy's assistant and caretaker, he was his executive officer and probably in charge of most of the actual work going on at the Holdfast.

Paddy sat at the head of the table, but the rest of them stood to better see the map and allow them to move the blocks around. At the moment, there were large green blocks in Hodenburg, near Picksbury, and in the Holdfast. Smaller blocks were in Yangmere and Ferchester, and then a number of even smaller blocks scattered in various locations. Large red blocks—denoting League forces—were at Hodenburg, south of Picksbury, and then smaller ones scattered around the borders.

"All right," said Aeron, "Rootwell has seven thousands in Hodenburg, Macsen has five thousands more at Picksbury, and we have around four thousands here. From your figures, Dilwyn, there are maybe another three or four thousands in the other garrisons or acting as pickets along the border. Nineteen or twenty thousands in all. That's quite a lot, really."

"Keep in mind that easily a third of those are newly raised levies. Untrained, underequipped, and with a lot of young, old, and women in them," said Dilwyn.

"Yes, I know," he said, thinking about his last sight of Nesta and Mererid, armed and armored, and ready to fight.

"And what's wrong with women, I might ask, you young whelp?" asked Mama Beata.

"Uh, why nothing…" stammered Dilwyn, clearly surprised. "It's just… just…"

"It's just that you think we women belong in the kitchen makin' you grub and not out there defendin' our homes, eh?"

"That's… that's… not what I…"

"Pah!" spat the woman. "I've heard it all before, so don't bother sayin' any more, Dilwyn Brynmor!"

Dilwyn wisely took her advice and said no more. He looked desperately at Aeron, and Aeron came to his rescue. "Ah, yes… so nineteen or twenty thousands, with some of them untrained. Now what about the enemy? When I was at the College, we saw some studies done by the League, looking at what strength they could mount. If I remember the figures correctly, they said that the human part of the League could produce about forty thousand men."

A lot of grim faces met him from across the table.

"Yes, that sounds like an awful lot, and it doesn't even include any sort of emergency musters they could call up from their larger cities and towns in a crisis, but those studies then broke things down into what could actually be put into a field army. The League needs to guard its other borders, and each duke and all the dukes' barons have castles of their own to guard. A lot of them aren't that popular with their own people, and they can't just march off with all of their troops and leave their castles unguarded. The study said that in practice, they could muster about twenty-five or thirty thousands. That's still a lot, but not an impossible number.

"Now Dilwyn tells me that the Duke of Berlonviche hasn't really committed himself to this war. He's not the most powerful duke, but we can probably subtract another four or five thousands. That's brings what we are facing down to around twenty or twenty-five thousands, an even more manageable number."

He straightened up from peering at the map. "So, with that as a starting point, what do we know about where the Rhordian field forces are right now?"

"Rootwell estimates he has ten or twelve thousands around him at Hodenburg," said Dilwyn. "He's been keeping us informed by pigeon almost every day."

"Good, good, that's what we were hoping for: his seven thousands holding down a much larger force."

"Yes, but they also have another force pushed out north of Hodenburg watching Macsen's forces at Picksbury. He estimates it at seven or eight thousands." Dilwyn picked up a red block and set it down close to the green one by Picksbury on the map. "Our scouts also report another force of two or three thousands on our eastern border near Ferchester." Another block was placed on the map. "Finally, there are a couple of thousands more in several groups that have been destroying the guardburgs along the border. We've evacuated as many of the garrisons as we could, but some weren't able to escape."

They studied the map for a while and then Culhwch spoke: "So Mister Cadwallader, what's you evaluation of this? Do you have a plan for us to follow?"

Aeron sighed. He'd been expecting a question like this but wasn't sure he had much of an answer. "Well, the Rhordians have some significant advantages, the most obvious one being numbers. They have more troops than we do, and if they wanted to push things to the limit, they could have even more. Another advantage is that most of their troops are better trained than ours, and their forces tend to be more heavily armored. And, of course, they have more warmages, and possibly more cannons and war machines."

"You make it sound hopeless," growled Culhwch.

"Not hopeless, sir, but we are in a position where we can only risk an open battle if we can shift the advantage in our favor."

"And how do we do that?"

"We do have some advantages. The biggest one is, I believe, that the Rhordians don't realize how strong we are - or where a lot of that strength is."

"What do you mean, Aeron?" asked Dilwyn.

"I'd been puzzling over why the Rhordians gave us a month to decide about answering their demands. Why wait?"

"I just assumed they didn't want to lay waste to the Shires," said Culhwch. "They clearly want to turn us into their serfs to supply them with all the food they need. They don't want to turn everything into a desert. So they are giving us a chance to think about it. They probably hope we'll think it's hopeless and give in."

"I'm sure that's part of it," said Aeron. "But I think another part of it is that they don't realize we managed to sneak the best part of our army - and about fifteen thousand civilians - out of Hodenburg without their knowing.

They think that not only is the whole population trapped there, but also nearly our whole army. All of them cooped up and eating the stored food. That food won't run out in a month, not even in six months, but they're hoping that we'll realize that given time, they can just starve us out. What they *don't* know is that we've got close to ten thousand troops outside their siege lines." He pointed to the green blocks at the Holdfast and Picksbury.

"I also think it's fair to assume that they have no idea what we are doing here at the Holdfast. The new weapons you are building and the new units to use them. If they did, they'd be sending a major force here - and they're not."

"So we have an advantage," said Culhwch. "What do we do with it?"

Aeron stared at the map for a while longer, and then he reached out and picked up the green block that was sitting on the Holdfast. "When we are ready, we move all of our forces here, south to join up with Macsen, and then make a surprise strike at the enemy forces near Picksbury." He placed the block he was holding next to the one representing Macsen's army and then pushed both of them up against the red one to the south of Picksbury. "If we can strike hard and fast—and with surprise—we smash that army, scatter it if we can, and then drive onward to Hodenburg. Then… well, we'll have to see what happens then."

"Surely, you'd keep going, join up with Rootwell, and try to destroy the army besieging Hodenburg, wouldn't you?" demanded Culhwch.

"Ideally, yes. But a lot will depend on how heavy our losses are in the first battle and what the Rhordians do once we show ourselves." Aeron nodded. "So that's the plan. But the first step is to get what we have here at the Holdfast ready to fight."

* * * * *

So they worked, hour after hour, day after day, with not nearly enough rest. Time was as big an enemy as the Rhordians. They had an enormous amount to do and an unknown amount of time to do it. They were assuming they had the month the Rhordians had given them, but that might be a very dangerous assumption. The enemy could resume their attack at any moment. Aeron sketched out plan after plan with different dates they would be enacted. If the enemy attacked in one week, they should do this; in two weeks, that; three weeks, another plan. He stayed up late every night working on them, because his days were full of other things.

As he'd promised Einion, he set up a school to train officers and sergeants to command the new units. He tried to draw the people from the existing trained bands that had come to the Holdfast. But as often as not, some of these 'veterans' resisted the new-fangled ways he tried to teach, and he ended up having to replace them, often with bright but completely inexperienced people from the new volunteers.

He drew upon what he'd learned at the College of Warcraft, both his own instruction and when he helped train those new recruits back in Eowulf. Trying to cram two years of training into a few days was very difficult, but at least none of his pupils tried to beat him up. He pared things down to the absolute bare minimum, and after a week, he turned his new officers and sergeants loose on their units, to relieve the temporary instructors he'd borrowed from the Light Horse, and watched what happened.

For the most part, the results were good. The volunteers were enthusiastic, motivated, and learned fast. By the end of the second week, the units were marching around, changing formations, and handling their weapons like people with far more experience.

Overhead, the *Windwalker* was practicing, too. They had fifteen of the amazing mechanical wing devices and the bold (insane?) people from Ej who operated them had come up with a way to use them in battle. The fliers could carry four small gunpowder bombs—or *grenades* as they called them - which they intended to drop on the Rhordian troops and then swoop away. A target range had been set up, and each day the airship would go aloft and the fliers - who were styling themselves *grenadiers* - would hurl themselves into the air and then swoop down and practice dropping their bombs on the targets. They quickly became quite good at it, although Aeron was skeptical about how useful they'd actually prove in a fight. Once the surprise wore off, he was afraid that magic or massed archery fire would quickly knock the grenadiers from the sky. Still, that initial surprise might prove very useful.

Meanwhile, the Light Horse had exchanged their horses for aralez, and they were training their mounts and themselves how to function. Gwenith and the two other people who had or once had the strange but wonderful creatures, were essential in making the transition. New weapons and armor were being provided them as well. Metal breastplates and helmets for the people, thickly quilted and metal studded 'vests' for the animals, and lances of an appropriate length for Shirefolk. Many of these things were imbued with magical properties to make them more effective.

"I guess you can't call us either 'light' or 'horse' anymore, can you?" joked Captain Einion.

"So what will you call yourselves?" asked Aeron.

"We're talking about it. I'll let you know."

Of equal concern to Aeron were the people crewing the cannons and other war machines. He believed that these could well be the difference between victory and defeat on the battlefield. Unfortunately, the Rhordians had equipment that was at least the equal of what the Shirelings were creating, and their crews would probably be far more experienced. At the College, there was an entire course of study devoted to such things, and the people he'd seen there seemed very professional. There was really nothing they could do about that except get their own equipment and crews into the best shape they could in the time they had. A practice range for them had been set up, and they spent long hours learning how to use their weapons.

One day, Dilwyn took him on a ride into Tanmill to show him some of the production taking place there. The workshops in the Holdfast were making the special and magical items, but most of the ordinary things were made in Tanmill. Of particular interest were the wheelwrights and wagon makers. They were producing the utterly vital carriages for the cannons, without which they couldn't get them to the battlefield.

"It took them a little while to get things set up properly," said Dilwyn. "None of them had built anything like this before, but now that they've got the hang of it, they are turning out several a day."

Aeron looked over the rows of carriages, lined up outside the workshop on the edge of Tanmill. "They look a little… small, don't they? Will they stand up to the shock of firing - and the shaking they'll get on the roads?"

Dilwyn smiled. "Yes, they are smaller than usual, but that's because our cannons are lighter than usual. You remember our tour of the armory at the College where Paddy talked about the spells they cast on the cannons?" Aeron nodded. "Well, by making the metal stronger, we can make the walls of the cannon barrels thinner - which makes them lighter. We've also put strengthening spells on these carriages. The result is we have artillery that only weighs about half as much as a normal gun of the same caliber. They will be much more mobile on the battlefield."

"Don't the Rhordians do the same thing?"

"Not as much as you'd think. They certainly do the spell casting, but they use it so they can make larger caliber guns on a normal carriage. Those big guns are fine for smashing castle walls, but aren't all that much more effective against troops in the field. And they are much less mobile - once they set them up, they rarely move them again. Ours should be able to run rings around theirs. You just need to figure out some way to make use of that, eh?"

"Thanks."

"But there's something else I want to show you while we're here. Come on." He led him down a road leading to another facility. There was a long shed and an open field beside it. The field had dozens of wagons parked in it.

"Ah," said Aeron, "We are going to need a baggage train to bring along the supplies the army needs. I know Mama Beata is baking her special bread around the clock and turning out tons of the stuff. Good to see you are ahead of the game on that, too."

"Yes, they are finishing three or four a day. We're also collecting every existing wagon we can from the surrounding countryside. But these new ones are a bit special, and we have you to thank for that."

"Me?"

"Yes, you. Here, let me show you." They walked up to one of the wagons. It was larger than a usual halfling wagon. "Remind you of anything?"

Aeron puzzled for a bit and then said: "The wagons we used to get out of Eowulf? The human-built ones?"

"Exactly. But it's not just the size. I remembered what you had us do with them and tinkered up a design." He went up to the side of the wagon and pulled down a folding ladder which allowed them to easily climb up into the cargo bed. It looked like an ordinary wagon except for…

"What are those levers for?" He pointed to two pairs of long wooden rods sticking up at the front and back.

"Let's find out. Grab hold of the red one at the front. I'll take the one at the back." Aeron puzzled, but he did as he was told. "Ready? Okay, pull!"

Aeron pulled on the lever in unison with Dilwyn, and to his surprise, a wooden panel rose up out of the side of the wagon going up to about head height. "Secure the lever in pace with that rope," said Dilwyn. He did so and then stepped back. The panel had four small loopholes through which a person could shoot.

"So, you've built wagons that are miniature fortresses! What does the other set of levers do?"

"It lowers a panel down to the ground so no one can get through underneath. Like I said, I was inspired by the way you fortified the wagons when the Rhordians attacked our train. And notice how they are designed to butt up very closely end to end. We could quickly create some very strong redoubts on the field to reinforce our battle lines."

"This is really clever, Dilwyn," said Aeron. "I need to give this some thought. How many of these will you have?"

"We've got about thirty right now, but we're finishing a couple more a day. Naturally, we're making the harnesses for the draft animals, too. Finding enough of them is proving a challenge as well."

"So, it all depends on how much time the Rhordians give us."

One week passed and then a second, and there were no significant moves by the enemy. The Rhordians strengthened their works around Hodenburg and finished demolishing the guardburgs along the southern and eastern borders and sent some cavalry probes deeper into the Shires, but that was all.

During the third week, they sent another message into Hodenburg - apparently believing the Shires Assembly was still there—and which Dunstan Rootwell forwarded to the Holdfast by courier bird. It just reiterated the earlier demands and warned that the League's patience was wearing thin.

"We haven't got much time left, I don't think," said Aeron when they held another strategy session. "We should call in whatever additional reinforcements we can and start getting ready to move."

At the end of the third week, the Rhordians lobbed a few cannon balls into Hodenburg, apparently as a warning of what would come if the Shirelings didn't yield. Aeron was becoming increasingly tense. If the enemy were to suddenly launch an all-out assault on the capital and take the place, it could throw all his plans into the midden heap.

By the start of the final week, the force in the Holdfast was coming together. They had three thousand infantry, the two hundred 'Picksbury Knights', as they had decided to call themselves, three hundred or so other cavalry, and over five hundred artillerists and engineers. That did not include the teamsters hauling the guns and supply wagons, or the crew of the *Windwalker* or their winged grenadiers. About a dozen mages and Paddy were coming along, too. They continued to drill, but they had most of their stuff packed and ready to move out on very short notice. Mama Beata had enough of the special bread for three or four days plus a few 'surprises' she wouldn't tell him any details about.

Finally, two days short of the deadline, word came that the Rhodians were moving. The army watching Macsen's army advanced on Picksbury, and Macsen, outnumbered almost two to one fell back, taking all but a thousand troops to garrison Picksbury with him. The enemy was building siege lines around the place. Aeron worried about what was happening to his family and home, they'd be almost smack between the two armies now. Another force advanced from the east and placed Ferchester under siege, too. No assault was launched against Hodenburg, but Rootwell reported that ammunition was being brought froward for the enemy guns.

"All right, everyone," said Aeron at a meeting of commanders, "Our time's up. Let all your people know we march at dawn."

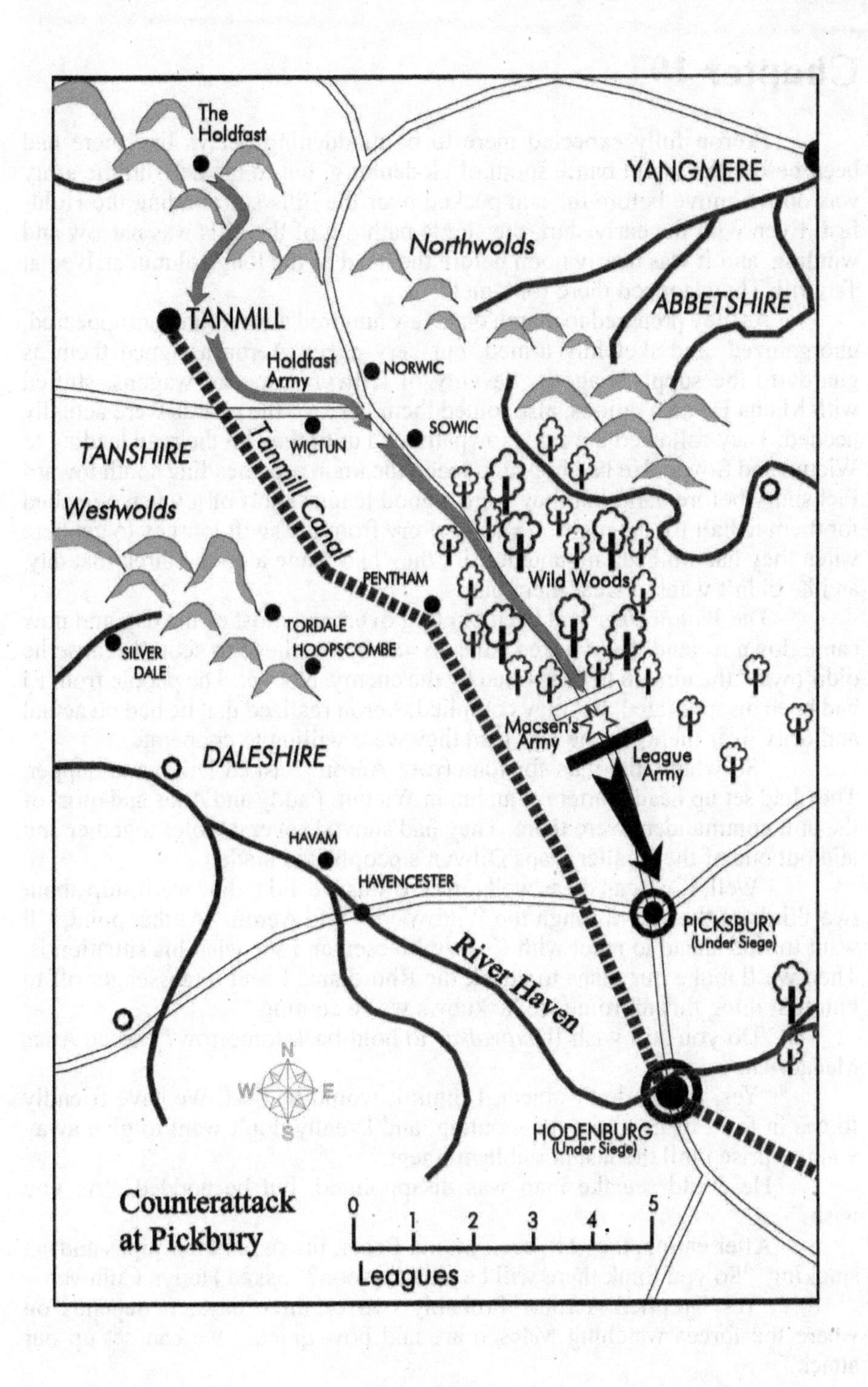
The Holdfast
YANGMERE
Northwolds
ABBETSHIRE
TANMILL
Holdfast Army
NORWIC
WICTUN
SOWIC
TANSHIRE
Tanmill Canal
Westwolds
PENTHAM
Wild Woods
TORDALE
SILVER DALE
HOOPSCOMBE
Macsen's Army
League Army
DALESHIRE
HAVAM
HAVENCESTER
PICKSBURY
(Under Siege)
River Haven
N
W
E
S
HODENBURG
(Under Siege)
Counterattack at Pickbury
0
1
2
3
4
5
Leagues

Chapter 19

Aeron fully expected there to be maddening delays like there had been before the awful battle south of Hodenburg, but to his delight, the army was on the move before the sun peeked over the hills surrounding the Holdfast. Even with the early start, the single path out of the hills was narrow and winding, and it was nearly noon before the head of the long column arrived at Tanmill. They stopped there for a meal.

As they prepared to march on, a few hundred new volunteers appeared, unorganized, and sketchily armed, but very eager. Aeron assigned them as guards to the supply wagons. Seventy of Dilwyn's special wagons, stuffed with Mama Beata's rations, also joined them here, so the guards were actually needed. They followed the canal towpath road until they hit the road leading to Wictun and Sowic. He had hoped to reach the main road heading south toward Picksbury before dark, but they were a good league short of it when he called for them to halt for the night. It was a far cry from the swift journey to get here when they had all been mounted. Still, they had made a good march that day, and he didn't want to wear them out.

The *Windwalker* had been circling overhead most of the day and now came down to land. He'd asked Anas to not fly on ahead to scout because he didn't want the airship to be spotted by the enemy. Not yet. The people from Ej had been disappointed, but they complied. Aeron realized that he had no actual authority over them, but he was glad they were willing to cooperate.

"So what's the plan for tomorrow, Aeron?" asked Dilwyn at supper. They had set up headquarters at an inn in Wictun. Paddy and Anas and most of the unit commanders were there. They had shoved several tables together and laid out one of the smaller maps Dilwyn's people had made.

"Well, if we can do as well tomorrow as we did today, we'll stop about two-thirds of the way through the Wildwood," said Aeron. "At that point, I'll want to ride ahead to meet with Conwy Macsen and see what his situation is. Then we'll make our plans to attack the Rhordians. I sent a messenger off to him first thing this morning, so he knows we're coming."

"Do you still wish *Windwalker* to hold back tomorrow?" asked Anas Macadrian.

"Yes, if you don't object. I think it would be best. We have friendly forces in front of us to do our scouting, and I really don't want to give away your surprise until the last possible moment."

He could see the man was disappointed, but he nodded. "As you wish."

After eating, they all, even Mama Beata, broke out their pipes and sat smoking. "So you think there will be a battle soon?" asked Heilyn Culhwch.

"Yes," replied Aeron. "Probably two or three days. It depends on where the forces watching Macsen are and how quickly we can set up our attack."

"And you're determined to attack?"

"Well, if we could somehow trick the Rhordians to attack us on ground of our choosing, that would be even better, but I don't think they'll..."

He was interrupted by the sound of hooves outside the inn and a cry: "Where is Commander Cadwallader? I need to see Cadwallader!"

"Missing Gods," said Culhwch, "that sounds like Macsen!"

They all got up from their chairs and hurried outside. A rider was just swinging down off his pony, and even in the dim light of evening, Aeron immediately recognized the rider as Conwy Macsen, the commander of the army near Picksbury.

"Over here, sir!" he called.

Macsen spotted him, and throwing the reins of the pony to a soldier, he strode over, a deep frown on his face. "There you are! At last! As soon as your messenger arrived I decided to come and find you myself. We've got a problem, boy."

"What's happened, sir?"

"I assume you got my message that the Rhordians have invested Picksbury?"

"Yes, we got that the other day."

"Well, I pulled my forces back, but the Rhordians are continuing to push me. They didn't stop and watch like they did after they surrounded Hodenburg. They're coming on and trying to bring me to battle."

"If our plans are working, they probably think you have the last mobile force left in the Shires," said Dilwyn. "If they can eliminate you, they think they'll have a free rein over everything except the cities."

"Yes, that seems likely," agreed Aeron. "So where are your troops now, sir?"

"I've pulled back almost to the edge of the Wildwood. If they advance again, I'll have no choice but to fall back into the trees."

"Would that be a bad thing, Conwy?" asked Culhwch. "We know those woods, and the Rhordians don't. If we bring up our force to assist you, we might be able to tear up their whole force."

Aeron frowned. "Yes... we might. But in the woods, we couldn't make any use of our cannons or the *Windwalker,* and our cavalry wouldn't be much use, either. We might be able to win, but it would be a close-quarters bloodbath. We wouldn't have an army left to advance on Hodenburg."

"Well, then what do you suggest, Cadwallader?" demanded Macsen.

"Can your forces hold them back one more day, sir?"

"Maybe... maybe. If we make a show of fighting, harry them with our cavalry, we might delay their attack for one more day. But what will that do? You're near to ten leagues away and I'm guessing you already marched all this day. Even if you start at first light tomorrow, you can't possibly get there before the end of the day after tomorrow at the earliest."

"That's true if we made a normal march. But if we left at dawn tomorrow, marched all day, and then all night, we could hit them before the next dawn. Hit them in the dark before they even know we're there."

"What? Are you crazy, boy? Even if you could get your people to do that, they'd be so worn out by the time they arrived, they wouldn't be able to fight!"

Aeron smiled. "Mama Beata? What do you think? Can your golden bread give my troops the strength to march ten leagues and still fight at the end?"

The stout woman pushed her way through the crowd to the front. "Can it? Can it, do you ask? It surely can! Ten leagues and twice ten leagues if you want! Add a dash 'o my pudding and you won't be able to hold them back when they get there!"

"Good, good! That's what I was hoping you'd say, Mama."

"And did I hear you say something about a night attack?"

"You did. I know it's risky and there's bound to be confusion and…"

"Don't you fret! One of those surprises I told you about will be just the thing. I calls it 'cats' eye'. It'll let you see in the dark like a cat."

"Mama! That would be perfect!"

"Thought you'd like it. But I'm guessin' that Mister Conwy, here, will be wantin' to get back to his army tonight. Perhaps he'd be willin' to try out my wares before he goes. Might make the journey a tad easier for him."

"Well, I don't know…" said Conwy, looking dubious.

"Nonsense! A loaf o' bread, a dash o' pudding, and a Cat's Eye Tart for desert! You can't leave without somethin' to eat, man!"

And in a twinkling, a table was set, the food produced, and Conwy had a dinner unlike any he'd ever had before. Aeron could almost see the food taking effect. His weariness faded away, his doubts became surety, and when he mounted a fresh pony, he rode off as if he could see the path like daylight. "I'll be expecting you tomorrow night!" he called over his shoulder. "Don't be late!"

"Should we feed the troops and get on the road right away, do you think?" asked Dilwyn.

Aeron calculated times and distances in his head and eventually said: "No, tell them to get to sleep right away. We'll let them rest five hours and then get them up, fed, and on the road. That ought to get us to Macsen's forces about four hours before dawn the following day. Should be enough time to get ourselves ready to attack."

"I hope you know what you're doing, Aeron."

"Yeah, me too."

* * * * *

The Holdfast Army marched. Mile after mile, league after league. There were short pauses now and then, but only to let the column—which inevitably got drawn out—close up again. Their seemingly tireless legs ate up the distance like nothing Aeron had ever seen. The only problem was that the bread didn't work on horses or oxen. The cavalry horses and the aralez weren't a problem, a ten league march was well within their endurance, but the beasts hauling the cannons and baggage wagons were going to start falling behind about dark, by his reckoning.

"It doesn't matter," he said when Dilwyn pointed that out as they rode along, side by side. "We won't be able to use the guns in a night attack anyway."

"You're taking a big risk, Aeron. I didn't study strategy at the College, but even I know night attacks almost never work—except for creatures like orcs and goblins and ratkin who love the dark."

"I know, I know. But it will be the last thing the Rhordians expect. And if it works, it could be decisive."

"And if it doesn't work, it could be decisive, too—for the enemy."

"Well, if you are dead-set against this, have Paddy and Culhwch remove me from command. I'm sure they'll listen to you."

"All right, all right, I'll stop worrying and shut up. You're in command."

"Still hard to believe that… I'm hardly more than a boy!"

"Well, Paddy believes in you and… and so do I." He leaned over in his saddle and slapped Aeron on the back.

"Thanks, Dilwyn. That means a lot."

"All right, let's go beat those bastards."

Shortly before noon, they reached the edge of the Wildwood, and Aeron halted for a quick, cold meal. Mama Beata's people distributed enough bread for four meals, along with two wrapped servings of her 'courage pudding' and strict instructions not to touch that until they were ordered to. They were given the food now on Aeron's instruction, because he feared that later the wagons carrying the rations would be far behind. One serving of pudding and one of bread were to be given to Conwy Macsen's people when they reached them.

They were soon on the march again, the trees along the road giving a welcome shade. It was late spring now and quite warm. Aeron was grateful for the clear skies; a heavy rain now would slow them down and ruin his plan.

About an hour later, he heard a faint rumble. With the trees muffling the noise, he couldn't tell what direction it was coming from, but he had no doubt what it was. Cannons. Macsen's force was engaging the Rhordians.

"It doesn't sound too bad," said Dilwyn. "A lot of long pauses between the rumbles. Maybe they're just feeling each other out."

"Maybe. But that doesn't tell us much. The two forces combined probably only have a score of cannons. With how long it takes to reload, there are going to be gaps in the shooting. We can't hear anything else from this far off, so a full-on battle could be raging, and we wouldn't know it."

"So what do we do?"

Aeron shrugged. "Keep marching. When we get closer, I'm going to ride ahead with an escort to meet with Macsen and find out what's happened and plan our attack."

They kept going, with only brief halts, and by nightfall they were well over halfway through the woods. The rumbles had stopped a while before that, and Aeron was worried about what that meant. If Macsen had been routed completely and was fleeing northward through the wood with the Rhordians on his tail, and Aeron's force ran into them while still in a march column… It was a nightmare scenario, but even if Macsen had been beaten, the Rhordians surely wouldn't continue a pursuit in the pitch dark under the trees. Surely…

They halted for supper, and afterward, Aeron gave orders to rest for an hour and then get marching again. He collected a dozen troopers from the Picksbury Knights and rode on ahead to find Macsen. Gwenith Parry was among them. He hadn't really spoken to her in a number of days, what with them all being so busy. She was mounted on an aralez which was a golden-brownish color with white paws and a patch of white on its muzzle.

"What did you name him?" he asked.

"I… I haven't given him one yet," said Gwenith. "With the battle coming, I didn't want… I didn't want…" Her voice trailed off to silence.

You don't want to get too close to him in case he gets killed like Fluffy.

"I understand."

They rode on, and it was fully dark now, almost pitch black under the trees. Aeron had eaten one of the Cars Eye Tarts at supper, and he could see the road clearly. Not quite like daylight, but good enough. There weren't enough of the tarts for everyone in the army, so only a few people in every unit would have them. They would have to guide their comrades as Aeron was doing for his escort.

They kept up a good pace, and it was only an hour later they heard hooves on the road in front of them. Aeron peered ahead and sighed in relief when he could see that it was a dozen Shirelings on ponies. He hailed them and they came to a halt and uncovered a small lantern. "Is Cadwallader here?" shouted one. "We're looking for Cadwallader!"

"And you've found him," he called back, riding up close so they could see his face. "Did Macsen send you? Where is he? What's happened, we heard the cannons."

"Yes, he sent us. We had a demon's own fight today, but we held them at the edge of the trees. Are you bringing help?"

"Yes, they're about an hour behind us. Take me to Macsen so we can make some plans."

They turned their ponies around and led the way at a good clip for perhaps a half-hour. Then they saw campfires ahead and soon rode into a camp where Conwy Macsen had his headquarters. The commander looked weary, but an unaccustomed smile appeared on his face when he saw Aeron.

"Well, we did as you asked, Cadwallader, we kept them out of the woods," he said. "They're camped out in the open, half a mile from the forest, right where you'll be wanting them, I expect. Where's your army? When will they get here?"

"They're coming up behind us, sir, maybe two hours back at the rate they're marching. Now, sir, you and I have to decide how to make use of them - and your people, too."

Macsen led him over to where a camp table and chairs had been set up near a fire and lanterns hung from the tree branches. A piece of parchment was on the table and a crude map had been drawn on it. "We danced with them all morning," said Macsen, "putting on a bold face, but pulling back if they tried to close. For a while, it looked like we could hold them all day, but after noon they got some reinforcements, looked like about five hundred heavy horse coming up from the south. They got bolder then, and we had no choice but to fall back. When we got near the woods, we stopped retreating, and things got serious. I lost about two hundred killed and wounded, but we forced them to deploy, and by then it was getting dark and we pulled back into the trees and they didn't follow."

"That was well done, sir. Once my people get here, we'll make then sorry they're here."

"My forces are worn out, Cadwallader," said Macsen. "They're not up to a night attack, can we let them rest until morning?"

"You remember your meal with us yesterday? When my force arrives, they'll have a similar meal for every one of your people."

"Really?"

"Yes, really. After what Mama Beata can do for them, I think they'll find the strength and nerve for what we need to do."

Macsen snorted out a laugh. "You know? They might at that."

"Good, now how certain are you of these enemy positions?"

They studied the map and talked and made plans until the vanguard of the Holdfast force arrived. It was near midnight, and it took several hours to get the food distributed to Macsen's troops and for everyone to eat. Soon thereafter, everyone was feeling so good and eager they had to work hard to keep them *quiet*. Another two hours was spent moving the Holdfast troops into position through the woods. The night-seeing tarts made that easier than he had hoped, but it still took time. Aeron was becoming anxious they would lose the darkness, but they still had an hour before first light when all was ready.

First to move out were the Picksbury Knights, they were to make a wide swing to the south, around the enemy's flank, and then into their rear to strike where the Rhordian cavalry was camped. They took one of the younger mages with them, and when they were poised to strike, the magician sent up a red blast of magic into the sky. It made no sound and was behind the way the enemy pickets would be watching, so Aeron hoped it wouldn't give the game away too soon.

But all the waiting Shirefolk saw it, and with only a few quiet commands, the entire force, nearly eight thousand of them, surged forward, out of the trees and advanced at a trot toward the Rhordian sentries, silhouetted by their own fires on a low ridge.

Aeron was on his pony near the center, and he moved along behind, feeling utterly useless. It was his plan, but there was now nothing he could do to help it succeed. Everything was in the hands of the troops.

The picket line was only a few furlongs away, and the rapid pace ate up the distance in what seemed an instant. The Shirelings, with the dark wood at their back, were nearly invisible, and the first shouts of alarm didn't come until they were nearly upon the humans. The shouts turned to screams as they were overrun by an unstoppable tide. At almost the same moment, they heard a great commotion from the enemy camp as the Picksbury Knights charged in from the flank and rear.

Up and over the ridge they went, the enemy camp was spread out before them only a dozen rods away. Most of the enemy seemed asleep with their campfires burned down to coals. But the noise of the attack had raised the alarm, and the Rhordians were struggling awake, grasping for weapons, trying to get into their armor. Officers and sergeants began screaming commands, and the few that had been on watch tried to get into formation.

Too late. The People of the Shires were upon them before they could create any real defense. True, the Shirelings' formations had fallen apart during the charge, but with the Rhordians spread out all over their camps, at the point of contact the attackers outnumbered then ten to one and simply crushed the humans. They swept into the camps, catching the enemy individually or in small groups, and cut them down.

Some small knots of resistance did form where the men had the time to grab their weapons and gather together in groups, but these were quickly surrounded and contained. For the most part, the Rhordian army disintegrated and fled southward. From where he was sitting on his pony, Aeron could see that the Picksbury Knights had routed the Rhordian heavy cavalry by simply stampeding the enemy's horses right through their camp. The battle seemed won…

A sudden flash of light tore away the darkness, and an ear-splitting roar of thunder shook the world. *Warmage!*

So, there was at least one Rhodian who was fighting back. The flash had come from off to his left, maybe two hundred paces away. He turned his pony in that direction and gave it the spurs. He had no idea what he would do if he found the mage, but he had to try and help his troops.

As he approached, a second blast of lightning half-blinded him, and he heard some shrieks from whatever poor souls had been struck. Damn it, why weren't the counter-magic standards working? Aeron's pony reared, but he forced it on; and a moment later, he came to what was clearly the center of the Rhordian camp. There were several large pavilion tents, one of which was on fire, and the other camp furniture and baggage you'd expect around a headquarters. In an open space was a small group of humans, and around them, a gathering crowd of Shirelings. During the battle south of Hodenburg, the enemy warmages had turned defeat into a route, but here, the Shirefolk showed no sign of fear despite a score of charred bodies lying in two distinct clumps.

Mama Beata's pudding...

The special food had banished fear in the Shires troops, and as he watched, arrows began to fly toward the humans. One of the humans, the warmage apparently, did something, and the arrows burst into flames before they could strike. But more arrows came as Shirelings were drawn to the combat. More and more arrows flew from all directions, and Aeron could see the strain on the human's face as he held them off. He let loose another lightning bolt against the archers, but this time, one of the special standards had been brought up close, and the bolt faded away before it hit anything. The man seemed so startled he lost control of his spell that was protecting him from the arrows, and at last one arrow struck him in the arm. The distraction broke the spell completely, and an instant later, the man was a pincushion, skewered by dozens of shafts. The men standing near him were also being hit.

"Stop! Stop!" Aeron screamed. "Cease your fire!" He had to shout it several times before the shooting finally stopped. He rode over to the pile of men and saw that at least a few of them were still alive. The Rhordian commander ought to be here, he'd love to take him alive if possible. He swung off his pony and started sorting the living from the dead. A crowd of his troops moved in to help.

The mage was very dead, as were a half dozen others, but a handful were groaning and wounded, and one fellow had miraculously not been hurt at all. The dead were dragged aside and the wounded guarded. Aeron looked them over and saw one with richer clothing than the rest. He looked closer and recognized the man. *The Duke of Hetronburg!* He'd seen him at the Grand Review in Eowulf. He had an arrow in his shoulder and another in his left leg.

"Get a healer over here!" he shouted.

He leaned over the duke and said: "Hang on, sir, we'll get you some help."

The man stirred, looked around in bewilderment, and then mumbled: "Better to let me die."

"That would be terribly rude of us, sir. You'll be taken care of." Yes, he certainly would: a duke as a prisoner would be invaluable. He stood up just as a dozen aralez approached. Captain Einion was with them and he spotted Aeron.

"Aeron! I mean Commander Cadwallader! There you are! We did it! We routed the lot of them!" Aeron walked over to him and indeed, the noise seemed to be settling down. Off to the east, the faintest hint of dawn streaked the horizon.

"How did you make out?" he asked Einion.

"Oh, it was glorious! We charged right into where they had their horses picketed. Y'know, they aren't too fond of aralez, and we stampeded the lot of them right through where all their riders were camped. Threw them all into confusion and we swept them away. Well, most of them. A few times they managed to clump together and try to make a fight, but that mage you lent us just tossed a fireball into their midst every time they tried, and that was that. We've got close to three hundred prisoners!"

"Well done."

More people were arriving now, Dilwyn and Macsen, and a few of the other mages. Aeron had deliberately kept them out of the fight, fearing that in the dark they might end up hurting friends as well as foes. It seemed like a good decision now. Dilwyn came right up to him, dismounted, and shook his hand. "We did it, Aeron, we really did it!"

"So it seems." He looked to Macsen. "What's the situation, sir?"

"Damn it, stop calling me *sir*, will you? Rootwell made us co-commanders of this army. But since you ask, *Aeron*, it looks like we've got this lot beat. We're collecting a lot of prisoners, and any that aren't dead or captured are running as fast as their long shanks can carry them toward Picksbury. I suggest we get after them and see how many more we can round up."

"Excellent idea, si… er, Conwy. It'll be light enough for those who didn't get one of Mama Beata's tarts to see clearly in a half hour or so. Why don't we let our people catch their breaths, get themselves back in order, and then get moving?" Macsen nodded and started spreading the orders.

Dawn revealed two armies, one victorious and the other defeated. Macsen's statement of a *lot* of prisoners didn't do reality justice. There were easily two or three thousand dispirited humans herded into an open field just south of their camp. About a third of them were hurt to some degree. Maybe a thousand more bodies lay scattered about. A great many horses had also been collected, and a dozen cannons, too.

The Shirefolk had paid an amazingly light price for their victory, about a hundred dead and twice that seriously wounded. Aeron and Macsen left about five hundred troops to guard the prisoners and collect booty while the rest of the army pushed on toward Picksbury. The cavalry, except for the Knights who were kept as a reserve, was sent ahead to capture stragglers and prevent the enemy from rallying. The plan was to for the rest of the army to keep right on advancing, all the way to Picksbury, lift the siege, and hurt the Rhordians as badly as they could.

Everyone was in high spirits and would have been even without the magic pudding. They had won a great victory, and the soldiers were soon singing as they marched. It was about three leagues to Picksbury, and Aeron expected to reach there a little after noon. Looking up, he saw that the *Windwalker* was far overhead. Apparently the people from Ej were tired of missing the show. He was slightly annoyed that they were showing themselves now, but eventually the secret was going to be lost and he really could use their scouting services today anyway. He had Anas's promise that they wouldn't use any of their flying grenadiers - he wanted to keep them secret until a critical moment.

As they advanced, they were almost constantly meeting small groups of cavalry escorting prisoners they had taken during the pursuit. The humans looked exhausted and dazed, and some of them were barely clothed - apparently rousted out of their tents before they could even dress.

"At this rate, there won't be any army left!" exulted Macsen.

"As long as the survivors can't rally on the besieging force and get themselves reorganized," said Dilwyn.

"There were fewer than two thousands of those," replied Macsen. "They can't stand up to what we've got here."

"Probably not," said Aeron, "But let's not let them rally. We've got a much bigger fight to win at Hodenburg, and we can't afford to lose anyone."

Windwalker had hurried on ahead and nearly disappeared from sight, but after about an hour was seen coming back. It got lower and lower and swung in over the army. Macsen's troops had never seen it closely before, and there were many cries of amazement. Aeron waved to Anas, and the airship closed in until it was just a dozen feet overhead.

"Hoy, Commander Aeron!" shouted Anas Macadrian, leaning over the railing on the side of the airship.

"I'm here! What did you see?"

"We saw a lot of humans running for their lives!" he answered a jubilant tone in his voice. "And it looks like the force around Picksbury has gotten the word, because they are packing up to leave. You better hurry if you want to catch them!"

"We surely want to catch them if we can. Can you go ahead and tell our cavalry to press on as fast as they can?"

"We'll try, but they're pretty spread out, running down the Rhordians. All right, see you later." The airship began to rise again and pick up speed.

By mid-morning, Picksbury was visible in the distance, and there was a great deal of smoke rising up from around it. "They must be burning any supplies or equipment that can't move," said Aeron. "If they don't burden themselves with a lot of baggage, I don't know if we'll be able to catch many of them."

"Our cavalry surely can," said Macsen.

"Yes, but if their infantry keeps its discipline, they can hold off the cavalry."

"But with that magic bread, we can keep marching and catch them when they drop from exhaustion. Can't we?"

Aeron shook his head. "Very tempting, but Mama Beata tells me that we only have enough of it left for a few more meals, and I want to save that for the next battle. Also, after a person has been living off the bread for a few days, once he stops eating it, he'll fall into a deep sleep for a day and a night. All your people should be fine since they only ate it for one meal. But the Holdfast troops are going to need a safe place to sleep. If we keep pushing on after the Rhordians, we could end up far too close to the enemy's main army with half our troops asleep. Once we get past Picksbury, we'll have to stop."

Macsen wasn't happy, but he saw the truth of the matter. Even so, the cavalry was capturing a truly remarkable number of prisoners, and by the time they reached the edge of Picksbury, there were thousands more being herded to the rear. It looked like only the small force that had invested Picksbury and a few of the hardier ones fleeing from the morning battle would get away. And they had left all of their baggage and cannons behind. This army had been wrecked as a fighting force.

Aeron halted on a little hill a couple of miles short of Picksbury and issued some orders for where to halt and camp once they were past the town. As he did so, he looked around and suddenly realized where he was. That lane that branched off from the main road…

"Wait here a moment," he told Gwenith, who was in charge of his escort. "I want to check on something. I'll be right back." He spurred his pony and cantered off, down the little lane.

He followed the tree-lined road for a quarter of a mile and then it turned a bit, and the trees opened out, and there was the Cadwallader homestead.

The stockade which had surrounded it was torn down in several spots and the gate was smashed. Beyond, he could see that the house and the barn were smoldering ruins.

Chapter 20

He sat staring at the place he had been born in, where he had lived nearly his entire life. He had halted the pony when he first saw the disaster, but now urged his mount forward. "Nesta! Mama! Da! Mererid!" He shouted out their names, but there was no answer. He rode through the ruined gates and into the farmyard. There were a great number of things scattered about: tables, chests of drawers, broken dishes, torn blankets, a framed painting. He recognized them all. A great weight seemed to descend on him, and he could barely breathe.

But as he sat there trying to take it all in, he slowly realized that there were things he was *not* seeing: bodies. Bodies, spent arrows, broken weapons; all the evidence of a fight were missing. The place had just been looted and then burned. *No one was here...*

With growing hope that maybe his family hadn't been slaughtered, he took one last look around and then galloped back the way he came. As he neared the main road, he saw a party headed for him, he recognized Conwy Macsen in the lead. "Aeron! Aeron!" he shouted. "They're fine! They're safe!" They both reined in their mounts when they met.

"Missing Gods, Aeron!" gasped Macsen. "I am so sorry! Forgive me! When the Rhordians advanced on Picksbury, I ordered all the people in the surrounding farms and villages to either fall back with my army or get inside the town. Your family is all in Picksbury. I should have told you, but with all that was going on, it totally slipped my mind. I'm so sorry."

Aeron didn't know whether to kiss Macsen or punch him in the nose. Instead, he just gave him a shaky smile and said: "Thank you. I was pretty worried there for a moment."

"I imagine you were! I came looking for you, and that girl on the aralez told me where you'd gone and I suddenly remembered I *hadn't* told you and, well, sorry."

"Like you said: we all had other things on our minds. No harm done, Conwy."

"Yeah, right," snorted the older halfling. "But come on, our troops are entering Picksbury, let's go find your family."

That seemed like a fine idea, and they were soon trotting down the road leading into the town. Aeron looked at the siege works the Rhordians had been building, but they clearly hadn't gotten very far on them. A few half-dug trenches and piles of logs waiting to be turned into pointed stakes for a palisade. Cannons stood abandoned before they could even be placed in revetments to fire on the town. Half-burned supply dumps and some unburned wagons, stray cattle and sheep probably stolen from nearby farms as food for the troops. They'd soon be feeding Shirelings as they had originally been intended. Small groups of prisoners sat under guard.

There were lots of townsfolk there cheering the incoming troops. They acted like they'd been under siege for months instead of just a few days, but the relieving army appreciated the welcome all the same. He wasn't sure how he'd find Nesta and the family in all this, but as it turned out, they found him. "There he is! Aeron! Aeron! Over here!" He recognized his sister Mererid's voice amid the din and turned to look. There they were! Mother and father, brothers, sisters, aunts, uncles, and cousins. And his intended. There was Nesta with the rest, her two children jumping, pointing, and shrieking next to her.

Without a thought, he was out of his saddle, forcing his way through the crowd, and he was soon locked in a mass embrace with those dearest to him. Suddenly, he was crying.

"Hey! Hey!" said his father. "Is this any way for the Conquering Hero to behave?" He was laughing as he said it, but there was concern on his face.

"I thought… I was afraid you were all dead," choked Aeron.

"Us?" said his mother. "Why, we were safe inside the walls here, *you* were the one out there fighting a battle!"

He almost blurted out: *Because our home is burned to the ground!* but caught himself. Unfortunately they saw the look on his face and realized something was wrong. His father stared at him with unblinking eyes. "What's happened, son?"

He knew that it was no time to lie. He took a deep breath and let it out. "I rode by the farm on the way here and it… it has been burned down." Every face was shocked, and several people gasped or cried out. "I feared you'd been there until I was told you had come here." He looked to Nesta, and she came up close and put her arms around him.

His mother was sniffling back tears, and several sisters were crying quietly, but his father reached out and rested his hand on his shoulder. "Buildings can be rebuilt and things replaced. All that really matters is that we're all here, alive and well."

"Yes," said Mererid, smiling bravely. "We are much luckier than many others. We'll put things right once this is all over!"

"Is it over?" asked his mother. "Everyone's saying you beat those terrible Rhordians and drove them away. Is the war over?"

"Oh, I wish it was, Mama, but I'm afraid not. We destroyed one of the League's armies, but there's another one down by Hodenburg. We still have to beat that one."

"And you have to go?"

"In a day or so. We're taking a rest here, but then we have to move on."

"If you're to rest, then you'll be staying with us at the town house," declared his mother. Oh yes, Da's house in the town that he used when he was here on business. With the whole clan here it must be packed, but a huge longing to be with his loved ones filled him up and he said yes. He found Macsen and made sure everything was being arranged for the Holdfast troops to sleep their full day while Macsen's own force and the garrison of Picksbury kept a lookout. Then he retired to the townhouse with the family and had dinner - an ordinary dinner. As he ate, he found he was getting sleepier and sleepier. Some time later, he found himself lying on a bed with Nesta, and Elin and Gethin curled up next to him. That was the last thing he remembered for some time.

* * * * *

He woke up a full day later, stiff, sore, and with a desperate need to use the garderobe. After finishing business, he sought out Nesta and found her chopping onions, helping Mama to cook dinner. Dinner? Yes a full day had gone by and it was dinner time again. "Oh you're awake," said Nesta spotting him. "How do you feel?" she asked.

"Like I could sleep another whole day," he replied with a yawn.

"Well, you ought to be allowed to, but I don't think they'll let you; that Macsen fellow left a message for you," she pointed to a folded piece of parchment on the table. He took it and saw that it was a summons to a meeting later that evening.

"So you'll be leaving tomorrow?"

"I imagine so. We'll decide tonight."

"It's not fair, you just got here"

"I know, but this victory will come as a huge surprise to the Rhordians. The less time we give them to react, the better our chances of winning the next battle will be."

"So there will be another battle." It was a statement, not a question.

Aeron sighed. "I can't see them giving up, so yes, there will certainly be another battle."

"Will we win?" She stopped her chopping. "Please don't lie to me, Aeron."

He looked away for a moment but then faced her again. "I don't know. It will be a much bigger fight than the one we just had. And we won't catch the Rhordians by surprise like we did this time. Still, we do have a few tricks up our sleeve that will give us an advantage."

"But it will be a hard fight. A lot of people will get killed."

"Yes, very likely."

"Please don't be one of them. I… I couldn't bear it." And then they were kissing, in spite of the fact that his mother and two sisters were right there in the room.

After dinner - a very quiet dinner - Aeron left and made his way to where Macsen had set up his headquarters, a large house which had been given for his use when he was here before the siege. All the commanders, all the artificers and mages and the people from Ej, were there. It was a large group and they filled the biggest room in the house.

To his embarrassment, they cheered when he arrived, and many slapped him on the back. He tried to brush it all off and went to sit next to Macsen. He expected that the older halfling would speak first, but Macsen motioned to him to begin. He looked around and cleared his throat. "Well, we won the first fight, and it was a very good win. We hurt the enemy badly and took close to four thousand prisoners, including the Duke of Hetronburg. My congratulations to you all. It was very well done."

"And to you, Aeron," said Macsen. "It never would have turned out that way but for you." He blushed at the praise from his former commander - and detractor. At that moment, it meant a lot to him.

"Maybe, but now we have an even bigger challenge. We can't just sit here and let the League recover and bring up more forces. Even with the losses we inflicted, they outnumber us by a lot. If we give them the time to collect all of those forces together and move against us, it will be a fight we can't win. We have to move south and beat the force they have besieging Hodenburg."

This produced a few cheers, but most of the people realized what a large task that simple statement really was. "So what numbers do we have here now, Conwy?" he asked his co-commander.

"Between what I had, what you brought, and the garrison here and a few other groups which have shown up, we have around ten thousands."

Aeron nodded, impressed. That was more than he expected, although he was sure that included poorly trained volunteers, teamsters, and supply train guards. And when they moved, they would have to leave at least a small garrison in Picksbury, plus troops to guard all those prisoners. Still, it was a force to be reckoned with. "And what's the latest reports from Rootwell in Hodenburg?"

"He says that he had about twelve thousands in the besieging force, but since the news of their defeat here reached them, they have been calling in reinforcements. About two thousand survivors from our fight have reached there and are being reorganized. A couple thousands more have arrived from the south and east. So right now, Rootwell estimates there are around three thousands manning the siege lines, all infantry and gunners, and the rest - twelve or thirteen thousands - are assembled north of the city to meet any advance by us. He says there are about three thousand cavalry - two thousand of it heavy - and the rest infantry and gunners. They are continuing the bombardment - you can hear the guns from here when the wind is right."

"Anything unusual?" asked Aeron. "I keep thinking about those mammoths the Duke of Targun Spire brought to the Grand Review. I don't how we'd deal with things like that."

Macsen laughed. "No need to worry about them, Aeron. I've met the Duke a few times at earlier Grand Reviews, and he treats the beasties like pets. He adores them, and he'd never risk them in an actual battle unless it was the absolute last throw."

"Well, that's good to know." Aeron did some figuring in his head. "So the total numbers are about equal, except a good part of our force is bottled up inside the city. If we hit them head on, they'll outnumber us in the field."

"But not by all that much," said Dilwyn. "And with our war machines and the *Windwalker* and the flying grenadiers and all the other things we've cooked up - literally in the case of Mama Beata's food - we should have a good chance."

Aeron wanted to say that at best they would end up with was a slaughter pen that would wreck both armies, but he could not dash their hopes. And there wasn't really any other choice that he could see anyway. They'd never get better odds than they had right now. The League had at least another ten thousand troops in scattered garrisons that they could bring here, while the Shires had scraped the bottom of the barrel and then scraped it again. Nearly everyone capable of carrying a weapon was here, and they wouldn't get any stronger by waiting.

"Very well then, unless there are any objections, we should march south tomorrow morning. Anas, we'd appreciate any scouting you can do for us in *Windwalker*, but please don't use your grenadiers, no matter how tempting a target you see. I have an idea for how to use them in the coming fight, and surprise is utterly vital."

The halfling leader from Ej nodded courteously and said: "It shall be as you wish, Commander."

A few dozen details about the order of march were discussed and settled, and then the group broke up. Aeron walked back to his father's townhouse through streets that were suddenly a lot busier, and the preparations began. He was feeling very tired. Nesta gave him a cup of warm milk and tucked him into a bed, and he was out almost immediately. At some point during the night, he woke up and discovered that she was in the bed next to him. He muzzily wondered what his mother would think, but he reached for Nesta and pulled her in close.

Departure the next day was at a reasonable hour instead of the dead of night. He said goodbye to the family and made his way to headquarters. Most of the troops were camped outside of town, but some, including most of the commanders, were inside Picksbury. He met up with Dilwyn and Macsen and their staffs and rode out through the gates.

The light cavalry was already heading out in front. Hodenburg was only a little over three leagues away, so they could start meeting the enemy at almost any time. *Windwalker* had been tethered just to the north of the town but was soon in the air and moving south. The infantry columns formed up and filed onto the road with the lighter artillery interspersed between them. The baggage wagons would come last. The whole column would probably stretch three or four miles, so it was possible that the front would encounter enemy forces before the rear even left Picksbury.

It was a cloudy day and cool for this time of year, and Aeron again hoped there wouldn't be any heavy rain. It would muck up the road and slow things down, especially for the wheeled vehicles. Much would depend on their artillery in the coming fight, and they couldn't afford to have it stuck in the mud. They did have a few showers but no heavy deluge. The clouds hid *Windwalker* for most of the day except when it came back to report. The reports usually consisted of a message dropped with a cloth ribbon attached. Due to the clouds, the airship had to come pretty low to be able to see anything, and Aeron worried that they might get low enough to get shot at.

The messages told him that the Rhordians had taken up a position only about a mile north of Hodenburg and seemed to simply be waiting for the approach of the Shires army. Sometimes there was a little sketch map included, but it didn't tell him much. As they marched, the sound of the bombardment got louder and louder; clearly the enemy had not abandoned the siege. Reports from the scouting cavalry said that the Rhordians had their own cavalry out in

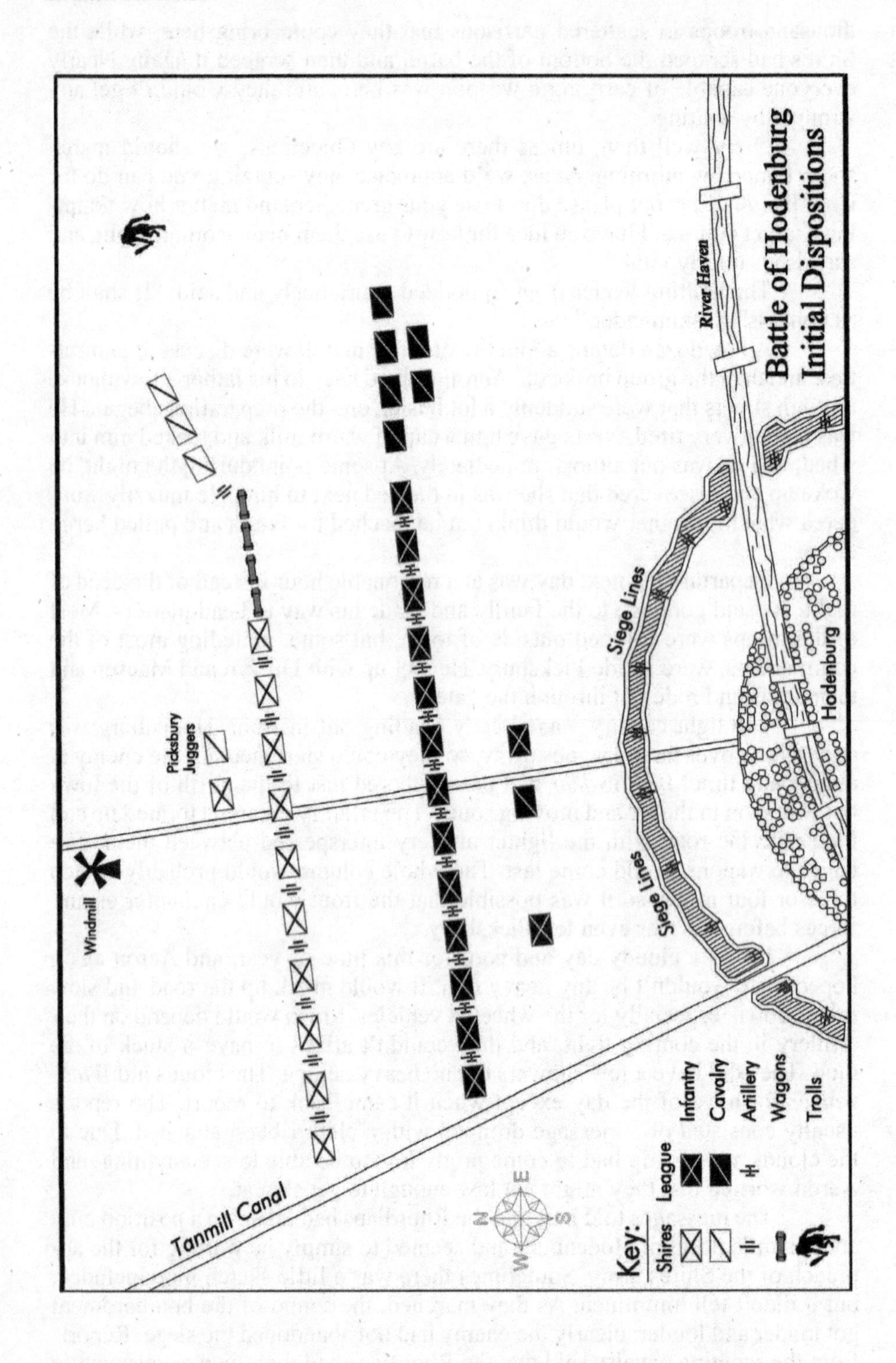
Battle of Hodenburg
Initial Dispositions
River Haven
Siege Lines
Siege Lines
Hodenburg
Picksbury Juggers
Windmill
Tanmill Canal
N
E
S
W
Key:
Shires
League
Infantry
Cavalry
Artillery
Wagons
Trolls

front as pickets, but they were not straying far from the main army.

"They certainly aren't being very aggressive, are they?" said Dilwyn after reading the reports.

"No, but they were content to just let us come to them before the first battle, too. Maybe they are doing the same thing now."

"Well, we aren't going to fall into their trap like last time," said Macsen.

Slightly after noon, they crested a slight rise and Hodenburg - and the enemy - came into view about a league away. Aeron ordered the head of the column to deploy into battle formation, screened by the light cavalry, and let the rest of the army catch up and deploy as well. This was a tense moment because if the enemy were to suddenly move forward and attack, the front of the army would have to fall back and try to deploy as best it could with the following elements. Aeron watched carefully, but the Rhordians stayed put, and he relaxed slightly. By mid-afternoon, the bulk of the army was in line and ready to fight. Some of the war machines were still coming up, and the supply wagons wouldn't be on hand until it was nearly dark, but they were basically ready to fight.

All the while this was going on, Aeron studied the enemy dispositions. There was a damaged windmill just behind the Shirelings' lines, and he climbed up there with Macsen and a few others for a better look.

The enemy had set up a strong line. Their left (the Shirelings' right) was anchored on the Tanmill Canal. The canal was about forty feet wide and five or six feet deep. Not a huge obstacle, but the banks were steep and another few feet high. Troops could not easily get across it without a bridge, and there weren't any on this particular stretch. There would be no hope of flanking them on that end. Of course once the Shires Army had its own right set there, they couldn't be flanked, either.

From the canal, the Rhordian line stretched about two miles east. Blocks of infantry were interspersed with cannons, and there were two walled farmhouses, one on either side of the main road, that had been turned into miniature fortresses. There was one group of cavalry in reserve near the center, but the bulk of the Rhordian horse was posted on their open right flank in a position where it could guard their own flank or threaten the Shires Army's left.

To their rear was another group of infantry in reserve, and then farther back were the trenches and palisade which had been thrown up around Hodenburg. The cannons and catapults placed there were still bombarding the city, and columns of smoke rose up here and there where buildings were on fire. It was too far to see clearly, but the city looked to have taken a battering.

The Shires Army finished its deployment, and its arrangement was almost a mirror image of the Rhordians'. Infantry from the canal, stretching eastward across the road, interspersed with cannons, and then most of the cavalry massed on the open left. The Picksbury Knights and a few bands of infantry formed a reserve. The line was significantly shorter than the Rhordians due to both lack of numbers and the simple fact that the humans were larger and took up more space. The enemy right extended at least eighty or ninety rods beyond the Shirelings' left. Clearly a danger spot.

The sun was invisible behind the clouds, but Aeron judged they still had an hour of daylight. "I want to advance our whole line about a mile forward. To just outside the range of their guns," he announced.

"Why?" asked Macsen.

"It's clear that the Rhordians want us to attack. They haven't made a move to attack us, even when we were deploying and vulnerable. And the truth is we *do* have to attack. Sitting here gains us nothing, and the enemy will only get stronger if we give them time. So, I want us to be in a position to start the battle immediately at dawn. I don't want to risk disordering ourselves by having to do a march in the morning just to get in range."

"Makes sense," said Dilwyn.

"All right," said Macsen. "Let's do it while we have the light." Messengers were sent out, and the army was alerted to move forward on a pre-arranged signal. Aeron was still slightly amazed that people were actually *listening* to him. Listening and obeying.

It took about half an hour to get the orders delivered. Cavalry were sent out to mark where the advance should stop. When it seemed like all the troops were alert and ready, a flag was waved from the windmill and a moment later everything was in motion. The advance was a bit ragged to his critical eye, especially the artillery, which had some troubles off the road, but overall it was well done. The Rhordians appeared a bit alarmed by this advance so late in the day, but when the line halted and then straightened itself out and didn't advance any farther the enemy relaxed.

"Let's get everyone settled in," he said. "We still need to get Mama Beata's food distributed - but *don't* let them eat it until breakfast! Also tell the troops to gather anything they can find to make barricades to protect themselves."

"I thought we were going to do the attacking, Aeron," said Dilwyn. "What use will they be?"

"They might be useful to rally on if we have to fall back," said Macsen. "Right, Aeron?"

"That, and I'm thinking that we might be able to induce the Rhordians to attack *us*."

"Oh? How?"

"I'll tell you later when we have a meeting. I need to talk to Anas and the Ej people." He turned to head down the ladder from the top of the windmill when someone shouted:

"Missing Gods! What are *those?!*"

He whipped around and looked the way the fellow was pointing. Off to their rear, following the road, were a dozen huge shapes, perhaps a mile or so away and heading in their direction. They were shaped like a person, two legs, two arms and a head, but they looked to be fifteen or twenty feet tall!

"Trolls!" exclaimed Macsen. "They must be from the Abbetsmoor, up near Yangmere. But what are they doing here?"

"Uh... I think I know," said Dilwyn.

"You do? What do you know?" asked Aeron.

"When we first got things rolling at the Holdfast, Paddy sent out requests to everyone he could think of for aid. A friend of his in Yangmere told him that he was going to see if the trolls would be willing to help. The people up there have traded with the trolls for years. Sometimes they'll hire themselves out for heavy construction work. They helped build the dam that created Yangmere Lake. That was the last we heard about it, but… well, here they are."

"Are they willing to fight? We don't have much in the way of construction to do just now."

"I've heard that trolls love a good fight," said Macsen.

"Well, we could sure use them, but we need to stop them!"

"What?"

"Stop them before they cross the ridge! I don't want the Rhordians to know we have them! Come on!"

They hurried down from the windmill, grabbed their ponies, and galloped to meet the approaching trolls. Up close, the creatures looked even more immense. They had scaly gray-green skin and long, trailing green hair. Most of them carried great wooden clubs, clutched in huge fists. They wore loincloths made of animal skins, and some also wore leather jerkins. All twelve of them also had better-made leather straps around their shoulders forming a kind of backpack in which a Shireling rode, peering over the trolls' shoulders!

A single Shireling riding a pony was in the lead, and he halted the group when he saw Aeron and the others pelting toward him. "Halloo!" he shouted. "Is Paddy Bobart around anywhere?"

Dilwyn came forward and said: "He's here. He's resting right now. Who are you?"

"Ah, well, don't wake him, but I'm Hopcyn Folant. Paddy sent me a letter a few months ago asking if I could get any of my trollish friends to help in the fight he thought was coming. It took me a while to convince them, but, well, here they are." He smiled and gestured at the figures behind him.

"Fight?" rumbled one of the trolls. Its voice sounded like a man with a handful of pebbles in his mouth.

"We fight now?" said another.

"Uh, tomorrow!" cried Aeron. "Fight tomorrow!"

"Eat?" asked a third. This was echoed by a half-dozen others.

"Uh, sure." Aeron looked to Folant. "What do they eat?"

"Oh, a sheep or two apiece ought to do for them... Well, we've been traveling fast to try and catch up with you folks, better make that three apiece."

"I'll see to it right away," said Dilwyn who hurried off toward where the quartermasters were establishing a supply dump.

"We will get you food," said Aeron. "But please sit! Sit down right here, and we will get you food."

Folant said something, and all twelve trolls plunked themselves down with an audible thud. The Shirelings riding on their backs dismounted and gathered near Folant.

Macsen put his hands on his hips and smiled. "Well if that don't take all. They'll sure come in handy. How do you think we can make best use of them?"

"I've got an idea about that. We'll talk at the meeting. In the meantime, do you think you scare up a dozen tents what we could use to cover these fellows?"

It was fully dark by the time they got all the commanders together to discuss their plans for the next day. Dilwyn had provided another map with colored blocks to indicate troops. The map was just a rough sketch, but it would do. Aeron stood up in front and took a deep breath. "So, we're here. The enemy is waiting for us to attack and try to relieve Hodenburg. They have the advantage in numbers, raw strength, and in a strong position. If we simply advance straight at them, we will be putting our heads into a meat grinder. We can't turn them on the right because of the canal, and they've massed all their heavy horse to our left to prevent us trying to turn them there and to threaten our flank if we do advance."

"So what do we do, Aeron?" asked Macsen.

"We are going to get them to attack us instead."

"You said that before, and I say again: how?"

"First, we are going to move all of our special wagons and their guards over to the left. I'm going to send all of our musketeers with them." He moved some blocks over to the left. "Once they're set up, that will extend our lines to be nearly as long as theirs. I'm going to send our new allies over there as well. If their heavy horse does try to attack us there, they will run into a nasty surprise. Next, once it seems the Rhordians are settled for the night, our whole force is going to advance five hundred paces straight toward them."

"Why?" asked Dilwyn.

"So that come dawn, our cannons will be in range of them. As soon as there's light to see, they will open fire."

"The Rhordians will just fire back with their own guns, Aeron. They have just as many, and they are heavier. We can't win a pounding match like that."

"No, you're right. But that is where the *Windwalker* and the flying grenadiers will come into play." He smiled and looked at Anas Macadrian. "Here's what I want you to do..."

*****

The movement forward was carried out very quietly in the dead of night. A score of Shirelings who had been given the last of Mama Beata's Cat's Eye Tarts were sent out with covered lanterns. They counted off five hundred steps and then exposed the lanterns only to the north. The Shirefolk could see the light, but the enemy could not. The troops started forward, the infantry helping to haul the cannons, their wheels wrapped in straw to muffle the noise. They left some of their people behind to keep their campfires burning, but the advancing troops, once they got to their stopping point, simply lay down and tried to sleep where they were. There appeared to be some stirrings in the enemy camps, but nothing more happened.

The supply wagons were too noisy to risk moving then, but they were kept ready to move at a moment's notice. Aeron wasn't happy about putting the mostly untrained wagon guards in such a vital position, but there wasn't much choice. Hopefully the well-trained musketeers would bolster their morale, and firing from the cover of the wagons, they should be very effective. He also assigned two of the volley guns to support them.

Having done all he could, Aeron tried to sleep. He dozed fitfully until he was awakened an hour before dawn. The order went out for all to eat the last of the golden bread. Aeron ate his small loaf, and in moments, his fatigue vanished and he was alert and ready for what lay ahead. There had been only a small amount of the Courage Pudding, and it had been cut into very tiny slivers so most of the troops would have a small bite. Mama Beata could not tell them if so little would have any effect, but it had been given out with instructions not to eat it until combat was nigh.

A faint reddish glow had appeared in the east, but everything else was still in darkness. The headquarters had spent the night by the ruined windmill, but with the advance of the army, it was now too far to the rear to be an effective location to command the battle, despite the excellent view if gave. Everyone mounted up and rode forward to a small farmhouse just off the road and a few hundred yards behind the battle line. Paddy Bobart came along in a carriage. The old artificer had not been looking well, and Dilwyn was afraid the huge effort to get ready had inflicted a heavy toll on him. Behind him, Aeron could hear the strange slapping noise the *Windwalker* made when its side panels were flapping. The airship was getting itself up and ready to play its vital part. The headquarters group consisted of Aeron, Macsen, Dilwyn, Paddy Bobart, another mage named Teged, and a dozen or so aides to run messages. Everyone else had dispersed to their own commands or stations, except Paddy who dozed in his carriage.

"Not long now," said Dilwyn, pointing to the growing light. "A lot of noise coming from the Rhodians; I imagine they've noticed our move forward by now."

"Probably. There's enough light now for the wagons to move. Have them take their position," said Aeron. Dilwyn immediately dispatched a rider. Shortly, they could hear rumbles and squeaks and groans from over on the left. "I hope our new friends stay put."

"Folant says they're amazingly cooperative as long as they get what they want."

"Well, if they want a good fight, they'll surely get it today."

Moment by moment, the sky got brighter in the east. There were some roiling clouds that were painted a garish, bloody red. It seemed all too appropriate to Aeron. "It's about time to get this started. I wish... I wish I could say something to all of them... thank them somehow..."

"You can, Commander," said Teged the mage. "I have a spell which will allow you to project your voice so everyone can hear."

"Really? I... uh, give me a moment to think about what I want to say." He thought about it, but nothing much seemed to come. The mage was looking at him expectantly, as were Macsen and Dilwyn. The dawn was coming, and he couldn't wait. He nodded to Teged, who made some motions with his hands, and suddenly a tingling filled Aeron's throat.

"People of the Shires," he began and flinched as his voice rang out across the fields. Heads turned in his direction from everywhere. "People of the Shires... battle is upon us. It is not a battle we wanted, we did not seek out this war, but it has been forced upon us." He hesitated, but then the words came to him. He knew not where they came from, but his voice became steady and sure.

"Will you suffer the wounds given to your country to go unavenged? Will you resign your parents-wives-children and friends to be the wretched vassals of a proud insulting foe? And your own necks to the halter?" He paused and then he was answered by thousands of voices shouting *No! No! Never!*

"I never doubted you! You have my thanks and the thanks of all our people! Now! Let us go on to victory! Let us drive the invaders from our soil! Let it begin!"

A huge cheer rose from the army, and a moment later, the cannons roared out all along the line.

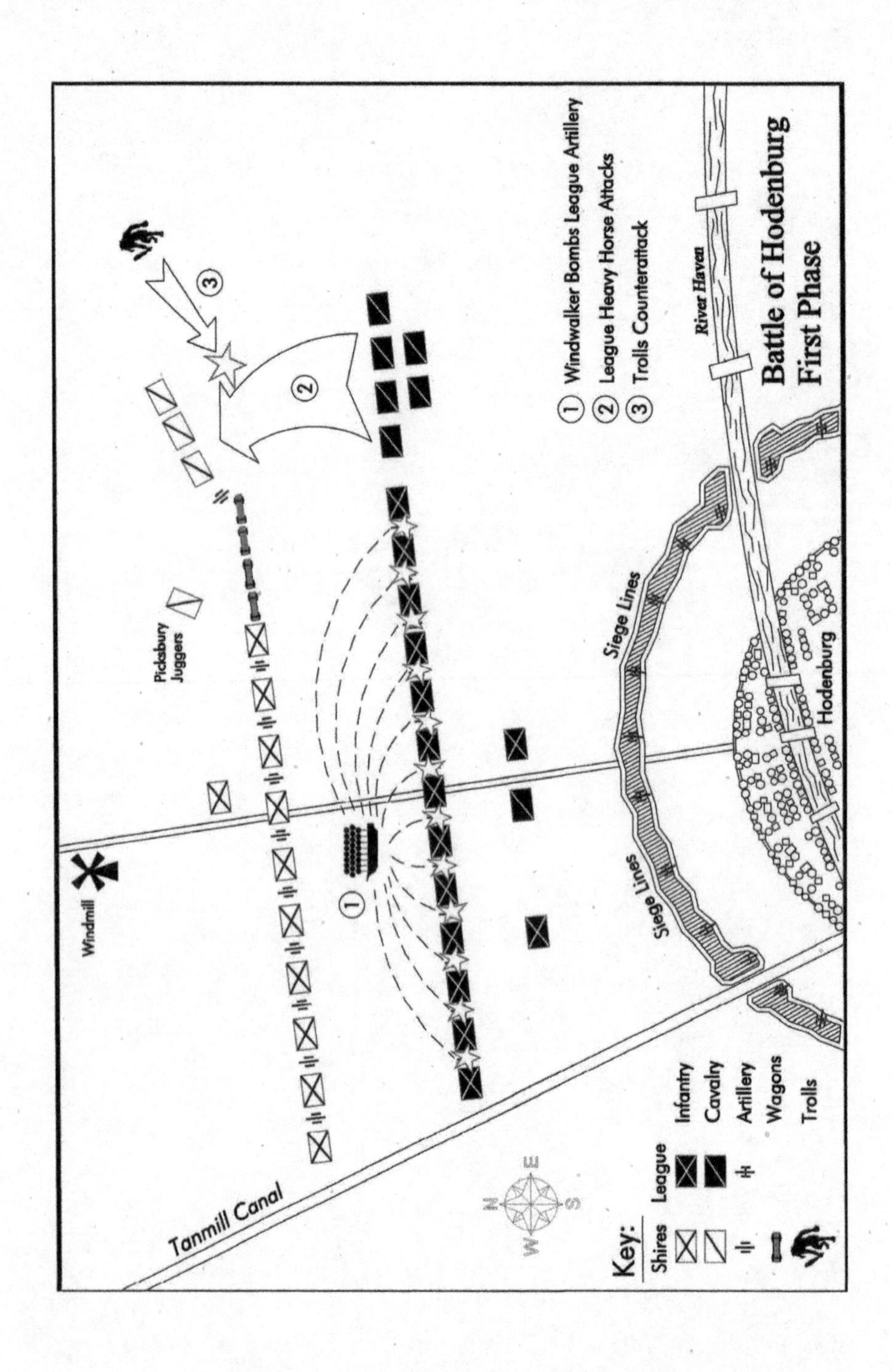
Battle of Hodenburg
First Phase
① Windwalker Bombs League Artillery
② League Heavy Horse Attacks
③ Trolls Counterattack
Windmill
Picksbury Juggers
Tanmill Canal
Siege Lines
Siege Lines
River Haven
Hodenburg
Key:
Shires
League
Infantry
Cavalry
Artillery
Wagons
Trolls
N
E
S
W

Chapter 21

The guns shook the ground, and clouds of smoke billowed out from them. It was still too dark to see what effect the shots had on the enemy, but it wasn't long before their own guns started firing back. A few screams rose between the shots, telling him that some of the cannon balls were finding their mark. The shot were just solid iron spheres that did their ugly work by literally tearing a person apart. A single shot could plow through a dozen ranks, mangling everything in its path. Due to the nighttime advance, the enemy line was only about a thousand paces away, well within range of most of the guns.

The initial fire for the Shires guns had almost been a regular volley, but now each crew loaded and fired as quickly as they could, unmindful of what their fellow gunners were doing. The next wave of shots was much more strung out, and soon the shots were randomly spaced. The Rhordians were the same, although they weren't firing their heavier guns nearly as fast.

Even so, they were doing damage and killing Shirelings. The headquarters people - who knew the battle plan - kept looking skyward at *Windwalker*, which was circling overhead in the growing light. "What are they waiting for?" growled Macsen.

"Spotting their targets," said Aeron. "They'll only get one chance at this."

Despite his statement, Aeron was growing impatient as well. He was losing troops he could not afford to. It was fully light now, and they ought to be able to… At last, he saw what he'd been waiting for: a dark speck detached itself from *Windwalker* and fell earthward. Then another and another. The specks fell and fell, and then the mechanical wings of the Sky Grenadiers spread wide and they continued to dive but steered their courses toward their targets.

The Rhordian artillery.

Down, down, the Grenadiers swooped. It was hard to tell if any of the Rhordians had noticed them, but there was nothing shooting at them as they pulled out of their dives, flew right over the guns, and tossed their grenades. Their bombs were too small to harm a big, heavy cannon, but they weren't actually aiming at the guns themselves…

Just as he'd learned at the College of Warcraft, to the rear of each cannon, a pit had been dug to store the ammunition. Cannon balls, wadding, and several hundred pounds of gunpowder in each one. The pits were close at hand for easy loading but kept the powder safe from flying cannon balls - but not from grenades dropped right in them. Large explosions began to erupt from just behind the Rhordian lines.

One after the other, the enemy cannons' ammunition blew up. Sometimes the explosions actually damaged the guns, but even when they did not, the crews were savaged and the ammo destroyed. Nearby infantry were knocked flat by the blasts. *Boom! Boom! Boom!* Red flashes and billowing clouds of white smoke, filled with hurtling debris, rose skyward. Not every magazine was hit on the first pass, but the Grenadiers, still moving at fantastic speeds, swung around and came back for another run.

More explosions billowed upward, but by now the Rhordians were past their surprise and began firing back. Arrows arced up and musketeers fired off their pieces, but it was the warmages that proved most deadly. Most spells only had a short range, maybe as much as a regular bow, but the Grenadiers were now close enough to be hit. Fireballs and lightning bolts stabbed upward, and the gallant fliers began to crash to the ground.

"Get out, get out of there!" hissed Aeron.

A few made the mistake of trying to climb upward, back to *Windwalker*, but their speed became so slow they were easy targets, and even archers were able to pick some off. The smart ones realized their only hope was to get back to friendly lines. They used the speed they still had and turned north.

Three of them made it.

One crashed just as he reached safety, cartwheeling across the ground and landing in a twisted heap. The other two landed more or less in one piece, although both were injured. The one who had crashed was rushed off to the healers, a bloody mess.

The whole battle had come to a stop during the amazing spectacle, but now it resumed. The Shireling gunners went back to work with a will, and only a single enemy cannon was replying. "Well, that worked!" said Macsen enthusiastically.

"But at what a cost. If I'd known most of them were going to die…"

"Aeron, most *us* could still well die," said Dilwyn. "Their sacrifice may have bought us… everything. Look, our guns are chewing them up, and they can't even strike back! If they want to win they'll *have* to attack! Exactly as you planned!"

He looked out over the field and saw that it was true. The Shires Army's guns were hammering the Rhordian infantry, tearing big chunks out of their formations. The humans were mostly just standing there, although a few units had flung themselves to the ground in hopes of avoiding the deadly projectiles. *They don't know what to do! We upset their plans, and they don't know what to do!* But he was sure they would figure it out soon enough. If they didn't want to stand there and get slaughtered, they would either have to move forward or move back. To retreat would put their backs right up against their own siege lines around Hodenburg, not a good place to be. So they would advance, and soon. But exactly how would they do it and where would they concentrate their attack?

A straight up frontal assault would bring them into range of the Shires archers, and the cannons would start using what was quaintly called 'scrap shot'. The cannons would be loaded with all sorts of sharp pieces of metal. When fired they would spread out and slice through dozens of men with a single shot. It was nasty stuff, but only effective at close range. So if they advanced straight against the infantry line, they would suffer terribly before they could close. *If I were them, I'd try to avoid that.*

An outflanking attack on the right was out because of the canal. So it was almost inevitable they'd try to strike the left with their heavy cavalry. If they could beat the much lighter Shires cavalry, they could roll up the flank of the infantry line, and then while it was trying to react to that, the Rhordian infantry would attack and finish things.

The location of the farm where they'd made headquarters didn't have a good view all the way to the left end of the line, so Aeron rode over that way a few hundred paces until he could see. At the very end of the line of infantry, the line of wagons began. Seventy of the special ones Dilwyn had constructed parked end to end extended the line almost five hundred paces. They had their parapets raised, and they were crammed with troops, including two hundred musketeers. Beyond their flank and well back were the bulk of the Shires cavalry. He couldn't quite see where the trolls were lurking, but he hoped they were over there somewhere.

"It looks like the Rhordian cavalry is up to something," said Dilwyn.

Aeron looked and saw that indeed the large mass of enemy cavalry was stirring. Due to their position, only a single Shireling cannon could fire on them, so they hadn't suffered much. The huge, dark mass slowly began moving forward, and just then, the sun peeked through a gap in the clouds and gleamed redly on armor and lance points.

"They're heading further out to the right," said Dilwyn. "To avoid the line of wagons, I guess."

"Yeah, they probably don't like the looks of them."

"Should… should we order the Picksbury Knights over here? To bolster our light horse?" Dilwyn was looking worried. Aeron was a bit worried himself.

"They're our only significant reserve. I don't want to use them up this early."

"But if the Rhordian heavy horse smashes our own cavalry and gets around our flank…!"

"I know, I know. All right, send a messenger and have the Knights move this way five hundred paces, but no further. Meanwhile, I want a closer look." He spurred his pony and cantered over to the left, taking the mage Teged with him. He rode quickly along the line of wagons, shouting encouragement and telling them to shoot straight when the enemy got close. Some of them cheered back, but most seemed to be peering anxiously at the masses of armored cavalry moving across their front. Except for the musketeers, the defenders were wearing a mish-mosh of regular clothing, ill-made armor, hastily made wooden shields, spears, hunting bows, scythes, and sickles. Aeron hoped they wouldn't be too heavily engaged.

He reached the end of the wagons where the two volley guns were placed and told the gunners to stand ready. They assured him that they were. Then he rode to the commander of the cavalry on that wing, a grizzled old fellow smoking a pipe named Siors Rheinallt. "You're going to have some action soon, I think, Captain," Aeron said to him.

"My boys and girls are looking forward to it, Commander," replied Rheinallt, blowing a smoke ring.

"You've got about twenty-five hundred Rhordian cavalry heading your way, Captain. Two thousand of them are heavy. You'll have some support from the troops in the wagons and the two volley guns. I've moved the Picksbury Knights up over there, and I'll send them in if you get into trouble, but I'd rather not commit them unless I really have to. Have you seen the trolls around anywhere this morning?"

Rheinalt laughed and pointed with his pipe stem. "The great smelly buggers are off that way fifty rods or so, hunkered down in a gully with those tents pulled over 'em. The fellow bossin' 'em around says they're itchin' for a fight. Sure hope he's right."

"Yeah, me, too," said Aeron. "All right looks like they are coming on, I'll leave you to it. Good luck." He turned his pony and rode around the right flank of the cavalry and fell back a few hundred paces to where he could see what was happening. From there, he could also see where the Shires Knights were waiting. He made eye contact with Captain Einion and held up his hand, signaling them to wait. If things turned bad, he could wave him forward.

The Rhordian cavalry was about a thousand paces away and coming on at a walk in a stately fashion. The heavy horse were formed up in squadrons fifty men wide and four ranks deep. Eight squadrons were lined up side by side with twenty or thirty paces between them, and two more were in the rear as a reserve. There was a screen of light cavalry out in front, a sensible precaution to make sure there were no unexpected gullies or fences—or traps—in front of the heavy horse. When they got to about four hundred paces, the light cavalry turned and fell back through the gaps between the squadrons, and the heavy horse picked up the pace to a trot. Aeron found it really rather thrilling - or would have been, if those men weren't coming to kill him.

It looked as though the Rhordians were planning to shift far enough to their right so they would pass about a hundred paces beyond the end of the wagons. Aeron doubted they had noticed the two volley guns yet. That would give them a surprise, but not enough to make a lot of difference. It was really up to the Shires cavalry to stop this attack, and Aeron didn't see any way they could. Bloody it, slow it down, but not stop it. The humans would smash back the lighter cavalry, Aeron would throw in the Picksbury Knights who would bloody them some more, but sooner or later the Rhordians would break through and swing around the flank. What should he do? He could bring up his small infantry reserve, but they couldn't stop heavy horse on their own. If he pulled any other infantry out of the main line, the Rhordian commander - who *was* in command over there anyway? - would see it immediately and send his own infantry forward, cannons or no cannons. He clutched the reins of his mount and held his breath.

Four hundred paces, three hundred, the sound of the warhorses' hooves was becoming louder and louder, and the ground was starting to shake, making his pony jerk nervously. Shouts rang out from the Shires cavalry and they started their counter-charge, moving forward in one big mob rather than ordered squadrons like the Rhordians. The gunners by the volley guns made ready…

It was at this point that the trolls decided to join the fun.

Aeron could just barely see where the huge creatures had been hiding, but once they stood up, he could have seen them from miles away. They threw off the tent canvas they'd been hidden under and charged directly toward the right flank of the Rhordian cavalry, which couldn't have been more than a dozen rods away.

Aeron didn't know a lot about trolls, but one thing he'd heard was that horses were *really* afraid of them. It was immediately apparent that he had heard right. The nearest squadron of heavy horse visibly *cringed* away from them. Which caused them to collide with the squadron immediately to their left. This forced those horsemen to their left, and the cringe just cascaded through the whole formation.

The trolls had looked slow and awkward when he had first seen them, but now that they were running, they moved with amazing speed. They smashed into the flank of the Rhordians, and in an instant, riders and even horses were tossed into the air as the trolls grabbed them and flung them aside, or just smashed at them with their clubs and great fists.

The enemy cavalry slid or was shoved even more to its left, toward the wagons. Just then, the two volley guns cut loose with all of their barrels, each one with a load of scrap on top of a cannon ball. The Rhordians were only fifty paces away, and the blast cut down a score or more of horses and riders in an instant. Their whole formation was becoming a jumbled mess, with all order and momentum lost. The mage Teged flung a fireball into the enemy midst for good measure, felling a dozen more. Moments later, the Shires cavalry slammed into them from the front with a crash that could be heard all over the battlefield.

"Missing Gods, look at that!" cried Dilwyn who had come up beside him. "The trolls and our cavalry are showing them right toward the wagons!"

And so they were. The trolls were stampeding the horses closest to them, and they were forcing the others further and further left. The Shires cavalry and the mound of bodies left by the volley guns kept them from getting past the wagons, and inexorably the whole mass was drifting to their left - Aeron's right - across the front of the wagons.

The Shirelings in those wagons were quick to take advantage. Puffs of smoke from muskets and arrows from bows lashed out from them as the Rhordians came near. The arrows probably couldn't do much against the heavily armored soldiers, but even the small Shireling muskets were capable of blowing holes right through breastplates and helmets. Riders and horses began to fall. The magnificent Rhordian charge had fallen apart completely.

The heavy horse, which normally made use of its momentum to smash through or over their opponents, were at a disadvantage in this sort of fighting, but their size, strength, and heavy armor still made them formidable opponents, and the Shires cavalry could do little more than keep them contained and let the musketeers and trolls do most of the killing.

And the trolls were surely doing that. If a heavy cavalryman could stab a charge-driven lance into a troll it might well kill it, but in this sort of close quarter fight, that was nigh impossible. Desperately trying to control their panicked horses, they poked with lances or slashed with swords, but the trolls shrugged this off like flea bites and struck back with blows that the heaviest armor could not turn. The Rhordian light cavalry which had fallen back was now reformed, but they could not get their horses to close on the trolls; all they could do was shoot arrows at them, risking hitting their own comrades, but a troll could be stuck as full of arrows as a pincushion and take no serious harm. Despite all the humans could do, the trolls smashed their way through the formation, herding the enemy before them.

Suddenly a blast of fire erupted around the trolls - and the humans close to them. The enemy must have sent a warmage with the cavalry. A number of humans and horses went down, but the trolls only seemed annoyed. A second fireball shot out, but with little more effect. Then a troll seized some luckless rider and hurled him a hundred feet through the air to smash into the group of riders from where the fireballs had come. No more spells struck the trolls after that.

"Guess we won't need the Picksbury Knights after all," said Dilwyn, staring in awe.

"I hope not," replied Aeron. "But what will the Rhordians do now?"

The answer wasn't long in coming. Horns began sounding along the enemy lines, and their infantry started preparing to move. The ones who had gone prone to escape the bombardment got to their feet and dressed their ranks. Aeron stared for a moment and then, leaving Teged behind to continue blasting the enemy cavalry, rode back to his central position near the farmhouse and hoped that things wouldn't fall apart on the left in his absence. Macsen met him there.

"Well, you got your wish," he said with a crooked grin, "they're attacking us."

"Be careful what you wish for," muttered Aeron. "It looked a whole lot simpler with wooden blocks sitting on a parchment map."

"Sure did. So what do you want to do?"

"Not much we can do except try to hold the line and hurt them as much as we can. I'll bring the Picksbury Knights back here as a reserve to charge anywhere the line starts to break." *Except the line could break in a dozen places at once.*

"Our archers will thin the bastards out," said Macsen, as if reading his thoughts.

But not nearly enough - and they have archers, too.

The Rhordian infantry lurched into motion, their lines rippling as they moved, rays of sunlight penetrated the scudding clouds and reflected off spearpoints and helmets. The defending Shires troops had constructed a few defenses as he'd directed, but there had not been enough time or ready materials to make anything substantial. Some small trees had been cut down and dragged in front of the lines as obstacles here and there, and some crude breastworks thrown up in other spots, but it wouldn't be enough to really hinder the enemy. Aeron's thoughts went back to when he was first training the Picksbury Light Horse and he was asked how a Shireling could hope to match a human's greater height, strength, and reach. He'd told them to gang up on an opponent, but the numbers here were nearly equal; there would be little opportunity for ganging up.

"Odd," said Macsen, "only their wings are advancing, the center is holding back for some reason."

Aeron looked and saw that he was correct. The Rhordian right and left wings were marching forward, but the center was holding fast. He had no idea why, but he was grateful for small favors. With no immediate threat in front of them, the cannons mounted in the Shires Army center were now free to fire to the right and left in support of the troops who were in danger. But they'd been firing non-stop for almost two hours now, and the crews were tiring and their rate of fire was falling. The Rhordian infantry had taken a beating, but they were professionals and kept going, despite their losses.

They came within bow range, and the Shireling archers opened up, sending showers of arrows at their foes. The human infantry wasn't nearly as well armored as the heavy cavalry, and some of them fell under the deadly rain. But to Aeron's surprise, the advance only went on a few more rods and then came to a stop. The infantry halted and hunkered down behind their shields, and then their own archers and musketeers began shooting. Over on the left, the humans faced not only that end of the Shires line but the section of the line of wagons not yet engaged with the Rhordian cavalry. Their arrows weren't going to be much use against the wagons.

The exchange went on for a short time, and then the Rhordian strategy became plain: their warmages went to work - or tried to. They had followed along behind the infantry line, each with several shield bearers to protect them. The range of their spells was short enough that they had to get within archery range to cast them. A half-dozen fireballs and lightning bolts streaked toward the halflings…

…and did nothing.

The flaming balls and crackling bolts just sputtered into nothing as they got close to the cringing infantry. Aeron gave a sigh of relief. The anti-magic standards were working! He'd seen one work at Picksbury, be he was glad that wasn't just a fluke. The troops had been told about the protective devices, of course, but they were as relieved as Aeron to discover that they actually worked. A cheer went up from the line.

And then another, when the lone Halfling warmages on either flank spit a fireball and a lightning bolt right back at the humans - and these got through to do damage. The duel of bows and magic went on for a while, neither side damaging the other very much, although the Shires Army cannons continued to mangle the Rhordian infantry.

But then the horns were blowing again, and there was movement in the enemy center. A new formation of infantry appeared, and they were clad in heavy armor almost like the mounted knights. Aeron peered through the smoke and said: "Those look like…"

"Duke Eowulf's personal guard," said Macsen. "I'd see 'em at every Grand Review. Veterans, every one of them, and damn fine troops. Coming right for us, Aeron. Better get your dog cavalry ready."

Yes, that was the only force he had, other than the trolls, who were still very busy, who could hope to match those men. But the guards were armed with halberds, and there were at least five hundred of them, and several thousand other infantry following behind them. The Picksbury Knights might slow them down, but they'd be chopped to pieces in the process. He sent a messenger to tell Captain Einion to get ready. And he sent several more to tell the artillery to shift their fire against the guards.

Well, this was it. The Critical Moment. He recognized it, but he wasn't sure there was much he could do to turn it to his advantage. If the Rhordian infantry pierced the center, the whole line would quickly collapse. He looked around, hoping to find some inspiration. There wasn't much at hand. The one band of infantry, maybe four hundred strong he'd kept as his final reserve, a bunch of headquarters people—there was Mama Beata, looking worried, a few healers, working feverishly to save the steadily mounting number of wounded, and a few others. Where was Taged the mage? Oh, right, he'd left him over to help on the left. And there was Paddy, slumped in his carriage. The strain was really telling on the old artificer. And even if he had the strength, snapping a few halberd shafts wasn't going to do much good here. Aeron nudged his pony and rode over to him.

"Paddy? I'm sorry, but maybe I wasn't the best choice for a commander. Things aren't looking too good, I'm afraid."

Paddy roused himself and looked up at him from under his bushy eyebrows. "No lad, I didn't make a mistake about this. And it isn't over yet."

"Aeron!" the sudden cry made him twist around in his saddle. There was Dilwyn. "Aeron, look at this!"

He rode back and stopped next to Dilwyn. "What now?"

"Look! Just behind the guards."

There was a large shape there, moving rapidly forward. The ranks of the Eowulf guards were opening up to let it through. "Missing Gods, what is that? It looks like…"

"Helga!"

Yes, that's what it was. The bizarre Iron Beast he'd seen back in Eowulf that nearly made him wet himself. The necromantic creation of Paddy Bobart with literally a mind of its own. "I… I guess they figured out how to get it going…"

"Yeah," said Dilwyn. "Look, they built a control cabin on the top of it, just like a normal Iron Beast. I'd assume there's a human crew in there. They must have installed the regular controls to make it go, but the rest of it is just like Paddy built it. Look at it move! It's gonna smash right through our lines!"

The huge machine was coming faster yet, leaving the guards behind. There was panic starting to form in the Shirelings facing it. It was still five hundred paces away, but people were already falling out ranks and heading for the rear.

"You're going to have to send in the Picksbury Knights," said Macsen.

"Not sure they'll do any good. I doubt even the aralez will go near that thing." Aeron could not tear his eyes away from the metal behemoth.

"Well, we've got to do something! It's going to rout the troops in front of it and then the guards, and all of the other troops following will spilt the army in two and roll it up in both direction!"

Macsen was right, but what could they do? He watched a cannon bounce a ball off the front of the thing with no apparent effect. Several others fired at it too but missed the rapidly moving Helga. The Shires infantry line in front of it was disintegrating and streaming to the rear. His last infantry reserves were faltering, too. As it got closer, he could see that the machine was almost unchanged except for the cabin on top. The two mechanical killing arms were folded back along the sides rather than deployed. Perhaps they hadn't found a way to operate those... *I wonder if Helga is still...*

The idea formed in an instant and a plan along with it. Jerking around, he said to Dilwyn: "Go talk to Einion. Tell him that on the signal he should charge, but avoid the Beast. Go around it and hit the guards."

"I could send a messenger..."

"No! Go yourself! He has to understand this *exactly*. Do it, Dilwyn!"

Dilwyn flinched at his tone but obeyed and rode off toward where the Knights were waiting. *All right, he's out of the way...*

"Aeron," said Macsen, "what are we going to do?"

"Something stupid. Macsen, if this doesn't work, you're in charge. Save as much of the army as you can." Without waiting for a reply, he turned his pony and galloped back to Paddy's carriage. He heard Macsen shout something after him, but he couldn't hear what, the noise of the battle was growing and growing. He reached the carriage and leaped from the pony onto the platform where the driver was sitting. The fellow was startled and then even more startled when Aeron physically threw him off the carriage and grabbed the reins. "Hang on Paddy! *Hyah!"*

He got the ponies moving and then turned the carriage directly toward the approaching Iron Beast. They galloped right past the stunned Macsen and through the crowd of fleeing Shires infantry.

They closed on the machine at a terrifying pace. One moment it was a good distance off and then the next it was *right there*. Aeron pulled on the reins to turn, but the horses, panicking, were already turning and much too fast. The carriage flipped over on its side, spilling Aeron and Paddy on the ground. Fortunately, it didn't turn all the way over, trapping them. The ponies broke free and galloped off.

Aeron scrambled over to where Paddy was lying and pulled him up to a sitting position. He seemed stunned but not badly hurt. Looking up, he saw that the beast was almost on them. He dragged Paddy to his feet and then shouted at the armored monstrosity, only forty paces away now:

"Helga! Helga! Friend!"

The machine came on, and he feared he'd made a dreadful mistake.

"Helga! Friend! Helga, Paddy's here! *Stop!"*

The beast seemed to falter, the headlong charge slowed... Twenty paces... fifteen paces... slower and slower...

It stopped ten paces away, steam puffing out from a dozen spots. The places where the eyes should have been had been dark, but now a red glow began to grow in them.

From the platform on top, Aeron heard voices: "Why are you stopping?" "I *didn't* stop! It stopped on its own!" "Why? What's wrong?" "I don't know!"

"Helga! Look, Paddy's here!" shouted Aeron. "Paddy! *Say* something!"

The old Shireling coughed several times and then said: "Hello, Helga. I've missed you. Did you miss me?"

The machine shuddered and more steam hissed out. Its head bobbed up and down and Paddy laughed. "Yes... Yes, Helga."

"Get this damn thing moving!" came the voice from above. "Crush those little bastards!"

Aeron could see that the Eowulf guards were catching up. They were running out of time...

"Helga!" he shouted. "Those men on your back want to hurt Paddy! They want to kill him! Don't let them! Stop those men!"

Helga became utterly still for a moment. Then a shudder ran through the whole machine, and the two mechanical arms unfolded. They twisted around, and the pointed ends reached in through the view ports on either side of the platform. From inside came voices crying out in alarm that quickly became screams.

The view ports were just large enough for the arms to fit through, but they weren't nearly large enough for a human to fit back out through them—but Helga didn't care. The arms, now covered in blood, came back out, dragging bits of the men who had been inside with them. Aeron swallowed to keep his breakfast down.

"Good... good work, Helga," he gasped. "But those men the men behind you. They want to kill Paddy, too. Turn around, Helga! Stop them from hurting Paddy!" Helga shook and shuddered but didn't turn. Then Paddy spoke:

"Do as he says, Helga. That's a good girl. Turn round and destroy those people behind you."

Helga twitched, and a strange moan emanated from it, but then it was turning, turning around to face the Eowulf guards.

"Helga, destroy," croaked Paddy.

Helga began to move. Straight toward the guards. The humans, totally surprised, stumbled to a halt. The men in front tried to retreat, but they were hemmed in by their close-packed comrades.

Helga smashed right into them.

Aeron had no idea how much Helga weighed - thousands and thousands of pounds surely - but it trampled right over the armored guardsmen, crushing them flat. The tusks on either side of its head skewered them and tossed them aside, and the mechanical arms swatted them like bugs. The beast crashed all the way through their formation and then turned and crashed through it again.

A few of the braver men slashed at it with their halberds but with no effect at all. Few survived to take a second blow. The heavily armored humans could not move very quickly, and Helga ran rampant through them, killing as it went. The enemy formation seemed to explode with men running in all directions trying to get away from the monster in their midst.

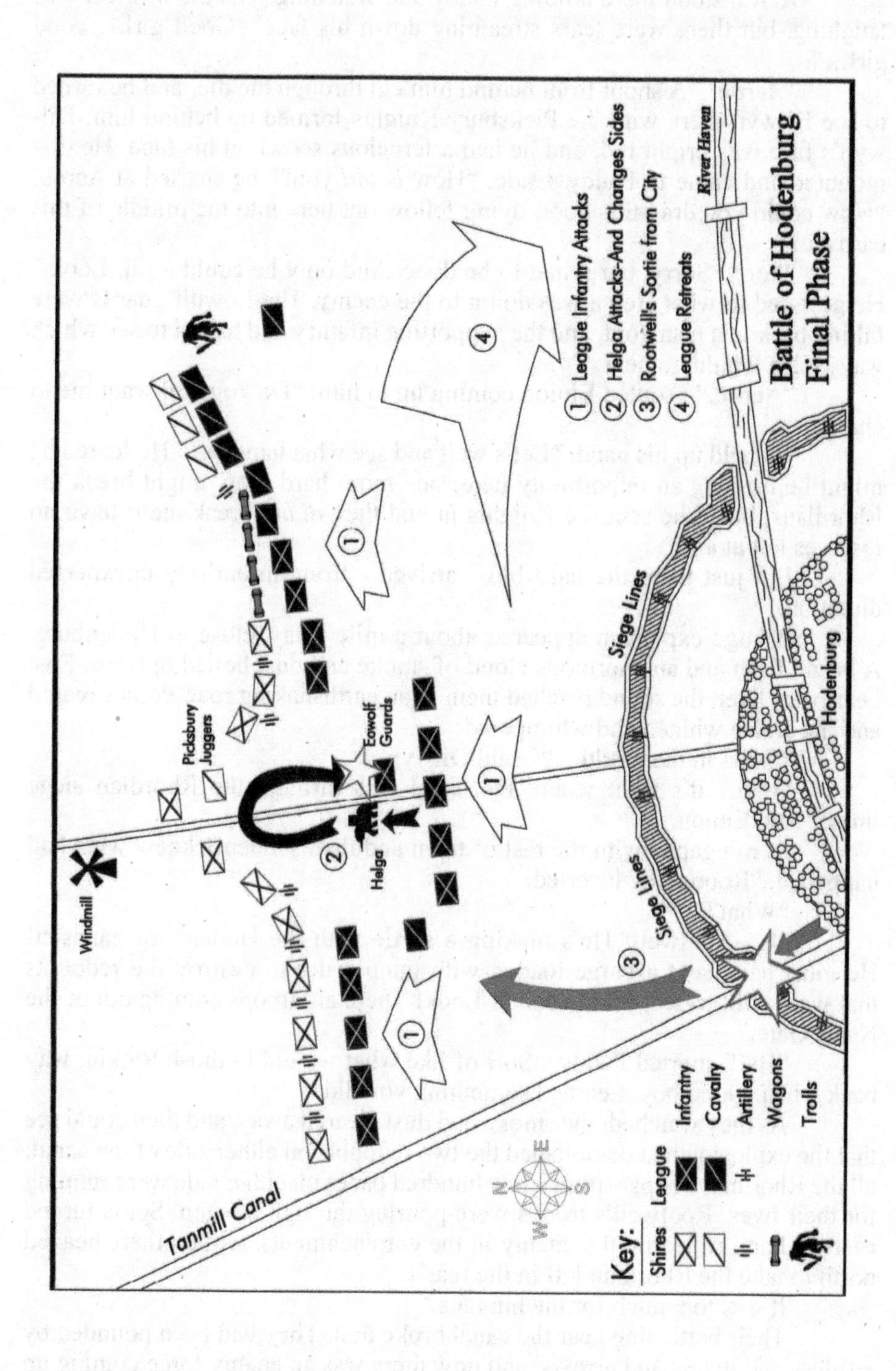
Battle of Hodenburg
Final Phase
1 League Infantry Attacks
2 Helga Attacks-And Changes Sides
3 Rootwell's Sortie from City
4 League Retreats
River Haven
Siege Lines
Siege Lines
Hodenburg
Picksbury Juggers
Eowolf Guards
Helga
Windmill
Tanmill Canal
Key:
Shires
League
Infantry
Cavalry
Artillery
Wagons
Trolls

Aeron stood there holding Paddy and watching. The old artificer was laughing, but there were tears streaming down his face. "Good girl… good girl…"

"Aeron!" A shout from behind him cut through the din, and he turned to see Dilwyn there with the Picksbury Knights formed up behind him. Dilwyn's face was bright red, and he had a ferocious scowl on his face. He dismounted and came to Paddy's side. "How *could* you?" he snarled at Aeron. "How could you drag this poor, dying fellow out here into the middle of this carnage?!"

"Sorry. Sorry, but it had to be done. And only he could do it. Look." He gestured to what Helga was doing to the enemy. The Eowulf guards were falling back in a near-rout, and the supporting infantry had halted to see which way Helga would go next.

"Aeron," shouted Einion coming up to him. "Do you still want me to charge?"

He held up his hand. "Let's wait and see what happens." He feared he might be missing an opportunity here: one more hard blow might break the Rhordians, but if he sent the Knights in and they *didn't* break, he'd have no reserves left at all.

But just then, the hard blow arrived - from an entirely unexpected direction.

A huge explosion appeared about a mile away, close to Hodenburg. A bright flash and an enormous cloud of smoke and dust boiled upward. Five heartbeats later, the sound reached them in an earthshaking roar. Ponies reared and the aralez whined and whimpered.

"What in the world…?" said Dilwyn.

"It's… it's right where the canal cuts through the Rhordian siege lines!" said Einion.

Aeron gaped with the rest of them and then suddenly knew what had happened. "Rootwell!" he cried.

"What?"

"It's Rootwell! He's making a sortie with the Hodenburg garrison! He must have sent a barge loaded with gunpowder to destroy the redoubts that were built to seal off the canal! Look! There are troops coming out of the North Gate!"

"Ha!" snorted Paddy. "Sort of like what we did to those Ratkin, way back when. Good boy. Learned something you did."

As they watched, the smoke and dust cleared away, and they could see that the explosion had demolished the two redoubts on either side of the canal; all the Rhordian troops within a few hundred paces on either side were running for their lives. Rootwell's troops were pouring through the gap. Some turned eastward and rolled up the enemy in the entrenchments, while others headed north to take the Rhordian left in the rear.

It was too much for the humans.

Their battle line near the canal broke first. They had been pounded by artillery and magic and arrows, and now there was an enemy force coming up on them from behind. They fell back and then headed east to get out of the rapidly closing trap. The center, already reeling from Helga's unexpected change of sides, was next to go. Helga was still coming after anything she could catch, and it was all simply too much. They started fleeing east, too. The only way out was to go around the eastern side of Hodenburg and then head south. The Rhordian right, fought to an exhausted standstill by the trolls, wagons, and Shires cavalry, had also had enough. They began falling back, too, in only slightly better order than the rest of their army. It all seemed to happen in an instant: one moment a raging battle, and now, a complete rout.

Aeron, unable to hold Paddy up anymore, slowly slumped to the ground, Dilwyn grabbing Paddy to keep him from falling.

"Aeron? You want me to do anything?" asked Einion.

He limply waved his hand. "See those people off, would you? Don't get close to Helga, though. I've got no idea what she'll do next."

"Right," grinned Einion. He gave the order, and the Picksbury Knights loped off in pursuit.

Macsen rode up a few moments later. "Well, this is quite a thing, ain't it?" he said. "What do you want me to do, Aeron?"

It was getting very hard to think. "Uh... why don't you go meet up with Rootwell? He's got to be over there somewhere. Just keep pushing them. Don't let them rally and reform."

"Yes, sir." Macsen flipped him an awkward salute and rode off. Meanwhile, Dilwyn started shouting for a litter bearer for Paddy. The carriage was a wreck, and the old Shireling was incapable of walking. It took a while to get one—there were so many other wounded in need—that by the time one arrived, the Rhordians were several miles away, disappearing around the edge of Hodenburg, with the Shires Army in pursuit. The field out in front of him was littered with dead and dying and a considerable number of human prisoners.

As they loaded Paddy up, Aeron felt strong enough to stand up and he followed along. After a while, someone showed up with a pony for him to ride, and he wearily mounted. He felt like he ought to be doing something, but he couldn't seem to think of what. The sounds of battle were fading, to be replaced with the cries and groans of the wounded.

He left Paddy and Dilwyn with the healers and went back to the headquarters by the farm. There were not all that many people there, but those that were there were laughing and shouting and all swarmed to welcome him. They shook his hand, and Mama Beata insisted he come down off his pony so she could give him a hug and a kiss. He thanked them all and then realized that was what he should be doing: thanking his people. He got back on the pony and began a tour of the army, looking for people to thank. It wasn't even noon yet.

It took him a few moments to realize that most of the army was gone - off chasing the Rhordians. But the ones who were left, he thanked. The healers and the wounded they were tending, the artillery gunners, and finally the people who had manned the wagons which had been so important in holding the left flank. There was no way they could join in the pursuit, so they were still there. He rode that way.

When he got closer, he was appalled to see the number of human bodies piled up in front of the wagons. When he'd left, the fighting had mostly been just the wagon guards shooting at the Rhordian cavalry. He hadn't realized that the fighting had gotten so heavy later on. And to the rear of the wagons, there were a lot of wounded halflings being tended to and a much too long row of bodies covered in tent canvas. "Missing Gods…" he hissed.

The Shires Army had taken a lot of casualties this day, but most of them were at least partially trained soldiers and many of them veterans of combat. The people in the wagons were neither. From the looks of things, they had become trained veterans in short order. Quite a few of them were women, a much higher proportion than in most of the trained bands.

He rode along the line, thanking the people and assuring them they had played an important role in the day's victory. Many looked stunned and exhausted, but most seemed to appreciate his gesture. Some of the people had made fires to heat water or cook meals. He saw one woman squatting next to a fire working on some stew. She looked a lot like…

"Nesta!"

He was off his pony and had her in his arms without a conscious thought. They clutched each other and then kissed for a long time. "What…? What are you *doing* here?!" he gasped when they finally broke apart.

"Defending our homes. Just like you," she replied. Her face was filthy, and tears had made little streaks through the dirt on her cheeks, but she looked as determined as anyone he'd ever seen.

Something in the tone of her voice got through to his befuddled mind, and he looked around. "Who else is here?"

She shrugged. "Your da, Bronwen, Gwilym, Mererid, Uncle Hywel, Uncle Pryce, some of your cousins…"

"Anyone hurt?" He held her away from him and noticed there was blood on her skirt. "Are *you* hurt?"

She followed his gaze. "Not my blood, don't worry."

"What about the others?" he was starting to panic.

"Your da got his arm broke by a Rhordian war hammer. Uncle Hywel, he got an arrow through his shoulder - Missing Gods, he was acting like a madman, 'cause of Madoc, I guess - and then Mererid…"

"What about Mererid? Was she wounded?" he demanded, his panic growing.

"She wasn't hurt, Aeron but, well, toward the end, the fighting got so hard and a Rhordian knight tried to climb into our wagon, and Mererid shoved her spear right through the opening in his helmet and he… and he fell. She's kind of upset right now."

"Oh no… and you were all here. All along. And I didn't know! Why didn't you tell me?"

"What? And have you worried to distraction and tryin' to figure out ways to keep us safe and maybe losing the whole battle because of it? No, we all agreed. We had to all crouch down in our wagons when you rode by before the fight so you wouldn't see us."

"I'm so sorry, Nesta, so sorry you all had to see this."

"Wasn't my first battle, as you might recall. And we got off lightly. Two wagons down from us, the humans got into it in force and killed everyone. We were trying to figure out how to drive 'em off when the retreat began."

It was all suddenly too much. Far too much, and he found himself sobbing like he hadn't sobbed since he was a boy. Nesta pulled him close, and they sank down to the ground. He cried while she gently rocked him.

Chapter 22

That evening, Aeron had pulled himself together enough to meet with the other commanders inside Hodenburg. Dunstan Rootwell was there along with Macsen and Dilwyn and Mama Beata, and a bunch of other people. The Rhordians had fallen back about three leagues before turning to make a stand. The Shires Army was too exhausted and disorganized to launch another attack, so they gave up the pursuit and fell back around the city.

The first reports on casualties had come in, and they were grim reading. The Shirelings had lost over a thousand dead and about three times that number wounded. The light cavalry had taken a significant portion of the total and was spent as a fighting force for the time being. The infantry had taken greater losses in total, but spread out over a larger number to begin with, they weren't in too bad shape, aside from being worn to a frazzle.

The Rhordians had taken a much worse beating. It would take longer to get an accurate count, but estimates were they'd lost maybe two thousand dead and probably twice that many wounded. About two thousand had been captured, but half of those were wounded, so there was some overlap. And they'd left all their artillery on the field or mounted in their siege works, so they were crippled in that department.

"We've hurt them," declared Rootwell. "Hurt them bad. The question now is what do we do next?"

"They've got ten or eleven thousands still able to fight," said Dilwyn. "We've got a bit more, but only a bit. Not enough for us to attack them with a real advantage, except for our artillery."

"But if we don't hit them now, they'll only get stronger," said Macsen. "You can bet they've got reinforcements heading this way as fast as they can march."

The discussion went on for a while, but they weren't able to form a plan everyone could agree on. Many of them looked to Aeron to simply give them an order, but he was too tired to even figure out what order to give, even if he was so inclined. Eventually, they decided to sleep on it and see what the situation was in the morning. Aeron got up, planning to ride back to where his family was camped.

"Oh," said Macsen as they were breaking up, "what about that thing, that Helga? It's still, roaming around on the battlefield. No one dares go near it."

"We'll have to ask Paddy in the morning," said Dilwyn. "He's still with the healers. We'll see if he can do anything with her."

* * * * *

But in the morning, Paddy was dead. He passed during the night, and the healers said it was simply his time and there was nothing they could do.

Helga had also stopped moving and although no one could say for sure, Aeron suspected that Helga and Paddy probably departed at the same moment. It was a tragedy, but with over a thousand other dead from the battle, it was hard to generate the proper emotions. Only Dilwyn was overly distraught.

"I like to think he's with Helga now," said Aeron after he got back into town and heard the news. "I'm really sorry, Dilwyn, but it was his foresight and wisdom which saved us here yesterday. You can be proud of the part you played in that."

"Thank you," he replied quietly. "And I'm sorry I yelled at you yesterday. I just... You did what you had to do. Just like Paddy." Aeron nodded, patted him on the back, and let him be.

Shortly after breakfast, scouts came back with the startling information that the Rhordians were gone. More scouts were sent out to try and make contact, and *Windwalker* went aloft and headed south to try and catch up with the enemy. Around noon, reports came in that the Rhordians had moved another three or four leagues and were now across the border and still heading along the main road to Eowulf.

"So what do you make of that?" asked Rootwell.

"Seems like they've had enough," replied Aeron. "In any case, there's no way we can chase them all the way to Eowulf and no point even if we could. We don't have the forces to lay siege to the place. Not and leave any sort of force guarding the Shires."

"So what do you suggest?"

Aeron shrugged. "Put ourselves back together as best we can. Tend the wounded, replace damaged or destroyed weapons and equipment. Have Mama Beata cook up some more of her food. Get ready for whatever happens. You might even want to send an emissary to try negotiating an end to all of this."

"What? Make peace? How could we ever trust them again?"

"We have to end it sometime. We can't keep all our people under arms indefinitely. They have crops to tend and lives to live. It's not like we can conquer the entire League and force a peace on them."

"You mean like they tried to do to us?"

"You saw how well that worked for them."

Rootwell chuckled, but he went away with a thoughtful expression on his face. Around nightfall, a fast rider arrived from Ferchester on the eastern border saying that the Rhordian force that had been besieging the town had also withdrawn and marched back into their own territory.

"They're pulling back completely?" asked Dilwyn.

"If they tried to continue the siege with a small force like that, they know we could just gobble it up," said Aeron.

"So for the moment, they can't get at us and we can't get at them," said Macsen. "A stand-off."

There was nothing to do but wait - and clean up the mess outside of Hodenburg. Several days passed, and the lightly wounded were patched up by the healers and returned to duty. The troops rested and tended to their equipment. Morale was high after the victory, but everyone was wondering what would come next.

What came next was the return of the Shires Assembly to Hodenburg from their exile in Tanmill. While it was nice to have the civil government back and the feeling of normalcy it bought, it also multiplied the number of opinions and voices in their strategy discussions. If there was no clear consensus before, it was even less clear now. Discussion turned away from military matters to economic ones. How long until the new volunteers could be allowed to go home? How much damage had been done to the crops? What sort of harvest could be expected and would there be enough to get everyone through the winter? When could trade be resumed? Who was going to pay for all this?

Aeron avoided the debates and spent as much time as he could with Nesta and his family. His Da was doing well, as was Uncle Hywel. Mererid was much quieter than her usual buoyant self, but she seemed to be dealing with things. He had an inspiration and sent her to see Gwenith, who had had a similar experience of killing her first person. They knew each other from family get-togethers but had never spent any time together before. Seeing and even riding Gwenith's aralez seemed like a balm for Mererid.

Everyone was talking about the battle and what they would do when they got home in about equal portions. Of course, the going home part was mostly about how they would do the rebuilding. Fortunately, only the main Cadwallader homestead had been burned. Uncle Hywel's newly rebuilt place had just been looted, and Uncle Pryce's farm, tucked in an out of the way hollow, hadn't been touched at all. There would be places for everyone to stay while they worked on the rebuilding.

Three days after the battle, the trolls announced they were going home. Four of their number had been killed in the final desperate melee on the left flank, but the survivors did not seem upset. It had been a 'good fight'. Aeron tried to convince them to stay with bribes of more food, but they refused. They made some necklaces for themselves by stringing the helmets of their vanquished foes together, grabbed a few other baubles, and then hoisted their fallen comrades on their shoulders and headed northeast, back to their moors.

Each day, Aeron would go out, supervising this or that, or conferring with people who were either far too sure of what needed to be done, or, like himself, unsure about anything. Each night, he'd come back to the family—who were sleeping in tents or under the wagons - and be asked what was going to happen next and when could they go home. He'd tell them since they were emergency volunteers, they could go home any time they wanted. This produced eye-rolls and icy stares.

Then, a little over a week after the battle, scouts reported that there was a large group of - they actually weren't quite what it was a large group of - approaching the southern border. Not an attacking force, it wasn't that large, but it was coming north along the road and would reach the border before the end of the day.

This produced wild speculation. A parley? If so, why so many of them? If not a parley, what then? They would have to wait to find out - and everyone was tired of waiting. But the next messenger left them even more puzzled. It was indeed a parley, but not only was there an unusually large delegation of humans - nearly two hundred - but they were accompanied by over a thousand

Shirelings! Prisoners taken in the early stages of the war, who were apparently to be freed!

"They wouldn't be freeing their prisoners unless they wanted to make peace!" declared Caradoc Lowri, a member of the Shires Assembly.

Lowri was prone to making excited statements, but this time, Aeron had to agree with him. It couldn't be a simple prisoner exchange since you don't release your captives until after the negotiations. So what was this all about? A peace overture, with the prisoners as some sort of gesture of good will?

It seems that they would find out shortly. Another messenger told that once they reached the border and stated their intentions, the humans, who were all mounted, hurried on toward Hodenburg with an escort at their best pace while the freed prisoners were left to be aided by the border patrol. Even more curious was the fact that there seemed to be a large number of women and children in the human party!

Bursting with curiosity, they anxiously awaited the arrival of this mysterious delegation who came into sight the afternoon of the next day. They rode in through the south gate of the city and were conducted to the central circle of the city. There was no building in the city large enough to hold the whole party and the Shires' leadership, so they met in the open. Fortunately, the weather was warm and fair.

The human delegation was led by the Duke of Berlonviche himself. He was the only one of the five dukes who had not joined in the attack on the Shires, so he was held in better regard than any of the others would have been. But his presence with this group was also a bit puzzling since his duchy was almost due north of Hodenburg. To be coming up the south road, he would have had to ride all the way around the Shires and then north again, a distance of almost seventy leagues.

Berlonviche and all the other humans dismounted and their horses were led away. The whole Shires Assembly and all the important military commanders and mages, including Aeron, were grouped a few dozen paces away to receive them. Several thousand other people, members of the army and citizens of Hodenburg, were gathered round to watch.

Berlonviche walked to within a few paces of the Assembly, and then to everyone's astonishment, he dropped to his knees and bowed his head. "People of the Shires," he said in a voice strong enough to carry, "I have come here to beg your forgiveness!"

A stunned silence followed which went on for so long that Berlonviche, getting no reply, went on: "We have been, all of us, betrayed!"

This finally prompted a response from Lowri. "Betrayed? How? And by who?"

"This war. This cursed strife between neighbors who had been friends for a century or more. It was all arranged, arranged by outsiders whose goal was to destroy us!"

"Outsiders? What outsiders? Who are you talking about?"

"At this moment, the City of Eowulf is under siege by the forces of Torvald Svendson, the mercenary leader."

"What?!" said a dozen voices, Aeron's among them. Svendson was a well-known mercenary commander from down south, in the regions of the Young Kingdoms near the Dragon Teeth Mountains. He was successful and respected as a commander, but his 'legion' was nowhere near large enough to besiege Eowulf!

"How can that be?" demanded Dunstan Rootwell. "How did he raise a force so large and come all the way up here?"

"It started in the spring," said Berlonviche. "Svendson suddenly had the money to take over a dozen other mercenary bands. Then he started attacking some of the smaller Young Kingdoms. Most of them are so small and so weak, he could easily conquer them. The first few resisted, and when he took the king's castle by storm, he put the king and all his family and followers to the sword to terrorize the others. It worked. After a while, he only had to march up to the castle and they would surrender. Then he took the king's family as hostages and added all the local troops to his army and marched on to do it again."

"We'd heard some rumors of this," admitted Rootwell. "But we never thought it could reach so far north."

"We have reason to believe that this is all some grand scheme coming from even farther south. That Lord Darvled fellow, he may be behind it all. He supplied Svendson with the money and directed his campaign."

Aeron frowned. He'd heard of Darvled. He was the one who started the 'humans first' campaign, persecuting non-humans. His two dwarf friends from the College of Warcraft, Vadik and Hagen, had warned him of something exactly like this just before the war started.

"All this spring," continued Berlonviche, "Svendson continued to grow, adding more and more troops to his army. All the while, his agent was pushing us, the Shires and the League, into a war. Now, when we are at each others' throats, he moved against Rhordia. I have come to ask - no, to *beg* - for your aid! Help us! Help us save the League and the Shires!"

The shock in the crowd was palpable - but so was the skepticism. There were angry shouts from the watching crowd until Lowri and Rootwell called for quiet. "You have proof of any of this?" growled Rootwell.

"We do!" said Berlonviche. He waved to some of his contingent, and a figure was hauled forward. His wrists were fastened with chains. Aeron recognized him at once. *"Jannik!"*

"Who?" demanded Lowri.

"He was the headmaster at the College. They appointed him after old Nedes retired. Several dwarf friends of mine said that he once worked for Lord Darvled."

"Yes," said Berlonviche. "We got information from Baron Gudman about that and watched him. We found proof of the accusation a week ago and put him to the question and he admitted all."

'The Question', the duke meant torture. Aeron could see terrible bruises on Jannik's face, and the man looked traumatized.

"This man was sent here to spread his master's poison, to turn us against each other, to prepare for this attack."

"Poison which your people lapped up without hesitation!" snarled Heilyn Culhwch, head of the Assembly. Many people nodded in agreement.

"Yes, yes, we were fools," agreed Berlonviche. "I can make no excuses for what my people have done. I can only ask forgiveness and beg for your aid. And you must aid us. If Eowulf falls, surely he will move against the other duchies—and against the Shires! Only together can we hope to prevent this!"

Negative shouts arose all around, and Lowri and Rootwell again had to call for quiet. "After all that's happened, how can you expect us to trust you?" asked Rootwell.

"I know it is asking much. But you can question Jannik yourselves if you like. And you can use your flying machine to see what is happening at Eowulf. But I realize that even that is not enough. We have brought back your own people who we captured. But we also bring hostages as pledges of our good faith." He gestured to the large group of people who had come with him. "These are the wives and children and grandchildren of the highest ranking nobles of Rhordia. Duke Eowulf's wife and children are here, as are my own. Some are from Targun Spire, Hetronburg, and Torffs Valem as well; many of our barons', too. We are placing our very future in your hands. If we prove false, their lives are forfeit, and we will lose all that is dear to us."

Aeron was shocked, and he could tell that everyone around him was as shocked as he. Lowri whispered: "It's true, I recognize a lot of the women from balls they held at Eowulf. They… they'd never do this unless they mean what they say."

The Shirelings were all so stunned that they were at a loss for words, looking from one to the other in bewilderment. Finally, Dunstan Rootwell said: "You've… you've given us a load of things to think about, Duke. We need to talk among ourselves. We'll find lodging for all of your… your dependents. If you'd be so kind, please keep yourself available to answer any questions we might have."

"Certainly, sir," said Berlonviche, rising to his feet and bowing.

It was a bit of a scramble to find secure lodgings for the humans. While almost none of the evacuated population of Hodenburg had returned yet, their houses, though empty, were much too small for humans. Most of the inns which did have higher ceilings and larger rooms to accommodate human travelers were occupied by army officers who had to be hastily evicted.

The Shires Assembly and all the higher-ranking commanders plus various other important people, like the mages and artificers and the people from Ej, retired to the Assembly Hall to deliberate. As Aeron was on his way there, he was hailed by a soldier: "Commander Cadwallader? I've got one of these humans here who's asking to see you. Demanding it, really. Claims to know you. You want to talk to him?"

Aeron almost told him to put him with the other 'guests' and he'd see him later, but then he hesitated. Who among the humans could know him personally? The only possible answer popped into his head. "Yes! Where is he? Take me to him!"

The abrupt answer took the fellow back, but he turned and led Aeron out into the circle and there was a shortish human waiting there with another soldier. "*Palle*!" shouted Aeron, breaking into a run. His old friend dashed to meet him, and they collided halfway with a thud.

"Aeron!" cried Palle. "Thank the Children you made it! I was worried sick about whether you got home safe, and I nearly fainted when I saw you there with the Shires' leaders. I could barely stop myself from running up to you in the middle of all the serious talking! Wouldn't that have been a sight?"

Aeron laughed, held Palle away from him for a moment, and then hugged him again, unmindful of the gaping soldier next to them. "I was worried that you'd gotten caught up in the battle around Hodenburg. I left word with our healers and the people guarding the prisoners to keep an eye out for you. But there were so many dead…"

"I *was* there," said Palle. "But I was still with the troops guarding the baggage train, so I was south of the town. And when everything fell apart, I was swept along with the rest of the rout."

"But what are you doing *here*?"

"I volunteered."

"What?"

"Well, right after the retreat halted south of Hodenburg, we got the word that Svendson had crossed the border and was marchin' on Eowulf. So we got moving again and managed to get to the city just before he did. I guess all the while, the dukes had been talking and interrogating Jannik and came up with the plan to send hostages and try to get you to join us. When I heard about it, I volunteered 'cause I know you, and I thought it might be good to have at least one friend here who might listen. I could scarcely believe it when I saw you with all the leaders here! I guess your wish to become an advisor to the Muster-Master came true after all?"

"Uh, well, something like that," said Aeron, not wanting to go into the whole story just then. "I have to go to this meeting, but first, tell me: how did they discover that Jannik was working for Darvled? Did you pass on the warning I gave you when you set me free?"

"Sure did. To my father, and he sent it on to Duke Berlonviche, and he was already on his way to Eowulf when everything broke."

"We were wondering how he got here so quickly. All right," he turned to the soldier and said: "I want you to keep Cadet Gudman here in case I need to bring him in to the Assembly to answer questions. Make him comfortable, get him food and drink, and treat him courteously, understand?"

"Uh, sure, sir." The fellow looked confused but compliant. Aeron slapped Palle on the shoulder and went into the Assembly chamber. Everyone looked up as he entered. "Problem, Aeron?" asked Rootwell.

"No sir, not at all." He related what Palle had told him and the circumstances. "So we can believe that part of their story at any rate."

"Assuming your 'friend' isn't lying to you," growled one of the Assembly members.

"The man saved my life and was a loyal friend for years," Aeron growled right back. "*I* don't think he's lying."

"Easy, son," said Rootwell. "We've got some hard decisions to make here, and we can't let our sentiments cloud our judgment."

"Yes, sir, you're right. But it seems to me it all comes down to whether or not we can trust the Rhordians. There's at least one Rhodian I *do* trust. We have to decide if we can trust the rest of them."

"Yes, that is the crux of the matter isn't it? So what do you all think? Can we trust Berlonviche and what he's told us?" Rootwell turned to look at the people gathered in the chamber.

"There's one thing we can check out for ourselves," said Anas Macadrian. "I can take *Windwalker* down to Eowulf and see if it really is under siege."

"This day's almost done, but can you go in the morning?" asked Caradoc Lowri.

"Weather's fair, we can leave right now," replied Anas. "With luck, we can be back here this time tomorrow."

"All right, but don't take any chances, we need you, Anas."

"Right." The Ej halfling took his leave and headed to his airship, leaving the rest behind.

"So, let's assume that Anas returns and can confirm that Eowulf is under siege. What do we do?"

"A large part of me says let the damn humans kill each other," said Fransis Drstan, one of the normally quieter Assembly members. "But another says that if this Svendson fellow wins, then it won't be long before it's our turn. Him and that Darvled look to be out to build an empire. Can't say I want to be part of it."

"Yes, that's the truth of it, I fear," said Rootwell. "If Svendson wins, he'll come after us. But if we help the Rhordians win then... what?"

This set off an intense debate. A few wanted nothing to do with the Rhordians no matter what future risks this might bring down on them. Others were more willing to help but wanted iron-clad guarantees about what came after. And a few, Aeron among them, felt that they had no choice but to help and right away.

During a pause, Aeron spoke up: "I'm no diplomat, my area of expertise is military matters. Along with the question of *should* we help the League is the one *can* we help them? Help them with any hope of success? We need to talk to Duke Berlonviche and find out how many troops Svendson has and how many the League can still muster against them."

The others, probably tired of the arguing about other things, agreed, and Berlonviche was brought in. "Duke Eowulf has maybe ten thousands inside the city," he said. "That's nearly all of the troops who came back from the battle here, plus the garrison that was left in the city, but he sent off most of the cavalry before the city was surrounded, thinking it would be more use outside than in. He sent that off northeast toward Worfmarch to join the other forces we were planning to assemble there."

"And what do you hope to assemble at Wolfmarch?" asked Aeron.

"I have six thousands headed there, the three thousands who were besieging Ferchester will go there, and Hetronburg, Targun Spire, and Torfs Valen are each sending about three thousands—all they have left. The Duke of Targun Spire will be in command when they are all assembled."

"So what… about eighteen thousands altogether? What sort of force do you reckon Sverdson has?"

Berlonviche hesitated, swallowed, and then said: "We estimate he has around forty thousands."

There was a long silence in the Assembly chamber. "Forty thousands?" asked Rootwell. "You're sure?"

"As sure as we can be. It could be a bit less—or a bit more. The bulk of it seems to be infantry and light cavalry. Not as much heavy horse as we would normally have with a force that size. Artillery is mostly lighter stuff, too. Ballistas and some catapults, not many cannons. No idea about warmages, but probably not too many—they don't seem to like the wandering life of a mercenary."

"So, forty thousands of them, and twenty-eight thousands of you," said Aeron, scratching his chin. "We could field ten or maybe twelve thousands, so that is just about equal numbers."

"We… we were hoping that you could free the prisoners you've taken," said Berlonvich. "If you can re-arm and re-equip them, that would add some to our forces. Uh… how many have you taken?"

"We have about five thousands," said Dilwyn. "But many of them are wounded. I doubt more than three thousands are fit for combat—although we did store their arms and equipment carefully, so there's no problem there."

"About equal numbers," said Aeron. "But ten thousands are stuck inside Eowulf. In a battle, Svendson could keep them penned up with half that number and send thirty-five thousands against us. Not the best odds."

"We've won with worse," said Rootwell. "But still, you are right, Aeron. An even fight like that could be a real bloodbath."

"Without your help, we would have no chance at all," said Berlonviche. "And once we're beaten, those forty thousands will be coming against you."

Yes, that was the hard fact they kept running up against. They sent the Duke away and talked for a little while longer, and then they adjourned for the night. They would meet again when the *Windwalker* returned with its scouting report.

The next day was tense. Aeron wandered from place to place, trying to help get the army ready for another campaign if it became necessary. Ammunition was gathered, rations stockpiled, animals tended, and Mama Beata had her cooks working day and night to cook up more bread and pudding. He visited with his family at noon and warned them what might be coming. They'd already heard, of course; the rumors were flying through the army. His eyes kept straying to the southern sky, looking for the airship.

It finally appeared just before sunset and came in to land outside the city. Everyone hurried to the Assembly chamber to meet Anas, who came in a short time later, looking out of breath. "Well, it's true," he said. "There's a large army surrounding Eowulf, and they are digging siege works."

"How large?" asked Rootwell and Aeron, almost simultaneously.

"We took some time to take a count - that's why we're a bit late getting back. I'd estimate somewhere between forty and forty-five thousands."

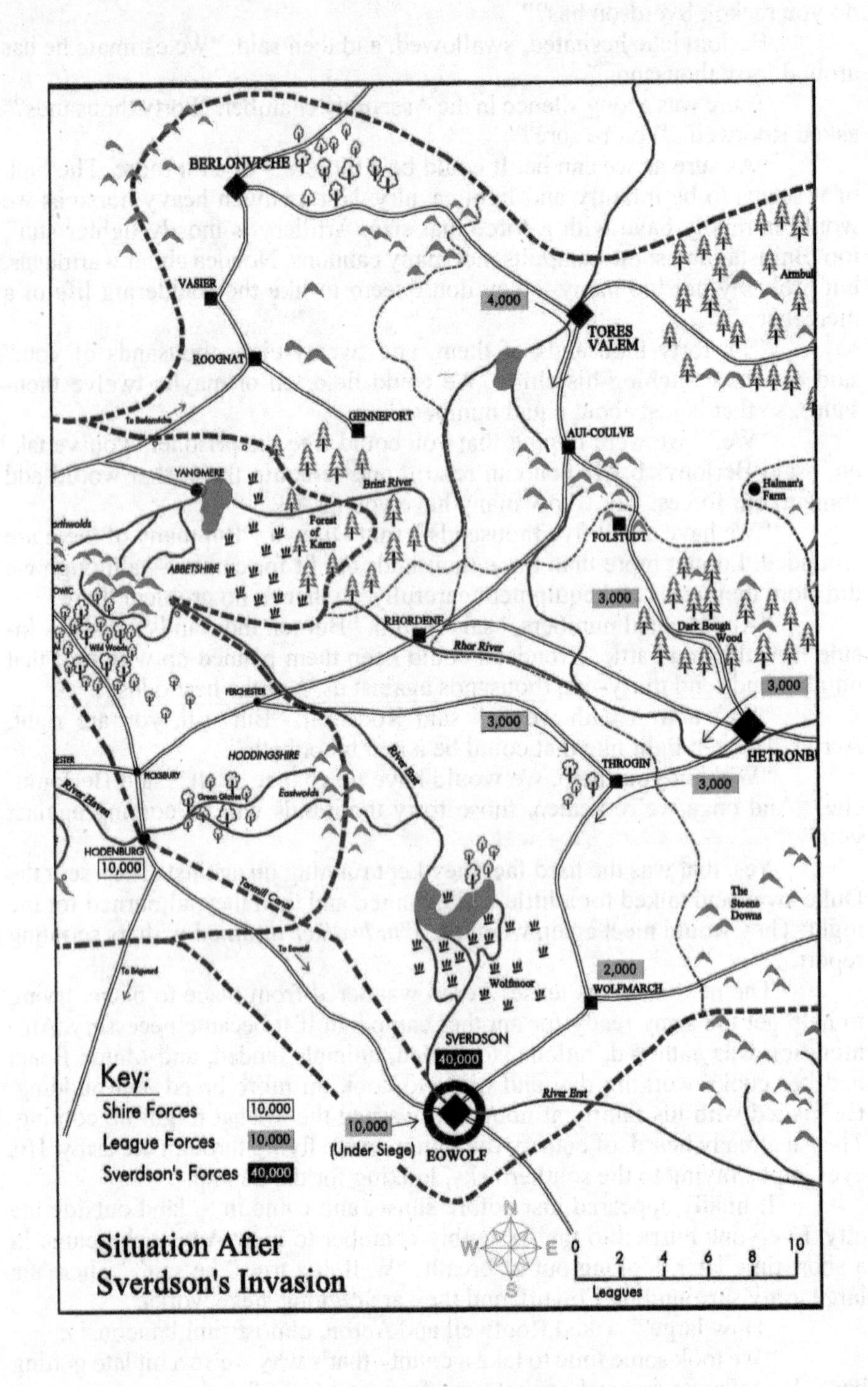
BERLONVICHE
VASIER
ROOGNAT
GENNEFORT
4,000
TORES VALEM
AUI-COULVE
To Berlonviche
YANGMERE
Brint River
Forest of Kame
Halman's Farm
FOLSTUDT
ABBETSHIRE
Wild Woods
3,000
RHORDENE
Rhor River
Dark Bough Wood
FERCHESTER
3,000
3,000
HODDINGSHIRE
River Brst
PICKSBURY
Green Glades
Eastwolds
River Haven
THROGIN
3,000
HODENBURG
10,000
Tonmill Canal
The Steens Downs
To Eowolf
2,000
WOLFMARCH
Wolfmoor
SVERDSON
40,000
River Brst
Key:
Shire Forces 10,000
League Forces 10,000
Sverdson's Forces 40,000
10,000
(Under Siege)
EOWOLF
N
W
E
S
0 2 4 6 8 10
Leagues
Situation After Sverdson's Invasion

A collective sigh filled the room. They were expecting this but all were hoping it wasn't as bad as Duke Berlonviche believed.

"Thank you, Anas," said Rootwell. "So, we now have as much information as we are going to get. The decision is up to us, and we have to make that decision and soon."

Dilwyn had provided another map and more wooden blocks. In addition to the green ones for Shires forces and the red ones for Rhordian, there were also yellow ones for Svendson's forces. While the debate went on, Aeron stared at the map and the blocks. It was a challenging situation. The enemy was all in one clump at Eowulf while the other side was in three different locations: The Shires Army at Hodenburg, Eowulf's forces inside the city bearing his name, and the rest of the Rhordian army gathering nine leagues away at Wolfmarch. If the Shires Army and the forces at Wolfmarch tried to advance on Eowulf independently, Sverdson's army would be in a perfect position to smash each one before the other could get close enough to help. The sensible thing to do would be for the Shires Army and the Wolfmarch forces to join up before advancing on the city.

The problem was that there was no direct line of march connecting them. There was a large lake and an even larger area of swampland called the Wolfmoor blocking any easy route from one to the other. The only practical route was a roundabout path leading through Ferchester and Throgin, a distance of thirty-five leagues, nearly a week's march. If the Shires Army tried to march to join Duke Targun Spire at Wolfmarch and Sverdson learned of it, he could send a force to assault Hodenburg, and there'd be nothing to stop it. If the League forces tried to come to Hodenburg, it was the same problem for them: the rest of the League would be wide open to attack.

He was so deeply thinking about the problem that Dilwyn had to nudge him when it came time to vote on whether or not to aid the Rhordians. He wasn't aware that there would be a vote, and it certainly never occurred to him that he would get a vote if one was taken. "Aeron? Aeron? What do you think? Should we help the Rhordians?"

"Oh! Uh, well, I don't think we have any choice. So yes, I think we should help them."

Caradoc Lowri looked around the room and said: "Well, it's not unanimous, but there's a clear majority: We'll help. Go bring in Berlonvich so we can tell him."

"Now all we have to do is figure out how to win," said Rootwell.

Aeron cleared his throat. "Well, I have an idea about that…"

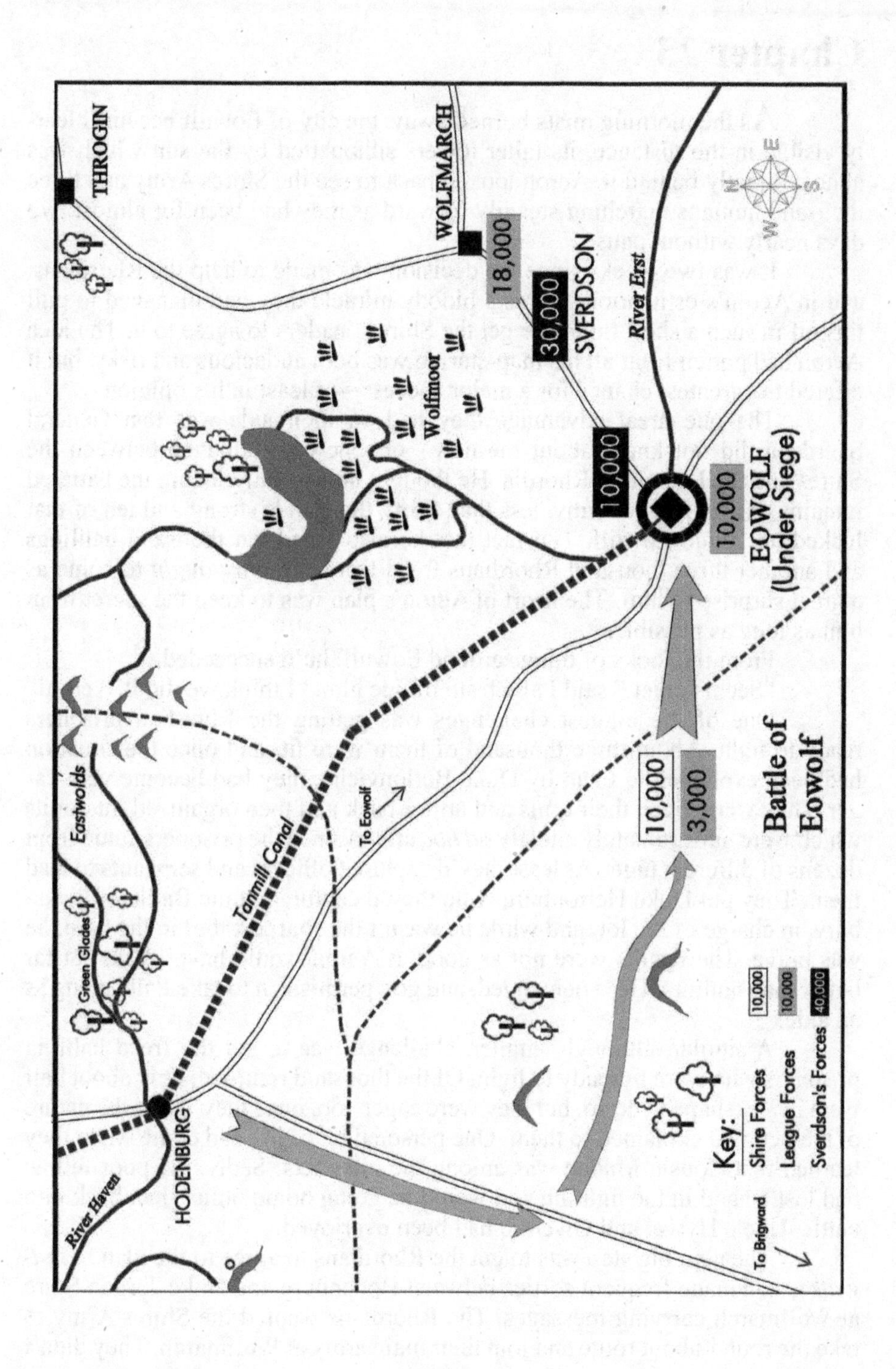
Battle of Eowolf
THROGIN
WOLFMARCH
18,000
30,000
SVERDSON
River Erst
Wolfmoor
10,000
EOWOLF (Under Siege)
10,000
Eastwolds
Tanmill Canal
To Eowolf
Green Glades
10,000
3,000
HODENBURG
River Haven
To Brigward
Key:
Shire Forces
League Forces
Sverdson's Forces

Chapter 23

As the morning mists burned away, the city of Eowulf became clearly visible in the distance, its taller towers silhouetted by the sun which was almost directly behind it. Aeron looked back to see the Shires Army and three thousand humans marching steadily forward as they had been for almost two days nearly without pause.

It was two weeks since the decision was made to help the Rhordians, and in Aeron's estimation, it was a bloody miracle they had managed to pull this off in such a short time—or get the Shires' leaders to agree to it. The idea Aeron had gotten from all his map-staring was both audacious and risky, but it offered the greatest chance for a major success—at least in his opinion.

The one great advantage they had on their side was that General Sverdson did not know about the new—or renewed—alliance between the Shires and the League of Rhordia. He thought he was only facing the battered remains of the League Army, less than thirty thousands strong and ten of that locked up inside Eowulf. The fact that he also faced ten thousand halflings and another three thousand Rhordians freed from captivity *ought* to come as a great surprise to him. The heart of Aeron's plan was to keep the secret from him as long as possible.

From the looks of things around Eowulf, he'd succeeded.

"Seems quiet," said Palle from beside him. "I think we did it, Aeron!"

One of the biggest challenges was getting the Rhordian prisoners ready to fight. About three thousand of them were fit, and once the situation had been explained to them by Duke Berlonviche, they had become very eager. They were given their arms and armor back and then organized into units which were, unfortunately, mostly *ad hoc* affairs since the prisoners came from dozens of different units. At least they'd captured officers and sergeants to lead them. They put Duke Hetronburg, who they'd captured at the Battle of Picksbury, in charge of the lot, and while he wasn't the sharpest tool in the barn, he was brave. The results were not as good as Aeron would have liked, but far better than nothing. He'd demanded, and got, permission to take Palle along as an aide.

A similar, although smaller, challenge was to get the freed halfling prisoners who were fit ready to fight. Of the thousand returned, only about half were in any shape to do so, but they were eager, too, once they'd had the nature of the betrayal explained to them. One personal bit of joy had come when they learned that Cousin Madoc was among the prisoners. Sadly, the poor fellow had lost a hand in the fighting and would be going home rather than back into battle. Uncle Hywel and Gwenith had been overjoyed.

The next big step was to get the Rhordians to agree to the plan. *Windwalker* had made frequent sorties between Hodenburg and Duke Targun Spire at Wolfmarch carrying messages. The Rhordians wanted the Shires Army to take the round-about route and join their main army at Wolfmarch. They didn't like the sound of Aeron's plan at all, but when it became plain that if they wanted the Shires' help they would have to accept it, they capitulated.

Aeron couldn't blame the humans for wanted things their way. It was a lot safer, but it would inevitably give away the big secret. Sverdson's scouts would surely learn the Shirelings were coming on their long march, and the advantage would be lost. If they made it look like there was no alliance and only strike at the last possible moment, they might pull off the surprise - as it seemed they had.

The siege lines around Eowulf were conducting business as usual. Catapults were lobbing stones into the city at intervals, and the troops in the trenches and the camps behind them were all involved in routine activities.

"They don't know we're here," breathed Dunstan Rootwell coming up beside Aeron. "You did it, boy!"

"*We* did it, sir. We all did it."

The key, of course was to keep Sverdson in the dark for as long as possible. The Shires made no overt moves to help the Rhordians or hurt Sverdson. The mercenary leader did send an emissary to Hodenburg, but he was allowed to see very little and was sent on his way with angry words to the effect: 'You humans are welcome to kill each other all you want, just leave us alone!' Aeron was quite sure that was all Sverdson wanted - until he'd beaten the League and could turn his attention to the Shires.

Then, when all was as ready as they could make it, the army had marched. Not down the main road from Hodenburg to Eowulf - that would be heavily patrolled by Sverdson's forces - but on the Brigward Road heading southwest. Mama Beata and her crew of chefs had been working almost nonstop to provide the Golden Bread and Courage Pudding for the whole army - enough bread for four days and pudding for one battle.

Once the march started, it only stopped for short breaks. It took two days and a night to swing around into a position due west of Eowulf, avoiding enemy scouts. Then, last night, the final approach began, across fields and hills, around forests, past farms and hamlets, guided by a number of people with the Cats Eye Tarts. It had been impossible to cover the whole distance and strike in the dark as they had at Picksbury, but they were here, and only shortly after dawn.

"I think they've seen us," said Rootwell, pointing to a pair of enemy cavalry that was galloping away as fast as their horses could carry them.

"Right, well, let's not give them any more warning than we have to," said Aeron. "Have the hornists sound the attack."

Horns began ringing out up and down the line, and the troops went into a slow jog. Or at least the Shirelings did, the humans down on the right end of the line just quickened their pace a bit. Having the humans come along and even giving them the special food felt strange, but they were here, they were eager, and they were needed.

They were still a full league away from the siege lines and would need the better part of an hour to reach them, so this would be no devastating surprise like they achieved at Picksbury, but the enemy was still at a big disadvantage. There were ten thousand of them, but they were spread out in a circle manning the siege lines around the city, and there was no way they could quickly concentrate their forces to meet the thirteen thousands bearing down on them. In addition, they could not ignore the ten thousand Rhordians actually in the city. If they left the siege lines unmanned, the garrison of the city would come boiling out, just like Rootwell's troops had done at Hodenburg.

The one factor that could thwart Aeron's plan was the Wolfmoor River which flowed through the city. It divided the siege lines in two. There was a stone bridge on the south side outside the siege lines, but on the north side, there was only a temporary wooden bridge the invaders had thrown up to allow them to move freely back and forth. If the enemy was able to quickly pull his forces on the west side of Eowulf across those bridges and destroy them, it could become very awkward to get at them. They could still get into Eowulf, but then they'd have to emerge from the city on the east side and attack the strong entrenchments of the besiegers; not a good situation. So they needed the bridges.

Aeron beckoned to a messenger. "Tell Captain Macsen to move out." The lad rode off at a gallop. He sent another order to Duke Hetronburg with the same order. Macsen was in command of all the Shires cavalry, including the Picksbury Knights, and his mission was to dash forward as quickly as he could and seize the wooden bridge on the north side. Hetronburg had no cavalry, but his men could run flat out and try to grab the south bridge.

The two flanks of the army surged forward, leaving the Shires infantry behind. They had no artillery, of course, the forced march and the roadless approach made it impossible to bring them. The guns and the supply wagons with an escort were only just now crossing the border and starting down the road to Eowulf. If all went well, they might arrive by the next day.

The *Windwalker* emerged from a cloud and cruised over the city, heading east to get a look at Sverdson's main army. Duke Targun Spire's army at Wolfmarch had made threatening moves toward Eowulf yesterday, and the invader had taken the bait. Leaving ten thousands to watch the city, he'd marched off with thirty thousands in hopes of smashing the last Rhordian field army and ending the war at a stroke. The airship had seen the move and reported to Aeron last evening that things were shaping up as he'd hoped. Aeron had conferred with Rootwell, and they gave the order to strike.

The infantry had covered half the distance to the city when the cavalry reached the north side bridge. The enemy had dithered for a considerable time before trying to evacuate their forces on the west side of the city, and not all that many had made it over the bridge before Macsen and his troopers reached it. Aeron could see the Picksbury Knights on their loping aralez leading the charge. He was still well over a mile away, so he couldn't see any details of the combat, but it was clear that a swirling melee had broken out and the retreating enemy began to stack up so their escape was at least temporarily blocked. Over on the right, he could see the Rhordian infantry moving around the curve of the siegeworks toward the south bridge, but he couldn't actually see the bridge from where he was.

The enemy trenches in front of him appeared empty, the catapults abandoned, so he directed the infantry to shift to their left to support the cavalry and hit the enemy in the rear. He and Rootwell and an escort rode on to try and get a better look at what was happening. Up ahead, a fireball blossomed in the enemy ranks. He'd sent Taged, the warmage, along with Macsen, and as he'd hoped, the enemy didn't have any mages to oppose them. He was quite certain they'd be all off with the main army. Why leave any behind?

Another blast ripped through the mercenary host, and as the Shires infantry closed in on their rear, helmets started going up on spearpoints, signaling a surrender. "Sure gave up easy," said Palle.

"Consider who they are," said Aeron. "Sverdson's army has a core of mercenaries, well-trained veterans, sure, but still men fighting for pay. The rest are men he's forcibly conscripted from the Young Kingdoms he's conquered. They have no loyalty to him or the other mercenaries. As long as things are going well, they'll obey orders and fight; but if things turn sour, they'll break - like they are now."

They came up and watched as the enemy threw down their weapons and surrendered. The cavalry had managed to capture the bridge and cut off the escape of about two thousand of the humans, who were now prisoners. Unfortunately, only a quarter mile beyond the river was the Tanmill Canal, and the enemy had managed to wreck the bridge across it, halting the pursuit temporarily. But the enemy was not trying to defend the line of the canal, they were continuing to retreat. Aeron ordered the men to get the bridge repaired as quickly as possible.

"Aeron, there are some riders coming out of the city," said Palle. He looked and saw a party on horseback riding across the open ground between the city walls and the trenches of the siegeworks. One was carrying a red and gold banner with the sigil of Duke Eowulf on it. It took them a while to work their way through the siegeworks, but Aeron and Rootwell were there to meet them when they did. Aeron had never met Eowulf face to face, but Rootwell knew him.

"Dunstan!" shouted Eowulf. "Thank the Children you made it!" Aeron saw Rootwell stiffen in his saddle and frown. The Duke's familiarity might have been appropriate a year ago, but after all that had happened, it was hardly so now. Still, Rootwell tolerated it and simply nodded his head. "Our men have seized the south bridge and the bastards are falling back. I'm sending out the garrison to join them. If you can take up the pursuit here, we can rout the whole lot of them!"

"We need to repair the bridge over the canal to get across, but as soon as that's done, we'll get after them," said Rootwell.

"Sir, my troops can get across right now," said Captain Einion coming up. "The aralez aren't built like horses, they can swim the canal and climb out the other side, despite the bank. Can I get moving, Dunstan?"

Rootwell looked at Aeron, who nodded back.

"Sure, get going. We'll be along shortly."

Einion smiled and rode back to his unit. Aeron followed along to watch. Sure enough, the aralez jumped in the water, and despite their armored riders, swam right across and clawed their way up the bank, seemingly without effort. Of course, then they nearly dismounted the whole command when they shook the water off themselves. Everyone, even Rootwell, was laughing at the sight of it. But the Picksbury Knights were soon in hot pursuit of the fleeing enemy.

It only took about an hour to get the bridge repaired, and then the rest of the cavalry joined the pursuit. It took longer to get all the infantry over the bridges, but by the time they were, the Rhordians from the city had emerged and the whole united force was forming up on the east side of the city. It was nearly noon by the time it was done, but with well over twenty thousand troops, it looked damned impressive.

By that time, *Windwalker* had returned and drifted low enough for Anas to shout down to them. "Sverdson's got the word about your attack now, and I think he's trying to turn to face you. The League forces from Wolfmarch had to fall back a bit this morning, but they are advancing now to harry Sverdson's rear. Looks like you might have a real fight before dark!"

Aeron agreed with that. "He has to strike now. If he waits until tomorrow, we have a good chance to link up the two armies, and then we'll outnumber him."

"What if he just goes after Duke Targun Spire's force and ignores us?" asked Rootwell. "Could we get there in time to hit him in the rear?"

Yes, that was a real concern, and the weak spot in his plan. If Sverdson simply ignored what had happened here and aggressively went after Targun Spire's forces, it could get very sticky. But what other choice was there? "Somehow, we have to get him to attack us instead of the Wolfmarch forces."

As they sat there watching the last of the army get in position to advance, a rider on an alarez came galloping up. Aeron saw that it was Gwenith.

"Aeron! Aeron!" she shouted.

Initially he was concerned that something bad had happened, but as she got closer, he saw a huge grin on her face and relaxed. "What is it?" he asked her.

"We found something! Something you just have to see!"

"What?"

"Oh, I don't want to ruin the surprise, just follow me. Come on!" she turned her mount and loped off. Aeron looked to Rootwell who shrugged and smiled. Soon, nearly the whole headquarters was galloping off after Gwenith. They came to an area where General Sverdson had obviously parked all his supply wagons. There were hundreds of them, all now captured and under guard.

"If nothing else, his troops will be getting hungry pretty soon," said Rootwell.

"Oh, it's better than that, sir!" cried Gwenith. "When we got here, most of them just gave up, but there was one group trying to get a half dozen wagons moving, and they fought like demons when we caught them!"

They arrived at the wagons in question and saw that indeed there were signs of a desperate fight and a number of human bodies piled up off to the side, and sadly, several dead aralez. Nearly the whole Picksbury Knights were now standing guard. Captain Einion was there, and he called them all over to one of the wagons and flung back the flap on its canvas top.

Inside, it was filled with treasure. Gold and silver candlesticks, plates, urns, chandeliers, and a number of locked chests and heavy canvas bags. One of the chests had been pried open and was filled with coins. "Wow!" cried Palle. "This must be the loot Sverdson stole from all the places he conquered."

"Even better, lad," said Rootwell, grinning. "Even better than that."

Palle looked at Aeron in confusion. Aeron grinned, too. "It's not just loot, Palle. This is Sverdson's pay chest. The pay chest for an army of mercenaries."

"I don't think we have to worry about how we'll get Sverdson to come this way," said Rootwell.

* * * * *

And so it proved. By mid-afternoon, they could see Sverdson's army coming toward them. *Windwalker* reported that the Wolfmarch forces were pursuing but were being delayed by a rearguard Sverdson had left behind. The combined Shires and League forces were drawn up to meet them. They had very little cavalry, but Duke Eowulf had been able to contribute about a dozen cannons which had been light enough to drag out of the city.

Of the ten thousand enemy who had been investing the city, about half had managed to make it back to the main army. The rest were killed, captured, or fled south. How much use the ones who made it back to Sverdson would be was unknown.

"So, around thirty-five thousands of them and close to forty thousands of us," said Dilwyn.

"Except we're divided into two almost equal groups, while Sverdson is all in one clump," said Aeron. "That gives him an advantage - if he can figure out how to use it."

"This Sverdson is an experienced commander, or so they say," said Duke Eowulf.

"But until this all started, I heard his mercenary force was only about four thousand strong. He hired himself out to be part of bigger armies. Now he's got a force near ten times that size. I'm wondering if he really knows how to handle anything that big."

"So what do you suggest we do… uh, Commander Cadwallader?" asked the duke. It was clear that Eowulf wasn't quite sure what to make of Aeron. A very young halfling who somehow was being treated as an equal by Rootwell and the other Shires commanders. Aeron himself still found it very odd.

He looked over the battle lines. The Shires troops were on the left and the humans on the right. Sverdson's force was deploying for battle about two miles away. He had quite a lot of cavalry, although most of it was light. There didn't appear to be any cannons, but there were some light bolt throwers. What would Sverdson do? What did Aeron *want* him to do…?

"Your grace," he said, turning to Eowulf. "I'd like you to shift a few thousand of your troops from your right over to reinforce the Shires army on the left."

"What? Why?" asked Eowulf. "That will weaken our right!"

"Yes, exactly. Sverdson will think we are afraid the *halfmen* are too weak to hold on their own and you are reinforcing them. He'll also see that his baggage train is over there, behind our right wing. He'll see it as an opportunity to turn our right and recapture the wagons."

"But we've already moved the treasure wagons inside the city walls," protested Eowulf.

"Yes, but Sverdson doesn't know that. He might even be hoping we haven't discovered them yet."

"So you want him to hit our right? Why? And what if he manages to turn our flank?"

"I do want him to attack there. If he hits us in force, your right can bend back until it rests on the abandoned enemy siege lines. If they try to get around you, they'll be disrupted by the trenches and stakes, and they'll be in range of your cannons on the city walls. Meanwhile, once he's committed, we will advance with our left. If Duke Targun Spire can attack the same place, we can crush Sverdson's own flank and link up our two armies."

Realization dawned on Eowulf's face, and the other commanders all nodded in understanding. "It's a good plan," said Rootwell.

Eowulf looked from face to face and finally said: "All right, it might just work. I'll give the orders at once."

"Thank you," said Aeron. Then he turned to Dilwyn. "Signal *Windwalker* to come down so we can give them the message to send to Targun Spire. Hurry, we haven't much time."

Things began moving, and before long, the human troops were marching from the right, across the rear of the army to reinforce the left - in plain view of the enemy. The airship rose up, flew over Sverdson's army, and they could see it descending beyond it. Targun Spire's forces weren't visible yet, but they had to be right over there somewhere.

"Aeron," said Palle, when they had a rare moment when nothing was happening. "How did you manage this?"

"Manage what?"

"You bein' in command here. Don't try to tell me you're not. Rootwell and the others, you try to pretend they are your equals or even your superiors, but they are constantly deferring to you when a decision has to be made. How did that happen?"

Aeron shrugged. "I was right about a few things. So they started listening, and then I was right about a few more things, and they listened more. I keep wondering how long it will last. All it will take is for me to be wrong about something once and it could all end."

"So you really were in command at the battle of Hodenburg? I've been listenin' to some of the others talking and that's what they've implied."

"I guess I was. I had a lot of help though."

"It was brilliant. All the Rhordian officers were talkin' about it during the retreat back to Eowulf. They kept wondering who the Shires' general was with Rootwell being stuck inside the city." He paused and looked out. "This is going to be brilliant, too. Remember when old Egilhard was talking about genius versus collective competence and all that back at the College?" Aeron nodded. "I guess he was wrong about you not bein' a genius."

Aeron snorted and shook his head. "I think it just comes down to victory going to the ones who make the fewest mistakes."

"Well, let's go out and not make any mistakes, eh?" Palle slapped him on the shoulder and laughed.

* * * * *

They made very few mistakes that afternoon.

As Aeron had hoped, Sverdson launched his main attack against the Rhordian right, and as he'd planned, the right bent back to the siegeworks. Sverdson's attack got all tangled up in the supply wagons and the trenches. Thousands of the enemy troops fell out of ranks searching through the wagons, probably looking for the pay chests. That flank was bolstered by Eowulf's company of mercenary ogres, who were not inclined to give way.

Once he saw the enemy was committed, he unleashed his own left, and they moved forward. If Targun Spire hadn't followed his instructions, that could have been a disastrous mistake, but the duke massed all his cavalry - and the two mammoths - on that same flank, and the two forces smashed through Sverdson's lines and linked up. Both armies then pivoted to face south, and the enemy force began to fall apart.

Sverdson's big weakness was that he really only had his original core of mercenaries with any personal loyalty to him. The other mercenaries had been hired and promised pay, and they knew perfectly well what the loss of the pay wagons would mean to them. The rest were men forced to be here because their liege lords' families were being held hostage back at home. They had every reason to hate Sverdson, and when the battle appeared to be a losing one, they began to break. Individuals, then squads, and then whole companies began peeling away from the battle lines and fleeing south.

Aeron had never seen a battle this large or imagined commanding one. It was much different than any of his previous fights, particularly because he never got anywhere near the actual fighting. He stayed at a safe distance and ordered people to go into danger. It was almost like moving Dilwyn's wooden blocks around on a map. Almost.

By dark, the whole enemy force had collapsed and was in full retreat. The Rhordian cavalry was in pursuit. The Rhordian infantry had a lot of prisoners to look after. The Shires Army, once it was sure that everything was under control, headed in the opposite direction. They marched through the dark, north along the road to Hodenburg. Around midnight, just as the last of the Golden Bread was starting to wear off, they met up with the supply wagons and artillery train coming the other way.

Still not willing to completely trust the Rhordians, the army bedded down for a two day nap behind the wooden walls of the supply wagons and protected by the artillery. Nesta and his family were somewhere with the wagons, but he was asleep before he could find them.

* * * * *

He'd gone to sleep in the dark and he woke up in the dark. He was delighted, but not really surprised to find Nesta snuggled down beside him. She woke when he stirred. "Hi, Beautiful," he said, reaching out and touching her cheek.

She smiled and stretched. "Good morning, my brilliant general."

"Morning? Is it? What day?"

"Just before dawn, two days since the battle. You've been sleeping a day and a half, I guess. You have such a cute little snore, you know."

"Really? I didn't know. So, what's been happening?"

"You mean with the war? About a hundred messengers have come looking for you. I have a stack of papers for you to read over breakfast. From what we hear, things are going well. That Sverdson fellow's army has fallen all to pieces, and they are fleeing south as fast as their long legs can carry them. I gather that the Rhordians are chasing him."

"Good, good. Just so long as they don't expect *me* to chase them. I feel like I could go back to sleep for a month."

"You've earned it, Love. But you need some food. We'll get breakfast going in a little while. You can eat, read your messages, and then take a nap."

It sounded like an excellent idea, and that is, in fact, exactly what he did.

For the next few days he, and the army, took it easy. Resting, repairing equipment, tending the wounded, and burying their dead. There were amazingly few of the latter. Except for the cavalry, there had been very little fighting during the initial attack, and then later, the bulk of the heavy fighting had been on the right of the line among Eowulf's troops. Once again, the Shires Cavalry had borne the brunt when they attacked on the left to link up with Targun Spire's forces, but the total butcher's bill was less than a thousand dead and wounded for the Shires.

The Rhordians had lost about three times that number, but still amazingly light for a battle this size - or this decisive. Sverdson's army had been virtually destroyed with nearly ten thousands taken prisoner and probably four or five thousands dead. A great many of the prisoners were the conscripted men from the Young Kingdoms. They simply wanted to go home.

"They will probably be allowed to," said Dunstan Rootwell. "The Rhordians are sending a force down south to free all of the kingdoms that Sverdson conquered, and the prisoners will go along as auxiliaries."

"What about the other prisoners? The mercenaries?" asked Aeron.

Rootwell shrugged. "Eowulf says he'll probably hire them himself. They are mercenaries, after all."

"Not sure I'd trust them."

"Nor I. But you know these humans," said Rootwell shaking his head. "The dukes are all talking about creating a sort of protectorate for the nearby Young Kingdoms. Maybe even bringing some of them into the League."

"I am *so* grateful I only deal with military things, sir. Politics makes by head hurt."

Rootwell gave him a strange and rather alarming smile.

*****

The following weeks saw the war wind down and finally sputter out. There was an elaborate ceremony in Duke Eowulf's palace where the duke's formally asked the Shirefolk for their forgiveness for their actions and where Shirefolk gave it. Oaths of eternal friendship were taken, but the Shires did not rejoin the League. They would remain allies, but independent. The old alliance was broken, probably forever, but the new one better suited everyone for the moment. This was followed by a huge feast. Aeron insisted that Nesta attend, and though a bit dazzled, she held up well in such high company.

After the meal, there was music and even dancing. Aeron and Nesta stayed off the dance floor but did mingle. At one point, he was almost tackled by Professor Egilhard from the College of Warcraft. The human demanded that he allow him to interview him about his actions in the 'Recent Unpleasantness,' as he called it for a book he planned to write. Aeron tried to placate him without promising anything.

The next day, former Headmaster Jannik was executed. Aeron did not attend, but to his delight, he ran into Sergeant Rolf on the streets of Eowulf that same day. His old company commander from the Academy looked a bit older but was the same large, gruff man he'd known from before. "Sergeant!" he cried. "I'm glad to see you well. With all that's been going on, I wasn't sure you'd survived."

"Oh, I'm the same as always. I spent the war safe here, nursemaiding the younger cadets. All except for the final battle, of course. We were all in the field for that. Managed to bring 'em all back alive, which is a miracle considering some of those lunkheads."

"I want to thank you for the gift of your dagger on the day I left. It saved my life not long after that. Unfortunately, I lost it later on."

"Just a bit of metal. Glad it served you well, even for a little while. But I hear you've gone on to bigger things than knife-fighting. Well done, kid. Really well done." They shook hands, and the sergeant went on his way, Aeron watching him go until he disappeared in the crowds.

Finally, they got the word they had all been waiting for: The army would march home. They wasted no time, and two days later, they were back at Hodenburg. It was decided that the volunteers would be disbanded but remain on call. The trained bands would be dispersed to be close to their homes but would remain on duty at least for a few months longer. The Shires' share of the captured booty would be used to help those who suffered during the war and to strengthen the Shires' defenses.

"Dunstan, I am going home, and I'm going to help my family rebuild our farm," he said to Rootwell one day.

The old Muster-Master held out his hand, and Aeron took it. "Thank you, Aeron," he said. "For all you did. And don't get too comfortable and domestic. I have a feeling I'm going to be needing your advice a lot in the coming days."

Aeron laughed. "If you need me, you know where to find me."

Chapter 24

Aeron and Nesta were married on the Fall Equinox. That was later than either of them wanted, but with all the rebuilding work to be done and the normal chores that happen on any farm, it just kept getting put off and put off. Still, by the day of the wedding, the house had repaired walls and a new roof and was nearly sealed up against the weather, and there was a small suite of rooms added for Aeron, his bride, and their two children. There was still a lot of work that needed to be done before it would seem like home again, but it was a good start.

The wedding drew a huge crowd and fortunately the weather was fair. A large pavilion tent had been erected to provide shade, and chairs had been borrowed from neighbors or makeshift ones made from sections of logs. Mama Beata had demanded to be allowed to provide the food, and it was extraordinary. Aeron wasn't sure just how much of her 'gastromancy' magic was in it, but everyone had a *very* good time. Mama Beata winked and slipped Nesta and him each a tiny sweet in gift-wrapped boxes with instructions not to eat them until bed time.

The guests included most of the Shires Assembly, all the higher ranked military commanders, including Dunstan Rootwell and Conwy Macsen, along with some lower ranking ones like Bevan Einion. Gwenith Parry was there, of course, since she was family anyway, along with all his brothers, sister, aunts, uncles, and cousins.

Palle, a newly graduate lieutenant, made the trip from his home in the Duchy of Berlonviche, and Dilwyn Brynmoor came down from the Holdfast with a few of his mages and artificers. Dilwyn was now the master of the Holdfast; Paddy Bobart had left it to him in his will. Sadly, all of the Ej halfings had gone home in the *Windwalker* several months earlier. "We're building an airship of our own," said Dilwyn proudly.

The ceremony itself was very simple, as such things were in the Shires, and went off without a hitch. After that, there was a great deal of music and dancing - which Aeron and Nesta joined in enthusiastically - and, of course, eating. The year's harvests looked like they would be good, despite the damage from the war, and Mama Beata was able to provide an ample feast.

The festivities went on all day, and Aeron found himself talking with a great many people. Most were just well-wishers, but some had other agendas. A debate, which Aeron had been vaguely aware of, had been raging for the last few months over the nature of the Shires' military. Some, like Rootwell, were arguing for a much more professional army drawn up on the lines of the Leagues', with more heavy cavalry and armored infantry and paid well enough that they could be kept on active duty the year round. Others, including several of the Assembly members, felt there was no need for that, and the military they'd had before was just fine—it won the war didn't it? Both groups were bending his ear about it, and he couldn't help but wonder why. "Do they really think I can influence what happens?" he asked in wonder to Nesta after they managed to escape another ear-bender.

"Do you really think you can't, Aeron?" she had replied with a smile.

Near the close of the evening, Rootwell cornered the newlyweds, and the old halfling talked for a while about the issues facing the Shires' military. Aeron had heard most of it from other people during the day, so he just nodded respectfully and told Rootwell that he agreed fully with the proposed reforms—which he did. "I'm sure you'll get it all figured out, sir."

"We'll see," he replied, peering at Aeron through a cloud of his pipe smoke. "But that reminds me, I have a wedding gift for you, boy."

"No need for that, sir…" began Aeron, but Rootwell waved him to silence.

"I'm getting too old for this sort of thing, son. I've told the Assembly I'm retiring at the end of the year. And I've recommended that you be the next Muster-Master. I can't see any of them daring to object."

"But… but…" sputtered Aeron.

"You asked for it! You came to my office all those months ago and offered your services. Very well! I accept, and that's what I want you to do: be my replacement." He nodded toward Nesta. "Evening, ma'am, and my congratulations and best wishes for the future." He turned and walked away into the crowd of revelers.

Aeron stood gaping at him with his mouth open before he finally gasped: "And he calls that a *gift*?!"

Nesta pulled him closer. "I'm sure he meant it as one. Now come on, Husband, let's go to bed. I foresee some very busy days ahead."

The End

About the Author

Scott Washburn is an architectural designer by profession, an avid reader of military history as well as long time re-enactor and wargamer. He has written books in the "Great Martian War" series, the author of The Terran Consensus and Across the Great Rift as well as contributing short stories to the "Beyond the Gates of Antares" books.

Tales of Mantica
Edge of the Abyss
Kings of War
Edited by
Brandon Rospond

TALES OF MANTICA
STEPS TO
DELIVERANCE
KINGS OF WAR
MARK BARBER

TALES OF MANTICA
DROWNED SECRETS
BEN STODDARD

TALES OF MANTICA
DROWNED SECRETS
BEN STODDARD

PIOUS
KINGS OF WAR
MARK BARBER

The Last
Hurrah
R.E. Waters